Enemies Domestic

A Lark Chadwick Mystery

SPEAKING VOLUMES, LLC
NAPLES, FLORIDA
2024

Enemies Domestic

Copyright © 2024 by John DeDakis

All rights reserved. No part of this book may be reproduced or transmitted in any form or by any means without written permission.

This is a work of fiction. Names, characters, places, and incidents are either the product of the author's imagination or are used fictitiously, and any resemblance to actual persons, living or dead, business establishments, events, or locales is entirely coincidental.

ISBN 979-8-89022-153-7

Enemies Domestic

A Lark Chadwick Mystery

John DeDakis

ADVANCE PRAISE FOR *ENEMIES DOMESTIC*:

"*Enemies Domestic* is John DeDakis at his best. Suspenseful, gripping, with a frightening dose of 'what could be.' Lark Chadwick, as feisty as ever, brings this story alive as she debates a decision only she should make. Except that's not how it works in a democracy on the edge." **~Carol Costello, former CNN Anchor; Special Advisor and Journalism Lecturer, Loyola Marymount University**

"*Enemies Domestic* simply must be read by every Christian, true patriot, and pastor in America. It is a gripping, courageous, and no-holds-barred fictionalized account of the dark and vicious forces that are at work in our land. The plague of Christian Nationalism is ripping our nation apart as its Nazi progenitor did in Germany a century ago. John DeDakis's premise is accurate—and terrifying." **~Cliff Kelly, Ph.D., former Founding Director, Institute of Public Affairs Journalism at Regent University (Virginia Beach, VA); former Professor of Digital Media Communication, Liberty University (Lynchburg, VA)**

"Once again, Lark Chadwick's adventures will leave readers slack-jawed and turning pages! But author John DeDakis's latest offering also delivers an important exploration of top-of-the-headlines social and political issues. It is quite simply a book for our ages." **~Diane Dimond, Investigative Journalist and Author**

"John DeDakis is the master of suspense. Just as you think *Enemies Domestic* is headed in one direction, DeDakis makes a sudden 90-degree turn. Keep turning the pages—there are more shocks ahead. This sixth book is his most controversial yet so don't expect any sugar coating as he courageously takes on the toughest political issues in today's world." **~Carolyn Presutti, Senior Washington Correspondent, VOA**

"John DeDakis's newest novel, *Enemies Domestic*, is a compelling story about a modern-day reality that truly captures the current state of affairs in our divided society and body politic. As we follow Lark Chadwick through her many twists and turns, we are confronted with the challenges facing our nation and the fragile state of our experiment in democracy. The plot couldn't be any more relevant and timely." **~Gail McCabe, Former Dept. of Defense Combat Journalist / Video Producer**

Books by John DeDakis

Lark Chadwick Mysteries
Fast Track
Bluff
Troubled Water
Bullet in the Chamber
Fake
Enemies Domestic

For Grace Jacobs
1934-2021
First a fan, then a friend.
May her memory be a blessing.

Author's Note

Even though I began noodling with ideas for this book in early 2019, things didn't begin to crystalize until 2022 when my wife Cindy and I began having intense conversations about what life might be like for my pregnant protagonist Lark Chadwick in a post-Roe v. Wade America.

The riot at the U.S. Capitol on January 6, 2021, also brought the need to write *Enemies Domestic* into sharp focus. That's when a mob, incited by then President Donald J. Trump, violently tried to overturn the 2020 election that Trump lost to Joe Biden.

What follows is fiction, but much of it is ripped from reality. Is the story far-fetched? I'd like to think so but, with every passing day in our current political maelstrom, I'm beginning to wonder about that. The United States is on a harrowing ride, and you're in for a harrowing read.

*I do solemnly swear (or affirm)
that I will support and defend the Constitution of the United States against
all enemies, foreign and domestic.*

~Oath of Office for all Federal Employees

Chapter One

This is a dumb idea.

That thought kept repeating itself as I stood next to President Will Gannon at the podium in the White House briefing room. No fewer than a hundred of my former colleagues eyed the president and me.

"Good morning, everyone," the president began. "The recent murder of my press secretary Ron McClain has left a massive hole in my staff. As I said in my statement last week, his loss is devastating. That's why, during this emergency, I've asked my trusted friend Lark Chadwick to be Ron's replacement."

I was doing my best to keep my face impassive, but my stomach was churning—and not just because of my recurring morning sickness.

A week ago, I'd been sitting in the most coveted seat in this briefing room—front row center—as the White House Correspondent for the Associated Press. Now I was about to be the voice of the presidency to my former colleagues, most of whom have advanced degrees in public policy and, in some cases, decades of experience covering politics.

This is a dumb idea.

I spoke those exact words to President Gannon two days earlier when he offered me the gig. I'd just left my AP job and we were working together on the biography I'm ghostwriting for him about his wife who'd died recently of pancreatic cancer. The working title is *Realist: The Life of Rose Gannon.*

I was sitting in the Oval Office on one of the two cream-colored sofas while Will paced in front of the iconic Resolute Desk. He prefers I call him "Will" when we're alone because he says he considers me his "First Friend" since Rose died suddenly a month ago.

At the time, her loss was an emotional body-blow for him, but he seemed to be bouncing back better than I was after my boyfriend Doug Mitchell died in February—five days after Valentine's Day.

"Lark," Will said, "I've been thinking about it, and I want you to be my press secretary."

"What?" Shocked, I looked up from my yellow legal pad. "Why?"

"You'd be perfect for the job. You know every journalist in the room, and you know their needs. Plus, you're tremendously popular right now."

That's because two weeks earlier he and I had made a joint appearance before the Senate Judiciary Committee in which we forcefully and dramatically put to rest a smear campaign of fake news that had been launched against us.

I shook my head vigorously. "With all due respect, Mr. President, I think this is a dumb idea."

"You'll be great." His voice oozed enthusiasm.

"You know I've got a short fuse and anger issues, right?"

He waved me off. "Yes. You're passionate. That's a plus."

We went back and forth about it for a few minutes, but Gannon's a persuasive guy. That's why he was elected president six months earlier. That's why his positives are above seventy percent in the polls right now.

"The country needs you, Lark." He paused and his voice softened. "*I* need you."

I gritted my teeth and shook my head. "Look," I sighed, "we're under contract to turn in the manuscript of Rose's biography in nine months. How about I do the press secretary gig on an interim basis until you can get someone more qualified to do the job?"

"Deal. But, for the record: I believe you're perfectly qualified." He extended his massive hand.

I stood, shook it, but added, "I still think it's a dumb idea."

"Duly noted," said the Leader of the Free World.

Now, as Gannon was saying all kinds of wonderful things about me to the White House press corps, I prepared myself to face their questions for the first time.

Gannon turned to me and stepped back. "So, Lark, I'll get out of your way and let you do your job." He gestured grandly. "The podium is yours."

To my surprise, my former colleagues applauded.

That eased my nervousness but, as I watched Gannon head toward the pocket door into the lower press office, I had mixed emotions. His departure was a strong affirmation of his trust in me to be his spokesperson, but I also felt lost at sea with the sharks circling.

As is always the case whenever the president is within earshot, reporters shouted questions at him about the latest rumor. One question stood out:

"Mr. President," a network correspondent in the front row asked, "is it true you're planning to nominate a woman to the Joint Chiefs of Staff?"

Gannon didn't pause or look back. He'd said his piece and would not be suckered into overshadowing his message: Lark Chadwick, 29, political neophyte, bumpkin from Wisconsin, had just been named White House Press Secretary.

I opened my briefing book, took a deep breath, and squinted into the bright lights.

This is a dumb idea, I said to myself.

"I'm much more comfortable asking questions than answering them," I said to the ocean of upturned faces. "But I'll do my best. Fire away."

It seemed everyone raised their hand and shouted my name at once.

"Lark!"

"Lark!"

"Lark!"

Even though the tradition is to begin with the front row, I have a soft spot in my heart for backbenchers, so I pointed blindly to a guy standing in the rear next to the wall on the Rose Garden side.

Big mistake.

"Lark," the guy began. He was in his forties, lanky, had a luxurious mane of black hair, and a red bow tie.

As soon as I realized who I'd called on, I saw my grave error. He represented a news organization I consider to be part of "The Rabid Right."

"Ever since the Supreme Court overturned Roe v. Wade," he said, "states have been passing their own laws about abortion. It's legal in some states, severely limited in others, and illegal in more than a dozen. This comes at a time when you have just publicly revealed that you're pregnant with the child of a man who died three months ago of a heroin overdose."

My knees nearly buckled.

A few reporters—most of them women—groaned loudly.

"My question," the guy continued, powering his way through the grousing, "are you, or are you not, planning to abort your unborn child?"

I gripped the podium so tightly my knuckles turned white. Taking a deep breath, I began to speak.

Chapter Two

"What was your answer?" Kris, my grief counselor, leaned in closer to hear my response.

We were sitting across from each other in her office at the Wendt Center for Loss and Healing on Connecticut Avenue in Tenleytown about four miles northwest of the White House. We'd been meeting since my boyfriend Doug died seventy-five days ago (not that I was counting).

Kris, a widow of about fifty, sat in an easy chair in front of the couch where I had nestled myself in a comfortable cocoon of cushions.

"I'll show you," I said, digging my iPhone from my messenger bag. "It went viral."

I found a clip on YouTube. It began with Gannon at the podium introducing me to the press corps. I was amazed at how calm and composed I looked when all my emotions were roiling.

"Here." I handed her my phone. "This is a good place to start."

It was fun to watch Kris as she viewed the unfolding spectacle. She held my phone between the thumb and forefinger of one hand, the other cupping her chin. As she listened to Gannon praise me, she smiled proudly as if I was her star student.

"Were you nervous?" she asked, glancing up at me.

"Big time."

"You don't look like it."

"I hide it well."

She scowled as Mr. Rabid Right wound up and delivered his fast ball down the middle: "Are you, or are you not, planning to abort your unborn child?"

"What a jerk," Kris whispered, her eyes riveted to the screen.

I'd already watched the clip a few times so I knew that during the, um, pregnant pause that followed, you could see my jaw muscles flexing. Then, instead of following my first impulse—storm from the podium to smack Mr. R.R.—I took a deep breath and drilled him with my eyes.

My voice was steel. "First: The answer is none of your business. What I do with my body is my choice and no one else's. *You* are *not* entitled to that answer."

"Good for you," Kris said, her eyes still glued to the screen.

My voice on Kris' phone continued: "Your question actually raises an important point, however. It shows just how untenable the situation is for women forced to face choices that will change their lives forever."

Kris nodded.

"Right now, in some states, those personal choices could lead to criminal prosecution. In all too many cases, single women with limited means to even support themselves, will now be forced—FORCED—to become single mothers in states that won't provide any assistance to help them care for the innocent life they are *required* to bring into being."

"That's so true," Kris breathed.

"So, thank you for that question," I continued. "You have demonstrated just how *cruel* the current situation is for women."

Kris hit *pause* and handed the phone back to me. "That was very powerful, Lark."

"Thank you." I put away my phone. "The honest answer is I still don't know what I'm going to do."

"Do you want to pursue this now, or do you want to talk first about the reaction to your statement?"

I waved a hand. "Let's talk about the abortion decision. I'm already being deluged—*deluged*—with interview requests, even from the late-night comedy shows. The producers say, 'Oh, Lark, we want to introduce you to the rest of the country.' But the real reason is they want to cast me as either the enemy or the hero of the abortion debate. Sorry. Not gonna go there. Especially if I don't even know where 'there' is for me." I was breathing heavily, and my palms were sweating.

"So, what's your current thinking about your pregnancy?"

"I've done my research. I have until August fourth to make my decision."

Kris looked quizzical. "How did you come to that conclusion?"

"The fetus becomes viable twenty-four weeks after conception and abortion will no longer be an option. I got pregnant on February sixteenth. August fourth is twenty-four weeks from that day. Today is May fourth so I've got roughly three months to make up my mind."

Kris shifted in her chair. "I recommend much sooner. The longer you wait, the more emotionally attached you'll be to the fetus. It'll be harder to make an objective decision. Plus, if you decide to have an abortion, you'll want to make arrangements in a timely manner. You live in Maryland, right?"

I nodded. "Silver Spring."

"Abortion is legal there until the twenty-fourth week of pregnancy. Same here in DC."

"What do you think I should do?"

Kris smiled. "Nice try. That decision is entirely up to you. My job is to ask questions to help you get your own inner clarity."

I scowled. "The last time we talked about this I told you I'd never considered being a parent. Married with children wasn't even on the horizon. Getting pregnant was an accident that grew out of both love and lust. But it was an accident. Now Doug is d—"

I stopped. A sudden pang of grief took me by the throat and gagged me. I snatched a tissue from the box perched on the arm of the couch and sobbed.

Kris waited patiently.

"Sorry," I finally blubbered.

"That's quite all right. Take your time." Her voice became gentle. "It's still fresh, isn't it?"

I nodded. "Shouldn't I have snapped out of it by now?"

"It's only been a couple months."

"How much longer will this pain and emptiness go on?"

"It could be a year—"

"Fuck!"

"—before you feel 'normal.'" Her fingers made air quotes. "Maybe longer."

I sighed. "Grief. Morning sickness. And now I've gotta decide if I'm going to get an abortion or face life as a single mom."

"There's also adoption."

"Yeah. I keep forgetting about that."

Kris smoothed her yellow pencil skirt but remained silent, waiting.

I thought a moment as I dabbed at my eyes with a second tissue. Finally, I spoke: "So, if you're not going to tell me what I should do, what's your guidance on how I should make this decision?"

"An excellent question. How do you normally make big decisions?"

"Impulsively." I laughed, but felt no humor. "There's got to be a better way."

"How would Lark Chadwick, the journalist, go about covering a story?"

"By asking questions."

"Of whom?"

"People who know more than I do about the issue."

Kris smiled and nodded.

I smiled, too. "I see where you're going with this. Who better to talk to than women who've had an abortion, single mothers who chose to have their baby, and women who have given up their children for adoption."

Kris nodded vigorously. "I think you're onto something."

"Finding all these women might be a trick, but I know where I can start."

"Where?"

"There's a group of expectant moms my OB-GYN told me about. Our first meeting is tomorrow night."

Chapter Three

Until a day ago, my only impression of what it's like to be the president's press secretary was formed by my brief time as a White House correspondent and by watching reruns of "The West Wing" and "House of Cards." The TV shows pretty much had it right: It's a whirlwind of activity and egos.

I was at my horseshoe-shaped desk in the West Wing at six a.m. Actually, it's not my desk. I still consider it to be Ron McClain's.

I sat with my back against the east wall. Out the window to my right, it was beginning to get light. I could see up the driveway toward the northwest gate. There was a flurry of activity on the left side of the drive nicknamed "Pebble Beach." Network reporters and production crews were gathering in the tented workspaces to go live for the early-morning newscasts with the White House as a backdrop.

On the other side of my office, a big-screen TV took up most of the west wall allowing me to keep an eye on the networks—mostly CNN, Fox, CNBC, and MSNBC, but sometimes C-Span, as well as all three legacy networks: CBS, NBC, and ABC. There was a small table by the north wall with a couple chairs. A long sofa took up the entire wall to my left, and two chairs were perched directly in front of my desk.

It felt spacious, but by nine it would be claustrophobic when my team assembled to anticipate the questions I'll be asked during my daily eleven o'clock briefing.

I used the quiet predawn time to whip through the morning papers, plus I used my laptop and phone to dip into the main wire services, including AP and Reuters, the U.K.-based wire.

The lead domestic story was my debut as PressSec and my answer to Mr. Rabid Right. Mainstream publications like *The New York Times* and *The Washington Post* played it straight. Same with *USA Today*. It's not a big deal for *The Wall Street Journal,* which focuses on financial news. There my debut got barely a mention. Fox, on the other hand, went ballistic, criticizing me for calling the questioner "cruel" and labeling me as a "dangerous role model for young girls tempted into using abortion as a form of birth control."

I sighed. *Gotta get yourself a tough skin, Lark.*

A knock on my door caused me to look up.

Will Gannon, wearing a dark gray suit, leaned jauntily against the doorjamb. It struck me yet again how much he looks like Justin Trudeau.

I stood. A reflex. "Good morning, Mr. President." I smiled. "You're up early."

"Hi, Lark. I could say the same for you. Got a sec?"

He didn't wait for an answer, simply turned on his heel and walked away.

Grabbing my phone and laptop, I scampered after him, catching up as he entered the Oval Office. I pinch myself whenever I'm in there, which has only been a few times so far.

It was brightly lit and decorated in golds and yellows—Rose's handiwork.

"Have a seat," Gannon said, pointing at one of the chairs in front of the Resolute Desk. The ornately carved desk, made from timbers of the British ship *HMS Resolute,* was a gift to the U.S. from Queen Victoria in 1880. It weighs more than half a ton.

The president took off his coat, uncinched his striped tie, and sat in the plush presidential chair.

"What's up?" I slid into one of the two chairs in front of the massive oak desk.

"It's gonna be a big day today, Lark." As he spoke, he rolled up the sleeves of his powder blue shirt to mid-forearm. "I'm planning to reveal what I'm calling my Reproductive Rights Restoration plan."

"Okay." I made a note, and inwardly cringed, fearing more unwanted attention on my womb.

"It'll be a Rose Garden event."

"What time?"

"Two o'clock."

"Cast of thousands?"

"Dozens."

"Who?"

"The vice president, attorney general, surgeon general, head of the CDC, my HHS secretary, leaders in the House and Senate . . . ."

I glanced up. "Both parties?"

"Definitely both parties. The Republicans aren't going to like it, but I want to make clear that I'm listening to them."

"What's in it?"

"You'll be getting a copy of my remarks from the speech office later this morning for distribution just before the event. They'll also provide you with a backgrounder."

"How much should I say at the gaggle and the morning briefing?"

The gaggle is an informal meeting in my office at seven with the wire service reporters and anyone else ambitious enough to come in that early.

"Give them a heads up about the Rose Garden event, but the less you know, the less likely you'll steal my thunder." He winked. "I want at least a few eyeballs for the rollout."

"Gotcha."

"Good job yesterday handling that first question. It was a rough one."

"I told you it's a dumb idea having me as your lightning rod."

"I couldn't disagree more, Lark. You handled it well."

"You knew I'd be asked, didn't you?"

"Well, I knew the issue might come up, but not as soon as it did and not as bluntly."

I harrumphed.

"I'm sorry to have put you in that position, but you're a tough person, Lark."

I scowled. "I don't like being the Poster Child for to-abort-or-not-to-abort."

His voice softened. "I know this is a tough time for you. How can I be supportive?"

I sighed. "It's enough to know you understand. That's huge to me. I'll be fine. I have a strong support system."

"Good." He turned his attention to a stack of papers on his desk.

"One quick thing, sir."

He looked up. "Uh-huh?"

"Are you, indeed, planning to appoint a woman to the Joint Chiefs? Some reporters are asking about that, but I've been referring them to the Pentagon. What can you tell me?"

"Her name is Mildred Jackson. She's a four-star Air Force General."

"When are you going to do this?"

"Tomorrow. It's going to be controversial."

"Why?"

"She's African American and a lesbian."

"Whoa."

"I know. Conservatives will focus on her race, gender, and sexual orientation; I'll focus on the fact that she's highly decorated, served with distinction in both Iraq and Afghanistan, and has a purple heart."

"Won't you have trouble getting her confirmed?"

He nodded. "Senator Carmichael is holding up *all* military promotions until I stop DOD from funding travel to states where service members can get abortions. Carmichael's gumming up the whole chain of command."

"So, what's your plan?"

"An end run. I'm going to appoint General Jackson to the Air Force position on the Joint Chiefs pending approval by the Senate. *Fait accompli.*" He stood. "Also, I want to keep the ball rolling on Rose's biography. Are you still good with that?"

I stood and edged toward the door. "I'm happiest when I'm busy, so I'm ecstatic."

He laughed. "Can we meet tonight?"

I grimaced. "I'm meeting with a group of expectant mothers tonight at seven."

He waved a hand in front of his face and returned to his seat behind the polished desk. "Go. I've been reading Rose's journals. I'll busy myself with that tonight. We'll figure something out."

I stood at the door. "Anything else, sir?"

"Nope. We're good for now. See you in the Rose Garden." He gave me a seated salute.

Chapter Four

I got back to my office at six-thirty surprised to see my friend Paul Stone sitting in one of the chairs in front of my desk. Paul is the son of my friend and mentor Lionel Stone. Until a week ago, Paul and I shared the AP cubicle as White House correspondents. He wore a blue sport coat over an open-necked pink shirt, no tie, and dark designer jeans.

"Hey, you." I brushed past him on the way to my desk. "The gaggle's not for another half hour."

"I know, but your life's just gotten super busy. Thought I'd squeeze in some 'us' time before your day got going."

I laughed. "It's already gotten going. I just had my first meeting of the day with the president." I took a seat at my desk. "What's on your mind?"

"I want to thank you."

"Oh? For what?"

"For making me think."

"Glad I could help," I chuckled, "but what have I gotten you thinking about?"

"My plans for gender transition."

"Oh. *That*."

He laughed. "Yes. That."

I put down my phone, folded my hands in front of me and gave him my full attention. "What are you thinking about it?"

As Paul composed his response, I took stock of him. He was early thirties, had close-cropped dark hair, and an open, wide-eyed face. My first impression of him when we'd met six months ago was his enthusiasm. Every sentence, it seemed, ended with an exclamation mark.

Paul said, "I'm thinking that you're right and I should slow down and think seriously about it before I do anything rash."

"It was hard enough telling your folks you're gay, right?"

"I'm bi." He paused. "Actually, that's not even right. Sexuality isn't binary. I consider myself pansexual."

"But your folks don't know that. And they certainly don't know you want to be called Paula."

"True. And I'm not ready to go there. Yet."

"But it's still on the table?"

"Yeah. But I came to tell you that I'm going to follow your advice to go slowly."

"How slowly?"

"I'm going to start meeting with a therapist who specializes in gender identity issues."

"Good idea. Big relief."

Paul looked surprised, almost hurt. "Why a relief?"

"Because I really care about you, Paul, like a brother."

My friend winced. "That's a micro-aggression, Lark, but I'll let it pass. This time."

I sighed. "My point is, I'd hate to see anything happen to you. If you're still trying to figure this thing out, I think it's better to talk it through with a professional rather than experimenting in front of close-minded, judgmental people."

Just then there was a knock on my open door. I looked up and Paul turned around.

Speaking of judgmental, standing in the doorway was Mr. Rabid Right himself wearing his trademark red bow tie.

Has he been eavesdropping? I wondered. "Hey, Roland. You here for the gaggle?"

"Yeah. Thought I'd drop by."

I motioned him in. "You haven't been a regular, but you're welcome to join."

As he took the seat next to Paul, I smiled to myself, realizing I'd unconsciously conflated his Rabid Right nickname with his actual initials: Roland Roberts. He's with the Christian Newswire, a right-wing livestreaming platform that patterns itself as the video version of the Associated Press. Its motto: "Truth You Can Trust."

Paul smiled perfunctorily at Roberts. "Hi, Roland."

"Hey, Paul."

The room was uncomfortably silent while I busied myself checking emails, texts, and the news while Paul and Roland sat next to each other wondering what to say next.

After a moment or two of awkward throat clearing and ass shifting, Paul said something innocuous to Roland about the weather, and Roland remarked about his Metro ride in from Crystal City.

Heavy stuff.

Soon, however, the room began to fill.

Harriette, my friend from Reuters, arrived a little before seven. She's in her fifties and has been on the beat twenty years.

The CNN White House correspondent, a woman in her mid-thirties, arrived next, followed by three twenty-something field producers from CBS, NBC, and ABC. They all took seats on the couch except for one who grabbed a chair by the table near the window. She seemed shy and new to the job.

"So, how's everyone doing?" I asked.

There were a few mumbles. It was early. I get it.

I turned my attention to the woman sitting by herself at the window. "You're the only one here I don't know. Tell me a little about yourself."

"Um, me?" she asked, clearly uncomfortable being put on the spot.

"Yes, ma'am."

"Hi, I'm Dorothy Rather with CBS."

"Any relation to legendary anchor *Dan* Rather?" I asked.

She blushed. "I wish. Everybody keeps asking me that."

"What's going to be happening today, Lark?" Harriette asked, impatient.

I folded my hands atop my desk. "The president has a two p.m. Rose Garden event where he'll be unveiling his Reproductive Rights Restoration plan."

Everyone began taking notes.

"In other words, Abortion Legalization Plan, right?" Roland sneered.

I ignored him.

"What're the details?" Paul asked.

"We'll release a backgrounder and the president's prepared remarks right before the ceremony."

"What can you tell us off the record, or on background?" Harriette asked.

"Nothing. I'm waiting to see it just like you all are."

Roland spoke up again. "Clearly, you and the president have a *special* relationship. Surely there's been some *pillow* talk."

I drilled him with my eyes. "That rumor was put to rest decisively last week, Mr. Roberts. There are no pillows, or special details involved."

He smiled as if he knew more about my relationship with the president than I did.

One of the field producers asked a nutsy-boltsy question about camera set-up arrangements, and if the two o'clock event would be a "hard start" at the top of the hour.

"Not sure about the hard start," I said, "but the president likes to stay on schedule, so I think it's safe to say that'll be your lead during the two o'clock hour." I paused and looked around the room. "That's all I've got. Anything going on that I should know about?"

The NBC field producer spoke up. "We just think it's neat that you're the new press secretary, Lark. Good luck."

"Yeah," chimed in the ABC producer sitting next to her.

"Thanks, guys. Sucking up will help a lot."

Everyone laughed and the meeting ended almost before it began.

I stood. "Roland, do you mind staying here for a minute?" I turned to Paul. "You too."

"Sure," they both said.

When the others left, I closed the door, returned to my desk, and stood next to it.

Paul and Roland remained seated.

"Roland, you've gotten off on the wrong foot with me."

"Lark, I—"

I held up my hand like a traffic cop. "You've got every right to ask me tough questions. That's your job. And I even understand the conservative agenda you're pushing. That's fine, too. But my personal life is off limits."

He started to speak, but I powered on. "Also off limits: insinuations about my relationship with the president. Unless you have *facts*, don't even go there."

He shot to his feet. "Or what? Are you threatening me?"

We were toe to toe. I could smell coffee on his breath. Hazelnut. "I have no power to threaten you. Your press credential is issued by the White House Correspondents' Association—your peers. Your job is to fairly and accurately report on President Gannon and, to the best of your ability, hold him accountable to the American people." I leaned toward him. "I. Am not. The story. My personal life is *not* the story."

"Why am I still feeling like I'm being threatened?" he sneered.

"I don't know, Roland. Your feelings aren't really my concern."

Roland jerked a thumb at Paul. "So, what's *he* doing here?" A snarl.

"He's my witness," I said. "Doesn't your Bible say something about having a witness present if you confront someone about an issue?"

Roberts looked stunned for a moment, seemingly surprised that I had even a remote acquaintance with the Bible.

"Isn't it your Bible, too?" he asked.

"My spiritual life is also off the table."

He snickered.

"I'm going to do my best to have a cordial, professional relationship with you," I said. "I will do my best to be responsive to your need and right to have access to the president and his policies. But I am telling you—not asking, *telling*, and in front of a witness—I will not tolerate questions or behavior from you that I consider personal harassment rather than a legitimate attempt to get and disseminate the news."

His face was turning almost as red as his bow tie.

Paul was now on his feet, eyes darting back and forth between Roberts and me.

"This sounds like a threat to me, Lark," Roland said.

"Paul, have I threatened Roland?"

"No. You haven't. You merely said you wouldn't—"

"Tolerate. I heard her," Roland said. "The threat is implied, not stated." He turned to me. "What does 'not tolerate' mean, Lark?"

"I guess we'll have to wait and see, Roland." I showed my teeth. It wasn't a smile.

Chapter Five

Paul left my office shortly after Roland. I now had about four hours to prepare for the morning briefing. One thing I was discovering quickly, however, is that there is very little time to ruminate and reflect—the job of White House press secretary is one interruption after another.

The first interruption was a Roland Roberts social media post—I checked the time—exactly seven minutes after our showdown:

Just met with Gannon's new spox Lark Chadwick. Day 2 of her tenure and already she's threatening me for asking pointed questions about her pregnancy. Message to America: The woke mob will not tolerate critical questions. The battle lines are drawn.

I felt myself redden and my pulse quicken. I'd barely been on the job a day and already my anger was at DEFCON 3. I took deep breaths, trying to get calm. If I allowed myself to get sucked into Roland Roberts' vortex, I'd never be able to have a normal life—it would be consumed by his relentless bullying.

I checked the Rolodex left behind by Ron McClain and found the phone number of Paige Summers, White House correspondent for *USA Today* and the current president of the White House Correspondents' Association. She didn't pick up when I called, so I left her a voicemail:

"Hi, Paige. It's Lark Chadwick. Could you please stop by my office when you get in? Thanks."

As I finished making the call, I looked up to see Ron McClain's number two standing in the doorway. I waved her in.

Nora Tomlinson is a birdlike woman in her late forties—tall, thin, nervous—as if she's about to take flight at any moment.

"Have a seat," I said, gesturing at one of the chairs in front of my desk.

As she sat, I got up and claimed the chair next to hers. She's now my assistant, but I didn't want to have my desk come between us.

"How are you doing?" I asked.

Her eyes were red-rimmed. Ron had only been dead a week, mugged and murdered on a D.C. street.

"Fine," she said automatically, even as the waterworks began again and she had to dab at her eyes with the balled-up tissue she'd been clutching tightly.

Today was her first day back after taking a few days off to grieve.

"It's good to have you back, but if you need more time, I completely understand."

She waved a hand. "I'll be all right. I need to stay busy, or I'll go crazy."

I nodded.

"How can I help, Lark?"

"I was going to ask you the same question."

She laughed, a mirthless "heh." Done dabbing, she fiddled with the tissue, hands on her lap. "You're certainly well acquainted with grief and loss. Tell me, does it ever get better?"

"Sometimes. For a while. But loss changes you."

She nodded. "Yeah."

"Any word on if they found the guy who killed him?"

Nora shook her head. "No. They're still looking."

"How long had you and Ron worked together?"

"Not that long. He was Lucia Lopez's deputy. When she quit, he moved up. Brought me over from the Pentagon where I'd been working in the press office."

"How'd you meet?"

"At one of the inaugural balls right after Gannon was sworn in. We had a great conversation about public policy. He must've picked up on my dissatisfaction with the job, so when Lucia left, he gave me a call."

I wondered if Ron and Nora had been an item, but decided not to ask. It was none of my business. Nora was married to Charles Tomlinson, an imposing Marine Corps general and Chairman of the Joint Chiefs of Staff. I had yet to meet him, but he was Mr. Personality compared to Nora's Shrinking Violet. Ron had been a gentle man and more her style.

"I'm certainly new to all of this." I gestured broadly to encompass the entire White House complex. "What do I need to know? How can I do this job well?"

"Do everything I tell you to do and you'll be fine." Her eyes twinkled.

I laughed, glad to see that, though grieving, she still had her sense of humor.

"There's just so much to absorb," I said. "It's overwhelming."

"That's where I can help."

"Thank God."

"Ron put together a good team."

"How does his system work?" I asked.

"Ron has three people in the press office—one for social media, one for news coverage, and one for policy issues. They briefed me regularly and I passed their reports to Ron every hour or so. That freed him to concentrate on the president's messaging."

"Sounds like a good plan. Let's keep that in place."

"Great. I agree."

"You've already seen Roland's post, right?"

She rolled her eyes. "Welcome to the hot seat. I don't envy you."

But something inside made me wonder if maybe she really did.

Chapter Six

As the clock ticked toward the eleven o'clock briefing, the pace of my day intensified. Even though I was now playing for the other side—my former briefing room colleagues would probably say "the dark side"—it felt pretty much like it did when I was a reporter: eye on the clock, pulse pounding as the deadline draws near.

At nine I met with my staff to go over the questions I would likely face. We inserted suggested answers into a loose-leaf, tabbed binder so I could quickly flip to the correct page containing a carefully worded response.

For the meeting, I sat behind my horseshoe-shaped desk. Nora sat on the couch to my immediate left, with the rest of the staff splayed out around the cramped room.

"By now you've all seen the draft of the bill the president plans to send to Congress later today on protecting women's reproductive rights. The guidance I'm getting from him is that we're not going to steal his thunder by releasing details until the two o'clock rollout. That said, what do you think I'm going to be asked and what's your guidance on how I should respond?"

Nora spoke first. "They're going to keep chipping away at you, trying to get you to pre-empt the president."

"I guess we need to come up with all kinds of fancy ways to say 'no comment,' right?"

She smiled. "Good luck with that."

A young woman in a far corner spoke up. "You're also going to be asked about Ron's murder."

"What do we have on it?" I asked.

The woman shuffled some papers in her lap and said, "The D.C. Metro police are investigating. No leads. No suspects. They believe the murder weapon was a hammer."

The entire room groaned in unison.

"Oh, my God," Nora whispered. She began to tear up again.

"The cops are otherwise playing it close to the vest," the woman said.

"That's just terrible. He was hit in the head?" I asked.

"Uh-huh."

I sighed heavily. "Okay. Thanks. I can refer people to the local cops, and to the president's statement last week."

"Reporters are always looking for conspiracies," someone piped up. "You're going to be pressed to speculate on all kinds of things."

"I'd do the same thing if I were back out there," I said. "If there's one thing I've learned from watching politicians, it's not to answer hypotheticals."

The meeting seemed to go on forever. I was briefed not only about possible abortion questions, but also on all matters economic, political, and international. I don't have a graduate degree, but I imagined this was how it felt to be prepped to defend a master's or doctoral thesis.

Ron McClain had assembled a sharp staff who prepared me well to face the minefields ahead.

The closed-door meeting broke up about fifteen minutes before the briefing. I had just enough time to dash to the bathroom, reapply my makeup for the cameras, and clear my head, but as I charged out of my office, I nearly collided with Paige Summers of *USA Today* standing outside the door.

Paige, early fifties, had been around Washington a long time. Gannon was the third president she'd covered. Her biography of Michelle Obama won a Pulitzer.

"Hi, Lark," Paige said. "I got your message. What's up?"

"C'mon in."

She entered and I closed the door behind her. "Have a seat."

She perched on the couch.

I sat in one of the two easy chairs in front of my desk and scooted it so I could face her. "I'm talking to you in your role as president of the White House Correspondents' Association."

She nodded curtly, hands folded atop her reporter's notebook, closed on her lap.

"Earlier this morning I had a run-in with Roland Roberts."

She grimaced. "So I saw."

"He has a personal agenda. It has nothing to do with covering the presidency and everything to do with smearing me."

She nodded. And waited.

"He showed up for the gaggle this morning, which is fine, but his questions insinuated the president and I have a 'pillow talk' relationship." I air quoted.

"His words?"

"Yup."

She eye-rolled and shook her head in disgust.

"I told him, in front of Paul Stone as my witness, that I will not tolerate him making my personal life the story."

"And he interpreted that as a threat, right?"

"Yes."

"So, why am I here?"

"I'm hoping you'll be able to help me out."

She scrunched her face, but said nothing.

"I don't have the authority to yank his press credentials, but the White House Correspondents' Association does."

Before I'd finished my sentence, Paige was already shaking her head. "No can do, Lark."

"Why not?"

"The guy's a certifiable asshole, but that's not a good enough reason to kick him out of the pool."

"But—"

She stood.

So did I.

"I wish I could help you, Lark. I really do. I'm sympathetic to your situation, but he works for a legitimate news organization. He's got a right to be here. Yanking his press pass will be seen as partisan and, frankly, won't be good optics for you, either."

I pursed my lips, an attempt to keep my growing anger in check.

"Want my advice?"

I nodded.

"He can be here, but you don't have to call on him or even give him the time of day. He feeds on drama and conflict. Ignore him. Take away his oxygen. My two cents."

I scowled. "You're right. Thank you for your candor."

She smiled. "Off the record?"

"Sure."

"How are you holding up?"

"Too soon to tell. It's a tough job."

"That's for sure." She headed for the door. "Hang in there. You're gonna be fine."

"Thanks, Paige." I smiled faintly, but my insides told a different story.

Chapter Seven

It's a mere forty steps between my office and the briefing room. During that walk, I clutched the canned answers in the dark blue binder to my chest like a life preserver.

In fewer than thirty seconds I'd entered the bright and stifling room. I set my briefing book on the podium, heart pounding.

"She's baack," one of the front-row network television correspondents joked.

"I missed you, Gary," I flirted.

Roland Roberts, instead of skulking at the back of the room, stood alongside the north wall, probably no more than fifteen feet from me. He was not going to be ignored.

I did my best to pretend he wasn't there but, to be honest, I was rattled.

"I've only got one item for you and then I'll take your questions."

Opening the briefing book, I took a deep breath, and read ponderously, my eyes locked on the page.

"The p-president has a Rose Garden event at two o'clock this afternoon. Hard start." Finally, I looked up, but focused vaguely on the back wall. "We'll assemble over there." I nodded to my right at the double doors that opened onto the inner colonnade and the Rose Garden.

"What's the event?" Paul Stone asked helpfully, knowing that I'd buried the lead in favor of house-keeping details, and probably sensing my nervousness.

I locked my eyes on Paul's, grateful for his friendly face. "The president will be introducing his plan for Congress to codify all the rights taken away by the Supreme Court when it overturned a woman's right to have control over her own body."

"Got any details?" someone hollered.

"We'll be handing out a copy of the president's remarks along with a fact sheet just before his announcement."

Roland spoke up. "Lark, why did you try to have my press credentials revoked?"

I ignored him, looked purposefully to my right, and called on the television correspondent sitting in the front row on the far end.

"Lark, isn't it true that even though the president remains extremely popular, his bill will be dead on arrival in a Congress that's majority Republican in both houses?"

Even though my staff had anticipated the question, and we had drafted an answer, I resisted the temptation to shuffle the pages of my briefing book in a frantic search for my reply. Instead, I winged it.

"We'll just have to wait and see. The president is a very persuasive person."

"So, he plans to expend political capital to get the measure passed?" the reporter followed up.

"Yes."

Paul Stone asked, "Is it safe to assume the president's measure will allow late-term abortions if the mother's life is at risk, or in the case of rape, or incest?"

"Without getting into the weeds, Paul, I think it's safe to say that everything that was legal during the fifty years after Roe will be reinstated under the president's plan."

The feel of the room—except for Rabid Roland—was not adversarial. I was beginning to relax, but I knew better than to get overconfident.

Every so often, Roland whined, "What about my press credentials?" but I was determined not to let him take up any real estate in my head, plus no one else picked up that line of questioning on his behalf.

Slowly and methodically, I worked my way toward the back of the room giving priority to the news outlets in the first few rows—CBS, NBC, ABC, CNN, Fox, AP, Reuters, *The New York Times*, *The Wall Street Journal*, and *The Washington Post*—outlets with literally millions of readers and viewers, not to mention world leaders and opinion influencers.

Most of the questions, as my staff predicted, focused on abortion. No one, thank God, asked about my own pregnancy.

Once again, there was a question from someone asking if the president planned to appoint a woman to the Joint Chiefs.

I turned to the appropriate page in my briefing book and tried to deflect the question quickly: "The president might have something on that tomorrow. In the meantime, President Gannon continues to urge Senator Carmichael, the chairman of the Armed Services Committee, to stop using his opposition to abortion to hold hostage national security."

"In what way is Carmichael threatening national security?" the guy wanted to know.

"The short answer is he's holding up hundreds of routine promotions. This bottleneck, I'm told, is creating turmoil and confusion in the ranks and threatens to undermine combat readiness and unit cohesion."

"In what way?"

"My counterpart at the Pentagon can do a more thorough job of getting those details for you."

I moved on. At the back of the room, the questions began to touch on more fringe and esoteric topics. By nature, reporters are always on the lookout for something new and novel—hence the word "news"—so I stayed focused and on guard against a misstep that could undermine the president and his policies.

About forty minutes into the briefing, I sensed that the reporters on deadline were anxious to file, plus I felt I'd succeeded in not stepping into any traps.

"Okay," I said. "That's all for now. See you at two. Be careful out there."

As I scooped the briefing book from the podium and turned toward the pocket door to the lower press room, Roland tried one more time: "Aren't you going to answer my question about my press credentials?"

I couldn't help myself. As I exited the room, I shouted without looking back, "No!"

Several reporters laughed, and a couple clapped.

Chapter Eight

As I expected, Roland used a social media post to keep alive his sense of victimhood even though he could remain in the briefing room unmolested mere feet away, taunting me with personal questions.

I was proud of myself for ignoring him, telling myself he wasn't on my mind, yet here I am blathering on and on about him.

Slowly, almost imperceptibly, I began to sense a hard protective shell forming around my heart. When I'm defensive, I can be peevish, and when I'm peevish, I lash out verbally—not the best attribute of a person paid to be an affable and popular president's mouthpiece.

Gannon's Rose Garden roll-out of his Reproductive Rights Restoration initiative went without a hitch. It already had the reporter-speak nickname "Triple-R." Example: "Lark, when will Congress formally get the president's Triple R initiative?"

I got through the rest of the day with no major dustups, or screw ups, but it felt like a combination treadmill and rollercoaster of one damn thing after another: fielding phone calls and texts from various reporters, plus a parade of staffers updating me regularly on relevant social media commentary and press coverage. Any quiet moment was spent reading Gannon's proposal.

By the time I was able to pry myself away from the desk, it was after six-thirty. I had just enough time to hoof it to the support group for pregnant women trying to figure out their options. Fortunately, it met in the Parish House of St. John's Episcopal Church on H Street on the other side of Lafayette Square, the park on the north side of the White House.

St. John's is known as "the church of the presidents" because every president since James Madison in 1815 has attended at least one service there.

I found the women sitting in a semi-circle of about a dozen metal folding chairs in the church undercroft. Following my grief counseling session with Kris the other day, I couldn't wait to get started following my curiosity. How did these women feel about their situations?

I slid into the vacant chair to the right of the leader just as she was getting the meeting started.

"Hey, y'all. I'm Loquacia Brown, the facilitator of this group." She wore her hair in long strings of colored beads. Her gray sweatsuit bulged at the stomach; she looked to be about four or five months pregnant.

"So, let me guess," I smiled at her. "Your mama named you Loquacia because you talk so much?"

The other women tittered.

"Nope." She shook her head and the beads clacked.

"Nope?" I raised my eyebrows.

"Nope. Opposite. And, as a baby, I didn't cry neither."

"Stoic."

She raised a finger. "Good word. Maybe Mom hoped I'd grow into the name."

"Did you?" someone else asked.

"Nope."

We all laughed.

Loquacia turned her attention to the rest of the group. "This here is what I like to call my mothers-to-be—or not-to-be—support group. If you're here, you're trying to figure out what you're gonna do next. Am I right?"

We nodded.

"And I'm assuming you either learned about the group from the flyer at the women's clinic, or were referred by a friend, doctor, or counselor, right?"

More nods.

"So, let's go around the room," she said. "Tell us a little about who you are and what your situation is. But before we do, I'll tell you a little about me. I'm twenty-three. Preggers with kid number two. Kid one was two years ago. Date rape."

A couple women gasped.

I asked gently, "Did you consider abortion?"

"Nope."

"Why not?"

"Guilt, mostly."

"What about adoption?"

"Couldn't kill it. Couldn't give it away."

I nodded.

One of the other women asked, "How do you feel about being a mom?"

She sighed. "It is what it is. A long slog. Every goddam day."

"Tell it, sister," one of the women said.

"Let's go around the room," Loquacia said, pointing at the woman to her left.

As each woman told her story, and the closer it got to my turn, a pattern was emerging of deep inner turmoil. The women ranged in age from sixteen to forty. Two were African American, one was Latina, a few of us were White. Their pregnancies were unplanned, but their situations differed.

The sixteen-year-old, just a shy kid, revealed that her father was the baby's daddy.

The forty-year-old told us she already had four children. "We've had to declare bankruptcy," she sniffed, dabbing at her eyes with a tissue. "We can't afford to have another kid."

There were a lot of tears among us.

After about twenty minutes, it was my turn. "Tell us about you," Loquacia said. "Why are you here?"

"I'm Lark."

"We know," someone said. "You're famous."

I blushed. "More like infamous, but whatever."

"How'd you get the name Lark?" Loquacia asked.

"My mom thought I was happy as a Lark, so it stuck."

"Are you? Happy, that is?" Loquacia asked.

I shook my head and reflexively put my hand against my tummy. "I'm conflicted. The pregnancy is a surprise. And the dad is dead."

"Oooo," someone said. "Single mom. That's gonna be tough."

I nodded. "I know."

"When you due?" Loquacia asked.

"The first week of November. I'm thinking about having an abortion."

Before Loquacia noticed, or could say anything, one woman took out her phone and used her two thumbs to type furiously.

By the time I got home that night, her post had gone viral.

By the time I got to work the next morning, Rabid Roland had turned it into a federal case.

"*CHADWICK PLANNING TO HAVE ABORTION,*" he posted.

His headline was false but try telling that to his seventy million devotees.

Chapter Nine

To my surprise—and immense relief—Rabid Roland was not in the briefing room to taunt me the next day.

Why not? I wondered, but immediately realized he was probably psyching me out. Making me wonder and worry about him even when he wasn't present. A master of intrigue and intimidation.

The press corps, now wise to the routinely false accusations of the extreme right, did not bite; I got no questions about the lie that I was "planning" to have an abortion. I still hadn't decided what to do, but the clock was ticking toward when I'd have to make up my mind.

The president had no public events scheduled. He planned to work the phones, privately lobbying members of Congress on his Triple-R initiative. His positive poll numbers allowed him to husband his energy.

Washington insiders, however, were telling me not to get lulled into thinking my job would be a breeze. There's always something unexpected that will take control of your life, they told me.

Our office also released a statement, without fanfare, in which the president appointed Gen. Mildred Jackson to the Joint Chiefs as the Air Force representative.

About six that evening I was dining with the president on the second floor of the Residence as we continued to work on Rose's biography. We set aside the dishes containing debris from my Cobb salad and his burger and fries. I opened my computer that sat next to papers and notebooks strewn across the mahogany table.

Gannon, a pained expression on his face, said, "There's something I need to discuss with you."

Uh-oh, I thought, but out loud I said, "That sounds ominous. What's up?"

He got up from the table and paced.

I waited patiently, worrying that I'd done something wrong.

Finally, he sat back down. "I've been reading Rose's journals." He shook his head. "I feel like a voyeur."

I nodded. "Did you come across something?"

"Uh huh." He scrunched his face but remained silent.

"Are you going to tell me?" I chuckle-prompted.

He took a deep breath and plunged ahead. "This is very hard for me to say out loud, Lark. I'm still having a hard time processing it." His face was flushed. He seemed to be struggling with a jumble of emotions.

Immediately, I turned serious and leaned toward him. "What is it?"

He could barely get the words out. "Rose wrote about having had an abortion."

I flinched. "Whoa. And this was news to you?"

"Yeah." He looked almost sheepish.

"When?"

"Twelve years ago."

"Before Grace was born."

"Right."

Grace, the Gannon's first-born, was eight. Her brother Thomas was a rambunctious four.

"What were the circumstances?" I asked.

The president rested an elbow on the table, a curled index finger trembled at his lip. "She felt the baby would get in the way of her career."

"Ballroom dancing."

He nodded.

Trying to keep my voice gentle, I asked, "Were you the father?"

He flushed, put his hand down, and glared at me. "Yes." His voice was indignant.

"I'm sorry, Mr. President. I follow my curiosity. I ask questions. You know that."

His voice softened. "I know. And for the record: tonight I'm Will. I need a friend."

"I'm here for you." A whisper.

For a moment, silence hung between us before he gave me a look and raised his eyebrows. "So, what's your next question?"

I grinned. "I've got a million of 'em."

"Start with just one."

"How do you feel about this? How did *she* feel about it?"

"That's two."

"Choose one."

Slowly, he groped for the right word. "I-I'm *surprised* at how I feel."

"Go on."

"I'm in favor of a woman's right to choose. I've campaigned on it. I'm even trying now to get it enshrined into U.S. law."

"But . . .?"

"But I'm personally opposed to abortion."

That was a surprise to me. "Do you think it's murder?"

He shook his head vigorously. "That's too strong a word. But living cells do die."

"So, why are you surprised at your reaction to what Rose revealed? What *is* your reaction?"

"I guess I'm . . . I'm . . . disappointed."

"Disappointed?"

"Disappointed in Rose."

"Disappointed at her decision?"

"Partly. But also I'm disappointed because she did it secretly without bringing me into the discussion." He snorted. "Hell, it wasn't even a discussion. It was a unilateral decision." His voice had taken on an edge.

"It was her decision to make." My voice was gentle.

"But I'd made a contribution." His voice rose. "Part of what she was deciding about was *mine*." He stabbed an index finger against his chest, a glancing blow.

I thought a moment. I didn't want to get into an argument with the President of the United States—even if he was my friend. How could I be helpful to him, but also understanding of Rose, which was our mission in writing her biography?

"Let's back up and regroup," I said after a moment. "And thank you, by the way, for your willingness to talk about this with me."

"You're my friend. I trust you."

"Thank you." I thought a moment, choosing my words carefully. "This is an extremely delicate, complicated, and potentially explosive revelation."

"Assuming it gets revealed to anyone outside this room."

"Yes."

"Do you have an opinion about that?" he asked.

"About what?"

"Going public with it in the book."

"I do." I gave a curt nod.

"What is it?"

"Take a guess."

"You're a full disclosure person," he said. "You're passionate about the truth—even if the truth hurts."

"You know me well, Will."

He bit his lip.

"May I make a suggestion?"

He nodded. "Please do."

"Let's set aside, for now, a decision about putting it in the book. Let's discuss, instead, your feelings."

He looked dubious. "Okay."

"I think the better you know your heart and mind, the more clearly you'll see a way forward."

"That sounds wise."

"You're disappointed in Rose. Let's talk about that."

He smiled. "Have you ever considered becoming a psychologist?"

I scowled. "More often than you'd think."

He chuckled.

"Disappointed in Rose," I said. "Go."

He got up and paced the room. "Disappointment. It's a fairly innocuous feeling. Certainly not as intense as anger."

"But disappointment, if given a chance to fester, could morph into anger," I said.

"That's not where I am now, though."

"In her journal, what did she say about her decision?"

He came back to the table heaped with a pile of notebooks, found one, and brought it over to me.

"She wrote about it a lot and struggled with telling me." He opened the notebook in his hand and began turning pages. "Ah. Here. Read this." He handed me the notebook and pointed at a passage.

Rose's handwriting was delicate and precise:

I feel guilty and selfish. I want my dancing career. I know that Will wants his political career. Eventually we want to start a family, but not now. Not this soon.

He doesn't need to know of my decision. For his sake, I choose to shoulder this personal torment on my own and by myself.

Torment. Such a dramatic term. But accurate? Oh, yes.

The far right pro-lifers depict people like me as callous about life, aborting without guilt or remorse for selfish reasons, justifying the decision because the fetus isn't human. Obviously, they don't know me. They don't know how I've agonized over this decision.

I have no idea when "life" begins. Ronald Reagan said that since we don't "know," we should "err on the side of caution." That makes intellectual sense to me, and I've pondered the wisdom of that argument but, in the end, I've rejected it.

And I've decided not to tell Will.

Why?

Because I know he will try to talk me out of it—and he'll probably succeed. I just feel that right, or wrong, the decision is mine.

Leading up to this moment has, indeed, been tormenting.

But how will I feel after I have the procedure tomorrow? Guilty? Relieved? Still tormented? We shall see.

I handed Rose's journal back to Will. "How did she feel afterward?"

"Based on the reading I've done so far, she felt all those things on and off, depending on the day and the circumstances. At first it was on her mind a lot, but then, as time went on, she wrote about it less frequently."

"Do you think she was at peace with her decision?"

He nodded. "For the most part, but every now and then, she'd second guess herself. Not for long, though, because—and this goes to the theme of the book we're writing—she was, as she called herself, 'a realist.' For good, or ill, she'd made her decision and moved forward with her life."

I was going to ask another question, but Will laughed suddenly.

"What?" I asked.

"I just remembered something."

"What's that?"

"Not long before she died, she told me about a dream she had. As she was recounting it, she referred to 'our three children.' I said to her, 'You mean *two* children, right?' For a moment, she looked confused before she said, 'Two. Right.' At the time, I didn't think anything of it, but I guess it shows that even more than twelve years later, the memory of what might have been still lurked in her subconscious."

"Interesting," I said. To myself, I noted: *Prepare yourself, Lark Chadwick. If you abort, you'll never forget what you've done. But will you regret it?*

After a moment's silence, I said, "Let's get back to your feelings. You're disappointed in her?"

"Yeah. *I* haven't worked things through yet. *She* had."

"Are you suggesting you, too, could come to accept her decision and forgive her for not bringing you into the conversation?"

He nodded. "I'm not sure I would use the word 'forgive' because it implies the decision she made to abort and keep it a secret from me was some sort of moral violation."

"You don't believe it's a right versus wrong thing?"

He shook his head vigorously. "No. I think that's what's wrong with this whole debate—we make things good or bad."

"You do see the huge contradiction in what you just said, don't you?"

He cocked his head, not sure what I meant.

"You just said it's 'wrong'—your word—to see things in terms of right and wrong."

He laughed. "I did."

"And that's the dilemma: we strive to be open-minded and non-judgmental yet we also have strong feelings about what's right and wrong."

"A dilemma, indeed."

"That brings us to the question of whether it should be in the book," I said. "It'll be a bombshell."

"I know."

"Toxic? Politically fatal?"

He stood. More pacing.

Chapter Ten

It was after nine when I walked out the northwest gate of the White House and into the balmy May night. Will had offered me a ride home in one of the cars from the White House motor pool, but I'd declined.

"I'd like to walk to the Metro. It'll clear my head and give me a chance to ruminate," I'd said.

"You still take the Metro? You know you have a parking place here."

"Yeah, but I still feel funny about having that perk. I don't want to become an elitist."

"You'll come around," he smirked.

"Probably. Sadly."

"It's safer, though." A gentle nudge.

"What do you mean?"

"Roland's latest rant that you're 'planning' to have an abortion is gonna stir up the nut jobs."

"Yeah. Maybe."

But nut jobs weren't on my mind as I headed across the Pennsylvania Avenue pedestrian mall and into Lafayette Square. Even at this hour, I felt safe. Not only were uniformed Secret Service agents everywhere, patrolling the White House perimeter, but Lafayette Square is also a haven for 24-hour-a-day protestors.

As I neared the 1853 Clark Mills statue of Andrew Jackson on his horse at the center of the square, my attention was drawn to two middle-aged women having an intense debate with one another.

I walked closer so I could hear better, the bill of my baseball cap tilted downward to obscure my identity.

Both of their faces were flushed. One woman carried a "Choose Life" placard. The other's sign read "My Body. My Choice."

As I watched and listened, I marveled at how they could disagree so vehemently, yet they both listened to each other and didn't interrupt. That, in itself, was noteworthy because for years political discourse had become so toxic that demonization of "the other" was an immediate default position.

Each woman argued passionately using examples from their personal lives.

Both women revealed they were nurses.

Ms. Pro-Life was dressed modestly and comfortably in a Washington Nationals hoodie, jeans, and bright pink walking shoes. She argued that when she was pregnant, an ultra-sound revealed a problem with the fetus. Some family members and friends urged her to have an abortion, but the woman went through with her pregnancy. She gave birth to a daughter with Down's Syndrome.

"If I'd listened to everyone else," she said, "I would have been deprived of my wonderful child and she would have been deprived of the life she's been living."

Ms. Pro-Choice wore wire rim glasses and had thick gray hair pulled back and tied with a rainbow-colored scrunchie. Amazingly, she actually took an interest in the other woman's story, asking, "What's your daughter's life been like?"

"She's had a difficult time of it, but she's very loving in spite of her struggles. She's an inspiration—to me and to others." The anti-abortion protestor nodded at the other woman's "Pro Choice" placard, adding, "I'm also in favor of choice, by the way."

"Really? That's refreshing. And surprising."

"The *real* issue of choice has nothing to do with abortion."

Ms. Pro-Choice looked confused, a reflection of how I felt, too.

Ms. Pro-Life continued. "The real choice is whether or not to have unprotected sex."

The other woman's face darkened. "But what about rape? What if the condom breaks?"

The pro-life advocate mimicked the other woman's tone of voice. "What about? What if? You're deflecting to tangential issues."

Ms. Pro-Choice scowled but I had to concede that the pro-lifer had a point. Trumpers used "what-about" arguments all the time to deflect, but now the shoe was on the other foot.

She jabbed a finger at the pro-choice sign. "Only one percent of rapes result in pregnancy, but rape is one of the allowable exceptions to abortion. My point is choices have consequences. The *choice* to have unprotected sex has consequences."

As I walked on toward the Farragut North Metro station, her words nagged at me: *choices have consequences*. I'd made an unwise choice to have unprotected sex with Doug. It was a moment when passion eclipsed wisdom. I realized that no matter what I decided to do about my pregnancy, I'd always wonder about the road I'd choose not to take.

At this hour on a Wednesday night, pedestrian and street traffic were light. I crossed K Street on the north side of Farragut Square at Connecticut Avenue, heading toward the Metro entrance on the corner.

I was lost in thought and, stupidly, not paying attention to my surroundings. When I looked up, a man wearing sunglasses, and a gray hoodie pulled over a baseball cap was striding purposefully toward me, a huge smile on his face.

He waved at me, but I didn't recognize him.

When he got to me, he threw his arms around me in an enthusiastic embrace. "So good to see you again," he gushed.

Before I could react or reply, he lifted me off my feet as if I weighed nothing, swung me around and, with his arms still encasing me in his straitjacket hug, toppled me into a minivan parked, side door open, at the curb on K Street.

"Hey!" was all I could say.

"Go! Go! Go!" the man hollered at the driver.

As the minivan bolted from the curb, the guy slid the door closed and stuffed my head into a canvas sack.

I couldn't see a thing.

Chapter Eleven

With all my might, I thrashed and struggled to break free, but the guy was too strong for me. In no time, he zip-tied my wrists and ankles.

This guy's good, I thought to myself. *Either he's an ex-cop, or ex-military.*

"Don't speed," he shouted at the driver.

I heard a metallic click. I don't know anything about guns, but it sounded like he was chambering a round.

Shit.

"Are we being followed?" he yelled.

"I don't think so." The voice belonged to a woman. Young. Scared.

As near as I could tell, we were driving northwest along Connecticut Avenue.

"The next chance you have, let's get onto some side streets and wind around. We're less likely to be seen by the cops than if we're on a main thoroughfare."

I didn't recognize his voice and he didn't seem to have any distinctive regionalisms.

"Okay," she said.

"Let me go," I hollered. My voice sounded especially loud to me because of the bag over my head.

"Shut up," he said. "Just shut it, bitch."

I writhed and tried to use my head to butt him, but it was useless. He'd done a splendid job of immobilizing me and holding me down on the floor, out of sight.

Soon the van slowed, turned right, then a quick left.

East on Desales, North on 17th, I reasoned, but then I got confused when the driver's zigzag pattern got complicated.

"Why are you doing this?" I yelled.

"Shut up."

He seemed to be fumbling for something, then I heard a *scritch* as if he was unspooling a roll of duct tape. That hunch was confirmed a second or two later when I felt him wrap something around my head so that the bag pressed hard against my mouth—a duct tape gag.

My anger suddenly turned to panic. Was I going to suffocate?

I tried to say "I can't breathe," but it came out as muffled gibberish.

Calm yourself.

Slowly, I took in a deep breath through my nose, held it, then exhaled slowly. Then again. Not only could I breathe, but doing so in a more mindful way eased my angst.

"Are we being followed?" he asked again.

"No. All clear."

"Okay. Look for an out-of-the-way place, a park maybe, so we can put our plates back on."

"Our plates." So, they're together. Married maybe? And if the van doesn't have license plates, I reasoned, *then any surveillance tape of my abduction won't be able to identify the owner of the van.*

Shit.

Plus the hoodie was pulled over his ball cap, so face recognition technology probably won't be any good.

Shit. Shit.

"How about here?" the woman asked after a while.

"No. Someone might come by walking a dog."

So far, they're being careful not to call each other by name, I noticed. *So far.*

I realized that I still had both my cell phones—my personal one, plus my government-issued one.

Maybe the cops can ping my phone and find me. This gave me a burst of hope.

The woman continued to drive. Slowly. Turning left and right at regular intervals.

She was meticulous about using her turn signals because I heard their distinctive *tick-TICK* just before she'd round a corner. The radio was off. All

I could hear was a *swish* as we passed parked cars. Occasionally, I'd hear a dog bark, a car honk, or a siren in the distance, but nothing that helped me get a handle on my whereabouts—or the two people who'd abducted me.

"How about here?" she asked again.

"Yeah," he said after a brief pause. "This is good."

The van came to a stop.

"Kill the lights," he ordered.

I heard her flip a switch.

"Here are the plates," he said.

Metal slid against thin metal as I pictured him handing her the license plates over the center console.

"Be quick about it."

She opened her door and got out.

A *whoosh* of cooler air swept into the vehicle. It was quiet outside. Were we in Rock Creek Park? I thought I heard rushing water, but couldn't be sure.

She slammed her door and soon I began to hear her attaching the license plates to the front and back of the vehicle. In fewer than two minutes, she got back in the driver's seat.

"Done!" she announced.

"Damn. I almost forgot."

"What?"

"Her phone."

Shit.

He began to frisk me roughly. He got a good feel, but no phone. Then I sensed him rummaging in my messenger bag.

"Here it is!"

Shit.

His breathing was excited as I heard him fumble with the case. "Here's the SIM card."

I heard a *snap*.

"Now they won't be able to track you," his voice a low growl in my ear.

"Won't she have two phones? One personal, one government?" the woman asked.

Shit.

"Yeah. Good thinking."

More rummaging.

"Got it!" he announced, followed almost immediately by another *snap*.

"Give 'em to me," she said. "I'll toss them."

"Not here. If they're able to trace her phones, this is where they'll look for them."

"What do you want to do?"

"Let's go home." For the first time since I'd been snatched there was less tension in his voice. "We'll deal with them—and her—there."

My tension, however, had just found more reasons to ratchet up a notch.

Shit.

Chapter Twelve

We drove in silence for what seemed like twenty minutes. The woman doing the driving had made so many turns I'd long since stopped trying to figure out where we were. Even if they'd stopped in Rock Creek Park to put their license plates back on, the park stretched for miles north and south through DC and into Maryland.

We could be anywhere.

Eventually the regular *swoosh* of parked cars going past the right side of the van sounded like we'd left the park and were back in a residential area winding again among side streets.

The hum of the tires on the pavement didn't vary for several minutes, but then the timbre changed, sounding as if we were going over a bridge.

It couldn't be Memorial Bridge over the Potomac, I reasoned, *or I'd hear more traffic.*

After about fifteen seconds, the sound changed back to solid pavement.

A short bridge?

The only short bridge over the Potomac I could think of was Chain Bridge, north of the District. My hunch was reinforced when the driver picked up speed and the turns became more gradual as if we were now cruising down a country road.

I'll bet we're in Virginia.

But why?

Where are they taking me?

What are they going to do with me?

To me*?*

When I was abducted, I'd heard what sounded like the guy chambering a round, but that was when the kidnapping was at its most precarious moment. I reasoned that the guy had been preparing or a possible shootout if someone had tried to intervene.

But that was at least a half hour ago. Since then, his breathing had slowed, and I sensed less tension from him. Plus, he never told me he had a gun, or in any way threatened that he'd shoot me. If he'd put the gun away, I didn't hear it. Maybe it was still in his hand, or on the back seat.

If he's ex-military, he's probably secured it again, perhaps in a holster.

My mind was racing, trying to be alert to my surroundings, trying to glean whatever I could about these two yahoos. If they simply intended to kill me, they would have done it by now. They could easily have shot me and then tossed me off Chain Bridge and into the Potomac.

Neither robbery nor murder seemed to be their motive.

I'd only caught a glimpse of the guy before he'd wrestled me into the van. He was White, muscular, and probably no more than forty.

The woman sounded White, and young, but I'd never actually seen her.

As my mind continued to spin, I figured that I was going to be held captive to extract a policy concession from the president—and maybe extort some money while they're at it. I wondered if this assault on my freedom and dignity was fueled by Rabid Roland's social media post amplifying the false report that I'd decided to have an abortion.

At times I tried to thrash and growl in protest, but it did no good. The guy's hold on me was firm. He had me wedged on the floor of the van, trapped between the driver's seat and the back seat. Trying to kick free or grunt my indignation was a waste of energy.

I tried to relax, but my heart and my mind were racing.

When the van finally came to a stop, it sounded like we were in a garage, the thrum of the van's engine bouncing off nearby walls.

When the woman turned off the motor, the sudden silence was deafening.

I heard her open her door and come around to the passenger side. My legs were pointing in that direction.

The side door slid open. She grabbed me by the ankles, turned me onto my back, then she began pulling me.

"Unlock the house first, hon," the guy said.

So, "hon." They're an item.

The woman let go of my feet. A moment later, I heard a key slide into a lock and a door opened.

Then she was pulling on my feet again.

When I was halfway out of the vehicle, the guy grabbed me under the shoulders so they were both carrying me into what seemed like a house with an attached garage.

I was determined not to make this easy for them, so I did my best to kick and wriggle.

The woman lost her grip momentarily and my zip-tied feet fell to what I sensed was the garage's concrete floor. Quickly, she recovered. Soon they carried me inside the house and through what seemed to be a long, narrow hallway.

As they carried me, they emitted various grunts and groans, but nothing intelligible.

After a moment, as I continued to struggle, I sensed that we'd entered another room. As we did, they swung me around so that now I was moving head first instead of feet first.

Then they stopped.

The man spoke as I dangled between them: "One. . . two. . ."

My body swung gently from side to side.

"Three!"

I was airborne for a second before I landed hard on my back onto what felt soft, like a bed. But, instead of lying on a bedcover, it sounded like I'd landed on plastic. That put the whole bed conclusion on hold, but at least whatever they'd thrown me onto was soft—like a mattress.

Then they left the room. And closed the door. And locked it.

I was alone. Still bound at my wrists and ankles. A bag over my head, duct taped against my mouth. In the dark.

* * *

I heard them walk away. Their voices were low, unintelligible.

The room was quiet. I tried to get my bearings and take stock.

I still had on my glasses but they were askew. I couldn't tell if they were broken, but the frame pressed into my forehead and right cheek.

Are they just going to leave me here to rot?

My stomach growled. It felt like it had been hours since the president and I had shared a light meal in the second floor Residence of the White House.

I needed to pee and assumed they'd come back soon to tend to me and maybe at least take the bag off my head so I could breathe better.

I assumed that at some point they'd talk to me and explain what was going on. Maybe they'd force me to videotape some sort of appeal to the president.

It seemed as though hours passed, but they didn't return. I heard them walking around upstairs. I thought I heard a television, and could have sworn I heard Roland's voice coming from it—or was my overactive mind playing tricks on me?

Once again, I took stock of my situation, both physical and emotional.

I began to draw on some relaxation and meditation techniques I'd learned over the past few months from Kris, my grief counselor.

I slowed my breathing. As I did, I focused on my body, fully aware of all my appendages, my chest, my stomach, my legs, my head.

I assessed my emotions. Anger seemed to be the dominant one.

How dare these assholes think they can control me.

For a moment, I lost my concentration and writhed in disgust. But the restraints were tight and doing their job effectively, so I stopped and gave in to the reality that I wasn't going to be going anywhere for a while.

More mindful breathing.

Amazingly—and totally out of character for me—I found myself trying to send positive (yes, *positive*) energy toward my captors. Other than robbing me of my freedom, they had not hit or tried to hurt me.

I'd heard fear in the young woman's voice at first.

They were a couple. That meant that at least on some level, they had the capacity to love—at least love each other, if not me.

But this wasn't about me. I was just a pawn, ensnared in the power play of two desperate people.

But what was fueling their desperation?

I sent them positive energy, hoping that some of it might eventually come back to me in the form of good karma.

I hadn't jettisoned my Christian faith since Doug died. Instead, Kris was helping me to see that spirituality—vital contact with the Divine—transcends religious dogma. Even before this moment, I'd been coming to feel more in touch with "God" than I ever had since being raised as an Episcopalian with my Aunt Annie back in Wisconsin.

So, as I lay on my back, bound and gagged in the dark, I was able to achieve a semblance of peace, even in the midst of my predicament.

But then my bladder began to badger me.

If they don't come back soon, I'm gonna wet my pants.

I rolled to my right side and sensed I was against a wall. Awkwardly, I maneuvered myself so that I could pound against it hard with my feet.

Bam! Bam! Bam!

I stopped to listen.

A TV was on, but unintelligible.

No voices.

And definitely no one was coming down here to take me to the can.

I tried again, harder this time.

BAM! BAM! BAM!

I stopped again to listen.

Thump! Thump! Thump!

At least one of them had heard me, but the thump on the ceiling was a definite message I interpreted as, *We hear you, and we don't care. Shit yourself, if you must.*

So I did.

That night, lying in the stench of my filth, I cried myself to sleep.

Chapter Thirteen

I didn't sleep well. The longer I lay there, the colder I got as the warm urine cooled against the skin of my buttocks and thighs. Any time I moved, it caused my feces to squish, emitting a fresh burst of gag-inducing toxicity.

In my mind's eye, I could see yellow and brown fumes enveloping me and slowly rising. I was basting in my waste.

Eventually, I began to hear the normal stirrings of a household coming back to life: a toilet flushing, the water rushing down a pipe somewhere between the walls; a television spewing unintelligible words into a room; muffled voices exchanging inanities.

Soon, I heard activity on the floor above me. The kitchen?

I heard my door open, but no one entered.

I turned toward the sound and tried to sit up.

"Mmmmmm! Mmmmmmmm!" is all I could say.

The door closed and I heard retreating steps. No doubt he (or she?) was just checking to make sure I was still there and had survived the night.

A few minutes later, the sweet aroma of frying bacon drifted into my nostrils. It helped to dissipate the smell of my steaming crap, but it was tormenting to know my captors were enjoying breakfast while I starved.

After a while, I heard the clatter of dishes, the scrape of chairs on a wooden floor, and water running into a sink. It was as if every sound brought an image immediately to my mind so that I could "see" what I was hearing.

By this time, I'd come to the conclusion that it would be wise to try to remain in the moment and not allow myself to think too far ahead. Doing so might cause me to jump to conclusions, or I'd begin to panic about worst-case scenarios that would sap all my energy—and sanity.

I heard the door open again and the rustle of clothing as at least one of them moved closer to the bed.

"How's she doing?" the woman asked from the doorway.

"Seems to me she's okay."

"Mmmmmmmm!" I said. Translation: "No. I'm NOT okay, you piece of shit."

"Pew. It stinks in here," she said.

"We need to get her changed and cleaned up."

No shit, I said to myself.

He futzed with the duct tape and snatched the bag from my head. The light was blinding. I had to squeeze my eyes shut before I could gradually open them and adjust.

He stood over me, leaning in, his face in shadow because of the ceiling light behind him.

I spit in his face. "Fuck you," I shouted. It felt *good.*

He gave me a stinging slap across my face that sent my glasses flying.

"Cletus, don't hurt her!" the woman shouted from the door.

He pulled back and wiped the spittle from his face with the untucked flap of his shirt.

The woman retrieved my glasses and placed them back on my face.

"Honest, hon, we don't want to hurt you," she said to me, her voice soothing and gentle.

"Yeah. Right." I snarled.

The lenses were badly smudged, and they didn't rest snuggly on my nose. The frame was bent and one of the nose pads had broken away causing the frame to dig painfully into the bridge of my nose.

The woman was pretty, almost angelic, with delicate features and dishwater blonde hair knotted at the top of her head. She wore jeans and a blue denim work shirt. So did he. His hair was close-cropped reinforcing my hunch he had military training.

"Why am I here? And where am I?"

The guy, Cletus, grabbed a chair from the desk next to the bed, pulled it close so it faced away from me, then sat with his Popeye forearms resting on the chair's back. His right forearm contained an intricately designed black tattoo of an upside-down hammer with lightning bolts radiating from the head.

"Here's the deal," he began. "You are our guest."

"Ha!"

"These are the rules of the house. One: you will remain immobilized until you earn the right to be trusted not to try to escape."

"Good luck with that," I said.

"Two. If you behave, you will be treated well."

"If I don't?"

"You already got a taste of my discipline. Three. You will be monitored 24/7 by one or both of us. You're not going anywhere."

"Why am I here?"

"You're smart. You'll figure it out."

I scowled and shook my head.

"Now we're gonna get you cleaned up, give you a change of clothes, and get you fed."

"That would be nice. It's the least you could do."

He pushed himself up and slid the chair back to its place by the desk.

"She's all yours, hon," he said to the woman. He stepped aside and made way for her to come to my side.

"Babe," she said to Cletus. "You need to free up her ankles so I can clean her up."

I could now tell that the bed they'd dumped me onto the night before was covered with a sheet of plastic. No doubt the plan all along was to break my spirit by having me soil myself. They'd pre-placed the plastic to protect the bedding.

Cletus moved to the foot of the bed and fiddled with the zip ties around my ankles. As he worked, I was able to get a better look at him. He was well built. Sturdy. Definitely handsome with blue eyes and a chiseled chin. I could see why the woman (*what the hell's her name?*) was attracted to him.

While he was freeing my ankles, the woman left the room briefly. When she returned, she carried cleaning supplies including rubber gloves and baby wipes.

He removed the zip ties, but continued to hold tightly onto my ankles. Leaning closer to my face, he said, "Let me be clear: you will *not*, I repeat: *NOT* try to kick my wife. Is that clear, bitch?"

"Let *me* be clear, you son of a bitch. If I am, indeed, your *guest*," I sneered the word, "then you will treat me with the dignity and respect I deserve as a human being."

He didn't answer. Instead, he loosened his grip on my ankles and stood back as his wife removed my two-inch pumps and daintily pulled off the bottom of my pantsuit. The act of exposing dried urine and feces to the air caused the stench to intensify.

She held her breath. It was clear she was trying to keep from gagging.

Interesting, I thought. *He's leaving the dirty work to her.*

She put on rubber gloves, balled up my ruined slacks and placed them on the plastic sheet next to me. As she worked, I studied her more closely.

She was petite, at least a foot shorter, and probably ten years younger, than he was. That would make her about five feet tall and thirty years old, maybe twenty-five—somewhere around my age.

She reached for my undies.

"Wait!" I ordered.

She stopped, surprised.

I looked at Cletus, glowering at me from the foot of the bed.

"I want *you* to step aside and at least give me a little privacy and dignity."

To my astonishment, he complied.

"Okay, go ahead," I said to her.

She began removing my panties.

"I know his name is Cletus," I said to her, gently. "What's yours?"

"Bon—"

"Don't answer her," Cletus shouted from the doorway. "She's just trying to weasel her way into your good graces."

Bon looked at me, gave me a shrug, and placed my thoroughly disgusting undies on top of my balled-up pants.

"Is it Bonnie?" I asked.

She didn't reply but gave me a look I interpreted as, *yeah, but it's our little secret.*

She used several wipes to clean off all the poop and dried urine on my bare legs. Cletus, meanwhile, stood guard at the door.

I laughed.

"What's so funny?" he asked, confused.

"Don't you see the irony?"

"Irony?"

"You two desperados are Bonnie and Clete." I laughed again. "You can't make this shit up."

She actually smiled, but Cletus said, "Fuck you," left the room, and slammed the door.

"Nice guy," I said to Bonnie.

"Actually, he is. He's just under a lot of stress."

"I'm sure he is. Kidnapping a U.S. government official and transporting her across state lines is a major *federal* offense. I hope you understand that by helping him, you're in deep doo-doo yourself." I nodded my head at the latest gob of my shit she'd just wiped from my ass and held in her gloved hand.

The sudden look of horror on her face showed that the metaphor had just become literal for her. The look passed quickly, however, and she continued to clean me, but she pursed her lips.

After a moment, Cletus was back, as intense as ever. While Bonnie continued to clean me, Clete returned to the foot of the bed and leaned in again.

"Okay, here's the deal," he said, his voice stern as if giving an order to one of the soldiers under his command, "Once Bonnie's got you squared away, you're gonna take a shower. You won't be able to get away because there are no windows in the bathroom, plus I'll be right outside the door—and I'm bigger and stronger'n you."

"Got it," I said. "Then what?"

"Clean clothes and breakfast."

"Charming."

"Are you always this lippy?"

"Always."

To be honest, my lippiness was a paltry cover for the dread I felt.

I looked around. As near as I could tell, the bedroom was windowless, too.

Finally, Bonnie finished wiping my lower extremities. She moved back and Cletus took her place. He yanked me to a sitting position, reached behind me, and removed the zip ties from my wrists.

My arms flopped limply at my side as blood rushed into them making them sting. I shook my arms to accelerate my circulation.

Clete then pulled me roughly to my feet.

Bonnie grabbed yet another wipe and gave a few swipes to clean off my rear end.

"Okay," he said. "Let's get you a shower. You stink."

He draped a heavy arm around my shoulders to steady me and guided me, almost tenderly, to the door.

The bathroom was just a few steps down the hall and on the right.

"Everything you need is in there, soap, shampoo, a towel. Bonnie and me'll be right outside the door waiting. Knock when you're done and Bonnie'll give you some clean clothes." For the first time, his voice was almost gentle.

"Thanks," I said. I meant it.

I entered the bathroom and the door closed behind me.

The room was cramped and dated—mid-fifties, I guessed. The sink was puke green, held up by two spindly metal legs. The toilet seat had a ruffled cover that resembled a green dust mop.

I looked at my reflection in the mirror. I was a horror.

My hair, never my finest feature, was a Medussa-like rat's nest of chaos. Dried mascara caked my cheeks. My smudged glasses were cock-eyed making me look as off kilter as I felt. I did my best to straighten them.

Sighing, I sat on the toilet and peed properly.

After wiping myself, I flushed, then removed my pantsuit jacket, blouse, and bra.

I turned to the bathtub, also green, and pulled aside the shower curtain decorated with yellow butterflies. A startled cockroach skittered down the drain.

Scowling, I adjusted the tub's hot and cold dials until the water temperature was just right before lifting the metal knob on the spigot. Water cascaded from the showerhead.

I stepped into the tub and let the warm wetness course over me. Gradually, the tension across the back of my shoulders eased and I began to feel human again. I almost started to cry, but caught myself in time.

You will not give in and give up, I said to myself sternly.

Slowly, I began to rub the bar soap against my skin until the lather was thick. The soap smelled good. I also shampooed my hair. I didn't recognize the brand but the aroma was sickeningly sweet like granny smith apples. But I was getting clean, so I didn't complain.

As I took my time washing, I let my mind roam. There's something about running water that gets me ruminating.

I assumed that by this time my staff would know I was late for work. It might still be a few hours before concern would turn to alarm.

I'd been snatched so quickly, I wondered if anyone had even noticed. Unless Bonnie and Clete used me to make a ransom demand, my disappearance would probably be a troubling mystery with reporters trying to find a connection to my predecessor Ron McClain's murder.

As I worked diligently to scrub away the grunge, my mind kept coming up with more and more questions:

Where am I?

Why am I here?

Just who are Bonnie and Clete?

Are they going to make a ransom demand?

Will they force me to record a plea to the president?

Will I be able to get through to Bonnie and somehow win her trust?

Will I be able to escape?

Will Clete try to rape me?

A pounding on the door interrupted my thoughts.

"Hurry up," Cletus hollered. "You're gonna use up all the hot water."

"I'm coming!"

To spite him, I extended my shower another minute.

Reluctantly, I turned off the water, stepped out of the tub, and dried myself with a towel of no better quality than what you'd find at a no-tell motel that rents rooms by the hour.

Before I'd finished, there was another knock on the door, lighter this time. The door opened.

"Here," Bonnie thrust a folded stack of clothing at me. "Something to wear."

"Thanks." I took the pile from her and placed it on the toilet seat then finished drying myself.

The ensemble she'd chosen for me was like hers: jeans and a flannel shirt. The jeans fit nicely, but the shirt was baggy. There were also fluffy slippers and panties.

"There's no bra," she called through the closed door. "I don't know what your size is."

"Thirty-four C," I said.

"I'll get you one later today."

"Thank you."

I dressed quickly, hung up the towel, and opened the door.

Bonnie greeted me with, of all things, a smile.

Cletus stood to her left—in the middle of the hallway I'd have to use if I ever wanted to try to escape—which I did.

"You hungry?" she asked.

"Starving. Literally."

She gestured toward the bedroom. (I almost referred to it as "my" room, but caught myself.)

Don't get too comfortable here, Lark.

When I stepped through the door, I saw a tray of food on the desk.

I took a seat. The plate was heaped with a tall stack of steaming pancakes drowned in butter and what smelled like real maple syrup. Two strips of crisp bacon were arrayed on either side of the pancake pile. A tall glass of OJ, but no coffee, completed the setting.

"Eat up," Bonnie chirped. "Now you're eating for two."

Chapter Fourteen

Eating for two? WTF!

For a moment, I stopped chewing, trying to fathom the import of Bonnie's statement.

If I'm eating for two, then my pregnancy is the reason I'm here. My mind was spinning. *If my pregnancy is why I'm here, maybe they're going to appeal to Will to withdraw his Triple-R bill.*

Even though both Bonnie and Clete were hovering over me in the background as if I were their fascinating new pet, I decided to take advantage of the opportunity to eat. So, while I shoveled pancakes and bacon into my mouth, washing it down with OJ, I tried to figure out my next steps.

I'm voraciously curious, so extracting as much information from them as I could seemed best. But, to a certain extent, questions reveal motives, so the less they could deduce anything about me and my thinking, the better.

I decided to make nice.

"Mmmm. This food is excellent, Bonnie."

"Thank you. There's more where that came from."

"Great."

"Seconds?"

"In a minute. Thanks."

As I chewed, I thought. Finally, without turning around, I spoke. "So, Cletus. What's the plan?"

"The plan?"

"Why am I here—and for how long?"

"You're here until I decide it's time to let you go." His tone was belligerent.

"And I'm here because . . . ." I let the question hang.

"Because you're a fertile myrtle and Bonnie isn't."

"What do you mean?"

"She can't have kids."

Bonnie began to cry. "We've tried, but I can't conceive."

"So, kidnapping me is the solution to your problem?"

"Maybe," she choked. "But it's bigger'n that. It's not about me, actually, it's about the baby."

"How so?"

"You said you're planning to kill it."

"I said no such—"

"Cletus and me decided to save it."

I let that sink in. Their decision to snatch me might have been a spontaneous decision after Roland made a big deal about my pregnancy. Were they making things up as they went, thinking long term, but hadn't really *planned* long term?

I stabbed the last piece of pancake with my fork and dragged it through a puddle of maple syrup, then put it in my mouth along with the last morsel of bacon.

"Mmmmmmm." I chewed slowly, then swallowed, stalling for time.

"More?" Bonnie asked immediately.

"Yes. Please." I slid my chair back to make room for her to take my plate. She picked it up and left the room.

I twisted in my chair to the left to look at Cletus who was sitting on the bed, forearms resting on his thighs.

"Are you planning to have me record some plea to President Gannon?"

"You mean to your lover boy?"

"C'mon, Clete. You don't really believe that shit about us, do you?"

He snorted. "Of course I do."

Obviously, the facts didn't matter to this guy, so I wasn't going to be able to change his mind.

I moved on.

"Am I going to have to record something?"

He shook his head. "Near as I can tell, they just think you didn't show up for work. Pretty soon they'll come to the conclusion that you couldn't take the heat so you got out of the kitchen."

I let his words sink in and thought more about them. As I did, Bonnie returned with another heaping plate, a pat of butter melting atop a steaming pancake pile doused with a generous smothering of maple syrup.

"Sorry I can't let you have coffee, Lark. Caffeine ya know."

"Right."

Actually, I'd forgotten. I'd been avoiding thinking much about the health of the developing fetus because I still wasn't sure I was going to go through with the pregnancy. I didn't want to get emotionally attached.

Attached to what?

What word do I use?

It?

Calling the fetus "it" seemed too impersonal because clearly something was growing inside me.

Baby?

I couldn't bring myself to use the word "baby" because I don't believe human life begins at conception in the same way the religious right does. To me, it's more likely that human life—spiritual life—begins when the baby takes its first breath—just as death occurs at our *last* breath.

But do I *know* that?

No.

The question "when does life begin?" is one of those unanswerable theological questions like, "How many angels are able to dance on the head of a pin?" Who the hell knows? Who the hell cares? Yet wars have been fought and people have been tortured and killed over such nonsense.

Even though I still had more than two months to decide whether to abort, if I didn't get away from these two wingnuts before August fourth, the decision would be made for me.

And that was entirely unacceptable.

Bonnie set the plate in front of me and I dug in again as if it was the last meal I'd ever have.

As I ate, I continued to mull my options. I could bolt for the door, but that would be futile—Cletus would be on me quickly and I'd be hogtied for sure. Best to be affable and accommodating, I decided.

"This sure is good, Bonnie."

"Thank you, Lark."

"Bonnie," I said after savoring a thoughtful bite, "Since Cletus tells me I'm a guest here, and you both seem to know so much about me, help me get to know you two better. What do y'all do for a living?"

"Don't—" Cletus tried to stop her but Bonnie was in Hospitality Mode.

"I work part time at Walmart and Cletus is a carpenter—like Jesus."

"How'd you meet?"

Clete tried again. "Bonnie. Hush now. Don't you see? She's trying to weasel information outta you."

"No she's not. She's just being friendly. She knows we don't intend to hurt her."

Obviously, Bonnie had already forgotten that Clete had given me a smack across the face. Had he ever hit her, too? If so, was she in denial about his dark side? Apparently.

Bonnie seemed eager to tell me the how-we-met-story. "Cletus had just gotten out of the Marines after two stints overseas—Iraq and Afghanistan."

"Thank you for your service," I said to him.

"Thanks," he mumbled.

"We met January 6th, 2021, at the U.S. Capitol building." Bonnie was talking rapidly.

"Trying to overthrow an election. Charming," I smiled, but seriously considered barfing.

"Cletus was bummed because he got there too late to get inside, but I was able to get him thinking about, um, *other* things," she giggled suggestively.

"Is this where you're both from?" I was hoping she'd let slip our location.

"Born and raised." She had a light southern accent.

"Fairfax?" I asked.

"Oh my no. Round Hill, Virginia. It's a little place outside Leesburg. We went to the same high school, but he's way older'n me so we didn't know each other growing up."

"What did you do in the Marines, Clete, or do you prefer Cletus?"

"I prefer 'sir.'"

"Were you an officer?"

"No, ma'am."

"Clete, then."

He harrumphed.

"What was your job in the Marines?"

"Infantry."

"A patriot."

"Damn straight."

"We both love this country, Lark," Bonnie said. "We're sick to death of the moral rot that's causing our great republic to crumble."

"Moral rot, like abortion?"

"Yes."

"And kidnapping?"

"Um," she said cleverly.

"Not if it's for a higher purpose," Cletus said, coming to her rescue.

"Let me guess." I looked at him. "Is the higher purpose to preserve the life of the unborn?"

"Exactly."

"And where does this fervor come from? Your religion?"

"Yes," Bonnie said. "We are trying to do God's will."

"What's your religious upbringing, and is it the same for both of you?"

"I was raised Southern Baptist." She pronounced it Babtist. "I was saved as an itty bitty but never really knew Jesus until I began attending Christ Fellowship. It's a nondenominational church. That's when the leader of my Bible study suggested I start listening to Roland Roberts' broadcasts."

By this time my gag reflex was on overdrive, but I was determined to milk these two for all I could get.

"What about you, Clete?"

When he didn't respond, Bonnie helpfully answered for him. "He was Catholic, but we both now go to Christ Fellowship and listen to Roland. He makes so much sense."

"Where do you get your news?" I asked.

"From Roland," she said as if it should be obvious. "He tells the truth."

"Have you ever met him?" I asked.

"No, ma'am."

"I have."

"I know."

"Would it matter if I told you I know for a fact that what he's reported about me is *not* the truth?"

"No, it wouldn't matter," Cletus finally spoke, his voice harsh. "That's because you are a lying, whoring, Jezebel. You speak for the Deep State. Your boyfriend, Gannon, is a puppet and a tool for all that's bad about this country."

"Uh huh." I was literally speechless. Their minds were made up based on Roland's lies and innuendos.

"Let me be sure I understand," I said. "Even though you've never met Roland Roberts, you're willing to believe what he says about me, even though I'm sitting right in front of you and am able to tell you the truth about myself."

"I don't believe a word you say," Cletus said. "The Bible says the devil is a liar. The truth is not in him."

"I'm the devil?"

"Not literally. How stupid do you think I am?"

I chortled. "Do you really want me to answer that?"

"You are doing the devil's work. Bonnie and I are doing God's."

"Do you intend for me to give birth here, in this room?"

"Yes, ma'am."

"And then what happens to me? What happens to the baby?"

Silence.

I looked back and forth between them. "You haven't thought things through, have you?"

More silence.

Chapter Fifteen

Their silence confirmed my hunch: they hadn't thought very far ahead. Therefore, I had to escape before they came up with a workable plan.

As soon as I began to realize I could be stuck here for months, I immediately got panicky and depressed. Quickly, however, I came to the conclusion I needed to think short term and not allow myself to settle in for the long haul.

I would try to think moment by moment. If I could endure just one moment, then the next one would be manageable, too. And the next. And the next. And during those moments, I would analyze and strategize.

After I downed the last of my OJ, Bonnie cleared away my plate and utensils and took them up to the kitchen where I heard her above me running water in the sink to do the dishes.

While Bonnie bustled about the kitchen, Cletus stayed in the room with me. He stood up from his place on the bed and walked to the other chair in the room against the wall at the foot of the bed. He dragged the chair to the open doorway where he took a seat, effectively blocking my exit.

"For the time being," he said, "either Bonnie or me will sit here and keep an eye on you so you won't be able to escape."

"Twenty-four seven?"

"Yup."

"That means you guys are being held captive, too."

He shrugged. "Yeah. But it's worth it because we're saving a life."

"It's gonna get pretty boring, Clete."

He grunted. "I'll figure something out."

"Do I at least get something to read to keep my mind active?"

He cocked his head as if reading was an alien concept. Come to think of it . . . .

When he didn't answer, I tried again. "Look, Clete, I have an active mind. I need to feed it. Plus, I think it's only fair that you allow me a glimpse into the outside world. Someday I'll be going back to my day job and I need to try to keep up with current events."

"The main thing is to keep you healthy."

"Good health includes good *mental* health. I need to feed my mind, not just my body."

He ignored me.

I tried a new tack. "Did you know my boyfriend served in Afghanistan?"

"Yeah. I heard that. Too bad he became a junkie."

I winced. "Doug wasn't a junkie. He was an addict."

"Same thing."

I felt hot tears beginning to form. "He became addicted to opioids when he lost a leg in a bombing. He earned a Purple Heart."

Clete shrugged. "Next time you see him, thank him for his service." A sneer creased his face.

"I c-can't." My voice broke. "He died of a heroin overdose a couple months ago."

Cletus looked down and picked at a cuticle. Meanwhile, Bonnie continued to clunk around upstairs.

I nodded toward the ceiling. "What does she do at Walmart?"

"Check out."

"Doesn't she have to go to work now?"

"She's part time. Off today."

"What about you? Do you work for yourself?"

He nodded.

"Clients? Gigs? How are you going to earn money while you're busy controlling my life?"

"I'll figure it out. Don't you worry your pretty little head about that."

"I'd like something to read now, please."

He swiveled his head toward the hallway behind him. "Hey, Bon?" he hollered.

The clunking upstairs stopped for a moment and her voice came through the ceiling. "Yeah?"

"Bring our guest a Bible, will ya?"

* * *

I spent the next couple hours reading a King James Version of the Bible while Cletus put in earbuds and listened to heavy metal music on his phone. I know it was heavy metal because the sound bled into the room. It's amazing his ears weren't bleeding, too.

After a while, I moved to the bed and lay down. Soon I was dozing.

When I woke up, Bonnie was sitting in the chair.

"Where's Clete?" I asked.

"He's around," she smiled, unhelpfully.

I listened, but heard no other sounds in the house.

Is Cletus away? Maybe I can overcome Bonnie and make a break for it.

I have anger issues, but I'm not a violent person. Something fundamental in me did not want to hurt Bonnie. Plus, in my condition, even if I got past her and made it out the door, she'd be coming after me, so I doubted I'd have the physical stamina to keep running.

What if she has a gun?

Even so, I began to casually look around to see if there was anything I could use to knock her out.

The room was barren: a bed, two chairs, an empty desk, a dresser with a lamp on it against the far wall.

Bonnie sat placidly on her chair listening to Christian music on her phone piped into her ear buds. I know the music was Christian because she sang softly along with the song. The catchy lyrics were: "Jesus, Jesus, Jesus, Jesus, Jesus, Jesus, Jesus, Jesus Lord."

The second verse was much like the first.

Oy.

I would have liked to have tried to extract more information from Bonnie by engaging her in conversation, but her ear buds were a barrier between us.

My mind returned to thoughts of how to escape.

I was still lying in bed, so I turned onto my left side, my back to the wall, and pretended to nap.

Enemies Domestic

I closed my eyes, but not all the way. Through the slit between my eyelids, I eyed the chair by the desk at the head of the bed and imagined how I'd pick it up quickly and efficiently, then bring it down onto Bonnie's head before she had a chance to react. After that, I'd bolt and hope for the best.

Bonnie's eyes were closed in ecstasy as she continued to mouth the words of the inane song.

Now's my chance.

Very slowly, I opened my eyes.

Very slowly and quietly I pulled myself up.

Very slowly I swung my legs to the floor.

Bonnie remained oblivious.

I looked at the chair. In one swift motion, I could grab it by the two sides, lift it over my head, take a long step toward Bonnie, and slam it onto her head.

I stood.

I reached for the chair.

Just then I heard the throaty growl of a motor pulling up in the direction of the garage where my captors had parked their minivan.

Cletus was back.

Chapter Sixteen

Before Bonnie noticed me standing, I quickly lay back down on the bed and listened as I heard the groan of the garage door opening. I still was unsure of the layout of the house, so I tried to listen closely to better understand the setting.

Based on the low rumble of his vehicle's engine, I pictured Clete's vehicle of choice as an alpha-male black pick-up truck. I couldn't tell if he'd driven into the garage and parked next to the minivan, or if it was a one-car garage and he was parked in the driveway.

I heard some clanking as if he was getting something metallic out of the back of his truck. A moment later, I heard the garage door closing, followed by a door down the hall opening. An instant later Clete appeared in the doorway behind Bonnie, still enraptured, eyes closed, listening to the Christian music on her phone.

He tapped her on the shoulder.

Her eyes flew open, startled. She yanked the buds from her ears and I could hear the tinny sound of the music more clearly. She turned her head to look up at him.

"All good?" he asked.

"All good. She's been sleeping, mostly."

"Okay. I got the stuff. You need a break?"

"Yeah. I need to go to the bathroom." She got up and went down the hall.

He took the seat she'd just vacated and looked toward me.

I'd been feigning sleep, but opened my eyes and glared at him. "Where were you?"

"You sure do ask a lot of questions."

"Yep. In your world women are supposed to keep quiet, huh?"

He grimaced, but had no reply.

Bonnie returned after a few minutes.

"I need to go, too," I said.

Clete stood and moved the chair out of the way. They both backed down the hall, clearing a path for me to get to the bathroom, but their bodies blocked my way so I wouldn't be able to dash down the hall and out the door—wherever that was.

I used the toilet and washed my hands quickly but left the water running as I quietly opened the medicine cabinet and drawers to see if they contained anything I could use as a weapon, or to facilitate an escape.

The only thing that might be even remotely useful was a small scissors in one of the drawers, but I decided to leave it there while I thought about how I might be able to utilize it.

When I opened the door, the two of them were waiting for me.

I went back to the bedroom and lay down on my back, hands laced behind my head.

"I'll be in the garage working," Clete said to Bonnie.

"Okay, Babe. We'll be fine." She moved the chair into the doorway and sat.

He gave her shoulder a quick squeeze, turned and left.

"What's he working on?" I asked.

"A project."

"Does it have anything to do with me?"

"You'll see."

"What were you listening to?"

"A Christian band—Blood of the Lamb." She unplugged the buds from the base of the phone. "Wanna listen?"

"That's okay. Thanks. I'm fine with the quiet."

She shrugged.

Down the hall in the garage, I heard Cletus banging around.

"Is his workshop in the garage?"

"Uh huh."

I heard some rattling and banging. Before long he came into the room carrying a metal post with a heavy chain attached to it. In the other hand, he carried an electric drill.

He knelt next to the head of the bed.

I turned onto my side to get a better view of what he was doing.

He pulled aside a throw rug next to the bed revealing a cement floor. The base of the metal post had three large bolts. He used the drill to embed the bolts into the floor. The sound of the drill was shrill, prompting me to stuff my fingers into my ears. Cement dust billowed up, but dissipated quickly.

In fewer than two or three minutes, Clete had installed the metal post, then he extracted handcuffs from his back pocket.

"Let's try these on for size." He grinned at me, grabbed my left hand, cuffed it, then connected the other end to the chain attached to the post.

"Really?" I said.

"Yeah. You won't be going anywhere for a while, so get used to it." He stood and looked down admiringly at the handiwork of locking down his handmaid.

I felt like crying but was damned if I was going to show any weakness to Clete. He didn't like lippy women, so I was determined to be as annoyingly lippy to him as I could.

"You're one strong guy, Clete."

"You bet I am."

"So strong you've got to handcuff a woman to control her. It's all about power with you, isn't it, tough guy?"

"Fuck you," he said, gathered up his tools, and stalked out of the room.

"Really, Bonnie? This is your man?"

"He's a good man. And I love him. He's doing this for me."

I'm Alice and this is my rabbit hole, I said to myself.

It wasn't until that evening that I discovered just how much this rabbit hole was distorting reality.

After uncuffing me, Bonnie served me an admittedly tasty and nourishing dinner—meatloaf, green beans, and mashed potatoes, plus a salad and whole milk to wash it down.

I ate slowly, quietly, thankfully.

When I was through, Cletus cleared away the dishes and Bonnie placed her laptop on the desk in front of me.

"We're just in time to see Roland's show," she said as she tapped a few keys.

Cletus returned with a big bowl of popcorn and sat on the bed. I was still at the desk where I ate. Bonnie sat on a chair behind me. We passed the popcorn bowl around and settled into a twisted version of movie night in lunatic fringe America.

To be honest, I'd barely ever seen Roland's show from start to finish—I could only stomach about two minutes before I'd have to change the channel.

Now I was a captive audience. Literally.

His show was slick, great production values. It began with a fast-paced open of quick video clips of Gannon, a shot of me at the podium, the iconic Truman Balcony of the White House, and the Capitol dome. Then Roland was front and center in a gaudy red sport coat and red bow tie.

"Good evening and welcome to this edition of the Roland Report. Tonight: more palace intrigue at the White House. Rookie White House Press Secretary Lark Chadwick, barely two days into her new job, is missing. Officially, the White House is tight-lipped."

There was a quick sound bite featuring Nora, my assistant, at the briefing room podium: "I have nothing for you on that," she said.

Roland continued. "Chadwick didn't show up for work today, but no one in the Gannon administration is telling me why. But I have my theories."

"You go, Roland," I said to the screen. "When there are no facts, you'll make them up."

"Hush, now, Lark," Bonnie said. "I want to hear this."

"Theory one: Gannon cynically threw Lark Chadwick into the role of his chief mouthpiece because she's his 'close friend.'" Roland used his fingers to pantomime exaggerated air quotes and winked in a "yeah, right" way. "Gannon knows she's pregnant and would be having to field questions about her condition even as he pushes his pro-death agenda."

"This guy is so full of shit," I muttered.

Roland was on a roll: "My theory is that Lark, who's already in over her head in a job she's clearly unqualified to do, has seen the light and dropped off the grid—too embarrassed to show her face in public. This after I reported that she has decided to have an abortion."

"Not true, Roland, you piece of shit."

"Speaking of friends," Roland continued. "This reporter recently overheard a conversation between Chadwick and her close friend Paul Stone, her former colleague at the Associated Press and son of the infamous Lionel Stone.

"Turns out, Lark is offering comfort and support to Paul Stone as he plans to have a sex change operation. Is nothing, not even gender identity, sacred?"

"What the fuck!" I shouted. I jumped to my feet, picked up the bowl of popcorn, dashed it against the screen, and stalked toward the door.

Cletus grabbed a fistful of my shirt and threw me roughly onto the bed.

"You're not going anywhere, bitch."

Chapter Seventeen

Anger has never been my friend. But, God, my outburst felt good.

Bonnie was in tears. The popcorn bowl had shattered against her laptop. Ceramic shards of the bowl littered the floor, along with plastic pieces of the broken computer, and a scattering of popcorn kernels like gigantic snowflakes.

But at least I'd silenced Roland.

An enraged Cletus glared down at me as I lay on my back in the bed. He drew back his right arm and made a fist.

"Cletus! Don't!" Bonnie hollered.

Clete hesitated, nostrils flared. For a moment I feared he'd smash me in the face, but the alarm in Bonnie's voice got to him. Instead, he grabbed my hand and slapped a handcuff onto my wrist, binding me to the metal post. Then he stormed out of the room.

Meanwhile Bonnie, whimpering on her hands and knees, began to clean up the mess I'd made.

"You broke my computer," she wailed.

"You kidnapped me and took away my freedom." My voice was steel.

She sniffled.

After a few moments, Clete was back with a broom and dustpan. "I'll get this," he said to her, his voice gentle.

Bonnie stood, face flushed, cheeks wet.

When Clete was done sweeping up the mess, he said to her, "Let's go."

Together they walked to the door, switched off the overhead light shut the door, and locked it.

I was alone in the dark handcuffed to a metal post with the rest of the night ahead of me to stew.

As I lay there, I let my mind roam.

One thing Roland said kept tugging at me: Was Will Gannon cynically using me and my pregnancy to advance his political agenda? What kind of *friend* would do that?

I remembered back to more than a year ago when Will and I had first met. He was governor of Georgia and a candidate for president. I was the cops and courts reporter for a kick-ass daily paper in Columbia, a small town about two hours southwest of Atlanta.

A story I'd broken prompted Gannon to capitalize on it. He'd scheduled a campaign stop in Columbia to tout his new initiative, but when I'd asked him tough questions about it, he'd faltered. His wife, Rose, stepped in on his behalf which began my friendship with her. Sadly, she succumbed to pancreatic cancer not long after he was sworn in as president.

At a time when both Will and I were grieving our losses, he made me his "First Friend," a deft way of sidestepping the mutual attraction we both seemed to have for each other but hadn't yet explored.

Friendship put our relationship at a safer arm's length distance. Good thing. I'm a nobody from Wisconsin and he's the frickin President of the United States and now, at forty-eight, the world's most eligible bachelor.

I'd told the president it was a "dumb idea" to make me his press secretary. Now, with every passing day, my observation seemed to prove its truth. I would not be lying here in the dark, handcuffed to a metal post, had I turned down Will's job offer.

My thoughts drifted to alarm for my friend Paul Stone's safety, not to mention the well-being of my friend and mentor Lionel Stone and his wife Muriel. They were still trying to come to grips with Paul's recent revelation to them that he's gay. Now, someone as despicable as Roland broadcasts a lie that their son is about to have gender reassignment surgery.

If someone could easily snatch me off the street and hold me captive because they believed I was going to have an abortion, what might some enraged sicko do to Paul simply because he believes he's Paula?

American politics—always fraught and violent—had come to a point where it was no longer good enough to win the argument, you had to demonize and demolish your opponent. Seeking common ground and compromise was seen as a moral weakness. It was now all about winning.

My thoughts also turned to my pregnancy. Something was, indeed, growing inside me—a part of Doug.

Damaged Doug.

If I chose to give birth, would the child have inherited Doug's addiction gene?

What would life be like for me as a single parent?

Parenting isn't for everyone. Loquacia Brown was resigned about parenthood, but that's far short of joy.

The woman protestor in Lafayette Square seemed passionate about being a mom, even though her child was born with Down's.

And then there were people in the world like Bonnie. She wanted children, but was embittered because she was barren. Not everyone goes to the lengths she and Cletus had, but her pain was real, and widely felt by a big chunk of the population.

I began to wonder what I'd do if I were still being held captive after August fourth, the last date when I could have a legal abortion. Would I, in desperation, be able to use a coat hanger to bring about my own abortion?

How would I even be able to get my hands on a coat hanger if I'm handcuffed to a bed for the next eight months?

The more I thought about coat hangers, the more I realized that's not me. I'm not some terrified teenager ashamed of being pregnant, panicked that her folks might find out.

Stewing in the dark brought my thoughts back around to my anger.

"Fight and flight." That's how Muriel Stone had once described my behavior several years ago. Since then, I'd made progress controlling my angry impulses, but my latest outburst, even though momentarily satisfying, had only made matters worse for me.

If it hadn't been for Bonnie's intervention, Cletus most certainly would have socked me in the face, maybe broken my jaw. But now I had alienated her, too, by breaking her laptop.

Sure. I had every right to be angry. But my righteous anger was only making my situation more bleak and dire.

My back was against the wall—literally. Now my anger seemed to have made it impossible to escape.

What should I do?

What could I do?

Nevertheless, I began to hatch a new plan.

Chapter Eighteen

I was in the middle of a vivid dream when Cletus shook me awake.

"Time to walk the dog," he snarled.

"Wh-what are you talking about?"

The chain rattled as he uncuffed me and yanked me out of bed.

"Taking you to the bathroom before you shit yerself again, bitch."

He jerked me so hard I thought he'd pull my arm from its socket. I almost had to run to keep up.

He shoved me into the bathroom and slammed the door behind me. If Bonnie wasn't awake, she was now.

For a moment, I stood stunned, still trying to get my bearings. There were no windows in this room, or the bedroom, so I had no sense of time or whether it was day or night. It felt pre-dawn.

I switched on the light and looked at myself in the mirror over the puke green sink. My hair was a mess—which it usually is anyway. My face was puffy, eyes baggy. I could only bear to look at myself for a moment before I became discouraged.

I turned on the hot water. While waiting for the water to warm, I stealthily locked the door. As I gathered my wits, I splashed water in my face.

The remnants of my dream were beginning to wear off. I dried my face and sat on the toilet, trying to figure out the meaning of my dream before it vanished entirely.

In the dream, I'd driven to a remote, rocky location. It felt like somewhere in the Middle East—where I've never been, except for in the movies, on TV, or in the news. For some reason, after I parked, I took a roundabout route on foot to enter a stone structure. Was I trying to evade detection? Not sure, but that's what it felt like.

As the dream continued, I kept climbing higher and higher, away from a gathering of young bearded men who were, it seemed, at a retreat center gathering for a group meeting.

As I continued to climb, I realized I'd gotten myself into a precarious position: I was now nearing the pinnacle of the stone structure but, when I looked down, I found myself feeling much like a kitten stuck in a tall tree. The angle of the slick marble buttress I'd climbed was so steep that if I tried to go back down, I'd easily lose my balance and tumble head over heels to my death on the building's stone floor.

In order to save myself, I risked having to reveal my presence.

It was at that point that Clete had roughly rousted me.

I must have dozed while still on the toilet because a banging on the door brought me back to consciousness.

"You done yet, bitch?"

"I'm coming," I said. "Just a sec."

I wiped myself, flushed, pulled up my jeans, and moved to the sink to wash my hands.

"I'm gonna take a shower," I announced.

"No. You're not. Not today. We can't use up all the hot water on you."

Shit, I said to myself. "All right. Gimme a minute."

I turned on the sink spigot and used the sound of running water to cover the sound of what I was going to do next.

Quickly, I unbuttoned and unzipped my jeans and pulled them down, along with my panties, then I opened the medicine cabinet door and removed the small scissors I'd noticed the night before.

Moving as fast as I could, I opened the scissors and sliced the blade into the pad of my left index finger. It stung.

Immediately deep red blood began oozing from the wound.

I dabbed the blood into the crotch of my underpants, which I'd pulled down to just above my knees.

"C'mon." Clete pounded on the door again. "I don't have all day."

"Almost done."

I squeezed my finger to get more blood to pool, then blotted and smeared more of it onto my panties, adding to the size of the bloody patch.

As I returned the scissors to its place in the medicine cabinet, I put my finger into my mouth to accelerate the coagulation. With my right hand, I grabbed a box of Band-Aids and extracted one.

The bleeding had stopped briefly, but my finger still hurt. I used both hands to unseal the Band-Aid, careful to keep my injured index finger extended and out of the way.

When more blood appeared, I jabbed my finger into the crotch of my panties once more, adding to the bloody stain, then I wound the Band-Aid tightly around my finger, grateful that the adhesive was clear and would be less obvious.

Cletus tried the door. The handle rattled.

"I'm coming, Clete."

I pulled up my pants, zipped up and buttoned the top button, then turned off the water.

When I opened the door, Cletus was glowering at me, his face a thunderstorm.

"I need to talk to Bonnie," I said, doing my best to look wild-eyed panicky.

"What for?"

"About my lady parts. You wouldn't understand."

He took me by the arm and hauled me back to the bed. With both hands on my shoulders, he pushed me to a sitting position, then reattached my left wrist to the handcuffs attached to the metal post.

"I'll go get her," he said, his voice gruff.

In a moment, Bonnie was at the doorway. "What's up?" Her face was impassive. I could tell she was still pissed at me for breaking her computer.

"I think my pregnancy is at risk," I said.

A look of horror came over her face. "What's wrong?"

"Vaginal bleeding. I just now saw it in the bathroom."

"Oh my God." She moved toward me. "Quick. Lie down," she ordered.

"I think I need to see a doctor," I said.

She ignored me. Instead, she unbuttoned, unzipped, and pulled down my jeans and panties.

"See?" I nodded at the blood.

"Uh huh." She placed her hand on my abdomen and pushed gently. "Any pain?"

What do I say? Pain can't be a good thing. "Yeah," I lied.

"Just a sec," she said.

She left and went into the bathroom where I heard the water running. After a moment, the water stopped and I heard her dry her hands, then rummage around for something.

In a moment, she was back wearing latex gloves.

"How far along is your pregnancy?"

"About thirteen weeks."

"Are you still experiencing morning sickness?"

"A lot." Another lie.

"What about cramping?"

I figured cramping can't be good, so I went with it. "Yeah. Lots."

"Okay."

She was inspecting the blood and looking closely at my vagina, but made no move yet to touch it.

"Have you had any pain going to the bathroom?"

"Yeah. Some." Another Pinocchio.

She used two fingers to more closely examine my vagina, then leaned back.

"Okay. Pull up your pants. You're gonna be fine." Her tone had shifted from concerned to annoyed.

"What? How do you know? Shouldn't a doctor be part of this?"

"No need." She folded her arms. "You're faking this."

"No I'm not. You saw the blood. Something's wrong. You, of all people, should care that I have a healthy baby."

"Oh, I do. And you will."

"How can you be so sure?"

"One. There's no blood in your vagina, only in your pants. Two. There's a fresh Band-Aid on your finger, and the packaging is in the trash in the bathroom. You cut yourself and spread the blood around."

"You're not a doctor. I need to see a doctor."

"No you don't. You'll be fine."

"How the hell do you know?" I sneered. "You're just a parttime check-out clerk at Walmart."

"Yeah, but I'm also a midwife. I've delivered hundreds of babies."

Her grin was triumphant as she removed her latex gloves with a snap.

Chapter Nineteen

After taking off her latex gloves, Bonnie turned on her heel, left the room, and slammed the door, leaving me handcuffed on the bed—and despondent.

Once again, I was alone in a barren room, trapped in a house with a desperate and barren woman, with only the Bible and my thoughts to keep me company.

I'm not anti Bible, but I'm certainly not warm to the King James Version which, at times, is barely readable—at least for me. The book, fortunately, was in reach. It was on the left side of the desk at the head of the bed. I could reach it by lying on my left side and extending my right arm to retrieve it.

The chains rattled against the cement floor and clanked against the metal post as I turned onto my back and opened the book. I leafed through the pages randomly, stopping at times to read a passage from Proverbs or Psalms, my two most favorite books of the Bible. But nothing jumped out at me.

After a few minutes, I returned the Bible to its place on the desk.

I wasn't totally immobilized. I could stand, and the chain was long enough that I could take two steps to sit at the desk. I could also do planks to keep my abs relatively toned—but I didn't do any of that.

I didn't feel like doing anything. I'd honestly thought that an alarmed Bonnie would immediately get me to a doctor—or get a doctor to come to me—which I hoped would increase my chances of escape.

Now I continued to stew about my predicament. And when I stew, I ask questions. And when I ask questions, they keep piling up and smothering any answers.

What's going on back at the White House?

Does Will know that I've been abducted, or is my absence baffling?

Now that I'm locked down, how am I going to get free?

Is there any way I can make peace with Bonnie and Clete?

Is there any way I can negotiate a relaxation of my restraints?

Is there any chance they will relax their guard and I can make a break for it?

All those questions were psychologically depressing. Sleep became a merciful escape.

* * *

I awoke with a start when I heard the door open. Cletus burst in and came directly to the bed, a stern look on his face.

In a flash I was worried about my personal safety. Was Bonnie at work? Was I alone in the house with Clete? Would he try to rape me?

Ever since being sexually assaulted a few years ago by my English professor, I'd had serious trust issues with men. Now I was at the mercy of a merciless man who was much stronger than I. He had serious misogyny issues. His anger at me was like a tensed spring restrained only by Bonnie. Now that she wasn't here (was she?) what might he do to me to establish his dominance?

All of that flashed through my mind in the moment it took for him to unlock the handcuff, pull me to my feet, and drag me down the hall to the bathroom.

"Do what you've got to do," he said gruffly and gave me a shove. He actually shut the door to give me a modicum of privacy.

As I took advantage of the opportunity to go to the bathroom, I decided on a new tack.

After I finished my business, I washed and dried my hands, then opened the door, greeted by Clete's perpetual scowl.

"Thanks," I said. "I appreciate that you're being attentive to my basic needs."

He grunted, but said nothing, just took me by the arm and guided me back to the bed.

To my surprise, and relief, he didn't handcuff me again. Instead, he grabbed a chair, positioned it in the doorway and sat, watching me as if I were some sort of curiosity at a zoo.

For a moment we sat quietly looking at each other.

"I'm sorry," I said.

"For what?"

"We've gotten off on the wrong foot. I have anger issues, it's my worst trait."

"One of many."

I shrugged. "Anyway, I'd like to try to start over with you."

A look of surprise crossed his face.

"I know that you care a lot about Bonnie."

He nodded his agreement.

"She's a good and kind person. I can tell."

"She is."

"And I've alienated her, too."

"Yeah. You have. Big time."

"I couldn't disagree more with what you're both doing to me—and why—but here we are, so I'm going to try to change and make amends."

"I'm listening."

I had no idea what I'd say next, so I let it sit there a moment while I thought. Questions are my comfort zone, so I tried one.

"Help me better understand you, Clete. As a person. What makes you tick?"

For the first time, he smiled. The transformation from stern authoritarian to something more relaxed was stunning. Once again, I could see why Bonnie had fallen for him. He was an Adonis. But I'd long ago learned that character trumps looks and, as far as I was concerned, this guy's character was depraved. Yet, even so, he was a fellow human being and I was now determined to try to understand him better.

"What makes me tick?" he repeated, trying out the question. "No one's ever asked me that before in quite that way."

"Let me ask it a different way: how are you different now than when you were, say, twelve years old? How are you different—and why?"

He became thoughtful, scratching his chin.

"Use both sides of the page if necessary," I smiled, doing my mightiest to inject levity to lighten the mood and lessen what had been thick tension between us.

"When I was twelve . . . ." His voice trailed off and I could tell he was trying to retrieve a memory. "When I was twelve I was already the man of the house."

"Why? What happened?"

"My daddy was a no good drunk. Beat up my ma, then left her for someone else."

"Were you the oldest?"

"Uh huh."

"Out of how many?"

"Seven."

"Catholic?"

"How'd you know?"

"An educated guess."

"You Catholic?" he asked.

I shook my head. "Episcopalian."

He cocked his head as if he'd never heard of it.

"Catholics who flunked their Latin," I joked.

He still didn't get it.

I tried again. "Same rituals, less guilt."

"Got it." A wry smile.

"How many boys? How many girls?"

"Six boys including me and one baby sister."

"So at twelve you're the head of the house riding herd over a bunch of rowdy boys."

"Yup."

"Must've been fun."

"Not really."

"How'd you handle it?"

He raised his right fist. "Power."

I nodded at his tattoo. "Is that what your tat is all about?"

"Damn straight." He looked at it admiringly. "Thor's Hammer. Strength, power, protection."

"What did you want to be when you grew up?"

"I was always good with my hands. Was good at making things and fixing stuff."

"Then what?"

"Soon as I turned eighteen, I got the hell out."

"Army?"

He looked offended. "Marines. Three hots and a cot."

"Meaning?"

"Three good meals a day, and a place to sleep."

I wasn't sure what to ask next, so I let the silence hang there. Often, this is the place in a normal conversation when the other person asks a question. But this guy seemed to like being on the receiving end of my curiosity. He sat in the doorway patiently waiting for my next question.

I thought about asking how he acquired his political views, but the phrasing that came to mind—"have you been a Fascist all your life?"—seemed a bit too provocative. Plus I felt a discussion about politics would undermine my purpose of trying to make peace through humanization.

Instead, I sat dumbly on the bed.

After a moment, he got bored, stood, walked to me, and reattached the handcuff to my left wrist.

"Good talk," he said, turning toward the door. "Thanks."

As he left the room, he closed the door. Gently.

Chapter Twenty

There's nothing like having your freedom taken away, to be trapped with no place to go, that helps you quickly discern the difference between what you can control and what you can't.

My brief conversation with Cletus gave me a glimmer of hope. He could have sexually assaulted me. Instead, he let me question him. I wouldn't say he allowed himself to be vulnerable—that would have been asking too much—but my lack of antagonism toward him may have helped to dial back his antagonism toward me.

My physical freedom was severely limited, but I still had my mind. That, too, had its limits. The biggest limitation: not knowing what was going on in the outside world. By now the people closest to me—Will, my staff, Paul, and perhaps Lionel and Muriel—probably knew I was missing and may be alarmed because going off the grid is out of character for me.

How were they reacting?

All I could control was how to behave in any given moment. Deep, mindful breathing became my friend, my go-to activity to stay centered and sane.

One surprisingly soothing thing I noticed is that when I breathed through my nose, it sounded like the undulation of ocean waves crashing onto a beach, then gently receding.

As I inhaled, I would think of someone; when I exhaled, I'd send positive energy vibes toward them. It was almost like non-verbal prayer.

Time no longer mattered.

With each breath, I found myself sending out positive energy, scattering it toward whomever, or whatever, came to mind.

Was this just a mind game?

Maybe.

By all accounts, I should be feeling angry, trapped, depressed, despairing, hopeless. And, to be honest, there'd been times that I'd felt that way. But mindful breathing seemed to be creating a byproduct of peace within myself. Peace that surpassed human understanding.

Mostly.

Not only did I send good energy vibes toward Will, Paul, Lionel, and Muriel, but also to myself—that I would be mentally and physically strong, not lose hope, and somehow find a way to escape.

I even—and this stunned me—I even was able to muster good thoughts for Bonnie, Cletus, and—of all people—Roland Roberts. When I observed this happening, I chuckled at the memory of a movie I'd seen as a kid. A little girl speaks a line about the story's villain: "He needs a mommy very, very badly."

Indeed, kid. Indeed.

* * *

As the day wore on, I could hear Clete rambling around the house. At times, he seemed to be watching something upstairs on television. Later, he'd putter a little in the garage. Other times I'd hear him clunking around in the kitchen. Once I heard the toilet flush.

Going to the bathroom must have reminded him that I had similar needs because he returned to my cell, unshackled me, and, without saying a word, guided me to the bathroom where he waited in the hall while I did my business.

I'd thought of more questions to ask him, but was disappointed when he silently recuffed me to the post and left the room.

I was losing track of time. In my mind's eye, I did my best to visualize a calendar.

As near as I could tell, two days had gone by since I'd been captured. In about 150 days the fetus would be considered viable outside the womb, and I would be precluded from having an abortion, even in my home state of Maryland where abortion was still legal.

Later in the day, just as my stomach was beginning to growl, I heard the motor of the garage door opener activate followed by the hum of Bonnie's minivan entering.

She cut the engine and came into the house through the door where I'd been carried two nights earlier.

"Babe, I'm home," she hollered.

My door opened and she stuck her head inside to check on me.

"Hi," I said, trying to be friendly.

She said nothing, closed the door, and clumped up the stairs to the kitchen.

I heard their muffled voices as they talked but couldn't decipher what they were saying.

Until now, the house had been relatively quiet but, with Bonnie's return, there was much bumping and banging in the kitchen. It sounded like she was making dinner.

Soon wonderful smells wafted down to me followed by the door opening and Clete bringing me a tray. Dinner was chicken, steamed carrots, a Cobb salad, and skim milk. The portion sizes were generous, and the glass was tall.

Even though Clete didn't unshackle me, I was able to maneuver myself to the desk and eat easily using both hands, the chain clink-clanking against the floor, the metal post, and the desk.

I ate alone.

Cletus and Bonnie ate upstairs in the kitchen. After a while, Clete returned to retrieve my tray. He didn't look at me.

After they did the dishes, they both returned, this time with what I assumed was Clete's laptop. He placed it on the desk and they each took a chair, while I sat on the bed.

"Where's the popcorn?" I asked, trying to lighten the mood.

They both ignored me.

Apparently, watching Roland's rants was a nightly ritual for them—and was going to be indoctrination for me.

His show always started at eight p.m. Eastern, so this was becoming the only way I knew for sure what time it was.

Apparently, watching Roland was how Bonnie and Clete got their "news." How many millions of others are out there, I wondered, for whom this is the only information they trust?

Frightening.

Once again, I was the lead story. But this time, it was clear that I wasn't just Roland's personal obsession. I was literally national news.

"White House Press Secretary Lark Chadwick has been abducted," Roland began.

"Uh oh," Cletus stiffened and leaned closer to the laptop.

"Acting White House Press Secretary Nora Tomlinson announced that stunner in today's White House briefing."

Roland's face disappeared from the screen and Nora's appeared. Her thin face seemed drawn and tense. She read from a carefully worded statement:

"Surveillance video reveals that Lark was snatched by a man wearing sunglasses and a hoodie as she approached the Farragut North Metro station at the intersection of K Street and Connecticut Avenue in downtown Washington."

Nora continued to speak as grainy black and white video of my abduction played on the screen.

"The FBI is investigating. The unidentified man grabbed Lark and wrestled her into a minivan which then drove off quickly. Authorities have been unable to identify the vehicle because it did not have license plates."

Roland's face reappeared. To my surprise, he seemed genuinely concerned and looked like an actual newsman, and not some clownish conspiracy theorist.

"President Gannon has not had any public events in the past two days. Nor has he made any direct, on the record statements about Chadwick's disappearance.

"Chadwick's abduction comes just weeks after the brutal bludgeoning death of her predecessor, Ron McClain. It's not known if the two events are related. DC police are investigating McClain's death which they are saying was a robbery gone wrong."

From where I sat, I was able to observe Bonnie and Clete as they watched the story unfold. Cletus was particularly troubled. His body was tense, his jaw muscles bulging.

Bonnie sat with her hand to her mouth, worried, I presumed, that somehow they'd been identified and it would only be a matter of time before a SWAT team surrounded their house, swooped in to rescue me, before sending them to separate maximum security prisons.

I, on the other hand, was elated to know that the indignity and injustice of my abduction was now front-page news commanding what I hoped was an all-out response from the Gannon administration.

Roland continued: "A motive for Chadwick's abduction is not known, but I'm told authorities believe it's the work of antifa who are trying to make it *look* as though she's been captured by anti-abortion forces who want to make an example of her *pro*-abortion views."

Cletus nodded vigorously at Roland's rank speculation, but I shook my head remembering how conservatives blamed the antifa anti-fascists for the January sixth attack on the Capitol in 2021.

"So far, there has been no ransom demand. Nor has any organization claimed responsibility for the kidnapping."

Roland moved on to other items.

I decided to weigh in.

"Looks like the Feds are on to you, Cletus. I hear face recognition technology is pretty sophisticated. And the FBI's involved. That tells me they were able to track the van into Virginia. They're coming for you two."

"Shut up," he shouted. "Just shut up."

Bonnie was crying.

Clete stood and slammed shut the lid of the laptop. "C'mon," he said to Bonnie. "We've gotta regroup."

Clete headed for the door with the laptop tucked under his arm. Bonnie was right behind him.

They left the door open and headed up the stairs leaving me alone, still shackled to the post. I walked as close to the door as I could, straining to make out what they were saying to each other, but all I could hear were muffled voices.

Chapter Twenty-One

Just when I was going to amble back to the bed, the muffled voices upstairs got louder—and more distinct.

"No, Bonnie. We can't do that!" Clete shouted.

"Why not?" she yelled. "The cops might be here any minute."

"Don't you see? If we put her in the van and hit the road, we're much more vulnerable."

Bonnie said something in reply, but I couldn't make it out.

"No!" His voice was stern. "And that's final. We stay put."

A moment later I heard footsteps coming down the stairs.

I tiptoed stealthily back to the bed and lay down. In a moment of inspiration, I grabbed the Bible from the desk and pretended to be absorbed when Bonnie stormed into the room.

"Oh. Hi." I tried again to make nice, but quickly checked to make sure I wasn't holding the Bible upside down by mistake.

Her face was flushed. She grabbed the chair by the desk and dragged it across the floor to the doorway, sat heavily, and folded her arms across her chest. It looked as though she was pouting.

I turned a page but wasn't reading.

Should I say something?

Bonnie sat in silence for a few minutes, then spoke, mostly to herself. "Dammit."

"What's up?" I tried.

"Dammit." Louder this time.

"Ohhh kayyy. Care to share?"

"Shut up, Myrtle."

Fertile Myrtle. She's still pissed at me.

I pretended to read.

She continued to stew.

"Look," I said, flopping the open Bible face down onto my chest. "I'm sorry I lost my temper last night."

Bonnie remained silent, but looked at me, surprised.

"My temper is my biggest weakness. I'm sorry I broke your computer."

Her face relaxed a little. "Thanks, I guess."

"You can understand how I feel, can't you?"

"Sure. But can you understand the way I feel?" she asked.

"I'm trying to. I never wanted to be a mom, or planned to be one, so tell me what it's like to be in your shoes."

She looked at me for a long time, maybe trying to gauge my sincerity.

I closed the Bible, placed it back on the desk, and swung my feet to the floor so that I was sitting on the bed, facing her, giving her my full attention.

Finally, she spoke. "I've always wanted to be a mom. Always. From as young as I can remember."

"Do you have a good mom?"

She shook her head. "Not anymore." Her voice cracked.

"What happened?"

"Cancer. I was twelve when she passed."

"I'm so sorry. That's such a tender time to lose someone that close. I never knew mine."

Bonnie looked at me, eyebrows raised. "Really? What happened?"

"Both she and my dad were killed in a car crash when I was an infant. I never knew them."

"Oh. That's terrible."

I nodded.

"Who raised you?" she asked. "Foster care?"

"My aunt. My crazy fucked up aunt."

"Jeepers."

I didn't want to make this conversation about me. I needed to swivel the spotlight back to her and get her talking more. "Was it your mom and her example that inspired you to be a mother?"

"Yeah. Kinda. I babysat right from an early age. I loved it."

"Did you want to have a big family?"

She smiled and actually chuckled. "Huge. I wanted scads of little babies. One a year."

As much as I wanted to barf at the thought, I also genuinely wanted to understand how anyone could want to so efface their identity. But then, in the same instant, I realized in a flash that motherhood *is* Bonnie's identity. Her purpose in life.

"Sorry. I don't mean to make you uncomfortable," I said, "but when and how did you come to realize that you wouldn't be able to be a mom?"

A distant look came over her. "Right after Cletus and I got married. We actually thought I was pregnant. I'd missed my period, so he said he'd be willing to marry me or, as he said it, 'make an honest woman out of you.'" She smiled at the memory.

"What happened?"

"I had a mis—" Her voice caught, and she had to pause. "I had a miscarriage." She tried to swipe away the tears now dampening her cheeks. "There were lots of tests and pretty soon the doctors decided I had to have a hysterectomy."

She sniffled, stood, and stepped into the bathroom for a second. When she returned to her chair, she had a box of tissues that she held on her lap.

"How long ago was that? Your hysterectomy?"

"Six months." She blew her nose.

"Did Clete want to be a dad?"

She shook her head. "Not really. But he's crazy about me."

"So, what am I? The mother for what will become *your* child?"

"Something like that. We're both just so dead set against abortion."

I wasn't sure where to go with this. I didn't want to make this conversation combative, but it wasn't easy. Sure, I could sympathize with Bonnie—but not empathize—yet life seemed to have played a cruel trick on both of us: She couldn't have children even though she desperately wanted them, whereas I was considering ending a pregnancy because I didn't want to be a mother and felt I'd be a poor one.

"Life's unfair, isn't it?" I said.

"It sure is."

Obviously, she didn't see the irony. She and Cletus were only focused on what was unfair to them. They were able to justify taking away my freedom because it served a greater good: preserving the life of a child that, they believed, would otherwise be aborted. Or, in their way of thinking: murdered.

I was not going to change her mind because she'd been so thoroughly brainwashed by Roland and others like him who preached the lie that mainstream journalism is nothing more than "fake news" purveyed by know-it-all elitists with a "socialist" big government agenda.

This conversation with Bonnie was reinforcing my hunch that if I wanted to in any way find common ground with her, and sympathy from her, I would have to appeal to her basic humanity, not her political or moral views.

That thought was exhausting.

I shook the slippers from my feet, pulled back the covers, and lay on my left side.

"You going to try to get some shuteye?" she asked.

"Yeah."

She flipped off the overhead light, but remained seated in the doorway.

"Are you gonna spend the night there?" I asked.

"Maybe." Light from the hallway behind her put her face in shadow so I couldn't read her expression, but her voice sounded resigned. "I need a little space away from Cletus."

That got me thinking.

I tried turning onto my right side. As I did, I made it a point to rattle the chain loudly.

"Dammit," I said. More shaking of the chain. More rattling. More thrashing.

"What's the matter?"

"I can't seem to get comfortable. I've been forced to lie only on my left side since I got here. I can't turn over because the chains are too restrictive."

Silence from her.

More thrashing and rattling from me.

"If you're gonna stay down here for a while," I said, "do you think you could uncuff me so I can finally lie on my right side?" I rattled the chain once more to punctuate my plight.

"Sure. I guess. At least while I'm here."

She got up and pulled the key from her jeans. I held up my left wrist and she unlocked the handcuff. It dropped to the floor with a clatter.

"Thank you," I rolled dramatically onto my right side and brought my left arm all the way around and placed it under my pillow. "G'night."

I heard her walk back to her chair and sit down.

My mind was racing. My heart began to pound. Might I be on the cusp of being able to escape?

Chapter Twenty-Two

I was so keyed up I couldn't have slept even if I'd wanted to. As I lay on my right side under the covers, I could see the shadow of Bonnie's head on the wall. She put in ear buds and soon I could hear snatches of her tinny Christian music wafting to me from her sentry post in the doorway.

Upstairs, the television was on, the laugh-track of a sitcom happening every five seconds, or so. At one point, Clete must have gone into the kitchen because I heard the refrigerator door open and close and the metallic *psht* of the tab as he opened a beer or soda.

I used my mindful breathing to stay focused on each moment, even as I sent energy vibes to Bonnie and Clete, hoping they would let down their guard and give me a chance to make a break for it.

But if I did try to get away, how would I do it, and where would I go? I had no idea where I was, or even what the weather was like outside. I had no cell phone or way to communicate with anyone. If I was in the middle of nowhere, were there any homes nearby? Could I trust the occupants to be sympathetic to me—or did they buy into Bonnie and Clete's lunacy?

I had no way of judging the time, but at least an hour passed.

Bonnie continued to sit in the doorway.

Clete continued watching television.

I continued to plot my escape.

After a while, Clete turned off the TV and I heard him walk out of the living room. The house creaked a little. He seemed to be going upstairs to bed rather coming down to check on Bonnie—and me.

A toilet flushed, then more silence.

The shadow of Bonnie's head on the wall in front of me bobbed in time to the music. Then she stood.

Shit. Is she going to cuff me and then head up to bed?

Instead of going upstairs, I heard her go into the bathroom and, out of habit, she shut the door.

Now's my chance.

Quickly, I threw off the covers, swung my feet onto the floor and into the slippers.

No sound was coming from the bathroom so she wasn't done yet. But was she doing number one, or number two? I prayed for number two—it might take longer.

Her phone wasn't on the chair so presumably she still had in her earbuds—less chance of any sound from me getting her attention—but I still had to be careful.

I took my pillow and placed it under the covers so that if she glanced in the direction of the bed, it might look as if my butt was facing toward her as I slept on my right side.

Would she notice that the slippers were gone? Maybe. But I prayed she wouldn't.

Stealthily, I tiptoed to the chair blocking the doorway. I picked it up, moved around it, then carefully set it down exactly as she'd left it.

Just then the toilet flushed.

Shit.

The light was on in the hallway. It led to a closed door that I presumed was to the attached garage. I couldn't take a chance on going out that way because the noise of the garage door opening would immediately alert Bonnie, and maybe Clete, too.

As I got to the end of the hallway, I heard Bonnie turn on the faucet to wash her hands.

I took a left turn at the end of the hall just as I heard the bathroom door open and Bonnie take her place on the chair in the doorway.

Slowly I crept down the hall, holding my breath, afraid that Bonnie would suddenly realize I was gone. But all I heard was silence from her end of the hall—and the booming of my heart.

After a few steps, I came to the end of the hall. To my left was a stairway to the second floor. To the right, a door to the outside—and freedom.

A sheer white curtain covered the window at the top half of the door. I pushed aside the curtain and looked out. An enormous black pick-up truck was parked in a cinder driveway in front of the closed garage door.

As quietly as I could I twisted the deadbolt and unlocked the door, opened it, and stepped outside, closing the door gently behind me.

The night was chilly. And silent.

All was quiet in the house behind me. Bonnie apparently had not yet noticed that I was no longer in bed.

The driveway was about fifty yards from the road. Tall bushes lined the right side. A spacious front yard with a big tree was ahead of me.

I sidled to my right, passed between the front of Clete's truck and the garage door, then scampered as fast as I could along the shrubs toward the road.

When I was about halfway to the road I heard Bonnie's scream.

Chapter Twenty-Three

To say Bonnie's scream was blood curdling would be a cliché. But, hey, clichés exist because they quickly convey a universal truth. And truth was, that scream had such an impact on the life-force within me that I staggered.

I'm a runner, but in that instant, I faltered and nearly fell, weakened by the fear that Bonnie and Clete would pounce on me at any moment and my restraints for the next eight months would be constant.

Running in slippers felt like I was trying to do the fifty-yard dash wearing fluffy clown shoes. But, somehow, I made it to the end of the hedge, ducked behind it, then peeked around it to look back at the house.

Bonnie had just opened the back door and was peering outside. She didn't see me, but I could hear her screaming.

"Cletus! Come quick. She got away."

A light came on in an upstairs window.

Time for me to move on.

Using the hedgerow as cover, I headed to my right, away from the house. I caught a quick glimpse of their mailbox by the side of the road. Their house number was 349, but there was no last name.

The road was narrow, two-lane, no center line, asphalt. I hoped I'd soon come upon a route number or street name that I could use if I could somehow find a phone and call 911.

It felt exhilarating to be outside for the first time in three days. It was early spring, but there was a chill in the air. I could see my breath.

The moon was only a sliver and I was heading toward it, East, I guessed. Stars were strewn across the sky because here in the boonies there were no nearby streetlights to fade the starlight.

Empty fields were on both sides of the road. That meant few places, if any, where I could hide. I decided to veer off to my right and go as deeply into the field and as far away from the road as I could get.

Apparently, it had rained recently because it didn't take long for my feet to sink into ankle deep muck, which sucked the slippers from my feet.

I kept running away from the road.

I heard the growl of Clete's pick-up as he revved the engine and threw it into gear. His tires scratched against the cinders in the driveway.

By this time I was barely fifty yards from Bonnie and Clete's house and perhaps another fifty yards deep in a field away from the road.

I lowered myself to a crouch as I saw his headlights reflect onto the grass berm across from the end of their driveway.

Clete turned to the right, the same direction I had run.

I flattened myself against the muddy field, but was able to peek to see what Clete would do.

He pulled to the side of the road, got out, and shined a powerful flashlight in my direction.

I pressed my head hard against the ground and held my breath.

The light passed across my location but didn't linger. He hadn't seen me.

When I heard his door slam, I dared to look up.

He drove a little farther down the road, stopped, got out, and once again scoured the field on both sides of the road with his flashlight, then got back into his truck and moved farther down the road for another rinse and repeat.

Just as I was about to get up and run farther into the field, I heard the garage door open and Bonnie revving the engine of her minivan.

I stayed crouched, waiting to see which direction she would go.

The lights from her vehicle got to the end of the driveway, then turned left, the opposite direction from where Cletus and I had gone.

Once I knew it was safe, I got up and ran farther away from the road.

The mucky ground was cold against my bare feet and sharp hay stubble poked into my tender skin. I ignored the pain and ran as fast as I could.

Good thing I kept looking back over my shoulder because soon I saw Cletus' truck returning along the road, stopping every dozen yards, or so, to once again scour the fields with his light.

Even though I assumed I was now beyond the reach of the flashlight's beam, I lay prone when Clete pointed it in my general direction.

When he moved on, so did I.

The ground sloped gently upward. A barbed wire fence was at the crest of the low hill. Gingerly, I tried to get over it, but it ripped a piece off my flannel sleeve and also stabbed me in the ball of my foot.

"Ouch!" My voice echoed.

I held my breath to see if anyone would respond to the sound.

A dog barked in the distance.

I got over the fence and limped onward.

On the horizon, I saw a light and went toward it.

It must have taken me about twenty minutes to get close enough to be able to identify the light's source: a 24/7 convenience store and gas station.

I crept closer and paused often to crouch and assess.

The gas station was at the intersection of two small roads. In order to get to it, I would have to cross one of them. I'd be exposed.

A small tree and some shrubs were on my side of the road just across from the gas station at the intersection. I made it there and hid for a while to watch.

The parking lot and gas pump lanes were empty, but floodlights drenched the area so brightly that the Washington Nationals could have played a game of night baseball.

Just as I was ready to dash across the road, I heard a vehicle approach the intersection from over my right shoulder. I crouched again at the base of the tree and held my breath.

A dark Lexus came to a stop, paused, then crossed the intersection and continued down the road.

I thought about waiting to see if a cop car would stop for donuts and a fill-up. Maybe I should have waited longer, but I was getting impatient—and was starting to shiver.

I said a quick prayer, looked in all directions, held my breath, and prepared to dash toward the building. Either this was the smartest decision of my life—or the dumbest.

I was about to find out.

Chapter Twenty-Four

I made it across the road easily, my heart rabbiting, and scampered in my bare feet to the entrance. A bell dinged as I entered.

The place was bathed in garish fluorescent light. No one was at the check-out counter.

I could be seen easily from the outside, so I made my way deeper into the store to a place behind shelves that shielded me from the road. Along the wall behind me, a row of glass-paneled refrigeration units hummed.

"Is anyone here?" I called out.

"Yeah. I'm here." A kid no more than twenty ambled around a corner and took his place at the cash register. He wore bib overalls and a baggy flannel shirt. "How can I help you?"

"I need you to call 911." My voice was pleading, urgent.

"Why? What's up?"

"My name is Lark Chadwick. I'm President Gannon's press secretary. I've been abducted, but managed to escape."

He looked skeptical. I guess presidential press secretaries don't come in here very often.

"It's been all over the news." I was beginning to sound exasperated.

"Yeah. I don't read the news." He gave me a crooked smile.

"I don't know exactly where I am, but for the past three days I've been held hostage near here. The mailbox in front of the house is 349, but I don't know the name of the road."

"Who'd you say you were again?"

Did I really need to spell it out for this guy? I was in the stationery aisle, so I grabbed a spiral notebook, a Sharpie, and scribbled quickly:

Lark Chadwick. White House Press Secretary. Held hostage by Cletus and Bonnie. Mailbox # 349.

I ripped the page from the notebook and rushed to the kid at the counter. His nametag read *Jimmy*.

"Please, Jimmy. Call 911 *now.*" I slipped him the piece of paper. "Tell the operator exactly what's written there."

He put the paper on the counter in front of him and started to reach for the phone. "Well okay then."

Just then the door dinged.

I looked over my shoulder.

Cletus stood in the doorway glowering.

Chapter Twenty-Five

"Put down the phone," Clete bellowed at the kid.

"I'm sorry, sir. This woman needs help." Jimmy stabbed the nine.

In one swift move, Cletus pulled a huge handgun from behind his back and rushed toward the counter.

"Put the phone down, motherfucker, or your brains are gonna be all over the back wall."

"Cletus!" I shouted. "You're supposedly pro-life. You put down that gun right now." I actually sounded to myself like a stern mother scolding her two-year-old.

His finger was on the trigger. For a moment he hesitated, then raised the gun to the ceiling.

Jimmy, meanwhile, fainted.

Clete took his finger off the trigger and quickly stuffed the gun into the back of his jeans beneath his untucked shirt.

"C'mon." He grabbed a fistful of my shirt at the back of my neck and pushed me out the door and to the passenger side of his truck. He opened the door, then the glove box, retrieving a zip tie. Working fast, he tied my wrists behind me, then lifted me into the front seat, got another zip tie, and shackled my ankles together.

I lay crumpled in the front seat of the truck for the few minutes it took for us to race back to the house. As he drove, he speed-dialed Bonnie.

Her voice came over the cab's speaker. "Hey, Babe. Any luck?"

"I've got her."

She sighed loudly, relieved. "Where'd you find her?"

"At the gas station on Possum Gap Road."

"Is she okay?"

"Yeah. The clerk was just about to call 911, but I stopped him."

I butted in. "Actually, Bonnie, I stopped Clete. Your man was about to blow the kid's head off. That would have added first degree murder to the charges against you two so-called pro-lifers."

She was quiet a moment, then: "Is that true, Cletus?"

"We're almost home. Get back there. We gotta figure out what we're gonna do." He ended the call.

"Want my advice?"

"No."

"Cut your losses and let me go."

"I'll take it under advisement."

"I'm serious, Clete. Do you really think this is gonna work, holding me hostage for the next *six* months? C'mon. Get real."

He turned into the driveway and gunned it toward the garage door. Bonnie was right behind us.

The two of them trundled me, hogtied, through the door and down the hall, tossing me onto the bed.

I tried again. "Guys. This isn't going to work."

"Shut up," Clete said.

"Maybe she's right."

"Thank you, Bonnie."

"Think about it, Babe. I know you want what's best for me, but maybe this isn't it. Lark's right. We didn't think it through."

In the distance, I heard a siren. Had Jimmy come to and called 911?

Neither Cletus nor Bonnie seemed to hear the distant wailing. They were too busy trying to decide what to do next.

In my mind's eye, I imagined Jimmy coming to his senses, calling 911, and reading my hastily scribbled note to the operator. Was it too much to hope that the cops would be able to pinpoint Bonnie and Clete's home and send a SWAT team?

Yeah. Probably.

From my zip-tied and contorted place on the bed, I tried again. "Look. Guys. I know now it's futile for me to try to escape. I get it. You don't trust me anymore. But are you really gonna keep me handcuffed down here for the next six months? Really? Six *months?* No exercise? No medical attention? You want this baby to be born, but how healthy do you think this kid's gonna be if my life is so restricted?"

By this time the sound of the siren had gotten so loud that none of us could ignore it.

"Shit." Cletus bolted from the room pulling the gun from under the back of his shirt.

"Cletus. No." Bonnie's voice was frantic.

"The cops are here," he hollered from down the hall. "They're coming up the drive."

"What are we going to doooo?" Bonnie wailed.

"It's time to give it up," I shouted. "Cut your losses. Otherwise it goes downhill from here. Is this the ditch you want to die in?"

I looked at Bonnie. She was terrified.

Chapter Twenty-Six

I held my breath expecting that at any moment Clete would begin shooting at the cops.

Strobing blue and red light from the cop cars reflected against the hall wall. Bonnie, her eyes wide with fright, had both of her hands clamped over her mouth.

From outside, a bullhorn squealed, then a metallic voice commanded: "Cletus and Bonnie Bauer. This is the Virginia State Police. We know you're in there. You are completely surrounded. Come out with your hands up."

"Do what he says, Babe," Bonnie shouted. "We fucked up."

Clete didn't respond. The silence coming from the hallway was ominous. His cell phone bleeped.

Clete must have been holding his breath because he expelled a burst of air and swore. He answered in a surprisingly contrite voice. "Yeah?" A pause, then, "Yes, sir."

Bonnie's hands went back to her mouth. "Oh, Jesus. Help us."

"I have a handgun, sir," Clete said.

"Jesus, Jesus, Jesus, Jesus," Bonnie prayed.

"Okay," Clete said. "I'm opening the door now and I'll throw it outside."

The back door opened and I could hear what sounded like a fleet of car engines in the driveway.

A bright white light replaced the blue and red strobe-flash reflections on the wall.

The bullhorn voice commanded, "Step out of the house with your hands held high."

"It's over, Hon," Clete called to Bonnie.

I heard the metallic click as Clete was cuffed.

"Who else is in the house?" a male voice asked.

"My wife and the girl."

"Is your wife armed?"

"No, sir."

"Where are they?"

"Down the hall."

A moment later, two men in tactical gear burst into the room, guns drawn.

"You!" one of them hollered at Bonnie. "On the floor. Face down. NOW!"

"Oh, Jesus, Jesus, Jesus," she wailed and dropped to the floor.

While the first guy frisked and handcuffed her, the other came to me and cut the zip ties binding my wrists and ankles.

I was free. But my nightmare was far from over.

* * *

An hour later, I was at FBI Headquarters in DC being debriefed. The sun had yet to come up, but the eastern sky was beginning to brighten.

Two FBI agents—a man and a woman—sat across from me taking my statement. By this time, I'd already received basic medical attention back at Bonnie and Clete's in an ambulance that had also been dispatched to the scene. The cuts on my bare feet were bandaged, I'd been given very comfortable slippers, and a warm windbreaker with FBI emblazoned in bright yellow lettering across the back.

The two FBI agents were patient as I went through every detail I could remember about my abduction and the time I spent in the custody of Cletus and Bonnie.

Orange light was beginning to brighten the eastern sky by the Capitol when the female agent's phone vibrated on the table. She took the call and immediately bolted to her feet.

"Yes, sir. She's right here, Mr. President. I'll put her on."

The woman handed me her cell.

"Hi, Mr. President," I said.

"Lark! I can't tell you how relieved I am to hear your voice."

"Thank you, sir. The feeling is mutual." I felt like a giddy schoolgirl.

"I'm sure you've been through quite an ordeal."

"You could say that," I laughed, grateful to be hearing a friendly voice.

"It's probably going to take a while for you to decompress, plus, when you're ready, I want to hear all about it."

"I've already given a statement to the Feds."

"I want you to be my guest this weekend at Camp David."

"That would be wonderful. Thank you, sir."

"You'll be joined by your friends Lionel and Muriel Stone."

"That'll be great. Thank you."

"I'm afraid I have some bad news for you, Lark."

"Oh?"

"Are you sitting down?"

"Yes, sir."

"Brace yourself. This won't be easy."

Is he going to fire me?

"Your friend Paul Stone was attacked yesterday."

"Oh my God! What happened?"

"Someone attacked him last night as he was arriving home after work."

"How badly was he hurt? Is he all right?"

Will paused, then, "He was bludgeoned with a hammer. He's dead, Lark."

Chapter Twenty-Seven

I arrived at Camp David late in the afternoon after stopping at my apartment in Silver Spring to shower and pack for the weekend.

The FBI had been able to retrieve my laptop and cell phones from Bonnie and Clete's. One of the agents gave me a new government SIM card but I had to stop by the AT&T store near my place to get a replacement SIM for my personal cell.

Lionel and Muriel Stone were waiting for me outside their cabin with Kris, my grief counselor, as a White House pool vehicle drove me into the compound. The president was expected to arrive by helicopter about six p.m.

The Stones stood side by side holding hands, their faces a portrait of anguish. They had already lost a daughter, now they'd lost their only remaining child—and my friend.

Lionel was pushing eighty. To me, he'd always seemed ten years younger, but on this day, he was stooped and a shell of his former self. Muriel, twenty-five years younger than Lionel, stood about half a head taller than him but she, too, seemed to have aged a decade.

Kris stood discreetly off to the side while I greeted Lionel and Muriel. We hugged and cried for several moments.

No words, just tears.

Muriel was the first to speak. "We're so glad you're safe, Lark." She cried into my hair as we hugged.

"Oh, Muriel," I blubbered. "I'm so sorry about Paul. He was my friend. He was a good person."

"I know." She could barely speak.

I held her tightly for a moment before releasing her to accept Lionel's bear hug.

"How you doin', kid?" His face was flushed and his voice husky.

"I'm okay. I'm good, but I'm so sad."

Kris stepped forward, arms outstretched.

I fell gratefully into her embrace. "Thank you for being here, Kris."

"The president called and asked me to come this weekend to support you and the Stones."

"How did he know to contact you?"

"Muriel told him about me when he placed a sympathy call to them."

I nodded.

Kris stepped back. "We can talk whenever you're ready—and for as long as you want."

"Thank you."

"Let's go inside and talk," Muriel said.

"I'll be at the cabin next door," Kris said. "Available to all of you."

The Stone's cabin was cozy. They sat next to each other on a sofa holding hands. I pulled an easy chair closer to them.

"We were so worried about you, Lark," Muriel began. "Are you able to talk about what happened? You don't have to."

"I've been talking about it all day with the feds. I'm more concerned about you two. What can you tell me?"

"I'd like to wring the neck of that asshole Roland Roberts," Lionel snarled.

"I know. Me too," I said. "I saw his report."

"You did?"

"His show was the only outside media I was allowed to see. That's how the two people holding me captive got their news, apparently."

"Were they in cahoots with Roberts?" Muriel asked.

I shook my head. "I don't think so. They're just ardent pro-lifers determined to hold me captive until I gave birth. When Roland falsely reported that I was going to have an abortion, they must've snapped. At least that's the way it seems."

Muriel nodded. "Same with the person who killed Paul."

"What happened? Any arrests?"

"Almost immediately," Lionel said. "A witness saw a guy shout 'faggot' at Paul before clobbering him with the hammer. The witness called 911. The cops got there right away and made the arrest."

"Seems like the crazies are getting desperate—and Roland's fueling their desperation," I said.

I was still talking with the Stones when there was a knock on the door. Muriel got up to answer it.

"Hello, Mr. President," I heard her say.

Lionel and I immediately got to our feet.

Will Gannon embraced Muriel and spoke softly in her ear.

"Thank you," she said.

As Will closed the door, I saw a Secret Service agent standing watch just outside. Gannon swept into the room and opened his arms to me.

I fell against his barrel chest. His arms surrounded me. He kissed me on the top of my head. His presence was tremendously reassuring and comforting. Not only did I not want this moment to end, but I selfishly wanted it all to myself.

After a moment, I stepped back and gestured to Lionel. "Have you met my friend and mentor Lionel Stone, sir?"

"Not in person. Only by reputation." Gannon smiled broadly at Lionel and extended his hand. "Again, I'm so sorry for your devastating loss, Mr. Stone."

Lionel's smile was tight but his grip was firm. "Yeah. Thanks, Mr. President."

"Can I get you some tea or coffee, Mr. President?" Muriel asked.

"Yes. Coffee, if it's no trouble. Thank you."

I moved to the kitchen area to help Muriel while the president and Lionel sat down together to get acquainted.

"I've read all your books," Gannon said. "Frankly, I'm relieved that you're no longer the *Times'* White House correspondent or I'd be toast."

Lionel chuckled mirthlessly. Small-talk chitchat is not his thing. Getting revenge on Paul's behalf was probably where his focus was at this moment.

When Lionel spoke, he removed all doubt. "We've got to stop that motherfucker Roberts, Mr. President."

"Lionel!" Muriel scolded.

Lionel coughed. "Pardon my French."

"Quite all right," Gannon chuckled. "I speak the same language."

"Is Roberts the puppet master behind all this crazy bullshit?" Lionel asked.

Gannon waited until Muriel and I distributed the steaming coffee mugs before he replied. "We're still looking into it. At this point, there doesn't seem to be a connection between the people who abducted Lark and the person who murdered your son. The only common connection is Roland Roberts' rhetoric. He's extremely influential, but at this point there's nothing we can find that suggests he's orchestrating the attacks."

"Who is 'we'?" Lionel asked.

"Homeland Security, FBI, the works."

Muriel took a seat next to her husband. I pulled up a chair and sat next to the president, positioning myself at an angle so I could face him and the Stones.

Will turned to me. "It wasn't until you didn't show up for work that we knew something had probably happened to you. I got the FBI to begin looking into it immediately."

"What did you learn?" I asked.

"Surveillance video picked you up leaving the White House compound. You were next seen being snatched outside the Farragut North Metro station. Facial recognition technology was unable to identify your abductor and we couldn't ID the vehicle because it didn't have plates. We lost it once it turned off Connecticut Avenue."

"What did you think happened?"

"We expected a ransom demand, but got nothing. Until you surfaced, we had no idea what had happened or where you were." His voice broke. "I was pretty worried about you, Lark."

"Me too. They were going to hold me until I gave birth."

"Yeah. I've been briefed. Then what were they gonna do?"

"Good question. I don't think they'd thought that far ahead."

"Did you feel your life was at risk?" Muriel asked.

I shook my head. "Not really. They're hard-core Christian pro-lifers. The guy's an ex-Marine and I'm pretty sure he's killed before, but in combat. He's certainly an alpha male chauvinist but my gut tells me they were eventually going to release me, then pull up roots and hit the road, or something half-assed like that."

Muriel nodded.

I turned to Gannon. "Do you think there's a connection between Paul's death and Ron McClain's?"

"Not sure. Maybe."

"The hammer?" Lionel asked.

Will nodded. "But it could just be a copycat."

"That reminds me," I said. "Cletus, the guy who held me captive, had an elaborate hammer tattooed on his right forearm. He called it Thor's Hammer. Plus, he's a carpenter. If he was able to stalk me, maybe he stalked Ron, too."

Gannon said, "That's interesting. I'll have the FBI look into that."

"Has a motive been established for the attack on Ron?" I asked.

"The working theory of the DC cops is robbery, but your tip could bring things into sharper focus."

"Was Ron gay?" I asked.

"Not that I know of."

Lionel shifted uncomfortably. He's an open-minded guy, but he's also an old guy. I knew Lionel wasn't thrilled to learn that his adult son was homosexual, but, until Roland's report, Lionel didn't know his son was still working through the whole trans thing.

As I studied Lionel's face it looked like a Vesuvius of unresolved emotions was coming to a boil.

Chapter Twenty-Eight

Will Gannon had only taken a few swigs from his coffee mug before he said, "I don't want to intrude any longer on your time together." He stood.

So did the rest of us.

"I hope you'll use the weekend to take advantage of the grief counselor I've arranged to be here."

"We will," Muriel said. "Thank you."

Gannon walked his coffee mug to the kitchen area and placed it in the sink, then moved toward the door.

We followed.

"Also, if you'd like, you're welcome to join me for dinner at my cabin about 7:30," he said.

"Thank you, Mr. President," Lionel said.

"Now I'd like to have a few minutes alone with my press secretary." He turned to me. "Will you walk with me, Lark?"

"Sure." I turned to Lionel and Muriel. "I'll see you guys later."

The sun was low in the sky as the president and I left the Stone's cabin.

The Secret Service agent who'd been waiting outside fell in step behind us as Will guided me along a path through the woods—the same path we'd walked a month earlier after I'd interviewed him for the Associated Press shortly after Rose died.

Will seemed to sense I needed to be quiet. We walked in silence until we reached the end of the trail at an outcropping of rocks that looked west over the rolling Maryland countryside.

Part of me longed for his touch, even a gentle hand on my shoulder, but we both knew the power dynamics wouldn't allow it. He was my friend, but he was also my boss. Even Rose had sensed the attraction Will and I had for each other, but we'd never spoken of it. Would we ever?

Frankly, at this moment, my emotions were in turmoil. Romance was the farthest thing from my mind. Plus, Will was still grieving the loss of his wife.

Now, not only was I mourning Doug, but I was also trying to absorb the madness that had killed my friend and former colleague Paul Stone, all while coming to grips with my unwanted pregnancy and the loss of my freedom at the hands of religious zealots who wanted to force me to give birth.

Will and I both needed a friend.

We both had one.

"Let's sit," I said.

We leaned against two boulders and contemplated the sunset. He had yet to speak.

I sighed.

He sighed.

"Thank you," I said eventually.

"For what?"

I spread my arms wide toward the horizon.

"For the sunset? You're welcome."

I laughed. "Seriously. For this weekend. I need this time to get my head back together before work on Monday."

"Oh, I think Monday might be too soon."

"I feel I need to get back to work."

"I know you do. But I'd feel better if you took time to decompress and process all of this. There's no hurry, Lark."

I nodded, unsure if I agreed.

We watched as a hawk circled lazily above us.

"The world is such a fucked up place," I said.

"I know."

"There's too much death. Too much senseless death."

"Yes. And you probably haven't heard the latest."

I looked at him, confused.

"On Thursday, the day you went missing, there were two mass shootings, both at elementary schools."

My jaw dropped. "How bad?"

"Bad. In all, thirty-nine people, mostly little kids, were mowed down by shooters using AR-15s they had legally. Both gunmen killed themselves."

"Oh my God. How awful." I let the news sink in. "Yet in the report I saw, Roland led with my kidnapping. Apparently, mass murder is barely a blip on his radar."

Will shook his head slowly, somberly.

The more we talked, the gloomier I felt. "I feel so helpless."

"I know. So do I sometimes." He shot me a worried look. "That's off the record."

"I'm retired from journalism."

"Good thing. I feel I can talk with you. I need a friend right now."

"Me too."

More silence. An easy silence.

The sun got lower, a bright orange ball on the horizon.

The beauty of the moment was in stark contrast with the leaden ache I felt. There'd been so much death—in both of our lives. Cancer, heroin addiction, trans-phobic hate, mass shootings, war.

In that moment, all of the world's pain overwhelmed me. I put my hands against my face and began to weep.

Will got up from his perch on the rock and came closer to me. Gently, he placed a hand on my shoulder.

The floodgates opened. I couldn't stop myself from sobbing.

I stood, turned to him and let the President of the United States comfort me in his arms.

Chapter Twenty-Nine

To my surprise, dinner with the president was more festive than I would have expected. That's partly because Will's two young children, Grace and Thomas, joined us for the first part of the evening.

Grace and I had formed a special bond over books the last time I was here. We picked up right where we left off.

I was sitting on a sofa, sipping a soda, when Grace sidled over to me and climbed into my lap as if it was a daily occurrence.

"Hello, Miss Lark."

"Hello, Your Grace."

She giggled. "You make me feel like I'm a princess."

"You are a princess. At least to me."

"And to my daddy. That's what he calls me sometimes."

Even though Grace's mother had been dead for only a month, Grace seemed resilient. I'd heard that kids are.

Her younger brother Thomas, who I was pretty sure had a crush on me, pranced in front of us, constantly trying to find my eyes to gain my attention and approval. He made loud mouth noises as he waved a scale model of Air Force 1 in front of my face, making elaborate loop d loops.

I winked at Thomas, but spoke to Grace. "What are you reading these days?"

"Ooooo," she squealed. "I'll go get it."

She jumped off my lap, but was back in no time waving a copy of E.B. White's *Charlotte's Web*. "Will you read to me, Miss Lark?"

"I certainly will."

Grace settled back into my lap. She must have just had a bath because she smelled of shampoo. Instinctively, I kissed her on the top of the head.

Am I warming up to the idea of motherhood?

For the next few minutes we were both entranced in the story while Lionel and Muriel talked animatedly with the president.

Dinner was low-key informal: tomato soup supplemented by grilled cheese sandwiches—a state dinner, this was not. Instead, it was homey and relaxing.

As Muriel helped Will clear the table, a sudden tiredness swept over me.

I stood. "It's been a long day and I've just hit the wall. I need to go to bed."

"I'll walk with you, Lark," Muriel said. "Let's leave the boys to solve the problems of the world."

"Will you join me in a nightcap, Lionel?" Gannon asked.

"I've stopped drinking—this time for good," Lionel said, "but if you've got ginger ale, I'll sit a spell with you."

"That can be arranged."

Muriel and I said our goodnights to Will and Lionel, then headed into the night.

Our cabins were next to each other so we walked slowly arm in arm.

"Have you had a chance to talk yet with your grief counselor since your rescue, Lark?"

"Not yet."

"I'm planning to talk with her tomorrow morning."

"What about Lionel?"

"She wants to meet with us separately."

"Really? How come?"

"She says the loss of a child is so intense that she prefers for couples to meet with her separately—at least at first."

I nodded. "Makes sense. It's not the same as marriage counseling, right?"

"Yes."

"How's marriage counseling going?"

"Pretty well. We're much closer now that I've found my voice and he's more willing to listen."

"Still, I'm worried about him."

"Me too."

"He seems to have a lot of anger," I said.

"Oh yes."

"Understandable, of course."

"Yes."

I gave her a worried look. "Does he own a gun?"

"No, thank God. I think if he did, he'd be tempted to use it on that Roland Roberts fellow."

"Uh huh." We walked a few more steps. "So, is he gonna meet with Kris?"

"I think so. I pray so."

"Maybe I'll give him a little nudge tomorrow."

"Please do. He definitely listens to you, Lark."

When we reached the point between our two cabins where we each had to go our separate ways, we hugged and said goodnight.

Five minutes later I was fast asleep in a warm and cozy bed.

* * *

On my first full day of freedom, the sun streaming through the cabin window woke me up. At first, I didn't know where I was because I'd slept so soundly.

I checked my phone—it was just after eight.

Out of habit, I went first to the website of my old employer, the Associated Press. News of my release was the top story there, on Reuters, CNN, and all the broadcast networks, as well as the *New York Times* and the *Washington Post*.

Shorter stories reported on Paul's murder.

The stories I read were accurate—as far as they went—but were incomplete. The AP version of my rescue was the most succinct and factual:

White House Press Secretary Lark Chadwick was rescued by Loudoun County, Virginia sheriff's deputies early Saturday morning. She'd been missing since Wednesday evening when she was forcefully abducted off a Washington street by a man wearing a hoodie.

Loudoun County Sheriff Wayne Jesper said a rural convenience store clerk alerted authorities to Chadwick's whereabouts when she managed to escape briefly and run to the store.

Dramatic surveillance video released by authorities shows Chadwick being recaptured at gunpoint.

The story linked to video of Clete aiming his handgun at the clerk. The clip contained no audio, but when I spoke sharply to Clete, he stuffs the gun into his rear waistband and shoves me out the door with him.

Sheriff's deputies surrounded the rural farmhouse where Chadwick was being held.

The gunman, identified as Cletus Bauer, 39, surrendered without incident, according to authorities.

Bauer and his wife Bonnie, 25, are being held without bail pending their arraignment on kidnapping charges Monday.

It's not clear why Chadwick, 29, was abducted.

The FBI is now in charge of the investigation.

Chadwick, a former AP White House correspondent, has been unavailable for comment.

Before leaving the White House for Camp David Saturday afternoon, President Gannon spoke to reporters.

"I'm thrilled to learn that Lark is now free and safe. I've spoken with her and she is in good spirits after her ordeal," Gannon said.

A separate AP story chronicled Paul's murder.

AP REPORTER MURDERED

AP White House correspondent Paul Stone, 32, was bludgeoned to death outside his Washington home Friday night.

DC police say he was hit in the head with a hammer.

An eyewitness told police the attacker shouted a homophobic slur at Stone and was apprehended at the scene without incident.

Arthur Van Doren, 24, a neighbor of Stone's, is charged with first-degree murder.

According to police, Van Doren became enraged when he heard an unconfirmed report on the Christian Newswire that Stone was planning to have gender confirmation surgery.

The Christian Newswire did not respond to repeated attempts by the AP to obtain a comment.

Stone is the son of Pulitzer-Prize winning journalist Lionel Stone.

Paul Stone's death comes 10 days after a similar fatal attack on White House Press Secretary Ron McClain. A hammer is also believed to have been used in McClain's death.

It's not known if the two incidents are related. DC Metro Police believe robbery to be the motive in McClain's death.

In a statement, AP Washington Bureau Chief Scotty Barrington wrote: "We are devastated by Paul's murder. He was a bright, dedicated, outgoing journalist of the highest caliber."

Just as I was beginning to wallow in feelings of profound sadness over Paul's death, there was a light knock on the door.

Thinking selfishly and foolishly that Will had decided to pay me an early morning visit, I scrambled out of bed, bounded to the door, and opened it.

"Hi," Lionel said. "I tried calling but you didn't pick up."

"I turned it off when I went to bed."

"Can I come in?"

"Sure. Have you had coffee?"

"Hours ago. But I'm ready for more."

As I tried to figure out how to fire up the cabin's coffee maker, I said, "You're up early."

"Couldn't sleep." Lionel took a seat at the kitchen table and crossed his legs.

"Yeah. I get that."

"I just finished meeting with Kris, your grief counselor."

"I'm glad you did. How'd it go?"

"Great. She's wonderful. Marriage counseling's been a bitch, but this one-on-one thing is excellent."

"I'm surprised to hear you say that. Didn't you tell me once you're not into psychobabble?"

"I did. But that's not how Kris operates. She'd make an excellent journalist."

"In what way?"

"She asks good, probing questions. She made me think and then got me to put into words what I was thinking and feeling."

"Yep. That's Kris. I know it's been just one session, but did you have any breakthrough moments?"

"I actually did, which is why I'm here."

"Oh? What's up?"

"You and I need to share a byline."

"I thought you'd never ask."

"No. I'm serious."

"What do you mean?"

"I've already checked with my friends at the *Times* and they're making room on tomorrow's op-ed page for you and me to write a guest essay."

"Really?"

"Yeah. Neither of us have made an official statement, plus you're Gannon's flack, so they consider you and me to be highly newsworthy."

"That's nice, but I don't have a clue about what we should say."

"That's why I'm here. We've got until five o'clock tonight to come up with something. We could write a first draft right now."

"All right then. I'm game. Let's give it a go."

I poured our coffees, brought them to the table, and took a seat next to Lionel.

Chapter Thirty

For the next two hours, Lionel and I sat at the round kitchen table talking and writing. Bright sunlight splashed into the room through the window above the sink.

"How should we do this?" I began.

"First let's talk through some ideas."

"Okay. What do you feel like saying?"

"I'm pissed that Paul is dead," Lionel growled.

"Right, but who are you pissed at?" I already knew the answer.

"Roland fucking Roberts." Lionel's eyes were fierce.

"Don't you think it's a stretch to pin Paul's murder on Roland?"

"Probably." He scowled, then turned to me. "What do you feel like saying?"

I put my head in my hands. "I feel so hopeless. The world has gone insane."

He waved a hand. "The world's always been insane." His voice was I've-seen-it-all gruff.

I nodded. "But what can our paltry 800 words do to change anything?"

"We can get people—powerful people—to do some serious thinking."

I held up my hands to frame the headline: "Breaking news: the world is insane."

He laughed. "Indeed."

I stood and toured the kitchen. "What do we want people to take away from what we write?"

"Excellent question. Your thoughts?"

"Saying the world is insane is stating the obvious. But can anything be *done* about it?"

"Let's explore that."

I looked at him, eyebrows raised. "You're serious, aren't you?"

"Sure. Think big. The world is fucking nuts. What can be done about it?" He jabbed an index finger at me. "Go."

As Lionel poised his hands over the keyboard, I stared out the window above the sink and thought a moment. A squirrel chased another up a maple tree.

"War is the craziest thing of all." I turned from the window and leaned against the granite counter as Lionel began to type.

"Keep going."

"In order to have a war . . ." I paused, groping for the next thought, "you have to have an enemy."

"And what constitutes an enemy?"

"An enemy poses a threat."

"What kind of a threat?" *Type, type, type.*

"There are lots of threats." I pushed away from the sink.

"List 'em."

I rubbed the back of my neck as I paced in front of Lionel. "The ultimate threat is to a person—or a country's—existence."

Lionel nodded vigorously. "Keep going."

"A person can feel their way of life is being threatened."

"How?"

"Their livelihood might be at risk, or their health, values, or freedoms."

"Get specific."

"History is full of specifics."

"Gimme examples."

I raked my fingers through my hair. "Um . . . The Civil War."

"Go on. How so?"

"The South saw Lincoln and the North as the enemy because his policies were a threat to their slave-based economy."

"Keep going."

"Hitler whipped up hatred for the Jews blaming them for Germany's problems."

"Keep going." Lionel's fingers thumped the keys.

My words tumbled out faster and faster. "The cold war. The Berlin Wall. Vietnam."

"Yes. Godless Communism versus Democracy's shining city on a hill."

"The struggle for civil rights." I stopped and looked down at Lionel. "You covered that."

He wigwagged his head. "I did but keep going. You're doing great."

More pacing. "Martin Luther King shined a spotlight onto the insanity of racism."

"And it got him killed."

"More insanity. Then there's the Middle East."

Lionel's fingers danced on the keyboard. "Oh, man. Talk about dysfunction!"

"And Trumpism."

"Yes. His war on truth, facts, science, and anyone who didn't put him at the center of their universe."

"Fake news." *God, I've been a victim of that.* "See what I mean, Lionel?" I stood in front of him. "How can you and I make a difference?"

"We can't."

I threw up my hands. "Then why bother?"

"We can take a stand. Make a start."

I rubbed my chin and thought. "It seems to me the only way we can end insanity is to declare war on it."

"Yeah, but didn't you just say war's insane?"

I pursed my lips. "So, what does *sanity* look like?"

"Oooo. I like this. Thoughts?" Lionel shifted his weight in the chair, prepared for more typing.

"Sanity . . . sanity . . ."

"Define it."

I darted to my laptop and typed *Merriam-Webster.com* into the browser, then *sanity* into the search engine.

The page loaded and I read aloud: "Sanity. The quality or state of being sane." I looked at Lionel and made a face. "Well, duh."

He waved a hand at me. "Go on. What else does it say?"

"Let's see . . . ." More scrolling. "Sanity also means soundness or health of mind."

"What's the derivation of sanity?"

I looked back at my screen. "It's Latin. *Sanitat*. It means health."

"Look up sane."

I did. "Rational. Mentally sound. Able to anticipate and appraise the effect of one's actions. Everything the world *isn't*."

"C'mon," he grumped. "It doesn't say that."

"The last part was my spin," I confessed.

As we talked, Lionel got me hunting for synonyms. I found balanced, clearheaded, and stable.

He sat back. "So, let's build on that. What does a sane society look like? What do sane relationships look like?"

"I like clearheaded and stable."

"Me too." He resumed typing.

I was now on a roll, thoughts coming together as I spoke: "To me, the struggle for interpersonal sanity, whether it's between nations or individuals, is the ability to see things clearly and not allow intense emotions to cause instability."

"What do you mean?"

"I mean that intense emotions, if not governed by clear-headedness, can lead to insanity."

"Interesting." Lionel sat back in his chair. "That's just what Kris and I were talking about this morning."

"Really? In what way?"

"She got me talking about my emotions. Especially my anger."

"Yesterday I could tell you were seething."

He nodded. "I've got every goddammed right to be angry. But using my anger to attack Roland Roberts would be the exact kind of insanity that will merely perpetuate the problem you and I are talking about."

"I've got an idea." I opened a Word document on my laptop and started a fresh page. "Pull your chair over, Lionel. Let's see if we can get this baby started."

Chapter Thirty-One

It was almost noon when Lionel and I finished banging out the first draft of our op-ed. We agreed to let it simmer, go our separate ways, then reconvene about four to put the finishing touches on it and file.

I felt a desperate need to talk with Kris, so I went to her cabin. She answered my knock right away.

"Good morning, Lark." Her smile was luminescent.

"I'm so glad you're here, Kris. Got some time? I need to talk."

She opened the door wider and stepped aside to let me in, but I remained rooted to the porch.

"Can we walk and talk, instead?" I asked. "I've been cooped up inside for days."

"Absolutely. Let me get a sweater." She was back in no time, swinging a dark blue wool sweater around her shoulders and tying the arms across her chest.

"What a magnificent place," she said as we began our trek along a trail that began near her cabin.

We took our time, strolling aimlessly. A month ago when I'd been to Camp David, my first impression was how large it is—125 acres. This time I was struck by how peaceful and secluded it is.

At first, we were quiet. Kris seemed content to wait for me to set the agenda.

I took a deep breath of the loamy air. "It's good to be free."

Birds chirped in the tall oak, maple, and pine trees along the path.

"What do you want to talk about, Lark?"

"There's so much I need to think through."

"Shall we begin with the kidnapping ordeal?"

"Sure." I picked up a branch from the ground and used it as a walking stick.

"What effect did the kidnapping have on you?"

"Ah. A nice open-ended question."

She chuckled.

I began with the events leading up to my abduction, then an account of my time in captivity and my attempts to build rapport with Bonnie and Clete, followed by my escape.

"I used your mindful breathing techniques," I said. "They really helped me to focus and stay calm."

"That's great."

I sighed. "Now I need to decide where my life goes from here."

"What thoughts do you have about that?"

"It's getting closer to decision time about an abortion," I said. "The clock is ticking."

"Yes."

"And I need to think about my role in life."

"Your role. You mean your job?"

I scowled. "No. It's bigger than that. Life is more than having a so-called 'dream job.' It's about what gives you joy."

"Good point. Very wise."

"I never really wanted the job of press secretary. I told the president it's a dumb idea, but then I agreed to do the job anyway."

"Do you regret it?"

My answer was immediate. "Yeah. I do."

"Why?"

I snorted. "It got me abducted, for one."

"How did you feel about the job before that happened?"

"To be honest, I hated it."

She waited a beat, then asked gently, "Why?"

"I felt like I was on the defensive the whole time. Right from the beginning, I was a target. The questions, especially from Roland Roberts, targeted me personally. And now I'm furious because Roland's incendiary rhetoric got Paul killed."

We walked in silence as Kris took in what I was saying. Finally, she said, "So, going forward, what are your fears?"

I didn't even hesitate. "Fear number one is getting attacked again, this time by someone who will kill *me*. I'm elated to have been rescued. But as long as I'm still in the spotlight, I'm also in the crosshairs. I'm not free—or out of danger."

"What are the other fears?"

"Fear number two: being seen as a quitter."

"What do you mean?"

"I hate the press secretary job, but if I quit, I fear I'll let down the president. Along with that, I'm afraid I'll disappoint people who support me, and I'm concerned it will show weakness to the people who want to harm me."

"And your pregnancy merely intensifies these fears?"

"Uh huh." Intense emotions were welling up, my eyes began to sting. I couldn't talk fast enough, my voice rising. "All the while I'm wrestling with my pregnancy, I'm in the spotlight, in the fishbowl. It feels like everyone has an opinion about what I should do with my body. They're so certain about my life, yet I feel so confused and clueless about it."

I began to cry.

We stopped walking and Kris waited patiently as I let the tears flow. This is what I liked about her. She wasn't uncomfortable with my emotions. She allowed them. She seemed to know that for me crying is an emotional safety valve. If I were to keep all this angst inside, my anger would build up steam and eventually explode.

Maybe this is why most, if not all, mass shooters are guys: they bottle up their pain. When they finally let it out, their tears are bullets.

Working with Lionel on the op-ed brought into sharp focus the grave risk to my own sanity if I don't do the work necessary with Kris to make rational, clearheaded choices about my next steps in life.

When Kris sensed that my sobs were dissipating, she asked gently, "So what are you going to do, Lark?"

"About the job?"

"And your pregnancy. You still have a couple months to decide. There's no urgency, but what's your thinking at this point?"

"I don't know yet. About either. That's why I'm glad you're here this weekend. Thank you."

"You're welcome."

We resumed our walk along a wooded path. Leaves were just beginning to bud, clothing the forest in green pastels.

Kris spoke. "You've already told me how you feel about your job. Let's set that aside briefly and talk more about your pregnancy."

"Okay."

"What are your current thoughts now on abortion, giving birth, and being a parent?"

"A *single* parent," I corrected.

"Yes. And did you know that today is Mother's Day?" She turned to look at me, gauging my reaction.

I shook my head. "Y'see? That's my point: I didn't have a clue it was Mother's Day. Motherhood is just not on my radar. I don't see myself as a parent. It's not something I ever wanted. I'd probably be a lousy one."

"What about abortion?"

"I just don't see myself doing that, either."

"Why not?" Her voice was gentle, not challenging.

"As far as I know, there are no fetal abnormalities. I suppose it's possible the child inherited Doug's addiction gene, if there is such a thing, but to end the pregnancy just feels selfish."

"What do you mean?"

"It's like getting rid of an inconvenience."

"Is that so bad?"

"Interesting that you would couch the question in terms of good and bad. Seems like that's what this whole abortion debate is about—good versus evil."

"Sad, but true. I suppose we can't get away from that. But, if I know you—and I think I do—the inner debate you're having with yourself is not so much about the rightness or wrongness of abortion, per se, but rather, your personal motives for having one. Is that correct?"

I nodded. "Yes. The abortion debate is really a religious debate. That's not what I'm talking about. I think the question comes down to what's right for *me.*"

"Fine. We can take religion out of the equation, yet I'm still hearing inner doubt."

"You are."

"So, if your doubts aren't inspired or prompted by religion, what's fueling them?"

"That's a really good and interesting question." We walked in silence a bit while my thoughts came into focus. "Just before I was abducted, I was listening to a couple of abortion protestors arguing in Lafayette Square. One of them said 'choices have consequences.' I've been thinking about that a lot."

"In what way?"

"Like it, or not, something is growing inside me. It's growing into something. Some *one.* And that gives me a sense of personal responsibility."

"A responsibility to care for it?"

"Yes. But also no."

She laughed. "Can you really have it both ways?"

"I can explain. I feel a sense of personal responsibility to take care of myself because doing so cares for the fetus. But once I give birth, I have grave doubts that I would be able to provide that child with the proper love and resources because of my lack of desire to be a parent."

"You mentioned that one of your fears is that to abort would be selfish."

"Right. I'd be getting rid of an inconvenience."

"But you're not against abortion per se, right?"

"Oh hell no. There are so many good reasons to have an abortion."

"Like what?"

"If the life of the mother is at risk."

"Okay."

"Rape. Incest."

"Uh huh."

"Grave fetal abnormalities."

"What if the mother already has a gazillion kids and this next one is one too many?" Kris asked.

"Then she has the right—or *should* have the right—to abort if that's her decision."

"If she chooses to abort, is she being selfish?"

"That's not for me to judge."

"What about if she's poor and single—which all too often go hand in hand? Isn't an abortion getting rid of an inconvenience?" Kris asked.

"It could be, but that's not my choice to make for another person, and certainly not my right to judge."

"Yet, wouldn't you be judging yourself as selfish if you decided to have an abortion?"

"Yes."

"Isn't that contradictory?"

"Not really."

"Why not?"

"Because," I said, "I feel it would be wrong for me to impose my values onto someone else. But I can certainly hold myself to my own standards of right and wrong."

"I see what you're saying, yet we live in a society of laws. Every day juries render judgments that impact the lives and freedoms of others."

"All true. But at least in Maryland, where I live, abortion is not against the law—and hasn't been for fifty years. So, the only 'law' at play for my decision, is what's right for me."

"And so, what's right for you, Lark Chadwick? Do you know?"

At that moment, it felt like a light switched on. As we continued to walk a forested trail at Camp David, Maryland, I could finally see a little farther down my own life's path.

I gave her a curt nod. "Yeah. I think I do know what's right for me."

It felt good to hear the strong resolve in my voice.

Chapter Thirty-Two

Kris and I continued to walk and talk. Soon the trail intersected with another and we saw the president approaching, accompanied by a Secret Service agent.

"There you are!" he called to me while we were still twenty-five yards apart.

"Hi, Mr. President," I replied. When he was a few steps from us, I continued. "Have you had a chance yet to meet Kris, my grief counselor?"

"I have," Will said, but shook Kris's outstretched hand, anyway.

"So good to see you, Mr. President," Kris beamed. "Thank you again for inviting me up here for the weekend. What a gorgeous place."

"We have FDR to thank," Will laughed. "And Ike for naming it after his father and his grandson. I'm just continuing the tradition of a place for retreat and reflection."

Will turned to me. "I was going to see if I could get in a bit of tennis before dinner. Do you play?"

"I do. But I didn't bring my racket or any gear."

He waved a hand. "Not a problem. I think we can get that taken care of."

Kris spoke. "We've covered a lot of ground today, Lark. Let me know when you want to talk again."

"I will. Thanks, Kris. I'm so glad you're here this weekend."

Kris held out her hand to the president. "Thank you again, sir."

He took her hand and smiled. "You're entirely welcome. To be continued."

As Kris turned and walked back toward her cabin, I fell into step with Gannon.

"How's the day been going?" he asked.

"Excellent. Kris has been a tremendously helpful guide as I try to think things through. How about you?"

"I love this place, but I sure do miss Rose." He sighed.

"Tennis is a great distraction. Did the two of you play often?"

He nodded. "Today Mitch was going to be my sparring partner." He nodded at the agent following us, "But I'd much rather play with you. I think my chances of winning will be better."

"Ha! I hate to disappoint you, but I'm actually pretty good. Was on the tennis team in college, plus I have no intention of letting you win just because you're the leader of the free world."

He laughed. "We'll see about that."

At the equipment shop next to the tennis courts, I chose a racket and changed into an outfit that felt good and looked great. I was a bit self-conscious about my pale legs, but the tennis shoes were of much better quality than my own.

As we walked onto the court, the president opened a new can of balls and we began to volley.

"I'm pretty rusty," I said after I hit a ball way out of Will's reach.

"Let the disclaimers begin." He bounced a ball, then gently tapped it to me.

We continued to hit the ball back and forth to get used to the feel of things. Will Gannon is extremely comfortable in his skin. He moves with grace and ease.

I, on the other hand, felt like an awkward and gangly fawn just getting her sense of balance.

"When did you first start playing tennis?" I asked.

"When I was ten. My dad taught me."

"Did you play in high school and college?"

"Lettered in it in high school. Played on the Vanderbilt tennis team in my undergrad years, but cut back when I was in law school. Since then, it's just been for recreation."

Once we had both limbered up, he said, "Should we play a set?"

"Okay. How 'bout two out of three?"

"You're on."

"What are the stakes?"

He thought a minute. "I'll let you know after I win the first set." He laughed at his own joke.

We volleyed for serve. He won with a sharp, angled shot to my backhand. *I'm toast,* I thought to myself.

His first serve was a scorcher, but I managed to return it. I then rushed the net and won the first point by slapping his return into a far corner.

"Uh oh. I'm in trouble already," he laughed. "Good shot."

We had some excellent volleys. I broke his serve in the very first game, but he came right back and broke mine in game two.

For the remainder of the first set we pretty much kept to ourselves and said very little. It felt good to be moving around. My pregnancy wasn't advanced enough to hinder me. I was barely beginning to show.

The president was working up a sweat and seemed to be taking the match seriously. I sensed that physical exertion put him in a zone where he was able to let his subconscious go to work as he wrestled with whatever decisions presidents wrestle with.

I had my own inner thoughts to ponder, so this was excellent alone time—together.

Athletics can be an excellent way to gauge another person's character. In Will, I noticed several things: determination, grace, honesty, and generosity. Several times, when it looked to me as if I'd hit the ball out, he returned it anyway with a hearty "great shot!"

I won the first set 6-4. He won the second by the same score. The third set was a back-and-forth battle. When I pulled even at 6-6, the president said, "Let's call it a tie. I don't want to lose you as a friend by trouncing you."

By this time I was exhausted and worried that I might not have what it takes to get to the end. I'm sure he was offering me a face-saving exit.

"It's a deal," I managed to gasp.

* * *

Will, shadowed by Mitch the Secret Service agent, walked me slowly back to my cabin after our tennis match.

"Dinner tonight is a cook-out at my cabin. Your friend Lionel Stone volunteered to grill the steaks."

"Awesome." I rubbed my tummy. "I need all the protein I can get."

"Lionel tells me that the two of you are working on an op-ed for tomorrow's *Times*."

"That's right."

"I wish you'd have cleared it with me first." His voice had a stern edge.

My stomach clenched. "I'm sorry, Mr. President. It didn't even occur to me."

"Lionel said it has something to do with declaring war on insanity."

"Right."

"I actually kind of like that, in principle."

"I was planning to talk with you about it."

"Talk to me now. What prompted your idea?"

"A lot of things: my abduction, Paul Stone's murder, the recent spate of mass shootings. I'm just feeling overwhelmed and powerless, like the world has gone crazy."

He nodded soberly. "Go on."

I turned to him. "A war on insanity could be a major policy priority for your administration."

"I'm listening."

"Your poll numbers are stratospheric. You've helped bring Democracy to China. Russia is no longer the threat it was. The economy is holding its own. You're not having to play defense on any major international crises that I'm aware of." I shot him a look to get a read on his reaction.

He smiled ruefully. "If you only knew. The world's a pretty dangerous place."

"Still, what I'm saying is that you have the influence to really make a difference in the long run by calling attention to the many ways we can break the cycle of insanity."

"The operative phrase is 'in the long run.'"

"A war on mental illness could be the cornerstone of your administration—your legacy."

"Yeah. Maybe. But if this idea of yours is to gain the traction it deserves, the rhetoric needs some tweaking."

"Okay. What do you suggest—and why?"

"First. Words like 'insanity' and 'mental illness' are fraught with all kinds of negative baggage. We use words like 'insane' and 'crazy' and 'nuts' so often and so casually that we don't realize we're stigmatizing and trivializing mental illness."

I nodded.

"Second. History has not been kind to presidential declarations of war."

"What do you mean?"

"LBJ declared war on poverty. A worthy goal, but his simultaneous escalation of the war in Vietnam blunted his program's effectiveness and merely weighed down the federal budget with an ever-growing Christmas tree of entitlements."

"Uh huh."

"Reagan declared war on drugs. Nancy Reagan's 'Just Say No' approach, though admirable, was simplistic and unrealistic—especially to the already addicted. Not only did she get a lot of ribbing, but the criminalization of marijuana possession ended up sending a lot of African Americans to prison unnecessarily."

"So, what do you suggest?"

"I suggest you back away from using war-like rhetoric."

I thought about that for a moment. "How about if Lionel and I call for a . . . national, um, *conversation* on mental *health*."

"Think bigger. Why not a global conversation?"

"Oh. I like that."

"Me too."

"Lionel and I will be meeting in another hour to put the finishing touches on our piece." An idea suddenly struck me. "How about if Lionel and I call on you in our piece to start a global conversation on mental health?"

He scowled.

"A global conversation on finding stability?"

He nodded slowly, pondering. "I think if you two call on me to do something along those lines, then I will be bound to answer. Seems to me if your idea is to succeed, it can't just be another federal program. It really needs to be a conversation with answers and ideas and energy and resources coming from the ground up, not the top down. I think you're onto something, Ms. Chadwick."

He gave me a playful poke on the shoulder.

Chapter Thirty-Three

The president and I said our goodbyes outside my cabin, then he and Mitch moved on. I went inside to shower before my meeting with Lionel to put the finishing touches on our op-ed.

Lionel knocked on my door promptly at four.

I opened it, a T-shirt wrapped around my head to minimize horrific hair frizz. "Hey."

He eyed my turban and bowed slightly. "Your highness."

I laughed. "You should have seen the humungous bath towel I had to use when I first got out of the shower. It was like carrying a huge fruit basket on my head." I let him in. "Take a seat."

He took his laptop to the kitchen table where we'd banged out our first draft. I went into the bathroom, unraveled the T, then quickly put some product in my hair to tame it.

When I'd finished, I took a seat at the table next to Lionel and opened my laptop. "Had a good talk with the president this afternoon about our idea."

"Yeah. I mentioned it to him, too."

"He likes it, but had some suggestions."

Lionel scowled, but said nothing.

"He's open to us calling on him directly to take action."

Lionel's eyebrows raised. "That's interesting."

"I'm really excited about this, Lionel. It feels like you and I are on the cusp of getting something started that might actually make a difference."

"Could be, but don't get your hopes up too high."

We each fired up our laptops and opened the draft of our piece. Lionel had been my first editor when, as a college drop-out at a low point in my life, I convinced him to let me write a follow-up story about the car accident that orphaned me when I was an infant. That story led to my first full-time job as a reporter with Lionel as my boss and editor.

Now, for the first time, we were working together as equals. Lionel has always been my mentor and guide. This time, however, it felt as though the tables had turned just a bit and he was willing to let me take the lead.

Is this a passing of the torch? I wondered.

As Lionel sidled his chair closer to mine, I began to write. He peered over my shoulder as the words poured out of me.

"Don't say anything," I said. "I know it sucks. Just let me get it down. Then you can work your magic."

"Deal," he growled.

When I finished twenty minutes later, it felt like my keyboard was smoking.

"Okay. Fix it." I angled my laptop at Lionel.

He pulled it to him, scrolled to the top and began reading. As usual, when he's in deep concentration, he breathes noisily through his nose.

"Good, good," he said frequently as he scrolled down.

Now and then he'd delete an extraneous word. Doing even a little thing like that gave a sentence so much more punch. He also corrected my myriad misspellings.

Here's how the piece gets started:

OPINION
GUEST ESSAY
LET'S STOP INSANITY

By Lark Chadwick & Lionel Stone

Ms. Chadwick is White House Press Secretary

Mr. Stone is the former National Editor of The New York Times and a Pulitzer Prize Winner

We are writing from a place of profound personal pain.

Lionel Stone and his wife Muriel are experiencing the loss of their only son Paul at the hands of a crazed killer.

Paul Stone, an AP White House correspondent, was Lark Chadwick's close friend and former colleague.

In addition, Lark was rescued Saturday after being abducted two days earlier by a husband and wife. The couple strongly opposed abortion and wanted to force Lark to deliver her baby rather than have the choice of terminating her pregnancy.

Our grief and anger are overwhelming.

But we are not the only ones experiencing these strong emotions. Pain is everywhere.

Nations war against each other. Political parties practice the politics of personal destruction. Families experience dysfunction. Mass shootings occur daily. It is the norm. Not news.

This insanity must stop.

It is tempting to call for a war on mental illness. In the 1960s, Pres. Lyndon B. Johnson declared war on poverty. In the 1980s, Pres. Ronald Reagan declared war on drugs.

Both wars failed.

It's time for something new. War itself is the ultimate insanity, but using warlike rhetoric to fight insanity is, at best, counterproductive.

Instead, we are calling on Pres. Will Gannon to initiate a global conversation on mental health.

We finished the piece by 4:50, ten minutes ahead of our deadline. Lionel placed a phone call to his friend on the *Times'* Op-Ed Desk to give a heads up that our piece was ready and on the way.

Then we went next door to pick up Muriel and walk to the presidential cabin for the evening cookout.

For the first time since my release a little more than a day ago, when I'd learned of Paul's murder, I had at least a glimmer of hope.

But it wouldn't be long before hope would give way to a sense of dread.

Chapter Thirty-Four

At the presidential cookout, I was in my comfort zone as a barn owl, mostly observing the festivities from the periphery.

Festivities is too strong a word, of course, because so many of us—Will, Lionel, Muriel, and I—were still carrying around a load of grief. But, because the gathering was seeded by additional people—presidential staff, Kris, and the president's children Grace and Thomas—there was more superficial gaiety than would have otherwise been present had it been a smaller gathering.

At one point, I sidled over to Muriel when I saw her accept a condolence hug from a stately African American woman wearing an Air Force uniform. As I got closer, I saw the four stars gleaming on the woman's epaulets and recognized her as Gen. Mildred Jackson, Will's recent appointment to the Joint Chiefs.

Muriel brightened when she saw me approach. "Millie, I want you to meet my friend Lark Chadwick."

The general wore gold wire rim spectacles and had an angular, but friendly, face. "So, good to meet you, Ms. Chadwick." Her handshake was firm, her hand smooth and warm.

"And you as well, general. Congratulations on your recent appointment."

"Thank you."

"Millie and I were roommates in college," Muriel beamed. "We haven't seen each other in twenty years."

"Really? I didn't know that. University of Wisconsin, right?" I noted.

General Jackson nodded and smiled. "Chadbourne Hall."

"Everyone referred to us as 'The Two Ms,' " Muriel laughed.

"Muriel was an English major. I majored in history and was in ROTC." General Jackson pronounced it "rot-see," the Reserve Officer Training Corps.

"I'll let you two get caught up," I said, backing away. "Wonderful to meet you, ma'am."

I retreated to my post at the periphery.

Will, I noticed, has a naturally extroverted personality. He mixed easily with everyone. If I didn't know better, I'd think he didn't have a care in the world.

A Naval steward worked alongside Lionel grilling steaks. I could tell he needed something useful to do and sharing the duties with a guy seemed to give Lionel a sense of purpose and male camaraderie that would have been lacking otherwise. Even so, when he wasn't bantering with the steward, there was a grimness in Lionel's countenance that reflected the deep pain of now having survived both his children.

Later, I noticed that Muriel, too, seemed dazed. Kris, sensing it, took Muriel aside and the two of them strolled away from the others to admire the flower garden that surrounded the backyard of Aspen Cabin where we'd gathered. I was glad that the president had arranged for Kris to be present, not only at Camp David for the weekend, but that he'd included her in the cookout.

I was content to slowly sip my ginger ale, but my reverie was interrupted when Nora Tomlinson, my number two, stopped by to chat.

"How are you, Lark?" she asked. "That's not just an idle question, you know."

"I'm good, Nora. Thanks for doing such an excellent job as my backup. I actually saw a short clip of you while I was being held hostage."

"Really?"

"Yeah. My captors love Roland. He's *must*-see TV for them. They made his show a *forced*-see for me during my captivity."

She rolled her eyes.

"Has Roland been making your life miserable?"

"He's such a jerk. I try to ignore him." She'd been holding a glass of red wine and took a sip. "Any idea when you'll be back?"

"Dunno. I need to talk with the president about that. I dread having to be in the same room with Roland, especially because his reporting inspired my abduction and Paul's murder."

Nora nodded.

"Part of me needs to be doing something useful, but another part of me isn't ready to be useful at the podium."

Just then a handsome man joined us. He looked familiar, but I couldn't place him. He was Nora's age, fifties, with close-cropped blond hair, blue eyes, chiseled chin, and looked fit in a white polo shirt.

"Have you met Charles, my husband?" Nora asked me.

"No, I haven't." I shook his hand. He gave mine a bone-crushing squeeze.

"Hello, Ms. Chadwick. I've admired you from afar for a long time, and Nora thinks the world of you."

"Thank you. Forgive me. I didn't recognize you out of uniform. Chairman of the Joint Chiefs, right?"

His already impressive chest puffed out a bit more. "That's right."

His smile gleamed. "Welcome back to freedom."

"Thank you. It's good to be outside again."

He started to ask me a question, but I just didn't want to get sucked into having to relive my ordeal for the benefit of someone else's curiosity even if he was the person who oversaw the entire U.S. military. I excused myself and drifted off toward a table piled with succulent red grapes, cheese, crackers, and other munchies.

As I left Nora and Charles in my wake, I noticed how I used to be gregarious, but now I was feeling uptight and defensive around other people, especially strangers. I didn't like this new Lark and made a mental note to talk to Kris about it.

As I pretended to take a personal and in-depth interest in the grapes on the table, I pondered my current predicament: I was still shaken by my abduction ordeal. No doubt I'd have to testify against Bonnie and Clete once they went on trial. That would mean more unwanted limelight for me.

I was also deeply troubled by the fatal attack on Paul, inspired by one of Roland's rants.

Thoughts of Roland made my stomach turn as I worried about having to face him yet again in the briefing room. He was taking up way too much psychological real estate.

I can't afford to let one obnoxious reporter get under my skin, I said to myself.

And then there was the pregnancy. I noticed that I no longer had a sense of urgency about obtaining an abortion, but I certainly had not gained a newfound sense of expectancy about becoming a mother. It felt like I was in pregnancy purgatory.

I suppose I should have been beginning to think more concretely about becoming a mother, but what was more exciting was the op-ed Lionel and I had just written. I hadn't yet seen it online, but it would be in the *New York Times* tomorrow.

I already knew Will was intrigued by the topic and I was energized by the idea of getting the world to begin to focus on finding ways to bring sanity to interpersonal—and international—relations. It would certainly be an uphill battle. And things wouldn't change overnight—or probably even within my lifetime—but I was thrilled by the possibilities.

I also wondered, and even worried a little, about the biography Will and I were writing about his late wife Rose. Had he decided how best to deal with what he'd learned about her secret abortion?

Yet, undergirding all these thoughts, bubbling just beneath the surface, was a vague sense that another shoe might drop and whatever sense of elation I had about being free might once again be suddenly snatched from me.

Chapter Thirty-Five

On Monday morning at 7:30, I was in the Oval Office, sitting in one of the two chairs in front of the president's Resolute Desk. President Gannon sat at the desk, leaning back, reflective.

I needed to be doing something productive but was not yet ready to face Rabid Roland in the briefing room, so Will agreed to have Nora continue as acting press secretary as he and I discussed how I could be helpful while trying to heal out of the limelight.

"That op-ed you and Lionel Stone wrote was excellent, Lark."

"Thank you, sir."

"I'm going to respond to it through Nora later today."

"What will be your official response?"

"That I'm giving serious thought to your call to action."

"That's heartening. Thank you. If I may be so bold, what are you thinking about doing?"

He stood, came around the side of his desk and took the chair next to me. "I'm thinking of declaring a national mental health emergency."

"Whoa!" My eyebrows went up. "Tell me more."

"Have you ever written a presidential address to the nation before?"

"Um, no. But thanks for asking."

He bounced to his feet and began pacing the room. I turned my chair around to watch as he walked and talked.

"Later today, I'm going to assemble my Cabinet to get their ideas. On Wednesday night I'm planning to address the nation on the issue. I want you at the Cabinet meeting today and I want you to write the first draft of my speech. A lot of people will weigh in on it, of course, but I'll have the final say. Working on this seems to me to be an excellent use of your time."

"I-I'm speechless, Mr. President."

He laughed. "So to speak."

For the next ninety minutes I took notes as the president and I brainstormed the outline of his address, and the points he wanted to make. I then joined him in the Cabinet Room as he met with the leaders of his administration.

Nora brought in the press pool. A CNN camera crew sprayed the room to get pictures of the event. A photog from *The New York Times* took rapid-fire still shots. *USA Today's* Paige Summers was the pool print reporter. She fired questions at Gannon as the photogs got their shots.

"What's the purpose of today's meeting, Mr. President?" Paige asked.

Gannon smiled affably but did his best not to commit news. "Good to see you, Paige. Thanks for being here."

"Do you have any comment, sir, on the *New York Times* op-ed calling for a global conversation on mental health?" asked the CBS reporter representing the major entertainment networks.

"Nora will be releasing my statement during the eleven o'clock briefing," Gannon said.

"But why not go on the record now?" the reporter badgered.

The president smiled but said nothing.

If presidents had their way, only photographers would be allowed in to take pictures. Past presidents had tried and failed to bar reporters, but it never ended well. The White House Correspondents' Association has had a long-standing rule that if reporters aren't allowed into the room, then the pool will not send in cameras, either.

"All right, everyone," Nora called. "Time to wrap it up."

Paige and the network correspondent continued to shout questions, but Gannon wasn't biting. Two minutes after entering the Cabinet Room, the press pool and the relentless shutter clicks and questions were gone.

The president sat along one side of the huge mahogany conference table surrounded by all the people leading the executive branch. I sat immediately behind Gannon, my back against the wall on the Rose Garden side of the table. Other staffers from the various departments also ringed the outer walls sitting behind their bosses.

Nora's husband Charles, in dress blues and bedecked with a chest full of colorful service ribbons, sat across the table from the president. Though technically not a member of the Cabinet, Gannon told me General Tomlinson, as Chairman of the Joint Chiefs, was attending the meeting at the behest of the Secretary of Defense who sat to Charles' left.

The brain power in the stuffy room could light the world for a century.

"Thank you all for being here on such short notice," the president began. "On Wednesday night, I'm going to be making an Oval Office address to the nation."

Everyone sitting around the table leaned toward the president and watched him intently as their staffs took copious notes.

"I'm going to declare a national mental health emergency."

Several members of the president's Cabinet nodded grimly.

Charles Tomlinson winced.

"If you could wave a magic wand, and resources were not an issue," the president continued, "what do you feel should be done to eradicate mental illness?"

The U.S. Surgeon General spoke first. "That's a pretty tall order, Mr. President. Isn't the idea of eradicating mental illness a bit far-fetched?"

"Oh hell yeah," Gannon said. "I'm enough of a realist to know that'll never happen. But I still think it's a worthy goal and that we should try."

For the next hour, the president went around the room, eliciting off-the-cuff ideas from his brain trust. I took notes on my laptop.

As the meeting drew to a close, the president said, "I want you all to go back to your departments today and brainstorm ideas. By noon tomorrow, I want each of you to provide me with at least five major things that can be done to turn around the scourge of insanity that seems to be gripping not just this country, but the entire world."

The Secretary of Defense spoke up. "With all due respect, sir, don't you think you're moving too fast on this?"

"I don't think I'm moving fast enough. I want to get a conversation going with the rest of the world as quickly as possible. Moving fast conveys a sense of urgency. As far as I'm concerned, the latest spate of school shootings is the last straw. We are facing a crisis. A crisis of mental instability. We must—all of us—do our best to turn things around. The stakes are very high."

Several members of the Cabinet nodded, but Charles Tomlinson slowly shook his head.

Chapter Thirty-Six

That evening, alone at my apartment, I curled up on my sofa with my laptop and smooth jazz. I craved a glass of Cabernet but settled for a non-alcoholic ginger ale. Even so, the mood I'd created was just what I needed and what I'd lacked for the past week—a peaceful almost womb-like setting where I could relax and put into words what had been swirling in my psyche like a tornado.

I'd never written a speech before. Not for myself and certainly not for a President of the United States.

Once again, I felt enormous gratitude for Will Gannon. Arguably, he was not only the most important person in the world—perhaps even the most popular—yet, for some reason, he not only valued my friendship and companionship, but made me feel truly seen as an individual. As a person.

During the day, I'd read past presidential addresses. Some were deadly dull because they bombarded the audience with facts and figures.

In my research, I noted that Jimmy Carter caught a lot of flak for a speech in which he described America as being in a state of "malaise." Republicans pounced on it as the antithesis of upbeat. Carter never lived it down and, consequently, it contributed to the perception that he was a weak president.

Instinctively, I knew I needed to be careful that Will wouldn't be painted with the same brush that doomed Jimmy Carter to only one term. I needed to find a tone that was upbeat while also sounding an alarm.

I opened my laptop, started a new page, and got off to a safe start:

Good evening, my fellow Americans.

For the next several minutes, my cursor blinked to the immediate right of the period, taunting me to write something profound.

I took a sip and listened to Miles Davis' soulful trumpet interpretation of "So What."

Long ago I learned from Lionel that the surest way to get trapped into the paralysis of writer's block is to freeze up, afraid of making a mistake.

"Just write," he'd admonish. "Sure, the first draft is going to be a steaming pile of shit. It's just the first draft, for Christ's sake. Get it all down. Write from your heart, without judgment. *Then* go back, pretty it up, and make it coherent."

So, with Lionel growling "just write" in my head, and out of the turmoil in my heart, I wrote the first sentence:

WHAT THE FUCK, AMERICA!!!!!!!!!!!!!!!!

Hmmm. Maybe a little too much?

Reluctantly, I pressed the *delete* key, and erased the cathartic primal scream I'd written.

I took a gulp from my glass, and a deep breath.

Calmer now—just a little—I tried again:

My fellow Americans, tonight I want to speak to you from the heart about a crisis of global significance.

Better. This felt better. For the next hour, the words flowed:

In just the past week, there have been two mass shootings at elementary schools. The innocent lives of more than two dozen children have been tragically cut short.

A week earlier, my press secretary, Lark Chadwick, was abducted, snatched off a public street just a few blocks from where I'm sitting. She was held hostage because of the false belief that she was planning to have an abortion.

During that time, a member of the White House press corps, Paul Stone, was brutally attacked and killed with a hammer simply because he was considering gender reassignment surgery.

These are not isolated events.

Instead, they mark an intensification of the viciousness that has permeated our political discourse since the 2016 presidential election.

Since then, our social media has been deluged with falsehoods.

QAnon conspiracy theories abound.

Millions of people really do believe that Democrats are blood-drinking pedophiles.

Trust in science, journalism, the judiciary, and government is at an all-time low.

Politics is now a zero-sum blood sport where collegiality and compromise are seen as treasonous.

In short: it would seem as though the world has gone mad.

And so, my fellow Americans, I'm coming to you tonight to declare a national mental health emergency.

I'm coming to you tonight to ask for your help.

We must find ways to bring our society back to a place of sanity and stability.

This crisis is grave because doing nothing threatens to undermine all that is good about this country and our people.

Let me be clear: I'm not here tonight to take away your guns, or to throw billions of your tax dollars at a problem.

Nor do I want in any way to call into question the sanity of anyone whose political opinions differ from mine.

Instead, I'm appealing to all of you—Democrats, Republicans, Independents, and even the politically disillusioned.

I'm reaching out to people of all faiths—and of no faith.

I'm appealing to corporations and individuals.

We must work together.

We must talk together.

We must try to find solutions to this crisis.

We must struggle together—from the ground up—to bring this country back to a place of stability.

We must struggle together—all of us—to find ways to replace the politics of demonization of The Other to a place where there is love for all.

I pledge to you that as long as I am your president, I will do all that I can to help bring this country back to a place of civility, stability, and sanity.

I'm not proposing an expensive and massive government program; I'm appealing to you—all of you—to begin today to find ways to change fear and fighting into love and peace.

Together, America, we can do it.

Thank you.

An hour later, my glass was drained—and so was I.

Chapter Thirty-Seven

"This is very strong, Lark." The president took off his reading glasses and set them down next to a printout of my speech that he'd been reading.

It was the next morning, Tuesday. We were in the Oval, the president seated behind the Resolute Desk; me perched in one of the two chairs in front of it.

"Thank you, sir. I know it's just a start, but I feel good about it."

"I like the tone, but something's missing." Gannon got up and paced.

"Policy proposals, right?"

"Yeah, but I purposely want to avoid being too prescriptive, at least right away. I believe there are a lot of good ideas out there that don't require federal spending."

"Maybe you can have a national town hall meeting to get people talking about it. Bring together experts in the field of mental health."

He paused to look out the French doors at the Rose Garden, hand at his chin, nodding. "Yeah."

I sighed deeply, involuntarily.

Will picked up on it right away, wheeled away from the window, and took the seat next to mine. "What's wrong, Lark?"

"Sir, I—I can't continue being your press secretary."

He looked stunned. "Why not?"

"I just can't."

"You've only had the job a week and most of that time—all but two days—you've been . . ." he paused, "otherwise engaged."

"I know. I feel like a quitter, like I'm letting you down."

He was quiet for a moment. I felt his gaze hot against the top of my head as I looked down, ashamed of myself for being a failure.

When he didn't say anything, I looked up at him shyly.

The look on his face was one of confusion mixed with empathy. We were both dealing with the loss of people we loved, but Will was powering through it as he shouldered the weight of the world.

I, on the other hand, was beginning to feel like I couldn't go on.

"Maybe you just need more time off," he said gently.

I nodded. "Yes. I do. But it's deeper than that."

"What do you mean?"

"I can't go back into that briefing room."

"Why not?"

"I can't face Roland Roberts."

"Why not?"

"He's a bully."

"Indeed."

"I just feel too weak right now."

"Right now."

I made a face.

"You feel that way now, but feelings change."

"They do, but I'm not so sure they will in this case."

"I know I sound like a broken record," he said, "but why not?"

"Because my abduction is a direct result of Roland's incendiary rhetoric. Roland has made me into a target."

"I'm a target, too. I get that."

"Do you?" I looked at him sharply. "Has your freedom ever been snatched from you?" My tone was stern.

"No, but it could happen. I live daily with the sober realization that anyone could take a shot at me at any time."

"But it's never happened, right?"

"Not yet."

"So, how is it that you're able to go on so easily, as if nothing has happened?"

"I have Secret Service protection. I can arrange it for you, too, by the way."

I shook my head. "Thank you, but something is changing inside of me. I've never liked the limelight, but now I'm in the spotlight—and it's unrelentingly white hot." I looked at him. "It's different for you. *You* sought it. *I* didn't."

He stood. More pacing, then plopped down next to me again, his face troubled. "I need you, Lark." His voice was barely a whisper.

"What do you mean?"

"I need you. Just like Rose was a source of stability for me, I see you as a very strong person. We have a connection. Your presence in my life is very reassuring."

"I don't know what to say."

"Don't say anything. Just think it over."

Time seemed to stand still, but the ticking of the grandfather clock standing against the wall over my shoulder marked the unrelenting passage of first one second, then two, then three . . . .

Chapter Thirty-Eight

"Thank you. And may God bless you, us, and the United States of America." President Will Gannon looked steadily at the camera, his Oval Office address to the nation now history.

The president's face was replaced on the screen by Wolf Blitzer's, then a wide shot of a panel of "experts" that seemed to extend into the next room.

I had turned down Will's invitation to be in the Oval Office with him "for moral support" as he gave the speech. "I don't want the press corps to see me skulking around," I'd said.

"Then will you watch in the Residence? We could do a debrief and watch the initial reaction."

I'd agreed and now awaited the president's return.

Most of the experts on the CNN panel were, predictably, fawning in their reaction to the president's speech. Much of what I'd initially written had remained, but the president, and his speechwriters, had added several things to give it more substance.

In declaring a national emergency, the president had deliberately refrained from grabbing any power to do things unilaterally. Technically, he still had vast powers, but he'd told me he wanted to hold them "in reserve."

I flipped to Fox News to see how they were handling it. Predictably, Republican leaders in both the House and Senate vowed to hold hearings and pass laws that would prevent the president from taking actions that would "strip Americans of their civil rights."

One twit flashed the peace sign and called it Gannon's "peace and love" speech.

"So, what's the verdict?"

I turned from my chair in the East Sitting room to see the president getting off the elevator.

Reflexively, I stood, but he waved me back to my seat.

He took off his dark blue suit coat and tossed it onto the settee by the window, uncinched his purple tie, and began taking off his onyx cuff links.

"Fox News hates you," I said.

"Breaking news." He took a seat in the chair next to me. "You hungry?"

"Sure. If you are."

He got up, snatched his suit coat from the settee and headed into his bedroom. "I could go for a burger. You?"

My first instinct was to ask for a Caesar salad, but I remembered those are now off-limits because they might contain raw eggs. "A Cobb salad would be nice. Thank you."

"I'll call downstairs and ask them to send something up," he hollered from the other room.

"Oh!" I called to him. "I just got this sudden craving for pickles and peanut butter."

"Um, okay," he said, uncertainly.

In a few minutes, he was back wearing jeans, moccasins, and a dark blue fleece hoodie emblazoned with the presidential seal.

"What did *you* think, Lark?"

"You did great, sir."

"It's Will. Please. We're in Friend Mode."

"Okay, Will. I thought your delivery was earnest and sincere."

"Thanks." He grabbed the clicker from the coffee table and began to channel surf, starting with Fox, then CNN, then MSNBC.

As he watched TV, I watched him.

He was clearly wired, energized by the personal impact he was having on the national psyche. He sat at the edge of his chair, right foot bouncing excitedly.

From time to time, he'd have a verbal reaction to what someone was saying: "Yes," he'd say, or, "Exactly." But mostly, he nodded in agreement—until he turned back to Fox, which had changed the subject to how he's "ignoring the invasion at our Southern border."

"They're so full of shit," he said.

I had mixed feelings about being here alone with the president. Before my abduction, our time together working on the Rose biography had been breezy and businesslike. But since my abduction, Paul's murder, and Will's unexpected vulnerable statement that he "needs" me, I was beginning to feel unsure of myself and of my feelings.

I'd always been attracted to him on a visceral level—what woman with a pulse wouldn't be? After Rose died, I'd sensed that he might have feelings for me. But we had an unspoken agreement that we wouldn't go there, even though there'd been widespread speculation that something might be going on between us.

Since my abduction, rescue, and learning of Paul's murder, I'd become a jumble of angst on top of pregnancy hormones.

During our conversation in the Oval Office the previous day, Will had put my mind at ease when he suggested—and I agreed—that I take a "leave of absence" from my role as press secretary. Nora would become "acting" press secretary.

That was a big relief. It freed me to continue being useful to the president, but in a behind-the-scenes role as ghostwriter of the Rose Gannon biography, plus unofficial "First Friend," a sounding board and companion.

But was there more going on beneath the surface?

When a handsome, dynamic, and recently widowed President of the United States tells you he "needs" you, what does that mean?

Do I need him?

The arrival of a steward with our food interrupted my reverie.

After the steward left, and we were seated at a small table, Will took an enormous bite out of his burger, while I picked at my salad.

"I thought you said you were hungry," Will said, his mouth full.

"I am, but I've been thinking, too."

"About what?"

I speared some lettuce with my fork and popped it into my mouth, stalling for time. Would I tell him that I felt I needed him, too?

"I feel . . . ."

"Go on."

I held up a finger indicating I needed to finish chewing and swallow.

Finally, I spoke. "I feel you're . . . really pumped about the speech." Yes. When in doubt, chicken out. Ignore speaking about the elephant in the room and throw the spotlight back onto the other person.

"I *am* pumped! Tomorrow I'm hosting a summit of mental health leaders across the street at Blair House to get the conversation started. Then I'm gonna hit the road."

"Oh?"

"Yeah. A series of day trips to every part of the country to kick-start this national mental health conversation." He turned to look at me and raised his eyebrows. "Will you come along?"

"Gee, I—"

"We could do more work together on the book."

"Um—"

"C'mon, Lark. It'll be fun." He wiggled his eyebrows.

"And you need me."

"Well, duh."

I laughed. "Okay. Sure."

"Yesss." He pumped his fist.

But fun for whom? I had mixed feelings.

Chapter Thirty-Nine

"I should be getting home," I said, putting my fork next to my salad bowl and wiping my mouth with a white linen napkin.

"Can you stay for a nightcap?"

"Remember? I'm pregnant. I can't have alcohol."

"But I can." He got up and went to the mini-fridge and opened it. "I've got ginger ale, too. Just sayin'."

"Thank you, but it's been a long d—"

"Good evening, Mr. President."

Both Will and I turned in surprise.

General Charles Tomlinson, Chairman of the Joint Chiefs of Staff, stood at attention just inside the doorway to the East Sitting Room. He wore his dress blue Marine Corps uniform. Four gold stars sparkled on his shoulders.

"Good evening, General." The president straightened from his position at the mini-fridge. "I don't believe I sent for you. Has something come up?"

"Yes, sir." Tomlinson turned to the two Secret Service agents who flanked him. "He's all yours."

The agents moved to the president.

"Sir," Tomlinson said, "You are hereby under arrest for treason."

"What is this?" the president said, raising his voice.

Before he could say or do more, one of the agents firmly gripped the president by the shoulders and spun him around while the other agent handcuffed his hands behind his back.

"What are you doing?" I shouted.

"Not now, Lark. I'm busy." Tomlinson said.

The president did his best to break free, but the two agents easily overpowered him.

"This is outrageous," Gannon said, his face red with rage. "I am the President of the United States. You have no authority to do this."

"I'm afraid I do, sir. For the good of the country, I'm in charge now."

"Stop! You have no right to do this," I shouted. I stood in the doorway and held out my arms trying to stop the two burly agents from manhandling the president to the elevator.

Tomlinson pushed me aside and the agents frog-marched Gannon to the elevator.

"Where are you taking him?"

"You'll see." Tomlinson said from inside the elevator. "Turn on your TV. I'll be making an announcement in about five minutes."

As Tomlinson punched a button in the elevator, the president's daughter Grace raced to my side where she saw her father in handcuffs.

"Daddy!" she cried. "Where are you taking my daddy?"

"Stay strong, Grace, honey. I'll be back," the president said.

The elevator doors closed.

Chapter Forty

Little Grace Gannon was inconsolable.

I knelt next to her and surrounded her in my arms. "It's going to be okay, honey. I'm going to do everything I can to help get your daddy back."

"I want my daddy," Grace cried into my chest.

"I know, sweetheart. I know. It's gonna be okay."

I was trembling with rage, frustration . . . and fear. Even as I was embracing Grace, I dug my iPhone out of my jeans and dialed the first person I could think of. He picked up immediately.

"Hey, Lark," Lionel said brightly. "What did you think of Gannon's sp—"

"Lionel!" I shouted. "There's a coup in progress. I was just with the president in the Residence when he was arrested."

"Whuh?" Lionel blustered.

Quickly, I filled him in, adding, "Tomlinson said he's gonna go on TV any minute."

We hung up. I dashed to the TV and turned it on, placed Grace on the settee, stood, and made another phone call.

"Nora!" I shouted into the phone. "What the hell is your husband doing?"

"He's saving the country, Lark." Her voice was smooth, oily.

"What are you talking about?"

"You'll see. I just alerted the networks. We're about to make a major surprise announcement."

"We? Are you in on this?"

"Gotta go, Lark."

Next I called Paige Summers, the head of the White House Correspondents' Association. She, too, picked up immediately.

"Paige! It's Lark. There's a coup in progress."

"What? What do you mean?"

Quickly, I told her what had happened, adding, "General Tomlinson is about to address the nation. Nora is in on it."

Next I placed a call to my old boss Scotty Barrington, the DC bureau chief for the Associated Press. He and I hadn't parted on good terms, but this was an emergency and I felt I had to get the word out.

He, too, immediately took my call.

"Hey, Lark. Long time no—"

"Scotty! There's a coup in progress. Gannon has just been arrested by two rogue Secret Service agents on the orders of Charles Tomlinson."

"The Joint Chiefs Chairman?"

"Yeah."

"How do you know this?"

"I was there. I saw it hap—"

"It looks like the networks are breaking in." He paused. "Holy shit. Tomlinson is speaking from the Oval Office. Gotta go. Thanks for the heads up, Lark."

I went to the settee, scooped up Grace, sat, and, with her on my lap, I watched in horror as a grim-faced Charles Tomlinson addressed the nation sitting where moments earlier President Will Gannon had declared a national mental health emergency.

"Good evening, my fellow Americans and fellow patriots. For those of you who don't know me, I'm Marine Corps General Charles Tomlinson, Chairman of the Joint Chiefs of Staff."

The shot of Tomlinson was medium wide. It showed the top portion of the Resolute Desk, pristine except for an iPhone, black fountain pen, and a sheet of paper. Behind Tomlinson, on a credenza, were pictures of Gannon and his family. On the other side of the window, the Washington Monument glowed in the background.

"There's a picture of Mommy, Daddy, Thomas, and me," Grace said as the camera slowly zoomed in for a close-up of Tomlinson.

"That's right, honey." I hugged her closer and we both watched.

Tomlinson appeared to be speaking without notes or a teleprompter. His bearing was authoritarian, regal, impressive.

"Moments ago, Will Gannon was placed under arrest by the Secret Service. He is being charged with treason."

"That's such horseshit," I breathed.

"Miss Lark," Grace said sharply, "You said a bad word."

"You're right, honey. I'm sorry. There might be more bad words coming from me before tonight is over."

She giggled, "Like 'shit'?"

"Yeah. Probably that one. And a few more. Hush now. Let's listen."

Tomlinson continued. "I'm in charge now here at the White House. Gannon has been taken to an undisclosed location where he will soon stand trial.

"Never in the history of this great nation have we ever been in more peril. Let me explain.

"Today my office intercepted a conversation between Gannon—"

"He's *President* Gannon, you asshole."

Grace giggled again.

"—and the President of China, Tong Ji Hui."

Will and the Chinese president had been close friends when they were both in law school at Vanderbilt. A year earlier, Tong, who had been China's defense minister, staged a bloodless coup against a bellicose president who was about to launch an attack on the United States. Since then, Gannon and Tong had been working together to help Democracy take root in China. As a reporter, I'd been on Gannon's state visit to China to cement in a new era of peace and cooperation between two formerly adversarial nations.

As Tomlinson spoke, he picked up his iPhone. "I want you to hear their conversation for yourself so that you can better understand the reason for the swift action I've had to take."

He punched a button on the phone. The camera zoomed in slowly for a close-up of the phone in Tomlinson's hand.

"Hello, my friend," came the recorded voice of the Chinese president.

"Hello, President Tong," Will said, his voice jovial. "I'm calling to tell you that things are now in place for you and I to be co-leaders of both the United States and the People's Republic of China. It's the first step in our plan for world domination."

"Holy shit," I breathed into Grace's hair.

The voice was definitely Will's, but what he was saying was a blatant departure from everything I knew about him.

"This must be a deepfake," I said out loud.

"What's that, Miss Lark?"

"It's when someone uses Artificial Intelligence to take your daddy's words and twist them into sounding like he said something he didn't really say."

"What's arma-fishall—"

"I'll tell you later. Let's keep listening."

Tomlinson switched off the recording. "Stunning and frightening to hear, I know. This is why I've taken immediate action to save this country from a takeover by Communist China, facilitated by former president Gannon. So, until Gannon's trial for treason is over, I am declaring martial law."

"What!?"

"The Congress and Supreme Court are hereby dissolved."

Tomlinson put down his phone, picked up a fountain pen, and, with a flourish, affixed his signature to a piece of paper.

When he finished signing the document, he looked up again, his ice-blue eyes boring in on the camera lens.

"Ever since Gannon was sworn in six months ago, my office and the patriots on my staff, have been keeping close watch as Gannon's woke policies threatened our country. Today was the last straw. Not only is he colluding with a foreign power, his so-called mental health emergency is nothing more than an insidious attempt to make us into a nation of weaklings, at the mercy of the evil powers in the world who wish us ill.

"But fear not, America. All will be well. I am in charge now. Soon, very soon, The United States will once again be restored to its place of primacy in the world."

For a moment, but only for a moment, I thought about impulsively storming into the Oval Office and interrupting Tomlinson's power grab, but even I realized how futile and self-defeating that would have been. I, too, would probably have been arrested—or worse.

But I needed to do *something*.

"Thank you. Good night. And may God bless this newly freed United States of America." Tomlinson's gaze was steely-stern.

The image on the screen switched from Tomlinson to Wolf Blitzer.

"We have just witnessed a coup. The overthrow of a duly-elected president of the United States." Blitzer looked stunned.

Chapter Forty-One

My adrenalin was pumping as I tried to take stock of the situation. Even though Charles Tomlinson had probably been working meticulously to identify and put in place like-minded people who would support removing Gannon from office, I reasoned there would most certainly be a powerful—and perhaps violent—backlash against Tomlinson and his supporters.

And then there was little Grace, little bewildered Grace, snuggling against me on my lap, wondering and worrying about the commotion swirling around her. She'd now lost both her parents.

Despite my concern for the country, my most immediate worry was what would happen to Grace and Thomas. Would Tomlinson leave the Oval Office and come up here to the residence where Grace and Thomas would be his hostages?

"Quick, Grace. I need your help." I jumped to my feet and placed her on the floor, then crouched so we were at eye level.

"What can I do to help, Miss Lark?"

"We need to wake up Thomas and go on an adventure."

"An adventure?" She looked dubious.

I did my best to make my face as bright and enthusiastic as I could fake. "Yeah. An adventure."

"Wh-what do you mean?"

"An adventure is fun because it's like taking a trip into an unknown future. It's . . . it's . . ." *Please, God. Give me the words. I'm groping here.* "It's a little spooky-dangerous because you don't know what's going to happen, but it's, um, thrilling, too."

She scrunched her face.

"You've read *Harry Potter*, right?"

She nodded.

"An adventure," I said, "is like what Harry, Ron, and Hermine go on all the time."

She brightened. "Oooo. That'll be fun. I love adventures like that."

Thank you, Jesus!

"Can Thomas come, too?"

"Absolutely!"

I grabbed her hand. "Where's your bedroom?"

"This way."

We bounded down the hall to the nursery.

"I'll wake up Thomas," she said. "You wake up Octavia."

"Is Octavia your nanny?"

"Uh-huh."

While Grace went to Thomas's bed to roust him, I knocked on the nanny's door, then entered.

"Octavia," I said to the woman, nudging her gently but firmly.

She stirred.

I shook her again. "You need to wake up. This is an emergency."

Octavia's eyes opened wide. "W-who are you?"

"I'm Lark Chadwick, the president's friend."

"Are the children all right?"

"Yes. They're fine, but there's been a coup. The president has been arrested and taken away."

"*Dios mio!*" She bolted upright.

"We're not safe here."

"Why not?"

"I'm afraid the children are going to be held hostage."

"Oh my God."

"We need to get out of here."

She threw off her bed covers, swung her legs to the floor, and stepped into her slippers. She stood and put on the pink robe that had been lying across the foot of the bed.

"Do you know of any secret passages?" I asked.

"Yes."

Quickly, she dashed past me to the children's room.

I dug out my phone and placed a quick call to Muriel.

"I need your help," I pleaded as soon as she picked up.

"Anything."

"I'm with Will Gannon's children at the White House. I'm concerned that Tomlinson is going to use them as hostages. I need to get them out of here so they're safe."

"Lionel and I will be right there."

"That's exactly what I need. Thank you."

"Where should we go? The Northwest Gate?"

"Maybe, but I'm not sure yet. Head in that direction. I'll call you back when I know more."

"We'll get rolling now. Thanks for calling, Lark. This is just a terrible situation."

"Thanks, Muriel."

I turned to see Octavia standing by the door to the nursery with the two children. She wore a windbreaker, jeans, and tennies. Thomas, still groggy, clutched a toy truck in his hand. Grace held a doll. They had lightweight coats over their PJs, plus they both wore tennis shoes.

"Where to?" I asked Octavia.

"Follow me."

We went into the main hallway. The place was empty, but suddenly the motor of the elevator began to whir.

"Someone's coming!" I said, my voice urgent. "Please tell me there's a back stairway."

"There is. This way!"

Octavia scooped up Thomas and I held Grace's hand. Octavia led us down a hall, through a doorway, and down a claustrophobic wooden stairway.

"Where does this go?" I asked, my voice sounding loud in the confined space.

"All the way to the basement," she replied.

"How can we get them out of the building and off the grounds?"

"There are secret underground tunnels that lead to the Eisenhower and Treasury buildings," she said. "There's also an exit onto Fifteenth Street."

"Why are we hurrying?" Thomas complained.

I wasn't sure what to say. I was proud of myself for not being alarmist with Grace, but that's hard to do when your nervous system is jangling.

Grace came to my rescue.

"This is part of the adventure, Thomas," she said.

"Cool. I love adventures."

When we got to the basement, there were two heavy steel doors on either side of the stairs, both closed.

"This one," Octavia said, reaching for the handle of the door on the left.

"Wait!" I said, grabbing her hand.

I depressed the door lever and slowly pushed it open a crack. About fifty yards down a brightly lit concrete tunnel, a Secret Service agent stood guard outside a set of double doors.

I'd barely opened the door, so he hadn't seen me. I closed it slowly and turned to Octavia.

"A Secret Service agent is blocking the way. We have to assume he's part of the plot." I nodded over her shoulder at the other door. "Where does that lead?"

"To the old swimming pool beneath the briefing room," she said.

"I have an idea." I slowly opened the door a crack.

No one was around.

I pushed the door open all the way. "Hurry. Follow me."

The area that had once been the swimming pool for every president between FDR and Nixon was now a tangle of wires and electrical equipment servicing the high-tech needs of the White House press corps.

As quickly as I could, I led Octavia, Thomas, and Grace along what I assumed was the north basement wall of the West Wing. At the other end of the room, we came to another closed door.

Slowly, I opened it. No one was there, only a stairway up to the lower pressroom, an area I knew well.

The area is a cramped warren of cubicles, like miniature phone booths, where some of the news organizations maintain a Spartan presence.

The cubicles were empty. I raced down the hall, Octavia, Grace, and Thomas close behind. I came to another stairway that I knew led up to the rear of the briefing room where the TV crews were set up.

"Hey, Lark."

I was relieved to see the friendly face of one of the older CNN photogs who'd been on the beat at least twenty years.

"Hey, Jay. I need your help."

"What's up?"

"There's a coup going on."

"No shit. Heavy stuff."

"I need to get the president's kids and their nanny out of here." I turned to show him Grace, Thomas, and Octavia.

Jay's eyes became saucers. "Ohhh kayyyy . . . ."

"I'm afraid that Tomlinson is gonna use them as hostages."

Jay nodded. "I was in Iraq at the beginning of the first Gulf War. Saddam Hussein used kids as human shields. Called them 'guests' of the regime."

"Is there a way we can somehow smuggle these guys out of here, like maybe in a couple of your big light cases?"

"Great idea." He turned and rummaged around beneath the huge console that stretched across the back of the briefing room. He found two black cases—one long and cylindrical, the other looked like a footlocker. Both were on wheels.

I crouched to be on eye level with Thomas and Grace.

"How would you guys like to become *invisible?*" I made my eyes as wide as they would go.

"Wow. Coooool," Thomas said, immediately warming to the idea.

"Here's how we're going to do it," I said to him, a big smile on my face. "You and Grace have to get out of here without anyone being able to see you."

"Okay," Thomas said.

"But it's going to be tricky."

"Okay," he grinned, excitement dancing in his eyes.

"You and Grace need to hide inside these boxes."

"Like hide and go seek?"

"Exactly. But it's gonna be dark in there."

His face fell. "I'm-I'm afraid of the dark."

"That's okay. It will only be for a few minutes. Just long enough to wheel you guys down the driveway and out the front gate."

Thomas scowled, unconvinced.

"Octavia and I will be right with you the whole time."

"Are you gonna be inside the boxes, too?"

"No, but we'll be walking right next to you. You'll be able to hear us talking." I held up a warning finger. "But don't talk back to us because you have to pretend you're invisible. Can you do that? It's the most important part of the adventure."

"Adventure!" Thomas said, once again beaming.

I turned to Grace. "Can you do this?"

"Yes, Miss Lark." She turned to Thomas. "It'll be fun."

"I get this box." Thomas jumped with both feet in front of the footlocker, definitely in Adventure Mode.

Jay unloaded the gear from the boxes, making room for Grace and Thomas who each scrambled into position.

We closed the lids and secured them, then I knocked on the top of the ebony footlocker. "Can you hear me, Thomas?"

He knocked from the inside. "Yup," came his muffled reply.

"This'll be fun," I called to Thomas, but I felt like I was going to throw up. I looked at Jay. "Let's get going."

"I'll push this one," he said. "Can you get the other?"

"Sure. No problem."

We headed for the double doors on the north side of the briefing room that emptied onto the walkway that led down the driveway toward the Northwest Gate.

As Octavia and I walked next to Jay, I began pumping him with questions.

"You were part of the pool for the Oval speech, right?"

He nodded. "What a shit show. Gannon was cool, but then we got word to stay in place."

"What happened?"

"I almost crapped my pants when Tomlinson sat behind the desk and announced martial law."

"Is the Secret Service in on this?" I asked.

"Seems so. The agents in the room had guns drawn. It was pretty tense."

"How widespread is this? Has there been any pushback?"

"None yet that I can see. Tomlinson must have had all his ducks in a row before he made his move."

"But certainly there's going to be a major backlash."

Jay nodded grimly. "It could get very messy. I'm just keeping my head down."

Fortunately, the guard shack at the Northwest Gate only inspects stuff coming into the White House. Leaving is a breeze, and, thank God, it was a breeze on this night, as well.

I breathed a little easier once we were on the Pennsylvania Avenue pedestrian mall. "Let's wheel them through Lafayette Square over to St. John's Church," I said to Jay. Once we're there, we'll be out of sight of the guards at the gate."

As is often the case during times of national crisis, a crowd was beginning to form in Lafayette Square, spilling onto Pennsylvania Avenue up to the fence facing the north portico of the White House. Faces were grim. The mood was tense.

As we walked, I called Muriel again. "Where are you guys?"

"We're at Sixteenth and K."

"Perfect. Meet me in front of St. John's."

Jay and I brought the cases to a stop on the stone patio in front of the historic yellow "church of the presidents" and released Gannon's children.

"That was fun!" Thomas said.

Grace, however, looked a bit queasy as she hugged her doll tighter than usual.

I crouched and gave her a huge hug. "You're being very brave, sweetheart."

As she threw her arms around me, she whispered into my ear, "I'm scared, Miss Lark. I'm really scared."

"I am, too, a little. But y'know what?"

"W-what?"

"Your big hug just made me feel a whole lot better."

As she hugged me once more, Lionel and Muriel pulled up in front of the church in their burgundy Volvo.

Chapter Forty-Two

St. John's Episcopal Church faces Sixteenth Street, now known as Black Lives Matter Plaza. It got its name in June 2020 as a rallying point for people protesting the murder of George Floyd by police officers in Minneapolis.

Riot police had used batons and tear gas to forcefully evict peaceful protestors from the area so that Donald Trump could awkwardly hold up a Bible for a defiant photo op.

In response, the DC Department of Public Works painted the words *Black Lives Matter* in bright yellow thirty-five-foot-tall capital letters on a two-block stretch of Sixteenth Street.

Now, this place was about to become Ground Zero for public reaction to the coup—from people who opposed it, but also from Tomlinson's supporters.

I feared things were about to get dicey.

Lionel maneuvered his Volvo into a U-turn so that he was facing north on Sixteenth Street, parked partially on the patio of St. John's, emergency lights flashing. Soon a cop was probably going to move him along.

It also looked like the street was about to be closed altogether because the plaza was quickly beginning to fill with concerned citizens converging on the White House, perhaps to hold a vigil, but possibly to storm the place to take back their government.

Lionel stayed at the wheel, but Muriel jumped out of the car. She embraced me in a huge, but furtive hug. "Thank God you're all right," she breathed in my ear.

I made hasty introductions and Muriel opened the Volvo's right rear passenger door.

With my arms outstretched, I herded the Gannon children toward the car. "Quick like a bunny, guys. Hop into the backseat."

Thomas literally started hopping.

"My friends are going to take you and Octavia to a place where it's safe."

The two children and their nanny clambered into the back seat.

As Muriel slammed the door, Lionel powered down the back window.

Octavia reached out her hand to me. "Thank you so much, Lark."

I grasped it and gave her an awkward hug. "These are my best friends in the whole world, Octavia. You'll all be safe with them."

"Aren't you coming, too?" Muriel asked me.

"You're taking them to your place, right?"

She nodded.

"I'll try to get there as soon as I can. I have to do something first."

Muriel gave me another quick hug. "God bless you, Lark. Let's hope this nightmare ends soon."

"Yeah." If I'd said more, I would have burst into tears.

As Muriel got into the front seat, I bent to look into the back seat and waved at the children. "Bye, guys. I'll see you soon." I tried to sound cheerful.

"Goodbye, Miss Lark," Grace said, doing her best to look brave.

"Love you," I called, tears welling in my eyes, but I'm not sure they heard me because Lionel was driving away.

Jay began closing and clasping the equipment cases.

"Thank you so much, Jay. Do you need any help?"

"Nah. I'll be fine. Thanks. You hang in there, okay?"

I gave him a quick hug and he headed back toward the White House, the metal wheels of the cases scrabbling along the pavement.

I stood on the curb in front of St. John's church and took stock of the situation, trying to figure out what to do next.

The crowd was getting larger. People were surging down Sixteenth Street, into Lafayette Square all the way to the north fence of the White House along the Pennsylvania Avenue pedestrian mall.

Sixteenth and H streets were now closed to traffic.

The faces of the people passing by looked grim, frightened. But others seemed to have a gleam of excitement. Everyone wore expressions of determination.

The idea that the government of the United States of America could be overthrown from within seemed preposterous to me. Sure, since the rise of

Donald Trump, we'd become deeply divided, but I'd always thought the grown-ups in the room far outnumbered the crazies who were willing to believe delusional conspiracy theories.

For things to have gotten to this point, I reasoned, Tomlinson must have slowly, painstakingly, identified a cadre of like-minded people at all the critical levels of government, especially in the military and within the ranks of the Secret Service.

He'd been able to physically remove the president from office, but it didn't guarantee the long-term success of his power grab. Surely, there were still people of integrity within the government who would push back and fight like hell to rescue the president and restore Democracy.

At this moment, even though I was still rattled by the recent murder of my friend Paul Stone, my unwanted pregnancy, the sudden and premature death of the baby's father, the bullying of Rabid Roland Roberts, and my abduction by Bonnie and Clete, circumstances beyond my control were forcing me back to the place where I didn't want to be: in the spotlight.

I was still President Gannon's press secretary. I had a duty to speak out against this travesty.

Chapter Forty-Three

I pulled out my cell phone and called Paige Summers.

"Hey, Lark." Her voice was tense. "I'm glad you called. I'm on deadline. I need a statement from you. What can you tell me?"

"I was going to ask you the same thing."

"Lemme file first, then we can talk."

"Here's my statement. Are you ready?"

"Go ahead."

I made it up as I went: "As White House press secretary, I'm calling on all *truly* patriotic Americans—civilian, military, law enforcement—to resist, *peacefully* resist this attempt to overthrow Democracy."

I heard Paige typing. "That it?"

"Yeah."

"Do you know where the president is right now?"

"I don't."

"Earlier, you told me that two members of the Secret Service were with Tomlinson when the president was arrested."

"That's correct."

"What exactly happened? Did they rough him up?"

"No. They simply handcuffed him and led him away."

"What about Tomlinson? Was he belligerent?"

"No. He was respectful. Called Gannon 'sir.'"

Paige tapped more keys. "What about Gannon? Did he resist?"

"He tried to, but he was outnumbered and was quickly subdued."

"Uh huh." *Type, type, type.* "Did Gannon say anything?"

"He shouted, 'I'm the President of the United States. You have no authority to do this.'"

"Was there a response?"

"No, other than Tomlinson telling the president he was under arrest for 'treason.'"

Summers was typing furiously. I stayed quiet to give her fingers a chance to catch up.

"So, the Secret Service is in on this," she said after a moment.

"At least some are, apparently. What are you hearing?"

"Not much. Most places are either unreachable or I'm getting terse no comments."

"What's going on around the country? Protests? Violence?"

"No violence. Yet. At least as far as I know. Mostly people seem stunned. Lots of sputtering and pearl-clutching on CNN and MSNBC."

"What about Fox News?"

"Amazingly, they seem to be leaning back and are actually reporting it as straight news."

"I'm speaking to you now in your position as president of the White House Correspondents' Association."

"Okay."

"I know you have a duty to report on all sides of the story—and that includes whatever bullshit Nora decides to spew at you . . . ."

I paused hoping Paige would laugh, but she stayed quiet, neutral. *She's a pro,* I thought to myself. To Paige, I said, "I want you to consider me to be the voice of the executive branch of whatever government still exists."

"Okay."

"I'm going to do my best to get in touch with my contacts at the other major news organizations, but can I count on you—at least for now—to be my personal pool correspondent?"

"You mean share what you tell me in dispatches to the rest of the White House press corps?"

"Yeah."

"I should check with my editor."

I felt my face flush. "How about you *inform* your editor?" My voice was steel. "Let me be clear: we're in uncharted territory. In this national emergency the profits of your newspaper should take second place to the preservation of the nation."

There was a pause, then Paige said, "I can tell her it's no different than when our paper is the designated pool rep of the day."

"Exactly. You distribute whatever I have for you to everyone else, but you still have free rein to do your own reporting."

"Yeah. I can do that. Sure. No problem."

"Thanks." I felt myself relax. "I'm going to make my own address to the nation to counter what Tomlinson has just done."

"As White House pool correspondent," Paige said, "let me arrange a conference call between you and the broadcast person who's got pool duty today."

"Who's that?"

"Just a sec. Lemme check." She paused and I heard her computer keys clicking. "It's Dorothy Rather at CBS."

"She's their new White House field producer. I remember her from the gaggle my first day on the job."

"I'll call her and patch her in. Hold on."

From my perch in front of St. John's, I could see that the intersection of Sixteenth and H was clogged with people. Some carried signs with competing messages.

One sign I saw read *Stop the Steal.*

Ironic, I thought. That was the mantra of those who felt Biden had stolen the 2020 presidential election from Trump.

Another sign read *Support Christian Government.*

Paige got back on the line. "I've got Dorothy Rather for you, Lark."

"Hi, Dorothy. Can you hear me?"

"Hello, Ms. Chadwick." She sounded upset.

"Call me Lark. Are you okay?"

"I just got off the phone with my dad. He thinks what's happening is wonderful. 'About damn time,' he said."

"I take it you don't agree with him?"

She sniffed. "No. But it's hard. He's my dad, y'know? But he's always given me grief for joining what he calls 'The Dark Side.'"

"Meaning journalism?"

"Yeah. But he calls it 'fake news.'"

"Where does he live?"

"Idaho. Coeur d'Alene."

"Is that where you're from?"

"Uh huh."

I sighed. "Well, frankly, Dorothy: you're dad's full of shit—no offense."

"I know. I know." She took a deep breath. When she spoke again, her voice was stronger, more composed. "Sorry about being so unprofessional just now, Lark. I'll be okay."

"Good," I said. "Here's what's gonna happen. As the pool producer for the networks, I need you to spread the word that I'm going to go live," I checked my watch, "fifteen minutes from now in an address to the nation. I'm speaking in opposition to what General Tomlinson just said."

"Will you be in the briefing room?"

"No. I've had to escape from the White House. It's too risky for me to be there. Tomlinson is probably going to do all he can to muzzle any opposition. I'm gonna speak from my cell phone. I'll livestream it, but I need you to hook me up to the other networks, too."

"Okay. Give me your number."

I did.

"I'll make some calls and get back to you as soon as I can."

"Thanks, Dorothy. Paige, are you still there?"

"Yeah. Let's keep this line open, but I'm gonna put you on hold while I spread word to the wires and newspapers."

In the few minutes I had to myself, I took a deep breath and tried to get my bearings.

Adrenalin seemed to be pushing aside my desire to run and hide. Once again, the thought of becoming a single mother was insignificant in comparison to the crisis at hand. Like it, or not, I had a sacred duty to be Gannon's voice to the nation. There was no time to be afraid, or even nervous.

For the first time since the coup less than an hour earlier, I had a chance to check my phone to see how the story was playing.

Every major news outlet was carrying it, but there were far more questions than answers. The only thing known for certain is that Gannon had been physically, but bloodlessly, removed from office. Joint Chiefs Chairman Charles Tomlinson had taken control of the government, dissolved Congress, and SCOTUS, and declared martial law.

Unanswered questions kept piling up: where is Gannon now? What does martial law mean? So far news organizations were free to report, but would there be a crackdown on freedom of the press? How widespread was this thing? For it to have gotten this far, it had to be fairly widespread. But what about pushback? What, if anything, was being done to overturn this?

I was still checking my phone when Dorothy and Paige got back on the line. "Lark," Dorothy announced. "The major networks are standing by, ready to go live when you give the word."

I looked at my watch: 9:52 p.m. "Let's go live at the top of the hour. Hard start."

"Got it," Dorothy and Paige said simultaneously.

A moment later, my phone vibrated with a bulletin from the Associated Press: *Gannon Press Secretary Lark Chadwick to make major announcement at 10 p.m. Eastern.*

Seconds later, my phone got similar alerts from *The New York Times, Washington Post,* and Reuters.

I noticed that people in the crowd were checking their phones. Apparently, they were getting those same announcements. In this time of confusion, the nation seemed hungry for information and a sense of equilibrium and understanding.

Before I'd had a chance to compose myself. Before I had a chance to decide what I was going to say to the nation—and probably the world—Dorothy Rather was back in my ear: "We're ready for you, Lark."

Quickly, I switched my phone to FaceTime, put myself on speaker, and turned the phone's camera so that it was pointing at me.

Dorothy spoke again, no longer the voice of a scared kid from Coeur d'Alene, Idaho. "Lark, you're live in five, four, three, two, one . . . ."

Chapter Forty-Four

I took a deep breath, said a quick prayer (*Help!!*), and began to speak.

"Good evening, my fellow Americans."

Strangely, I could hear my own voice coming from many of the cell phones of people in the crowd filling Black Lives Matter Plaza.

"My name is Lark Chadwick. I'm President Gannon's White House Press Secretary."

I spoke slowly, deliberately, doing my best to give the next thought a chance to compose itself before I spoke it into existence.

"As you probably know by now, President Gannon was taken into custody less than two hours ago by General Charles Tomlinson, Chairman of the Joint Chiefs of Staff."

Every fiber of my being wanted to use all the vulgar insults I could muster to excoriate Tomlinson. Instead, for once, I thought it best to take the high road.

Be factual. Be calm, I kept telling myself.

"I was an eyewitness to the moment when President Gannon was handcuffed by two Secret Service agents and led away, leaving behind his crying eight-year-old daughter Grace."

A woman standing near me said, "Oh my God."

"Within a few minutes of President Gannon's arrest, General Tomlinson physically occupied the Oval Office. On live television, with the stroke of a pen, he declared martial law, dissolved the government, and put himself in charge."

I felt my blood beginning to come to a boil. If I wasn't careful, I'd lose my cool and begin sounding like a spittle-sputtering lunatic.

"General Tomlinson then played for you a doctored audio tape—a deepfake—making it sound like President Gannon had committed a treasonous act. Don't be fooled. I know Will Gannon. I know his heart. He loves this country. He loves you."

A murmur swept through the crowd, but one man standing on H Street shouted, "That's bullshit."

I ignored him. "Never before in the history of the United States of America has a duly-elected president been deposed, overthrown. Never in the history of the United States has the Constitution been torn up and your rights shredded. Never in our history have the institutions that are the vital checks and balances against the abuse of power been destroyed."

I was starting to speak quickly. Too quickly. My emotions were whipping me forward.

Dial it back, Lark. Dial it back.

I paused and took a breath. The earnest face looking back at me on my phone appeared as though she was about to cry.

"At this time, I don't know where President Gannon has been taken."

"What about his children?" the woman standing near me shouted.

"But I can assure you that his two young children, Grace and Thomas, are safe."

As I spoke, I began to worry about my own safety. Even though I hadn't announced my location, people in the plaza had turned to look at me. And not everyone in the crowd was friendly.

"General Tomlinson has said the president will now be tried for treason. In the meantime, I'm calling on all of you to be calm. For things to have gotten to this point, it would appear that General Tomlinson has the support of some very powerful and influential people at many levels of government, beginning with the Secret Service and the military."

So far, I'd managed to keep a lid on my emotions—and my rhetoric. But I was now at a point where I needed to be forcefully persuasive.

"For several years now—way too many—we have been a nation divided. For far too long we have been at a point where we can no longer agree on basic facts. For far too long, there has been an erosion and an evaporation of truth and, consequently, trust.

"Just two hours ago, President Gannon appealed to you—all of you—to begin working together to turn this nation away from the instability of delusional thinking."

"Peace and love, baby!" some asshole shouted.

"Tonight, I'm speaking specifically to those of you in the government who are appalled at the current situation. I'm also appealing to all of you. Just regular people who are now caught in the crosswinds of bewildering powers seemingly beyond your control. Maybe you've taken Democracy for granted. Maybe you've taken your freedom for granted. But now freedom and democracy are at risk. Freedom and democracy are in peril."

Slow down, Lark. Not so fast. You're getting carried away.

"I'm calling on everyone, both inside and outside of government. Resist this current tyranny. Resist. But do it peacef—"

I was still speaking, but I could no longer hear my voice coming from the hundreds of cell phones in the crowd around me.

Charles Tomlinson had just pulled the plug.

Chapter Forty-Five

As soon as the live feed of my impromptu speech went dead, the crowd grew restive:

"Awww."

"Oh no!"

"What the fuck?"

By this time, news cameras had gathered around me, their lights shining on me starkly. Jay from CNN was among them. Even though I knew that I was no longer speaking live to the nation, I still had people in front of me. Plus, I hoped—and prayed—that my words would be recorded and rebroadcast.

I raised my voice.

"It looks like General Tomlinson's military dictatorship has just pulled the plug on me. But I will resist. I will persist. I will continue to speak out against his treachery."

Now, rather than calmly speaking into my phone as I had been, I had to shout to be heard by the people near me. Now I had to project my voice as far as it would carry.

I'm not really a public speaker. In fact, I can't remember a time, other than the few White House briefings I'd conducted, when I'd had to speak in front of a big crowd. I should have been cowed and intimidated. Instead, I was energized.

It helped that the people standing nearest to me cheered my last statement in which I'd accused Tomlinson of treachery.

Now, the dynamic felt different.

No longer was I speaking intimately, one to one with people all across the country—and perhaps around the world. I'd pictured them listening on their car radios, watching on their phones, or on their laptops, or even gathered in their family rec rooms, or sitting alone in their apartments.

Now I was no longer speaking to a mass, but unseen, audience; I was now addressing what had morphed into a political rally.

The mood had shifted and, I observed, so had mine, along with my rhetoric.

Intimate communication leaves room for subtlety and nuance; speaking to a large crowd requires brevity and passion.

I adjusted on the fly.

"We as a nation are in uncharted waters," I hollered. "But we have weathered vicious storms in the past.

"More than 150 years ago, our country was torn apart by a long and bloody Civil War. But we came through it. The nation survived—and even thrived.

"Fewer than a hundred years ago, our nation was attacked and we were drawn into World War Two—a war on two fronts against tyranny. And, once again, we prevailed.

"On September 11, 2001, we were brutally attacked again, but we stuck together. We prevailed.

"Now a military dictator, a man who claims to be a patriot, has stripped you of your freedom.

"We must resist.

"We must persist.

"We must take back our country."

Someone hollered, "Yeah!"

Another shouted, "Resist."

Someone else started to chant: "Resist! Persist!"

The chant spread like a wave throughout Black Lives Matter Plaza.

It spread through Lafayette Square.

Soon I could hear people chanting my words along the Pennsylvania Avenue pedestrian mall in front of the White House.

"RESIST! PERSIST! RESIST! PERSIST!"

No doubt, Charles Tomlinson could hear it in the White House.

I wanted to say more. I wanted to urge peaceful resistance, but I realized, to my chagrin and regret, that peaceful resistance was a subtlety I no longer had the power to articulate and explore with this crowd.

Instead, I waited. For a time, I joined in with the crowd, pumping my fist in the air as I shouted defiantly, "RESIST! PERSIST!"

The sound of the crowd chanting was thunderous. It gave me hope that eventually the tide would turn against Tomlinson.

But even as I joined in the chant that I'd started, I began to worry. Not everyone was caught up in my enthusiasm. I could tell by looking at the scowling expressions of some people that they were in agreement with Tomlinson, but they were holding back because they knew they were outnumbered, at least in this crowd, but they must have sensed that the military power of Tomlinson was on their side.

We had emotional energy, the power of our indignation.

He seemed to have military might, the power to easily strangle the life out of our resistance.

So, it shouldn't have been a surprise—but it was—when a canister of pepper gas exploded just above my head.

Chapter Forty-Six

BANG!

Immediately after the deafening explosion, it felt as though a thousand tiny pin pricks hit my face. My entire head was blasted by searing heat.

I couldn't see.

I could barely breathe.

The crowd began to scream and scramble to get away as more explosions rocked the plaza.

In the commotion, someone grabbed my hand. "This way," a man said.

I managed to hold tightly to my phone as the person holding my hand pulled me toward the front entrance to the church.

Several other coughing and gagging people also shouldered their way into the building.

"This way!" the man hollered to everyone.

He led us through the nave and down a stairway.

I let go of his hand and grabbed the handrail. As I staggered down the stairs, I was still having trouble seeing and breathing but the immediate blast of heat that I'd felt had dissipated.

At the bottom of the stairs, the man shouted, "This way."

We followed the sound of his voice.

I tried opening my eyes, but they burned so badly, I could only keep them open for brief blinks.

Each furtive glance helped me to get my bearings. The man leading us wore a dark sport coat and a white clerical collar.

As near as I could tell we were somewhere beneath and beyond the church sanctuary.

"There's water here," the man said.

My eyes, though still burning badly, were beginning to clear, but I was having trouble catching my breath. We were in the hall outside a kitchen near a drinking fountain and bathrooms.

I pocketed my phone and dove at the drinking fountain, turned on the spigot, and placed my face directly into the stream of running water. I used one of my hands to bathe my face and eyes with the cool water, then stepped away to give someone else a chance.

Other people were doing the same thing at the sink in the kitchen. Some had gone into the bathrooms while everyone else used water bottles to flush the tear gas from their eyes, and the eyes of those who didn't have water with them.

"Those fucking pigs," someone hissed, but, for the most part, no one spoke. Most of what I heard were people huffing to catch their breath. Several women were crying.

The cleansing water helped a lot. My face still felt flushed. I was now able to see better, but I was still wheezing.

"Thank you," I said to the man who'd rescued me.

He was pouring water from a plastic bottle into the eyes of a middle-aged woman.

"You're welcome." He turned to face me. "Are you all right?"

"I'm getting there. You're a life saver."

He shrugged. "We were having a vestry meeting. Came outside to see what was going on. You were great. Very inspiring."

"Thanks." I held out my hand. "I'm Lark."

He took it. "I know. I'm Felix, the rector here."

"May the Lord be with you," I said. "I'm a fellow Episcopalian."

He smiled. "Really?"

"Lapsed, actually." I blushed.

"That's okay. Glad I could help."

Gradually, the others were also finding relief and were milling about aimlessly, still trying to catch their breath and get their bearings. In all, there must have been at least thirty people down here.

Someone read out loud from what he was seeing on his cell phone: "Tomlinson has just declared a retroactive dusk-to-dawn curfew."

"Retroactive? You mean the curfew's already gone into effect?" I asked.

"Apparently," the guy said.

"That makes no sense."

"Wait. There's more." He read from his phone: "White House Press Secretary Nora Tomlinson says her husband is granting a one-hour grace period for the Eastern and Central time zones to give people a chance to get home and off the streets." He looked at me. "Aren't *you* White House Press Secretary?"

I smiled ruefully. "That was BC—Before the Coup."

"You're all welcome to stay here," Father Felix told the crowd. "Consider this your sanctuary." He spread his arms wide to encompass the sacred space.

People were gradually catching their breath and getting their bearings. Many talked quietly in small clusters, consulted their cell phones, or tried to call loved ones.

I pulled out my cell and called Muriel.

"Hello, dear," she said.

"Hi, Muriel. Did you get home all right?"

"Yes. We're fine. Lionel is playing horsey with little Thomas and I'm reading with Grace. They're adorable. It's just like—" Her voice caught.

"Like when Holly and Paul were little?"

"Uh huh," she managed.

Holly died in a fall off a cliff along the Inca Trail while hiking to Macchu Picchu in Peru a year before I met the Stones. Now they were reeling once again, this time from Paul's murder.

"Did you hear about the curfew?" I asked.

"No." She sounded alarmed. "What will you do? And where are you? We were able to listen to your speech until it got cut off."

I quickly brought her up to date, telling her about the tear gassing.

"Oh, dear. This is so terrible. I think you should come here."

"Do you have room?"

"Of course we do, and the children adore you. Actually," she giggled, "I think Thomas has a crush on you."

"I don't want to impose, but—"

"Nonsense. You are *never* an imposition. We love you, Lark. You're family."

I felt myself beginning to tear up. "Thank you, Muriel. I love you guys, too. I'll try to get there as soon as I can."

When I hung up, Father Felix was standing near me, but at a respectful distance, waiting for me to get off the phone.

"Do you need a ride somewhere?" he asked.

"I have friends about five miles from here who'll let me crash there for the night."

"I don't mind giving you a lift."

"You're very kind. Thank you. What are your plans?"

"I'll spend the night here. I should be able to get back in plenty of time before the curfew goes into effect."

Part of me irrationally felt that it was somehow my fault that everyone down here in the church basement had been subjected to the tear gas assault so, before I left with Father Felix, I addressed the people.

"Is everyone all right?"

There were nods all around, some sniffling, and a few "yeahs."

"Let's thank Father Felix for being our rescuer."

People began to clap, but Felix aw shucksed and gestured for everyone to hold their applause.

"How many of you work for the government?" I asked.

A few people raised their hands.

"How many of you took an oath to defend the Constitution?"

A few additional hands went up.

One guy said, "Hundred-and-first Airborne Division."

"*Hoo*-ah," another guy called out.

"Okay, then," I smiled, feeling I was among friends and kindred spirits. "Then you remember that you took an oath to defend this country against all enemies, foreign and *domestic.*"

I pointed in the general direction of the White House. "We now have a domestic enemy who has taken control of the country. All of us now have a sacred duty to take this country back."

There were murmurs of assent.

"I'm not exactly sure how we're going to do that. But I do know that violence only begets more violence. An armed insurrection now will make the Civil War look tame. Yet somehow, all of us—individually and together—must look for ways to resist.

"Tomlinson is thinking and acting like a so-called 'strongman,' but he's so paranoid and insecure that he has to use dictatorial tactics to do that. Let's not be cowed into submission. Keep persisting in resisting. Godspeed to you all."

There was more applause.

I turned to Father Felix. "Let's get going."

Chapter Forty-Seven

Felix led me up a back stairway to a small driveway behind the church. It was next to a manse that housed the church offices. He pressed a button on his key chain that unlocked with a beep his sensible hybrid SUV.

"What kind of gas mileage do you get in this?" I asked as I clambered into the passenger seat and buckled myself in.

"It averages fifty miles per gallon."

I whistled in amazed appreciation.

He pushed a button to start the engine—which was almost completely silent—and began backing out onto H Street. "I'd like to get an all-electric someday, but there aren't enough charging stations online yet."

The sting and smell of tear gas was still in the air, but H Street and Lafayette Square were now devoid of people.

Felix backed into the empty street, shifted into *drive* and headed East. "Where to?"

"Take the first left."

He turned onto Vermont Avenue then pulled over and began fiddling with his GPS. "What's the address?"

I gave him Lionel and Muriel's house number on Quesada. "It's just off Utah at Nebraska Avenue," I said.

"Thanks." He set the coordinates.

The route read-out on his dashboard screen showed that the twenty-minute drive would take us up Sixteenth Street then left on Military Road. Arrival time: 10:55 p.m. Felix would easily be able to get back to the church before the 11:30 "grace" curfew.

We made a left off Vermont onto I Street. Before making a right to go north on Sixteenth, I looked south toward the White House. It looked like it always had, bathed in bright light, but now surrounded by what looked like National Guard troops. Black Lives Matter Plaza was barricaded.

As Felix turned onto Sixteenth, I said, almost to myself, "This is chilling."

"But it's not unexpected."

I turned to look at him. "What do you mean?"

"Our church has been studying White Christian Nationalism. This coup shouldn't have come as a surprise to anyone."

"Why not?"

"The country has been heading step by step in this direction since 1960." He chuckled to himself. "And it's ironic."

"Ironic?"

"I came to the U.S. from Cuba in 1960 not long after Castro took over. I was part of Operation Peter Pan."

"Peter Pan?" I laughed. "What was that?"

"It was organized by the Catholic Church to encourage Cuban parents to send their children to live with families here as a way to rescue us from Communism. I never saw my dad again."

"That's so sad."

He pursed his lips. "Yeah." He paused, regaining his composure. "I grew up in freedom, yet now this country has fallen into the hands of a dictator, too. Ironic."

"But you say you saw this coming?"

He nodded. "There's always been right wing extremism in this country, but it began to take root in 1962 as a reaction against the Supreme Court decision abolishing prayer in school. It accelerated in 1973 when the court legalized abortion. It went mainstream in about 1979 when Jerry Falwell founded the Moral Majority."

"Wasn't that the beginning of the so-called 'family values' movement?"

"Exactly. By the time Ronald Reagan was elected president in 1980, evangelical Christians had effectively infiltrated the Republican party."

"Wasn't Reagan's mantra 'government isn't the solution to our problems, government *is* the problem?'"

"Right."

As we drove, I was struck by how empty the streets were. It was spooky, as if America—what was left of it—was holding its collective breath waiting for the other shoe to drop.

"So, tell me more about this Christian Nationalism thing your church has been studying," I said.

"It springs from the bogus belief that America was founded to be a Christian nation."

"And white?"

"Oh yes. Racism has been baked into this country's DNA since the 1600s."

"But certainly there's been progress."

"What progress there's been has been arduous and, at times, violent."

"But haven't Christians been at the forefront of the fight for Civil Rights? MLK was a Baptist minister."

"Right. The term 'Christian' is fraught. It's certainly not monolithic. But ever since the 1980s, an ultra-conservative strain of it has been steadily gaining traction."

"How so?"

"You put your finger on it a minute ago: family values. Evangelicals saw the Roe v. Wade abortion decision as evidence that the country was going to collapse due to moral depravity. There was also a resentment that undeserving welfare cheats," he turned to look at me, "read: Black people," he returned his attention to the road, "were taking the hard-earned wealth from the rich. Socialism."

"Sounds familiar."

"Am I preaching to the choir?"

"Sort of. But I want to know more about this so-called White Christian Nationalism. I've heard of it, but I don't know much about it."

"It's been taking root gradually, but I became alarmed about it when Trump was elected president with the enthusiastic help of evangelicals. It made no sense to me. The evangelicals were supposedly pious and personally moral, yet they embraced a man who was neither pious nor moral."

I shook my head. "Seems like it was more about power than piety."

"It all came to a head January 6, 2021."

"The riot at the Capitol."

"Uh huh, but Republicans portray it as a 'tourist visit'—not a big deal. White evangelical Christians were at the forefront of the insurrection. They believed Trump's Big Lie that Biden had stolen the election. Most of the Republican party did, too. The GOP had essentially become a Trump cult."

"Yeah, I remember Trump actually called for getting rid of the Constitution."

Felix nodded vigorously.

"But that was then," I said.

"Yes, but the virulent religious extremism didn't go away. As we now know, it's just gotten more treacherous—fueled by the delusional lies of QAnon and amplified by social media with messages stoking fear about socialism, abortion, trans-gender, immigra—"

"Right. I know all this. But I've always felt that these were just extremist nut jobs."

"And you wouldn't be wrong. It's just that now there are so many of them—millions and millions—that their power and influence has reached what appears to be a critical mass, seeded throughout the government."

The map display directed Father Felix to exit west onto Military Road, so he turned on his blinker and complied.

I said, "It seems as though Tomlinson has been able to build up such a powerful network of true believers that they now hold the upper hand."

"The upper hand against what I call the sane Constitutionalists who revere the rule of law rather than raw political power."

I sighed. "This is so depressing. How does this end? How can we turn this around?"

He shook his head.

"*Can* we turn it around?"

"I just don't know," Felix said, his voice weary. "Castro held onto power for fifty years. We might have to take the long view, Lark."

I folded my arms across my chest. "Nope. Not gonna wait that long. Something's gotta be done *now*."

As I sat back against the seat, I began worrying yet again about what had become of Will Gannon.

Chapter Forty-Eight

Before I got out of Father Felix's car in front of Lionel and Muriel's, he and I exchanged contact information and promised to keep in touch.

As I reached for the door handle, he touched my left sleeve. "God bless you, Lark. You'll be in my prayers."

"Godspeed, Father Felix. And thank you."

The porch light was on, a warm and welcome sight to me as I walked quickly to the stone stairway of their red brick 1940s Federal style home. Someone had scrawled *Sven* into the once wet cement of the sidewalk.

Through the picture window to the left of the front door, I saw Muriel get up from where she'd been sitting in the living room and walk briskly to the front door. She must have been watching for me.

By the time I'd gotten to the top step, she was opening the door.

She gave me a hug and whispered, "The Gannon children and their nanny are asleep."

Lionel stood behind Muriel and gave me one of his bear hugs once Muriel stepped aside. "Good to see you again, kiddo."

"Thanks, guys for taking me in yet again."

"Do you want some tea to unwind before bed?" Muriel asked.

"Only if you'll join me."

"Of course." She trundled off to the kitchen.

I set my messenger bag down by the door and followed Lionel into the living room. He sat in a powder blue wingback chair to the left of the fireplace; I chose a spot facing him at the end of the sofa next to the bay window.

For a moment, we just looked at each other, too overwhelmed by the events of the past few hours to say anything.

"What a day," I finally said, cleverly.

"What's the plan?" he asked.

"I wish I knew. Will you be my sounding board?"

"Sure. And I promise not to sound bored." He winked.

I eye-rolled.

Muriel returned carrying a tray with three steaming cups of tea, plus a small plate of cheese and crackers.

"How are the children?" I asked Muriel.

"They're fine. Grace is very polite, but a bit reserved. I think she's rattled, but having her nanny here steadies her. For Thomas, this is just a great big adventure."

"Where are they?"

"They're all in the basement guest suite. We're putting you in our guest room upstairs."

"Thank you." I turned to Lionel. "What's the latest news? I haven't had a chance to read anything."

"So far, it would seem that the fourth estate is still up and running."

"No censorship?"

"Not as far as I can tell—except when you got muzzled."

"How widespread is this thing? Has there been backlash?"

"There have been pockets of resistance and some isolated violence."

"Deaths?"

"None reported."

"This can't have been bloodless. What about the vice president? The secretary of state? The leaders in Congress?"

"You're talking the chain of succession."

"Right."

"Nothing. Nada."

"That's not good."

"No. It isn't."

"What do you think has happened, dear?" Muriel asked Lionel. She sat next to me on the sofa.

He shook his head slowly and shrugged. "Dunno."

"Murdered?" I asked.

"Maybe."

"You would think that by now there'd be serious pushback against Tomlinson from the Secret Service," I said.

"Yeah," Lionel agreed. "Perplexing. Maybe there has been, but we just don't know about it yet."

"And the military? Where would they have taken him?" I wondered.

"You last saw him in the hands of the Secret Service," he said to me.

"Obviously, they were rogue agents. But the entire detail couldn't be in on this, could it?" I wondered.

Lionel shrugged. "Could be. You didn't hear any gunfire, did ya?"

"No. Somehow the two agents who cuffed Will were able to spirit him out of the White House before anyone else knew what was going on."

"You're assuming he's no longer in the building."

I nodded. "Don't you agree?"

"Yeah. Makes sense they'd get him out of there, but where would they take him?"

"It seems to me," Muriel said, "a military base wouldn't be safe because it would be too easy for a counterinsurgency to get him back."

"I hate to say this, but maybe they executed him." Lionel's voice was gentle, almost a whisper.

I shut my eyes and held my breath. "No. I can't go there. Unless I learn otherwise, I'm going to proceed under the assumption Will has been moved to a place that only he and the coup plotters know about."

Lionel nodded. "*He* might not even know where he is."

"True." I took a sip of tea, mint, and was immediately reminded of my last conversation with Rose Gannon. She'd told me chemotherapy had ruined her appreciation for mint tea.

"Here's a thought," Lionel said. "Maybe all presidents, once they're elected, have a GPS computer chip surgically implanted in them so they can be found in case something like this happens."

I laughed. "You've been reading too many thriller novels."

Lionel's face remained stern. "Maybe. But ya never know."

"That would be wonderful," Muriel said, her basic hopefulness shining through, as usual.

"Did Gannon ever mention anything like that to you?" Lionel asked me.

I shook my head.

He shrugged. "Doesn't mean it didn't happen. It would be top secret so he wouldn't necessarily have told you."

"One can only hope," I said.

"It might explain why things are so quiet," Muriel offered. "Maybe the grown-ups in the military—the ones who haven't joined the plot—know where he is and are secretly and quietly planning an operation to rescue him."

I snapped my fingers. "Muriel! You've just given me an idea."

"I did? Really?"

"What about your old college roommate? The one you introduced me to at Camp David."

"Millie?"

"Right. General Jackson. The new head of the Air Force. Did you exchange contact information?"

"We did." Muriel got up and headed for the kitchen. "Let me get my phone."

She was back in an instant and sat next to me thumbing the keys.

"Do you think she's part of this?" I asked.

"I'd be surprised, but there's only one way to find out." She stabbed more keys and put the phone to her ear. "I'm calling her now."

I sidled closer to Muriel and listened to her side of the call.

"Hello, Millie. It's Muriel Stone." She paused briefly, then continued. "I'm sorry to be calling so late, but—"

I could hear a tinny voice coming from Muriel's phone but couldn't make out the words or gauge the tone of voice.

Muriel spoke again. "Yes. That's why I'm calling. I'm here with Lark Chadwick, President Gannon's press secretary." A pause. "That's right. You met her briefly at Camp David last weekend. Lark would like to speak with you if that's all right."

General Jackson must've agreed because Muriel handed her phone to me.

I had no idea what I'd say, but opened my mouth and this came out: "Good evening, General. Thank you for taking our call."

"It's quite all right, Ms. Chadwick." The general's voice was strong, but tired. "I saw your speech earlier tonight. Very brave. Very impressive. How can I help?"

"Thank you, Ma'am." I hesitated, not sure exactly how to couch my question. Finally, I took a deep breath and plunged ahead. "I don't know how best to ask this, so I'll just be blunt: are you loyal to General Tomlinson, or are you loyal to the Constitution?"

There was a long pause.

Oh shit, I thought, *is she beginning to trace the call?* I almost hung up, but then she responded:

"I took an oath to defend the Constitution against all enemies, foreign and *domestic.*"

"Are you saying that you believe that your immediate boss, the Chairman of the Joint Chiefs, General Tomlinson, is a domestic enemy?"

"You're goddam right."

I let out the breath I'd been holding. "Thank you, General. That's a huge relief to hear."

Other than a grunt, Mildred Jackson didn't reply.

"As you can imagine, General, I'm now trying to figure out how widespread this plot is, and where the president is now."

"At this point, Ms. Chadwick, I'm sorry to say that I'm flying blind."

"You don't know where he is, either?"

"Negative."

"Hunches? Theories?"

"We believe he's still alive . . ."

Thank God.

". . . but we don't know where."

"Does he have a GPS chip embedded in him?"

"I cannot speak to that." The cadence of her voice was crisp and precise.

"For the sake of discussion, let's say that he does."

"As I said, Ms. Chadwick, I can*not*—and will not—speak to that."

"Okay. Is there reason to believe that he is being held at some sort of government military facility?"

"Negative."

"How can you be so sure?

"No military assets appear to have been utilized in the coup operation."

"Does that surprise you?"

"Actually, it does not."

"Why?"

"Using military assets and facilities would be easier to trace, making it easier to launch countermeasures. A more likely scenario is that the president is being held at the redoubt of some off-the-books private militia."

"That's your working assumption?"

"Affirmative."

"Have you been able to determine how widespread support for the coup is?"

"Negative. We're still trying to figure that out."

"But this is a huge country. Hundreds of thousands of civilians and military personnel swore an oath to defend the Constitution," I said, my voice rising. "This plot certainly seems widespread, but it can't be everywhere. That just seems impossible."

"I agree. But sadly, I believe support for the coup within the ranks is more widespread than you'd think."

"What makes you believe that?"

"Several reasons. First: ten percent of those charged for offenses during the 2021 January sixth insurrection were veterans. Some were active duty. Second: Coinciding with the insurrection, more than one hundred retired generals and admirals supported the fraudulent claim by the Trump people that the 2020 election was stolen by Joe Biden."

"But that was a long time ago."

"Not long enough. Traditionally, the U.S. military has reflected American society. But since the 1970s, when we did away with the draft, those within the ranks have become increasingly conservative, prone to believe conspiracy theories that the system is rigged against them."

I finished her thought. "Consequently, they're more likely to support a strong commander, not the Constitution."

"Affirmative."

"How many people are we talking about?"

"Let's see . . . we've got roughly two million active duty and reserve troops. I would guess that the infection rate is at least, at *least* ten percent. Maybe more."

I did some quick calculating. "That would be roughly 200-thousand troops."

"Or more."

"That's a lot of people who can gum things up."

"Affirmative."

I sighed. "Thank you, General." I gave her my contact information, she gave me hers, and we agreed to keep in touch. I then briefed Lionel and Muriel on what General Jackson told me.

"I think I need to begin working the phones to find out who else, if anyone, is still loyal," I concluded.

"Loyal to President Gannon?" Muriel asked.

"No," I replied. "Loyal to the Constitution. The country is bigger than one person."

Lionel chimed in, mansplaining to his wife, "Dictators want people to be loyal to them. That's the litmus test."

"Oh. I see. Yes. Of course." She looked hurt.

I began to think out loud. "Assuming I'm able to get through to key people in the government, it will still come down to trust."

Lionel nodded. "Even if you can get through to the vice president, members of the cabinet, and Congress, there's a good chance someone who's part of the plot will be listening in. That's gonna put a damper on open, honest communication. You lucked out getting through to Jackson." He stopped and nodded deferentially to his wife. "Thanks to you, Muriel."

She smoothed her skirt, but said nothing, yet I could tell she appreciated Lionel's affirmation.

Lionel turned his attention back to me. "But it sounds like Jackson's having a hard time coordinating a counterinsurgency."

I nodded, placed a square of Swiss cheese on a Triscuit, and announced, "Time for me to do what I can to turn this thing around."

I worked late into the night, reaching out to my counterparts in every branch of the government, trying to ascertain the length and breadth of the coup, trying to discern who was friend—and who was foe—and trying to figure out the whereabouts of my friend Will Gannon.

Chapter Forty-Nine

At first light on Thursday morning, I was awakened by a chorus of birds chirping in the trees outside Lionel and Muriel's. Sometime during the middle of the night, I'd slipped off my shoes, reclined on the living room sofa, and fell into a fitful sleep.

The normal sounds of nature were comforting. The birds didn't care that where they lived was now in the hands of a dictator. The birds only cared about feeding themselves and their babies, flying, washing in birdbaths, and simply hanging out—being birds.

Life goes on, I realized.

For these few quiet moments at the beginning of a new day, my life was going on—as was the new life growing inside me. By this time, I'd tentatively decided not to have an abortion, but I was still coming to grips with the idea of being a single mother. I was definitely *not* warming to *that*.

The abortion decision was complicated. I realized I'm not morally opposed to it per se. But, because there were no known abnormalities with the fetus, and because giving birth would not put my life at an extreme risk, I didn't feel in my heart that I could, in good conscience, terminate the pregnancy.

In addition, although a part of me feared that the child might inherit Doug's addiction gene, that didn't seem to be a strong enough argument to abort.

I was now leaning toward going ahead with the pregnancy, because growing inside me was all that was left in this world of Doug and the love we had for each other. I suppose on one level, that's a sappy reason to have a kid, but emotions are powerful things—and I still had strong emotions about Doug and our all-too-brief time together, strong emotions that are a byproduct of pregnancy.

Also, as I lay on the sofa, I realized, *It's my body. I can still choose to have an abortion for any reason, including simply not wanting to be a mom.*

Throughout the night, I'd been reaching out to all my government contacts. I began with my press office staff.

At the time of the coup, not even twelve hours ago, most of the members of my press office staff were already home. When I contacted them, a few of my staffers made it clear they were loyal to Nora and abruptly hung up on me.

But the majority told me they were aghast at Tomlinson's treachery. They vowed to work from within the press office to secretly undermine and obstruct Nora's efforts to firm up her husband's usurped power, even as they sought to keep me informed, and to find like-minded compatriots elsewhere in the government.

My attempts to find allies in the Vice President's office, as well as at State, and among the Congressional leadership were met with silence. No one answered my repeated calls, or responded to my voicemails and texts, leading me to wonder and worry. Had their phones merely been confiscated or—worse—had the people next in line for the presidency been executed?

I had better luck finding allies in the lower echelons of the Justice Department and the FBI, but I had to be careful here because, especially in the case of the FBI, these people had the power to track my cell phone and pinpoint my location. As the reluctant public voice of opposition to Tomlinson's coup, I felt I needed to be very careful about the possibility of an overt attempt to silence me—or worse. For that reason, I went into my phone's settings and did my best to find ways to make me invisible and untraceable.

My best hope for a counterinsurgency resided in the active-duty military, but General Jackson had made it clear she didn't know where the president had been taken. Consequently, as sunlight began to tentatively shine into the living room, I was resigned to being in the dark about any possible plan that might be in the works to rescue Will, punish the coup plotters, and restore our Democracy to its duly-elected guardians.

I was clinging to the hope that the reason things hadn't become violent—at least as far as I knew—was because only a few people actually knew where Gannon was. Consequently, there'd been no bloody pushback among those loyal to the Constitution. For now, I believed—based on nothing more than hope—that the Constitutional Loyalists at all levels of government were engaged in a feverish search for the president.

Muriel was the first in the house to arise. She came padding down the stairs in her slippers and powder blue robe. She gave me a quick "good morning" as she passed through the living room on her way around the corner and into the kitchen to fire up the coffee pot.

Octavia, the Gannon children's nanny, was next. She came tiptoeing up the basement stairs to the kitchen and began whispering with Muriel.

It wasn't long before Thomas, followed by Grace, bounded up the basement stairs.

As Muriel and Octavia began making breakfast, the children found me on the sofa, still gaining my bearings after not getting nearly enough sleep. I had yet to recline in an actual bed in the guest bedroom upstairs.

Thomas jumped on me excitedly. "There you are! Let's play horsey!" he shouted.

"Let's not and say we did," I laughed. "How did you sleep, guys?"

"Okay, I guess," Grace managed. Then she climbed onto the sofa and cuddled with me. "I miss my daddy," she whimpered.

"So do I." I kissed her on the top of her head.

Muriel entered the living room carrying a steaming mug of coffee for me and placed it on a coaster by the bay window.

"Thanks," I said, continuing to cuddle with Grace.

Lionel came downstairs next. "Morning," he croaked.

"Horsey! Horsey!" Thomas shouted, jumping off me and dashing to Lionel.

"I'm too old for this," Lionel said, but he obediently got down on all fours and Thomas clambered aboard.

"Giddy-up!" Thomas hollered.

Lionel, I must admit, seemed to be enjoying himself.

"Go see if your nanny and Muriel need any help in the kitchen," I said to Grace as I began to sit up.

Grace jumped to the floor and ran to the kitchen.

Lionel, meanwhile, managed to crawl around the side of the sofa and deposit Thomas on the floor in front of me.

"That's enough for now, Cowboy." Lionel slowly got to his feet with various creaks and pops then collapsed onto the sofa next to me. "Where'd you get that?" he asked, nodding at the coffee I'd just begun to sip.

"Muriel," I said, blowing on the hot brew. "She likes me."

"Are you allowed to have coffee?"

"My doctor says one or two small cups a day is okay."

"Muriel," he called. "Got any coffee for *me*?"

Before he'd even finished barking the question, Muriel was rounding the corner from the kitchen, carrying Lionel's coffee in a gray and black *New York Times* mug.

"Here you are, Dear." She handed it to him.

"Thanks." He picked up the control wand for the wide screen TV positioned above the fireplace. "Let's see what's going on in the world," he said, pointing and clicking. "I heard something about a regime change?"

I frowned. It was too early for gallows humor.

CNN, apparently, is Lionel's news channel of choice because that's what popped up first. By this time, it was seven a.m. and the hour's top stories were just beginning.

On one level, it was comforting to see that some things in the country still felt normal—like a newscast.

The lead story was—duh—the coup.

And, as near as I could tell, CNN was playing it straight.

The news program opened with a series of quick shots—pictures of Gannon delivering his Oval Office address; Charles Tomlinson, in full uniformed regalia, also sitting at the Resolute Desk, signing a martial law proclamation; followed by a quick shot of me addressing the crowd in BLM Plaza; and ending with clouds of tear gas enveloping Lafayette Square as mounted police began clearing away the crowd.

A pair of anchors—one male, one female—sat at a desk in front of a huge video screen. One of them threw to the network's White House correspondent standing at a new position—outside the Northwest Gate. The shot didn't just include the White House in the background, but also the north fence. Standing outside the fence, shoulder to shoulder, were armed National Guard troops.

I wondered if CNN had been able to find out anything more than I had during my overnight phone calls.

"Turn the volume way down so the news about their dad doesn't upset Grace and Thomas," I said to Lionel.

As Lionel faded down the sound, I leaned in to listen.

The female anchor turned to look at the image of the White House reporter on a monitor. "Lyle," she said, "have you been able to learn how widespread this coup is?"

"Sadly, no. At this hour, we still have not been able to find out where President Gannon is. Nor have we been able to confirm just how widespread the plot is. CNN is proceeding under the assumption—and it's just an assumption—that the coup has support at all levels of the federal government, but it's not clear how wide or deep that support is."

As the newscast continued, viewers were brought up to date on the events that had occurred earlier, beginning with Gannon's Oval Office address in which he declared a national mental health emergency.

CNN played an extended clip from the speech I'd largely written for Gannon. As I watched and listened, it seemed like that was so long ago.

Gannon's image was followed by a sound bite of Tomlinson declaring martial law, then the White House reporter came back on the screen.

"We're standing by now for a live interview with General Tomlinson that, we're told, will be conducted by Roland Roberts of the Christian Newswire. We'll bring it to you live when it begins in the next few minutes."

"Oh, that should be entertaining," I cracked to Lionel. "Wonder if Roland will be asking Tomlinson how *he* feels about my pregnancy because all men are entitled to weigh in on what I should do with my body."

Next, CNN threw to excerpts from my appearance in front of St. John's church next to Black Lives Matter Plaza. To my chagrin, CNN judged that the most newsworthy thing I said was when I repeatedly shrieked "Resist! Persist!" to the crowd.

The image of me whipping up a crowd was jarring to see because it's so out of character for the person I feel I am. Even before the coup, I was way out of my comfort zone—first, as press secretary, and now as the voice and face of the opposition.

When I was a journalist, I was happiest. I loved being able to follow my curiosity. I loved not having to be partisan because I'd learned from Lionel early in my career that good and reasonable people populate both the left and the right. I'd learned that no one political party has a corner on truth and righteousness. I'd learned that the strength and beauty of Democracy is found in the give and take of opposing ideas in an attempt to find consensus.

But now those days seemed not only like a distant memory, but like an elusive reality that would never return. Yet it was comforting to see that some news organizations were still—at least for now—allowed to report the facts.

As much as it annoyed me that Roland would probably just be lobbing softball questions, I hungered to learn more about what Tomlinson was going to say—even as I knew it was going to be complete bullshit.

Chapter Fifty

Speaking of bullshit, Lionel and I didn't have to wait long before Roland's interview with Tomlinson began.

As it was getting started, Lionel quickly checked the other networks—cable and broadcast—and all of them were carrying the Oval Office conversation.

Lionel nudged me. "You're going to need to respond to this, so take good notes."

"Shit. You're right." I dug inside my messenger bag, pulled out my reporter's notebook and pen, and opened to a fresh page.

Roland and Tomlinson sat in low-backed chairs in front of the iconic presidential desk. General Tomlinson was not in uniform. Instead, he wore a dark suit, crisp white shirt, and bright red tie. He looked . . . presidential, not like the military dictator he actually was.

Roland, wearing a red, white, and blue bow tie, began affably. "Good morning, Mister . . ." he paused and laughed. "I'm not even sure what I'm supposed to call you. Should I address you as 'General,' or 'Mister President'?"

"Let's go with 'Mister *Acting* President.' I'm only here for the time being."

"Does that mean you're planning to hold an election?"

"Yes. Eventually. A free and fair election. *This* time."

"When will that be?"

"Haven't decided yet, Roland."

"Will you be a candidate?"

"Of course."

"But won't you have to resign from the military?"

"No. Not at all. This country needs a strong leader."

"What can you tell us about Will Gannon? Where is he, and what happens next?"

Tomlinson waved a hand dismissively. "Gannon is in custody at a secret location."

"A military base? Guantanamo?"

"No."

"Why not?"

"Too risky. He still has allies in the military so he needed to be taken to a place out of their reach."

"And where is that?"

Tomlinson smiled. "Nice try. Next question."

Roland obeyed. "Why did you find it necessary to remove Gannon from office?"

"Gannon is the embodiment of the woke mob."

"What do you mean?"

"Bigger and bigger government. More and higher taxes. Globalism. Open borders. Pandering to minorities—the tail wagging the dog. Winking and nodding at the moral rot of abortion and sex changes. Should I go on?"

"I see your point."

I couldn't help myself. "Of course you do, Roland, you sanctimonious piece of shit."

Roland continued. "So, what prompted you to take action at this particular time?"

"The last straw was Gannon's declaration of war on mental illness."

I wrote *mental health emergency* and underlined the clarification so forcefully my pen tore into the paper.

Tomlinson continued, "Can you imagine? The President of the United States declaring that his country is full of crazy people?"

"He didn't!!" I shouted.

"Before I acted—and acted decisively—we were inches away from Gannon and his toadies declaring that anyone against him is mentally ill and should therefore be involuntarily institutionalized, or to be more precise: carted off to political correctness re-education camps. I was forced to act preemptively because it wouldn't be long before the government would also be coming to disarm the populace."

"Right," Roland agreed.

I couldn't scribble fast enough. "This is such bullshit," I said under my breath.

"So now that you're in charge," Roland continued, "what are your plans?"

"I plan to restore this great country to its Christian roots."

"What do you mean?"

"This country was founded as a Christian nation embodying Christian principles. We've lost sight of that. Pluralism and unchecked immigration have diluted and replaced those principles. I'm going to turn back that tide."

"How?"

"First, no more of this L-G-B-T-Q . . ." he paused for effect, "R-S-T-U-V-W-X-Y-Z alphabet soup nonsense."

Roland laughed.

"It will take some time and will require much patience. But eventually I envision an Illiberal Christian Democracy along the lines of what Viktor Orban put into place in Hungary. I've already taken the first step by rescuing America from Will Gannon."

"Will there be a trial?"

"Yes."

"When?"

"Soon."

"On what charges?"

"High treason."

"Got specifics?"

"Stay tuned."

"If convicted?"

"Treason is very serious, Roland. It's a matter of life . . . and death." Tomlinson turned and looked directly into the camera. "America, I am your warrior, I am your justice, I am your retribution."

His smile was chilling.

Chapter Fifty-One

As soon as Roland's interview with Tomlinson ended, I was on the phone to Paige Summers.

"I assume you were watching," I said to her when she picked up.

"Oh yes. Do you have a response?"

"I'm going to hold a presser in about half an hour, so I need you to spread the word."

"Where's it gonna be?"

"On Zoom."

"Why?"

"I think my location needs to be kept secret. I could be Tomlinson's next target."

"Okay. I'll spread the word. Send me the link as soon as you can."

"Gotcha. Thanks, Paige."

Just as I was finishing scheduling the news conference on Zoom and sending the link to Paige, Octavia entered the room, her cell phone bleeping.

"*Dios mio!*" she said, "It's the president."

"Quick. Put him on speaker," I ordered.

"Hello, Mister President," she said. "How good to hear your voice."

"Hello, Octavia." Will Gannon's baritone was buoyant, almost FDR-confident. "It's good to hear your voice, too."

The sound of his robust voice caused my heart to do an involuntary flip. I was about to say something, but the president kept speaking.

"I don't have much time—and my captors are listening on speaker. I'm calling to check on Grace and Thomas. Are they there?"

"Yes. I'll get them." We all followed her as she moved into the kitchen. From the top of the basement stairs, she called down to them. "Children! Come quickly. Your daddy is on the telephone and wants to talk to you."

Even though Grace and Thomas are little, the sound of their feet on the wooden stairs was like thunder as they raced to the kitchen.

Before they reached the top of the stairs, Will spoke sternly to his captors. "Now that you know that I've made contact with my children, this is a *personal* phone call so I'm going to talk with them privately, not on speaker phone."

"Hi, Daddy! Thomas bellowed.

"Hi, Tiger," Will said. His voice caught. "H-how are you?"

"I was playing horsey with Mr. Lionel," Thomas exclaimed.

"That's great. Is Grace there, too?"

"I'm here," Grace said, stepping to the phone in Octavia's outstretched hand. "Where are you and when are you coming home?"

"It's still dark where I am," Will began. "I was taken away in a small, fast jet plane. But I hope to be back soon."

I whispered to Grace, "Ask him if he's still on speaker phone."

"Miss Lark wants to know if you're still on speaker phone."

"No," Will said. "Not right away."

Immediately, I realized that Will's captors could only hear his side of the conversation, but he was making it sound like he was only talking with his children. To me, "no" meant "I'm not on speaker."

Will asked another question: "So, guys, tell me everything you've been doing. Don't leave anything out."

"We've—" Grace began, but I stepped in.

"It's Lark, Mister President. Roland Roberts has just done a live Oval Office interview with Charles Tomlinson. Tomlinson was wearing civvies and wants to be called 'Mr. Acting President.'"

"That's wonderful," Will exclaimed as if talking with Grace. "Tell me more."

"Tomlinson has declared martial law, dissolved Congress, and the Supreme Court, and plans to put you on trial soon for treason."

"Uh huh," Will said with exaggerated enthusiasm. "Tell me more about the games you've been playing."

I had no idea what he meant, but I assumed he wanted me to continue with my surreptitious briefing.

"There has been no word from the vice president or the leaders in Congress, but there's no indication they've been killed, either."

"Nice!" the president exclaimed.

"Can you give me any hint about where you are, sir? If it's still dark where you are, then is it safe to assume that you are somewhere out west?"

"Of course," Gannon gushed. "That would be wonderful."

We both knew that he could only respond to yes/no questions. "Of course" meant to me that he was, indeed, somewhere out west. He probably didn't know exactly where he was, either, but at least I had something to go on.

"Are you well, sir? Are you being treated humanely?"

"Yes. Splendid," he replied. "I have to go now, but I want you guys to know that I lov—" His voice caught again, and he had to stop to regain his emotional balance. "I love you very much and I hope to be back with you soon."

"Bye, Daddy," Grace said, tears streaming down her face.

"Bye, Dad," Thomas yelled. "When you come back, can you bring me an airplane like the one you were in?"

"I will, Buddy."

Then the line went dead.

Chapter Fifty-Two

For a moment, no one spoke. We just stood staring at the quiet cell phone resting in the palm of Octavia's hand.

My emotions were aswirl. I was relieved to hear Will sounding so strong, but the times he faltered briefly, overcome by emotion, was a hint that he must know his situation is dire.

Have I just heard his voice for the last time?

That thought was too monstrous to consider.

I was the first to break the silence with a clever, "Well!"

"Yeah," Lionel offered.

"Let's go play," Thomas said to Grace. He dashed down the stairs, Grace following reluctantly.

As Octavia pocketed her cell phone, I turned to Muriel and hugged her. I couldn't help myself, I had to cry.

Muriel held me tightly, but said nothing. Words wouldn't have helped anyway.

As quickly as I could, I tried to get a grip on my emotions.

Lionel handed me a paper towel and I blew my nose.

"Okay," I said, catching my breath. "I've got a presser to do."

"Let's get you set up in the guest room upstairs," Lionel said. "It'll be quieter there."

I returned to the living room, scooped up my messenger bag containing my laptop, put my notebook into it, and headed up the stairs.

The Stone's second-floor guest room is tiny. The bed was off to the right against the back wall by the window. A small desk faced a window opposite the door. Available light from the window would be adequate and, with the closed door as a neutral backdrop, I reasoned that no one would be able to ascertain my location.

I placed my laptop on the desk, lifted the cover, and sat down. I opened Zoom, scheduled my news conference to begin in fifteen minutes, then forwarded the link to Paige.

During the few minutes I had to myself, I riffled through my notes as I gathered my thoughts and jotted down a few talking points. I then clicked on the link and started my Zoom session.

I was stunned—but shouldn't have been—to see a wall of faces peering back at me, many of them familiar from my days in the White House briefing room. It was a full house—100 participants.

This was the first time I'd faced them since before my own abduction just seven days earlier.

Emotionally, I'd come a long way since then. At first, I was elated and exhausted following my rescue, but I was then sent reeling with the news that my friend Paul Stone had been murdered as a reaction to Roland's false report that Paul had decided to have gender reassignment surgery.

Just three days ago, I was so shaken about the prospect of having to face Roland's bullying in the press room, that I gave in to my fears and, yes, cowardice, and convinced Will to grant me a reprieve in the form of a leave of absence.

Now, because of the events of the past few hours, I was so pissed I couldn't wait to take on Roland, or whoever else stood in the way of Truth and Democracy.

Before I began to speak, I quickly scanned the gallery of participants. I didn't see Roland and a part of me actually hoped Paige had decided—finally—to exclude him from this gathering now that he was clearly in league with Tomlinson and his coup.

Without knowing for sure, I proceeded under the assumption that my remarks were being carried live online and on national—and probably international—radio and television.

"Hello, everyone. Thank you for being here. I have a brief statement to make, then I'll do my best to answer your questions. Can you all hear me?"

I paused. Several people nodded or gave me a thumbs up.

"Let's be clear about what's going on here," I began. "Within the past hour, we have witnessed a so-called interview with a man who actually looked presidential. He wore civilian clothes. But he is anything but a civilian.

"The man who now occupies the Oval Office is a four-star General in the United States Marine Corps. Charles Tomlinson is the Chairman of the Joint Chiefs of Staff. He's in charge of the entire United States military. This means the United States is under military occupation.

"Just last night, on live television from the Oval Office, you saw him, with the stroke of a pen, rip up the Constitution by declaring martial law and dissolving the other two branches of government—judicial and legislative. They have been a check and balance against a dictatorship since this country came into being in 1776.

"I suppose some of you feel that it's about time that a so-called 'strong man' takes charge. We've been building toward this moment for decades beginning in 1964 when Barry Goldwater accepted his party's presidential nomination by stating, 'Extremism in defense of liberty is no vice.' And in 1979 when the Reverend Jerry Falwell founded the so-called Moral Majority.

"Virulent and violent right wing Christian extremism intensified over the years with the massacre of eleven people at a synagogue in Pittsburgh, and the attempted abduction of Michigan Governor Gretchen Whitmer in 2020.

"And then there was the attack on the Capitol building on January 6, 2021, by a largely extremist Christian mob of people who believed the lie that the presidential election was rigged against Donald Trump.

"Now the extremists have taken over. If you're white, and male, and fundamentalist Christian, that's great. But woe to you if you are a person of color, Jewish, Muslim, atheist, gay, transgender, or dealing with an unwanted pregnancy. Your rights are kaput."

I paused to take a breath.

"Look. I really don't want to make a speech. That's not who I am. But I do want to say that in the so-called interview Roland Roberts just did with General Tomlinson, you witnessed the attempted gaslighting of America—and the world.

"Let me do my best to correct the record."

For the first time, I looked down at my notes.

"First, President Gannon did *not* declare war on mental illness. General Tomlinson twisted the president's words. I helped write that speech. We deliberately stayed away from using war-like rhetoric. The president's emphasis was on mental *health* not illness.

"Under the Gannon administration, there is not a plan to take away your guns. And under the Gannon administration, there is not a plan to institutionalize political opponents as mentally ill. Those are lies from hell spoken brazenly from the Oval Office by a military dictator who has single-handedly shredded your rights."

I felt my anger coming to a boil.

"It's best that I stop here and take your questions before I say something extremely intemperate."

Paige Summers asked the first question. "Lark, have you been in touch with the president? Do you know where he is?"

I winced. I did not want to lie, but I also didn't want to let his captors know that I was listening in on Gannon's phone call with his kids in which I deduced that he was being held captive somewhere in the Western United States.

By asking two questions, Paige had unwittingly given me an out. I chose to answer one and not the other.

"No," I said honestly, "I don't know where the president is—"

Just then I was saved from having to lie when the door behind me burst open.

"There you are, Miss Lark," Thomas bellowed. "Let's play horsey!!"

He galloped into the room.

Chapter Fifty-Three

At first, I was disoriented by the noisy interruption, but then I saw on my screen the commotion behind me.

"Horsey! Horsey!" Thomas scampered toward me, his head bobbing into view, a panic-stricken Octavia right behind him.

"I'm so sorry, Miss Lark," Octavia stage whispered. She scooped Thomas into her arms. "You can't be in here, Thomas." Her voice was soft, but stern. She wheeled around and swiftly exited the room, gently closing the door behind her.

"Was that President Gannon's son Thomas?" Paige asked.

I shut my eyes, gritted my teeth, and told the truth. "Yes. Both Grace and Thomas are safe with their nanny."

"Where are you?" someone asked.

"I'd rather not say for reasons I hope are obvious. We are in uncharted waters as a country and I doubt that dictators like it when anyone challenges their integrity and their authority."

The news conference continued for another few minutes before I ended it. I'd said my piece. I wanted to end it as soon as possible before my message became eclipsed by side issues.

Actually, my message had already been upstaged by Thomas' dramatic entrance. To many people, it was probably just an amusing interruption. But to me it was mortifying because I feared that Tomlinson might now try to seize Grace and Thomas and use them as pawns to further subdue their father.

In addition to feeling on the defensive—as I always do when I'm facing the press corps—I was also feeling nervous that Tomlinson would make a move to silence me. Ultra-patriotic extremists had already abducted me once. Was it about to happen again—or worse?

I ended the news conference with another urgent appeal for peaceful resistance to Tomlinson's usurpation of presidential power.

"I truly believe there are many people in government who remain loyal to the Constitution. They took a solemn oath to defend it. We must find Will Gannon. We must restore him to his rightful place as president. We must take back our country. Thank you."

I couldn't click on the *End Meeting* button fast enough.

After closing the lid of my laptop, I dashed to the door. When I opened it, Lionel and Muriel were standing with their backs to it, on guard against another possible Thomas incursion.

"What the hell just happened?" I couldn't hide my exasperation.

Muriel turned to me. "We're so sorry, Lark. Lionel and I were watching you in the other room and didn't notice that Thomas had escaped from his nanny."

"Yeah. Sorry." Lionel seemed genuinely chastened—not his comfort zone.

I threw up my hands. "What do we do now? Do you think Tomlinson is going to figure out where I am?"

Lionel shrugged. "Dunno. It's possible, I guess."

The three of us walked down the stairs and back to their living room.

"I think I need to leave," I announced.

"Why? Where will you go?" Muriel asked, alarm in her voice.

Before I could reply, Lionel spoke. "You're safe here, Lark. Out in the world, you might be at risk. You're a thorn in Tomlinson's side. I'm sure he wants you out of the way. The first place they'll look for you is your apartment—assuming they haven't done so already."

"Yeah, but don't you think this is where they'll look for me next?"

Muriel and Lionel exchanged anxious looks. "They might," Muriel said, "but not necessarily."

"Maybe we could keep you here," Lionel said, "but build some sort of secret hiding space for you in case Tomlinson's goons come looking for you and Gannon's kids."

I shook my head. I didn't like it, but didn't have an alternative plan. "I just wish I could get a better bead on where Will is. Once we know where he is, there's an excellent chance that Constitutional Loyalists in the military can rescue him and bring Tomlinson to justice."

"Easier said than done," Lionel sighed.

"No shit." I sat down hard on the sofa and placed my head in my hands.

Chapter Fifty-Four

My head was still in my hands when I heard my cell phone ring.
Nora Tomlinson.
I hesitated, then decided to pick up.
"What do *you* want?" My voice dripped with derision.
"Lark. We need to talk." She sounded breathless, urgent.
"About what?"
"Not on the phone. In person."
"Nope. I don't trust you, Nora. If you've got something to say, say it now."
She hesitated, then took a deep breath. "My life's in danger."
"Yeah. Right. And mine isn't? Cut the crap."
She was silent a moment, breathing heavily. Was she crying?
I waited.
And waited.
Finally she spoke, a whisper. "Charles had Ron McClain killed."
"What? Why?"
"Charles just revealed to me that he ordered the hit."
"Why?"
"So that I, as Ron's number two, would be elevated to be in a key position in Gannon World."
"Better positioned to support the coup, right?"
"Uh huh." She sniffed. "Neither of us expected that Gannon would name you to be press secretary."
"And you bought the story that Ron was murdered by a random mugger?"
"Yes."
"But why would he tell you he had Ron murdered?"
"He sensed that my loyalty was wavering. 'I killed for you,' he said to me."
"Then he told you what happened?"

"Right. He's still tight with the guys who were in his unit in Afghanistan. They're very loyal to him. He ordered one of them to kill Ron."

"Why are you telling me?"

"Because I had no idea about the extent of Charles' plans, or his treachery."

"Oh, c'mon. You married the guy. You couldn't be that dumb."

"Apparently, I am." She actually laughed.

"So, why are you telling me all of this?"

"I want to help. I want to, as you said just now, 'take the country back.'"

Is this some sort of trick? I wondered.

"That's admirable, Nora, but I still don't trust you."

"I don't blame you."

"Do you know where Will is right now?"

"Not exactly."

"Got a hunch?"

She paused. A long one. "Probably Idaho."

"Why there?"

"It's become a gathering point, almost a Mecca, for White Christian Nationalists."

"If you *really* want to help—and I'm still not entirely convinced that you do—then you need to find out and let me know *exactly* where Will is. Otherwise, you're still an enemy to me."

"Okay. I'll do my best."

"Do better than that."

I ended the call.

Chapter Fifty-Five

A few hours later I was pacing nervously at the intersection of Tennyson Street and Oregon Avenue NW, a residential area just a few blocks away from Lionel and Muriel's house. Oregon Avenue is at the West edge of Rock Creek Park, a bucolic, heavily wooded swath of land that makes DC bearable.

I wore running shoes, jeans, a dark blue hoodie, a Nationals baseball cap, and sunglasses—doing my best to be incognito.

After hanging up on Nora, I'd placed a quick call to Dorothy Rather at CBS and asked her to meet me here for an off-the-record conversation. I'd only been waiting about ten minutes when a black sedan with an Uber sticker approached on Oregon from the south, turned left onto Tennyson, pulled to the curb, and stopped.

Dorothy emerged from the right rear and began looking around uncertainly.

"Over here," I called.

She waved, said something to the Uber driver, slammed the back door, and the guy drove off.

As she trotted across the street, I noticed that she had on walking shoes even though she was dressed for work.

"Hi," Dorothy said brightly. "I love this cloak-and-daggery stuff."

"This way," I said looking both ways before crossing Oregon and entering the park along a trail shrouded by gigantic trees that were just beginning to bud.

Dorothy had to walk fast to keep up.

Once we got more deeply into the woods along an asphalt walkway, I turned to her.

"Thanks for meeting with me, Dorothy."

"Sure. Of course."

"Let's sit down."

"Okay."

We sat on a nearby bench, one of several at various points along the path.

Dorothy was about five years younger than I, probably only a couple years out of college but already in an important job at CBS.

Before I could say anything, she pulled out her phone. "Just a sec. I need to tip the Uber driver and give him some stars."

I liked her more already.

She quickly thumbed her phone, then put it away. "Okay. Ready. What's up?"

"The last time you and I talked, you were upset because your father was in support of the coup."

She sighed heavily. "Yeah."

"How are you two getting along? Have you talked since?"

"Not really. I'm pretty pissed at him."

"Tell me more about him."

She gave me a look. "Why?"

My turn to sigh. "Let's back up."

"Okay."

"This conversation needs to be on deep background."

She frowned. "When you called, you said it was off the record."

"I know. But the stakes are super high."

"So, now I can't even use what you tell me? At least off the record lets me use your information without naming you as the source."

"That's right. We're in Deep Throat territory."

"You mean like Watergate?"

"Uh huh."

"How so?"

"During Watergate Bob Woodward's chief source, nicknamed 'Deep Throat,' was actually Mark Felt, the assistant director of the FBI. Woodward was never allowed to quote him even off the record. Instead, Felt's information pointed Woodward and Bernstein in the right direction."

"So, they had to confirm Deep Throat's information elsewhere?"

"Exactly."

"And you're offering to be my Deep Throat?"

"Yes."

She thought a moment. "Flattering. But why?"

"I can't tell you unless you agree that we're on deep background, not just off the record."

"I dunno, Lark."

I stood to leave. "Never mind."

"Okay. Okay." She waved her hand, her voice urgent, impatient. "Just wait. Lemme think about this."

I stood looking down at her. She was young, but she was smart. I realized if I had been her during my reporting days, I would have been just as skeptical, just as reluctant, just as wary about being used as a tool by a possibly corrupt politician whose personal agenda might conflict with finding the truth.

As Dorothy pondered her dilemma, I sat next to her again. "I know what you're thinking," I whispered.

She nodded slowly. "I'm sure you do. You've been here yourself, right?"

"Right. It's all about finding out the truth—and trust." I turned to her and found her eyes. "Do you trust me?"

She looked down. "I don't know who to trust anymore." She scowled. "The world's gone crazy."

"No shit."

Dorothy took a deep breath. "Okay. What the hell." She looked at me. "Yes. I trust you, Lark. I'm cool with deep background. What d'ya got?" She pulled out a notebook.

"No notes," I said.

"Really? Come on."

"Really. This'll be easy. You won't need notes."

She scowled, slapped her notebook shut, and put it away.

Before speaking, I appraised her again. It felt as though I was looking at a younger version of myself, but a person more mature than I was at her age. It confirmed my initial hunch that I, too, could trust her.

I spoke slowly, choosing my words carefully. "I have reason to believe that President Gannon is being held out west at some kind of redoubt, a fortress that's not connected to the U.S. military."

"Like something run by a private militia?"

"Yeah. Maybe."

"How do you know this?"

"I don't."

"Then what makes you think it?"

"I can't say."

She gave me the side eye.

"This is where you come in," I said.

"How?"

"You might be in a position to find out."

"'Out west,'" she said, quoting my words back to me. "Do you think Gannon's in Idaho?"

"Dunno. But your dad might."

"And you want me to *ask* him?" She seemed aghast at the idea.

"Not exactly. Tell me more about him. He's a Tomlinson sympathizer, right?"

She nodded and pursed her lips.

"What does he do for a living?"

"Retired military. Worked in IT."

"Is that what he's doing now in the private sector?"

"Uh huh. Owns his own company."

"What about your mom? Are they still together?"

Dorothy nodded. "Yeah. She's the good wife. Does whatever he says. Dutiful."

"What was it like growing up in . . . where'd you say you're from, Boise?"

"Way farther north. Coeur d'Alene. It was oppressive. Suffocating."

"In what way?"

"My folks are fundamentalist Christians."

"And you're not?"

"Not anymore. But I was."

"Why aren't you anymore?"

"Let me count the ways."

I didn't respond, just waited.

"You mean you want me to count 'em?"

"Yes, please," I nodded.

She began ticking off the reasons on her fingers in rapid succession. "The patriarchy. The racism. The legalism. The philosophical inconsistencies. The close-mindedness." She turned to me, eyes blazing. "Should I go on!?" Clearly, she was pissed.

"I get the picture."

Her voice softened. "Don't get me wrong. I love my parents. I had a good upbringing. But their life isn't mine. I had to get away."

"Like all the way across the country away?"

"Exactly."

We were quiet a moment. I was groping, feeling my way with no clear plan for how to move ahead, how to find Will, how to restore the country to sanity and stability.

I hoped to heaven that powers stronger than I am, with more resources, were doing all they could to find and rescue the president—and Democracy—but it felt as though the burden was entirely on me, yet I had so little to go on.

It was heartening to me that it sounded like Nora Tomlinson's loyalty to her husband was, indeed, wavering, but she had yet to prove her trustworthiness.

Dorothy Rather seemed to be my only hope.

"I need your help, Dorothy. The *country* needs your help."

"Geez, Lark. No pressure."

I laughed. It felt good.

"Let's think this through." I sat back against the bench. "There's so much we don't know."

"Yeah. Like where the hell's the prez?"

"Exactly. And, frankly, I think you have a good chance of finding out."

She looked skeptical.

"Let's spitball this," I said. "How do you feel about taking a trip home to try to mend fences with your dad?"

Her face darkened.

"Hear me out, okay?"

She nodded, unconvinced.

"Tell me about your gig at CBS."

She did a double take. "What's that got to do with my dad?"

"Nothing directly. But my hunch is being a White House field producer for a major network means you have some major chops."

"Chops?"

"Skills."

"Such as?"

"Let *me* count the ways," I said, falling into Dorothy Speak. "Flexible. Attentive to detail. Able to stand up to diva correspondents and demanding managers. Unflappable."

"Oh, I flap a lot," she laughed.

"But you get my drift," I chuckled.

"Yeah. But what's this got to do with my dad?"

"Think of him as a demanding manager."

She nodded slowly. "That's not a stretch."

"Let's assume that President Gannon is being held somewhere in or near Coeur d'Alene."

"Okay."

"Even if your dad doesn't know where the president is being held, he might know someone who does."

"I see where you're going with this. You want me to work him like a source, right?"

"Yeah. Think you can?"

She inhaled slowly and raised her eyebrows. "Maybe."

On impulse, I added. "Maybe I could come, too." I gave her a huge smile. "Road trip!!"

Dorothy Rather turned and gave me a mischievous smile.

Chapter Fifty-Six

"You're gonna do *what!?*" Lionel stood before me in his living room, jaw dropped, hands on his hips.

"I said I'm taking a road trip to Idaho with Dorothy Rather of CBS."

"I heard you the first time. This is just crazy, Lark."

We were toe to toe. "No, it's not. It'll be an adventure. And keep your voice down. I don't want to upset the children." We could hear them laughing as they played below us in the basement.

Lionel lowered his voice to an intense whisper. "Help me understand why—and how—you think you're gonna pull this off without getting yourself picked up by Tomlinson's goons."

"Which do you want first, the why, or the how?"

"The why."

"I need to find Will and rescue him."

"Tilt at windmills much?" he sneered.

"What the heck does *that* mean?"

"You should read more. Don Quixote. It's literary shorthand for being delusional."

"I know it sounds crazy."

"Sounds??"

"Okay. Is. But I need to at least try to find him before it's too late. I can't just sit around here and do nothing."

"This makes no sense, Lark."

"I know. I won't argue, but I just need to go."

"But how? How are you going to be able to stay off the grid and not get yourself caught up in Tomlinson's dragnet?"

"Dorothy's gonna drive. I'll use a burner phone, I'll take cash, not plastic, so my movements can't be tracked, and I'll be disguised in a baseball cap, hoodie, and sunglasses."

"I don't like it."

"You're just jealous."

He smiled. "Yeah. A little."

Just then Muriel came back from her shopping excursion carrying two bags. "Here are the burner phones you asked me to get, Lark."

Lionel looked at her incredulously. "You're in on this, too?"

"Of course!" She beamed.

* * *

The next morning, Dorothy picked me up. She drives a hunter green Mazda Miata convertible. I winced when I saw her park at the curb. It would've been nice if she drove something innocuous like a Ford Focus sedan. But no. Now we would be the target of come-ons from every frat boy, horny trucker, and lonely business traveler for the next two thousand miles.

We stopped first at the Wells Fargo on Connecticut Avenue near Chevy Chase Circle and I went inside to withdraw three thousand dollars.

"Did you have any trouble getting the time off?" I asked as we drove north along Connecticut Avenue toward the Beltway.

"Not nearly as much as I expected." Her sunglasses rested atop her luxurious thicket of strawberry blonde hair. "I told them I felt I needed to mend fences with my coup-supporting family, plus I pitched it as a possible series of pieces designed to get the pulse of America in this new era."

"And they bought it?"

She nodded. "I told them I'd send them video vignettes for the website that are illustrative of where the country is right now—slice of life stuff."

We merged onto I-495 at the top end of the beltway and headed west. Tomlinson's dusk-to-dawn curfew had been lifted. Our plan was to get to Coeur d'Alene as quickly as we could on Interstate highways 70, 76, 80, and I-90 through Pittsburgh, Toledo, Chicago, Wisconsin, Minnesota, Iowa, South Dakota, Montana, and Wyoming.

If martial law meant checkpoints, we might need to take back roads. We decided to play it by ear.

The trip would also give me a better opportunity to get a sense of what the country was like now. And I was grateful for this opportunity to get to know Dorothy a bit better. My first impression was that she was both shy and introverted, but the farther we drove and talked, the more I was discovering that she could be winsome and engaging.

"These video vignettes, are they how you plan to earn your way into an on-air career as a correspondent, or anchor?" I asked.

"Oh, God no."

"Why not? You're gorgeous. The camera will love you."

She made a face. "I hear that a lot, mostly from some of the male hotshots at the network. But I think their not-so-hidden agenda is to make me feel obligated to provide them with sexual favors in exchange for them helping me with my career."

I nodded.

"What about you, Lark? Why didn't you become a network correspondent? The camera loves you, too."

Her question reminded me that, unlike most people who love to hear themselves talk, Dorothy was a reporter with a surplus of curiosity. I'd have to be careful not to reveal too much of myself.

"Back in Wisconsin, when I was still working for Lionel Stone at his weekly newspaper, I had a boyfriend who tried to entice me into getting a weekend anchor gig at the station where he worked."

"How'd it go?"

I laughed at the memory. "It was a disaster. I suck as a broadcast journalist. I was much more comfortable in print."

"And yet here you are as the face of the presidency."

"Life doesn't turn out the way you expect." Before she could ask another question, I quickly got her talking again. "Tell me more about you. Dorothy is an interesting name. I haven't heard it since *The Wizard of Oz.*"

Dorothy let out a throaty laugh. "You nailed it. My parents *love* that movie. I didn't like my name at first, but now I think it's kind of retro hip. Makes me sound more mature."

I laughed when she purposely mispronounced "mature" as mah-CHURRRR, feigning a Valley Girl accent, then sat up straighter and made a show of putting her hands at the responsible ten and two o'clock positions on the steering wheel.

"How'd you get the CBS gig?" I asked.

"I did an internship there my senior summer. They liked me and I liked them."

"Where'd you go to college?"

"University of Maryland."

"College Park?"

"Yeah."

It was a good school in suburban DC that cranked out many good journalists primarily because it relied on adjunct professors with hundreds of years of experience at high-powered, influential media outlets in the nation's capital.

"Two more questions," I continued. "Why not on camera, and what do you like to do best behind the scenes?"

"I'm shy. I'm just not an out-front person. But I'm also curious. You said the other day that I'm attentive to detail and that's really true. As you already know, there are so many details and moving parts involved in getting a story on the air. I love that stuff."

"It's hard to believe you're shy." I spread my arms to take in our surroundings. "This is a pretty in-your-face set of wheels you've got here, ma'am."

She laughed. "I've learned to act bolder than I feel. The confidence comes later." She paused. "Sometimes."

We drove in silence for a while. I could tell that Dorothy would be good company. I liked her. A lot.

Traffic was light as we drove northwest away from DC. All the commuters were going the other way on I-270 as we angled past Rockville and Gaithersburg before linking up with I-70 West at Frederick, Maryland.

At one point, we saw a military convoy heading toward DC. At a roadside pitstop I'd read a historical marker that said that the interstate system was created by President Eisenhower. He saw the need for it way before he became a celebrated commanding general during WWII.

As a young soldier, the historical marker stated, Ike was aghast at how bad the U.S. highway system was when he had to convoy across the country from DC to San Francisco in 1919. A lasting legacy of his presidency is what is now the interstate highway system.

As I took note of the convoy passing us on the other side of the median, it was obvious to me that Charles Tomlinson was now effectively using the interstate system to bring reinforcements to protect the nation's capital from the woke mob of enlightened people who wanted to take the country out of his clutches.

As Dorothy and I headed west, I noticed that, in many ways, the United States under the military dictatorship of Charles Tomlinson looked and felt pretty much the same as it did under the leadership of Will Gannon—and maybe that was exactly the look Tomlinson was going for.

Our first chance to take the country's pulse came just east of Pittsburgh when we stopped for gas.

While Dorothy filled the tank, I went inside to use the restroom and to get a cup of coffee and a snack.

When I returned to the car, she was in a spirited conversation with a guy—no surprise there, she's a Guy Magnet. As I got closer, I was able to hear their conversation.

The guy—T-shirt, backwards ballcap—was mansplaining to her. "This country has needed a strong leader for a long time. I've been saying for years that we need a benevolent dictator. Someone who'll take control and get stuff done so that things are less chaotic."

"And you think Tomlinson is that person?" Dorothy asked.

"Abso-fucking-lutely."

"Why?"

"Ain't it obvious?" He was going to say more, but then he noticed me and did a double-take. "Whoa! Who's this? Your big sister?"

"We're friends," I said, pulling the bill of my ballcap lower and wanting to get the hell out of there before being recognized.

He stuck out his hand. "I'm Dan."

I gave it a firm shake. "La—" I almost blew it but recovered quickly with the first name that popped into my head: "Louise."

He turned to Dorothy. "Don't tell me. You're Thelma?"

She laughed. "No. But we *are* on a road trip."

"Where you heading?"

"Idaho."

"Why?" He chuckled as if Idaho was nowheresville.

"To see my folks—and to get a feel for the country under the new regime."

"Are you some kind of reporter?"

"I'm a field producer for CBS."

"Ah, the Lamestream Media." He nodded knowingly.

"Where do you get *your* news?" I asked.

"The Christian Newswire." He must've seen my jaw drop because he continued defensively, "I've got to have my opinions reinforced."

"Actually," I said, "you need to have them *informed*."

"Where do you get *your* news?" he sneer-asked.

I pointed at Dorothy. "CBS is pretty solid, but there are a lot of reputable news organizations out there."

He snorted.

"We've gotta get going," I said, not wanting to get into an argument with this ignorant lout, but before I could get back into the car, Dorothy cut in.

"Mind if I do a quick interview with you for a piece I'm doing for the network?" she asked him.

"Sure. I guess." He stood up a little straighter.

This guy might think CBS is fake news, but he can't wait to be on it, I noticed.

Dorothy pulled her cell and a lapel mic out of her purse. She plugged the mic into her phone's charging port before clipping it to Dan's shirt. She then opened her camera app and began shooting.

"State your name, please," she said, all no nonsense.

"Daniel L. Lamberti."

"So, Dan, what do you think of General Tomlinson's coup?"

"'Bout damn time."

"Why do you think so?"

"Gannon was weak. Plus there's evidence that he sold out the country to China. Seems like Tomlinson stepped in just in time to stop that traitor."

"Does it bother you that Tomlinson has done away with all the checks and balances that have been in place since the country's founding?"

"Not at all. Look around. Things are normal. We're now being guided by a firm hand. That's the way I see it."

"Thanks," Dorothy said brightly, stopping the camera and returning the mic and the phone to her purse.

"When's it going to be on the air?" he asked.

"Dunno yet. Right now I'm just getting person on the street interviews—or, in your case, person at a gas station. You're my first victim, so it'll probably be a while."

He pulled out his wallet, plucked a business card from it and handed it to her. "My email's on there. Gimme a heads up when it's gonna be on, okay?"

"Sure." She slid his card into her purse.

"Nice talking with you, Dan," I lied.

Before we left, Dorothy got a few quick shots of Dan filling his pickup truck.

"What an asshole," I said to her when we were back on the road.

"I know."

"We need to talk to more people." I held out my big bag of Cheetos so she could keep me from eating them all.

"What do you say we get off the interstate and meander some back roads, get a better feel for the country?"

I scrunched my face. "We need to get out to Idaho fast."

Dorothy nodded. And thought. After a moment, she asked, "How 'bout a compromise?"

"I'm listening."

"Let's do some back-roads meandering from time to time. We'll do our best to make progress, but in each new state, let's leave the main road and get some local color."

"That sounds good. Okay."

We made good time on I-70. Our next pitstop was near Columbus, Ohio. Dorothy steered us off the interstate and onto a back road. Immediately I noticed that it felt like we were getting a more granular look at the country than what seemed to be a superficial view from the speedy superhighway.

Ohio is both beautiful and boringly flat. Spring planting was well underway. We saw lots of tractors in fields. In some ways, the scenes reminded me of my upbringing in Wisconsin.

We found a gas station next to a greasy spoon diner so, after we filled up, we parked and went in to get a bite to eat, choosing seats at the counter in order to better strike up a conversation with someone.

I sat down on a stool to the right of an older woman I judged to be in her seventies.

"More coffee, Maude?" the waitress asked, her coffee pot hovering over Maude's mug.

"Yes. Thank you, Priscilla."

Priscilla poured.

"Hi, Maude. I'm Louise." I held out my hand, marveling at how smoothly the lie rolled off my tongue. "Are you from here originally?"

Maude took my hand and gave me a friendly smile. "All my life. Are you from around here?"

"My friend and I are just passing through on our way out west." I gestured to my right. "This is Dorothy. She's with CBS News doing interviews with people, asking them about that power shake-up in Washington."

"I don't pay attention to the news," Maude said.

"Mind if I do a quick interview with you?" Dorothy asked, pulling out her phone and lapel mic.

Maude blushed and laughed self-consciously. "I don't mind, but I think you'll find out pretty quickly I don't really know much about politics."

"That's okay," Dorothy said. "You only have to be an expert on what you believe."

Dorothy got up from her stool, came around behind me, clipped the mic onto Maude, then stood so she could get a better angle.

"State your name, please."

"I'm Maude Blanchard."

"And what do you do here in . . . where are we, anyway?"

"We're in Catawba, Ohio. I'm a former housewife. My husband passed about ten years ago, so I'm a widow now, too."

"So, what do you think about the ousting of President Gannon by General Tomlinson?"

"I heard about it, but I don't really have an opinion."

"Why not?"

"I just don't pay attention to politics. They're all corrupt, if you ask me."

"Why do you think so?"

"It's been going on for decades, the screaming and shouting and accusing. Don't know who to believe anymore, so I just tune it all out. It's just noise."

"Thank you."

"You're welcome." Maude smiled sweetly and waited for Dorothy to stop recording, then added, "That wasn't so bad."

"See? I knew you'd be a champ," Dorothy beamed. "I'll just take some video of you having your lunch and that'll be it. Easy peasy."

Priscilla The Waitress brought Maude's blue plate special and while Maude took the wrapping off the napkin that encircled her utensils, Dorothy began filming the event. When she finished getting her shots, she re-took her seat on the stool next to me.

After Priscilla took our orders, Dorothy asked if she could interview her, too.

"The place isn't too busy now, so sure," Priscilla said. Her hair was dyed pink and she had an elaborate sleeve of tattoos along her entire left arm.

Dorothy mic'd her up and centered her in the frame. "State your name, please."

"Priscilla Kemp."

"How long have you been working here?"

"Two years."

My ears perked up when she added, "I'm a single mom. Making ends meet is hard."

"What do you think about the shake-up in Washington?"

Priscilla shrugged. "I'm too busy to pay attention."

"Doesn't it bother you that Democracy appears to be dead?"

Another shrug. "Not really."

"Don't you vote?"

"Nah. What good would it do? I'm a nobody with no power."

Dorothy ended the interview and, while she got pictures of Priscilla bustling about the restaurant, Maude began chatting me up. It was a delightful conversation. I could feel my blood pressure dip because it was refreshing to be able to talk with someone about something other than politics.

As Dorothy and I worked our way west, we fell into a rhythm: every 200 miles, or so, we'd leave the interstate and roam a back road looking for another slice of life to investigate and chronicle.

We took turns driving, deciding to drive straight through to Idaho but agreeing to stop at a well-lit rest stop if we both needed to sleep at the same time.

As we drove, it became increasingly clear to me what a vast and beautiful country the United States is. It's also extremely homogeneous. Many places look the same, especially when viewed from the fast lane of the interstate. There's a certain comforting familiarity with road signs and traffic patterns. Pittsburgh looked a lot like Columbus; Columbus looked a lot like Indianapolis—and so it went until we got west of the Mississippi River at La Crosse, Wisconsin.

I would have loved to have done some sightseeing, or reconnecting with friends in the Badger state, but our mission was deadly serious. I was under cover, and we had no time for tourism. I wondered: Will this country ever get back to those carefree days?

However, the more people we talked to, the more I began to think that the country was very much unchanged. The farther away Dorothy and I got from

Washington, the farther away we seemed to be getting from the turmoil that had rocked our world.

Yes, some of the people we talked with had strong opinions either for or against the Tomlinson coup, but the vast majority of people Dorothy and I encountered really didn't seem to give a damn that their duly-elected president had been physically removed from office and would now soon be on trial for his life facing allegations—false allegations—of treason.

As we drove through red state after Gerrymandered red state, I also began to wonder and worry what I would do if suddenly there was a problem with my pregnancy. What would happen if something went wrong and my life was threatened by a pregnancy emergency?

I did some Googling. The results were demoralizing.

"Listen to this," I said to Dorothy.

"What've you got?"

"It's a piece in Kaiser Health News about abortion."

"Okay."

"It says here that seventy-five percent of the OB-GYNs in Idaho, where it's a felony to perform an abortion, are thinking of leaving the state."

Dorothy threw me a worried look. "What if the mother's life is at risk for something like an ectopic pregnancy?"

"The ban was total until the Idaho supreme court allowed for that exception, but when a pro-life legislator tried to soften the law with language to save the life of the mother, it got shot down."

"That's terrible. Why?"

"Let's see . . . ." My eyes scanned the article until I found the answer and read from the piece: "One Republican legislator said the list of conditions was endless and so broad that *everything* became an exception to take the life of a potential child."

"So, the OB-GYNs are getting outta Dodge?"

"In droves. They're afraid of getting busted and going to prison for doing their jobs."

During our 2,500-mile trip, Dorothy and I made more than a dozen stops, interviewing people at each place. No one recognized me. The trip took a total of forty hours.

We pulled into Coeur d'Alene, Idaho just as the sun was coming up on Sunday, May 17, barely four days after Will Gannon had been removed from office and taken into custody.

As was her habit, Dorothy caught the latest CBS news at the top of the hour on her car radio. The 8:00 a.m. newscast started this way:

Acting President Charles Tomlinson says former President Will Gannon will go on trial tomorrow morning for treason. The trial will be televised and CBS plans to carry it live.

Dorothy and I exchanged looks of horror.

Chapter Fifty-Seven

Dorothy and I were still absorbing the news as we were driving past a church—a magnificent building constructed almost entirely of what looked like crystal. A huge blood-red cross stood at least twenty feet tall on the spacious concrete apron by the church entrance.

The service must have already started because I saw a solitary figure hurrying toward the front door. The woman wore a chic blue suit and looked vaguely familiar.

"Whoa. Slow down," I ordered.

"What? Why?"

"I think that's Nora."

"Tomlinson?"

"Uh huh."

Dorothy pulled to the curb and we both watched as Nora—it was definitely her—got to the front door of the church and entered, sunlight flashing off the glass.

"Let's go to church," I said.

"You're on."

Dorothy found a place to park and we walked briskly past the gaudy cross and into the building.

"Let's sit in the back. I don't want her to see or recognize us," I said, slipping my hoodie over my head.

The service was already underway when we arrived.

This was the first time I'd been in church since Rose Gannon's funeral at Washington National Cathedral. This place was, in every way, the opposite of the Cathedral.

The sanctuary was like a television studio or Broadway theater with a grid of spotlights on the ceiling.

The congregation was lustily singing a hymn I recognized from my Episcopal upbringing—"Jesus Christ is Risen Today"—but the traditional organ was replaced by a rock band front-and-center on the stage. The lyrics were projected prominently onto a gigantic screen that took up the entire back wall of the stage.

The drummer sat on a pedestal behind plexiglass baffles, his bass drum thumping like a heartbeat. Stretched across the stage in front of him were two teenage guys playing electric guitars.

A young woman, wearing a denim jacket, stood center stage in a lone spotlight. Her eyes were closed in ecstasy as she sang into a hand-held microphone.

To me, this mega-church-with-a-back-beat felt less like worship and more like a slick, professional performance.

Nora, even though she'd arrived late, was sitting near the front on the aisle.

The place was nearly full—perhaps 500 people, all white. Instead of pews, there were plush individual seats. Dorothy and I slipped into two of them in the right rear, as far away from the center aisle—and Nora—as we could get.

As near as I could tell, everyone in the church but Dorothy and I had cumbersome five-pound Bibles on their laps. The only way we fit in is that most people were dressed as informally as we were.

The hymn ended with a flourish and a cymbal crash.

The congregation applauded.

The band seamlessly segued into a rock version of "Amazing Grace." Dorothy sang along, but I've got a terrible singing voice, so I just mouthed the words.

Many in the congregation stood and raised their hands in prayer and praise.

I looked around and noticed at least three television cameras focused on the stage. This was one slick production.

When the song ended, one of the guitar players, a guy, led the congregation in an extemporaneous prayer in which every phrase began with, "Lord, we just really . . ."

At the end of the prayer, the musicians shuffled off the stage, those in the congregation who'd been standing sat, and a rugged-looking guy with a shaved head and short, dark beard carried a Plexiglas lectern to center stage. He wore a dark blue sport coat, a white shirt open at the neck, and jeans.

"Open your Bibles to Joshua 6," he ordered in a nasally voice.

Pages rustled.

The guy sitting to my left poked me. "Where's yer Bible?"

I gave him my best I'm-a-dope look. "I forgot it."

"Here. You can look along with me." He turned immediately to the correct page and angled the book so I could see, too.

"Thanks," I whispered.

"This guy is *so* good," my seatmate said, nodding toward the pastor.

I had my doubts, but listened as politely as I could, biting my tongue the entire time.

The pastor wielded the hand-held mic as skillfully as any stand-up comic I've ever seen.

"The title of my sermon today is 'From Joshua 6 to January 6th—and Beyond.'"

"Oh, man. This is gonna be good," the guy next to me gushed.

The pastor continued. "A lot of the stories in the Old Testament are—let's face it—old."

The congregation tittered.

"But Joshua 6 is as timely as today's headline that Will Gannon goes on trial for treason tomorrow."

The congregation burst into applause.

I glanced quickly at Nora. She, too, was clapping.

"You are all twenty-first-century Joshuas," the minister said when the applause died down.

"Joshua was Moses's successor. Joshua was commissioned by God Almighty to take control of Israel which was occupied by the Canaanites. For far too long, the United States has been like Canaan—full of idolatry and sexual perversion."

"Amen!" someone called out.

As if he'd just thought of it, the pastor said casually, "Haven't you always wondered why it is that grown men wearing lingerie want so badly to read to your eight-year-old boy at the library?"

Many people laughed heartily.

The pastor's smile turned to a scowl as he said, "During the fifty years that abortion was legal in this country, seventy-million babies were murdered on the altar of child sacrifice." His voice caught and he had to pause.

A murmur went through the crowd.

When he recovered his emotional equilibrium, his voice was strong. "But back in 2021—January 6th, to be exact—things began to change."

"Oh yes!" someone else shouted.

"Back then a whole lotta Joshuas—including many in this room—began to rise up against the Democrat oppression of a rigged election."

"Speak it, brother."

"Just like Joshua did back in the Bible, you circled the Capitol. You circled the Supreme Court. You circled what had become symbols of oppression."

"Oh, yes!"

"Granted, the walls didn't come tumbling down like they did in Joshua's day, but they were breached. They began to crack. They began to crumble."

"Yes, Lord."

"And you Joshuas have kept the faith." With every sentence, his voice rose in intensity. "You didn't stop believing that the Lord would prevail. You didn't stop believing that justice would conquer. And now here we are on the cusp of a new day. A bright and shining day. A day—tomorrow—when, with a mighty shout, the walls of oppression will finally fall and the DC Demon will be gone for good."

The pastor's face was red. The tendons in his neck stood out. He was shouting.

The people jumped to their feet, including the guy next to me. The church was filled with loud shouts and applause.

Dorothy and I sat in stunned silence.

My eyes zeroed in on the text of Joshua 6:20-21: *When the trumpets sounded, the army shouted, and at the sound of the trumpet when the men gave a loud shout, the wall collapsed; so everyone charged straight in and they took the city. They devoted the city to the Lord and destroyed with the sword every living thing in it—men and women, young and old, cattle, sheep and donkeys.*

Was this going to be the next step in Charles Tomlinson's America?

I felt sick to my stomach and, even though I was trembling all over, Dorothy and I managed to escape the church before anyone—especially Nora—recognized us.

Chapter Fifty-Eight

"Jesus, that was terrifying," Dorothy said when we'd gotten outside.

"I know."

"What's next?"

"Let's get off the street and back to your car so we can regroup."

"I'm starving."

"Me, too. But we have to stay focused. I need to find out where the president is being held. Nora might be our only chance to find out."

"Should we follow her?"

"Yeah. That's what I think."

We got to Dorothy's Miata and kept our eyes fixed on the church's front door. We waited for more than half an hour, our tummies growling in unison the entire time.

Finally, the glass front door opened and people began streaming out. The pastor stood at the door shaking hands with everyone as they left.

When Nora got to him, he grasped her extended hand with both of his and patted the top of it. They beamed at each other then she said something. He nodded and I saw him mouth what looked like, "Thank you, sister."

On impulse, I pulled the phone out of my jeans, called her number, then watched as Nora fished her phone from her purse.

"This is Nora," she said in her best business-official voice.

"It's Lark."

Nora winced. "I don't recognize this number."

"I'm calling you on a burner phone, just checking in since our last chat. Where are you?"

"I'm just leaving church."

"Where's that?"

"It's a small non-denominational church just off Connecticut Avenue."

An obvious lie and a confirmation that, as I'd feared, she couldn't be trusted. I was still on my own.

"Any luck finding out where the president is being held?" I asked.

"I'm still working on that."

"I heard he goes on trial tomorrow."

"That's right."

"And it'll be televised."

"Uh huh."

"C'mon, Nora. You're the press secretary—actually, I still am, but whatever. Surely, you're at least making arrangements for pool coverage."

"There'll be no press access. Charles will supply the feed and the networks will have their access that way."

"What's your role?"

"Making sure they have the link that gets them plugged into our feed."

"Don't you have to be on the scene?"

"Not really. I can do it all from my desk at the White House here in Washington."

"The last time we spoke you said you had a hunch Will is being held someplace in Idaho."

"Uh huh."

"Have you been able to confirm that?"

She hesitated. "N-no. Not yet."

"The clock's ticking, Nora."

"I know."

"What happens if Will is convicted?"

"Firing squad, I guess."

I winced. "Will that be televised, too?"

"I don't know, but I wouldn't be surprised."

"Jesus, Nora. The stakes are pretty fucking high. Don't you have anything better to do than to go to church?"

"I believe in the power of prayer, Lark," her voice indignant.

"So do I, but has the Almighty told you yet where the president is being held?"

"I'm working on it."

"Work harder." I hung up, steaming.

I watched as she held her phone out in disgust and glared at it. She then stuffed it into her purse and stalked down the street to her car, a deep blue Beemer.

"She's lying," I said to Dorothy. "We need to follow her. I think she knows exactly where the president is."

Chapter Fifty-Nine

The top was down on Dorothy's Miata making us more conspicuous.

"Quick!" I yelped. "Put up the top."

Dorothy pouted. "Aww. It's such a nice day."

"Dorothy! C'mon!"

"Oh, all right." She deftly reached behind and easily pulled the compact top up and over us, securing it with a *click* to the windshield.

I pulled down the bill of my ballcap and slunk lower in the seat. My hair was tucked inside the cap and my sunglasses were in the "on" position.

As Nora's Beemer glided past us, we pulled in behind her, but at a discreet distance.

"This is fun. Just like the movies," Dorothy gushed, gripping the steering wheel tightly at ten and two.

I merely grunted. The stakes were too high for this to be fun.

After a few blocks, Nora pulled into a gas station.

We drove past, then found a place to park where we could watch. Nora was talking on her cell as she filled up her tank.

Soon she replaced the nozzle, screwed on her gas cap, and continued driving north on U.S. 95.

"Where do you suppose she's going?" Dorothy wondered.

"I think that Will . . . um, the president . . . is being held at some sort of heavily fortified remote location, like a ranch."

"That's the second or third time on this trip you've referred to Gannon as 'Will.' Are you sure there's nothing going on between you two?"

I pursed my lips. Busted.

"I mean it doesn't matter to me," she said. "He's hot and now he's single—and so are you."

"We have what I'd call a very close friendship that preceded my time as his press secretary. He insists that I call him Will when we're alone. It's a lonely job and he craves having a friend. But—believe it, or not—our relationship is professional."

"Okay. I believe you."

"You're probably the only person in the country who does, so, thank you."

"Sure thing." Dorothy shot me a worried look and changed the subject. "If Nora leads us to some kind of compound, you're not thinking of busting in, are you?"

I shook my head. "No."

"So, what's the plan?"

"If she enters what looks like a place where the president is being hidden, then I'll get in touch with my contact at DOD and get the ball rolling on a rescue mission."

"Seems highly speculative."

"It does, but it's our only hope. The military might be able to do some recon to determine if—and where—the president is, then launch a raid to get him back." I turned to look at her. "And this is when I'll need your help, too."

"My dad, right?"

"Right."

"He's not my biggest fan."

I nodded. "Let's just find out what we have. Maybe then we'll have a better idea of how to play your dad."

"Maybe *you'll* have better luck with him."

"I doubt that. You heard at church what people here think of people like me. You may not be popular with your dad, but he might consider me to be the devil incarnate."

She chewed her lower lip. "You've got a point."

I nodded toward Nora's Beemer. "She's got her blinker on."

Dorothy put her blinker on, too.

"No," I nearly shouted. "Turn it off."

"Why?" She turned off her blinker but slowed down.

"It'll be too obvious that we're following her."

Nora turned left.

"Go straight," I commanded.

"But we'll lose her."

"No, we won't."

As we passed through the intersection, I turned my head to check on Nora. "Now quick make a U-turn and go back to the intersection."

"Okay."

Traffic was light and Dorothy was able to guide her Miata into a looping left turn onto the gravel shoulder on the other side of the road, then she floored it sending stones flying as we bolted toward the road where Nora had turned a few seconds earlier.

"See?" I said after we made the right turn. "She's farther ahead, but we can still keep her in view without it being obvious to her that she's being followed."

"You should be in the CIA," Dorothy quipped.

We were now driving through farm fields, but up ahead they gave way to timberland on both sides of the highway. No one else was on the road, so I patted myself on the back for having Dorothy make the maneuver that kept us off Nora's radar.

Soon, after the road entered the wooded area, Nora slowed, then tapped her brakes.

"Slow down and stay back," I directed.

Dorothy obeyed.

Nora stopped. Then made another left turn.

"Okay. Step on it," I said. "Let's see where she's gone."

"Should I follow her to the left?"

"No. But go slow. Let's see where she went first."

As we approached the place where Nora turned, I could see that it was some sort of private drive. Two black Cadillac Escalades flanked the driveway, their front grills facing the road.

"Keep going," I said. "But don't look."

"Okay." Her hands white-knuckled the steering wheel. "This is giving me the creeps."

"Me too."

I did my best to keep my head facing toward the front, but I shot my sunglasses-shrouded eyes to the left to get as good a look as I could at the place where Nora had turned.

In the few seconds it took for us to drive past I noticed several things: The entryway was flanked by tall tree-trunk timbers that held a wooden plaque over the driveway. An imposing metal gate blocked the entrance and a fence of black metal bars stretched to the left and right along the front of the compound.

I didn't catch the inscription carved into the wooden plank above the gate, but it looked like it might be the name of some sort of ranch.

The two Escalades each contained four men in dark suits and sunglasses. Probably Secret Service. A similarly dressed man carrying an AR-15 assault weapon stood menacingly in front of the gate.

"These guys mean business," I said softly to Dorothy. "They've got the weapon of choice of mass murderers and school shooters everywhere."

"No shit," she breathed.

"Keep driving."

"Ya think?"

Once we'd driven past the gate, she accelerated.

"Is anyone following us?" I asked, my voice tense.

She eyed the rear-view mirror. "No. Or at least not yet."

"Keep going."

"Oh, I'm going. You don't need to worry about that."

We kept driving until the road curved to the right and we were no longer in view of the guards at the gate.

"Pull over," I said. "Let's regroup."

Dorothy drove onto the gravel shoulder and put on her emergency flashers as I pulled out my phone and opened my map app.

The blue dot had us located in the middle of nowhere on a county road surrounded by thick woods.

I found on the map the driveway where Dorothy turned and noted the coordinates on Google maps.

"Are you thinking what I'm thinking, Dorothy?"

"I'm thinking we are the only two people in the world—other than the insurrectionists—who know where Will Gannon is right now."

"I think you're right."

I hit speed dial on my phone.

Chapter Sixty

Air Force General Mildred Jackson picked up my call immediately.

"It's Lark."

"What've you got?"

"I think I've found Gannon."

"Excellent. Where?"

"Got a map?"

"Affirmative."

"It's a heavily fortified compound about ten miles northeast of Coeur d'Alene, Idaho."

"What are the coordinates?"

I gave them to her.

"Copy that."

"I'm looking at it on the satellite view."

"Me too."

"I see several buildings."

"Yeah. That'll make it tricky. He may be there, but we don't know exactly where. What are the fortifications like?"

"Dunno for sure." I told her about the metal-barred fencing, the gate, and the heavily armed Secret Service detail out front.

"Is there any chance you can poke around the perimeter and see what else you can see?"

"And risk getting caught?"

"I know it's a big ask, but Gannon goes on trial in less than twenty-four hours. Whatever we do, we've gotta do it fast. Your eyes will help speed things up."

"Don't you have drones?"

"Yeah. That'll help."

"Use drones."

"I will, but I sure could use your help, too."

"I'll think about it."

"Okay. Let me get the ball rolling here. Lemme know asap what else you're able to learn."

"Deal." I hung up.

"What's next?" Dorothy asked.

"You need to go home, and I need sleep, a shower, and food—not necessarily in that order."

"Same here."

"You'll be able to get all of those things at your place."

"What about you?"

"There were a whole lot of motels on the U.S. 95 strip near the church. Let's see if I can get a room there. Then you go home. We can regroup later this afternoon."

"Sounds like a plan. Should we go back the way we came?"

"Too risky. Those agents looked like they're on a hair-trigger and we're way too conspicuous. They'll come after us in a heartbeat. Go straight and we'll loop back to 95."

"Okay." She turned off her flashers and continued down the country road.

Soon we were back on the main highway and, not long after that, we were back in Coeur d'Alene. We stopped at a nondescript, cheap no-tell-motel-looking place on the outskirts of town. I figured, correctly, they'd be less likely to check my ID, especially since I was paying cash.

I signed in for two nights as "Louise Chatworth" and forked over ninety-five dollars in cash. The guy actually checked my ID, but because I'd chosen an alias that resembles "Lark Chadwick," he didn't bat an eye.

Once it was clear that I had a place to stay, Dorothy drove on to her parents' house on the southern outskirts of town.

My motel room was on the scuzzy side of basic: a threadbare carpet, cigarette burns on the bedside table, a rickety desk, a faucet dripping noisily in the bathroom, with towels as substantial as Kleenex tissues.

The bed was rock hard. I fell into it without even bothering to take off my clothes and slept soundly for the next five hours.

It was after three in the afternoon when I dragged myself into the bathroom and took a long, luxurious shower—once the water finally began to run hot.

I was drying my hair when Dorothy called me on my cell.

"What's up? How's it going with your folks?"

"They want to meet you, Lark."

"You're kidding. Don't they think I'm a Jezebel?"

"If they do, they haven't said so. My mom insists you come out for dinner. She's very hospitable that way."

My stomach must've recognized the word "dinner" because it let off an enthusiastic growl.

"Okay. Dinner. Thank you. I accept. What about your dad? Any progress there?"

"Maybe. He seems to have mixed feelings about the coup."

"Does he know anything about where Gannon might be?"

"Not sure of that, either. I've been careful not to push too hard. We're on speaking terms—and that's a lot."

It was five when Dorothy picked me up. As I got into her car, I began having second thoughts. I'd been incognito and off the grid, but now I was about to meet a man who, at least initially, had been in support of the coup. Was I letting my empty stomach lure me into a trap? Was Dorothy's dad connected to the plot? Was I about to be turned over to the coup Gestapo?

As we drove toward my rendezvous with dinner, I was beginning to lose my appetite.

Chapter Sixty-One

On the way over to the Rathers', once I'd confirmed with Dorothy that her folks drank alcohol, I prevailed upon her to stop at a liquor store so I could pick up a bottle of wine—as a peace offering.

Having spent almost every minute of the past forty-eight hours crammed into Dorothy Rather's tiny Miata with her, I could tell she'd had a good upbringing, but that didn't prepare me for the opulence of her parents' home. To say it was "palatial" would be an understatement.

When we arrived, Dorothy's mom greeted us at the top of an imposing marble staircase at the front door. She wore elegant camel-colored twill slacks and a peach twin set and a simple pearl necklace.

I immediately felt like an underdressed slob.

"Hi, Mom," Dorothy said as she walked into the foyer. "This is Lark Chadwick."

I extended my hand and smiled. "Hello, Mrs. Rather."

"Call me Bea." She took me by the hand and led me to where her husband stood smiling just inside the front entrance beneath a towering crystal chandelier. "This is Jerry."

Jerry wore linen slacks and a navy-blue blazer over a pale blue shirt, open at the neck. "Hi, Lark." He shook my hand in a firm, but not overpowering grip.

"Hi, Mr. Rather. It's great to finally meet you." My smile was tight. I still had no idea what to expect, but at least in the initial moments of our meeting, I felt welcome.

I'm ashamed to admit it, but I'd badly prejudged her parents, especially her dad. I confess I have no personal respect for people who buy into conspiracy theories based on flimsy-to-no facts.

Yes. I can be intolerantly judgmental. It's one of my biggest character flaws. I was wrong about The Rathers.

Dorothy's mom was gracious, warm, and personable. Dorothy's dad was friendly, affable, and seemed to be open minded.

Bea Rather took the wine from me, handed it to her husband who walked it into the kitchen. She then swept us to a cozy sitting area near a stone fireplace so big we all could have sat inside it.

Gouda cheese, crackers, and an assortment of red and green grapes were arrayed on a coffee table.

In a moment, Jerry was back, standing over us. "What would you all like to drink? We have the wine Lark brought, soda, or something stronger."

"I'll have ginger ale, if you have it," I said. "Thank you."

Jerry took everyone else's order, then disappeared into the kitchen as Bea, Dorothy, and I settled in.

We made small talk about the trip until Jerry returned with our drinks, then took at seat next to his wife.

The Rathers were making me feel welcome. By that I mean they were making me the center of attention, not realizing that's the exact opposite of my comfort zone, so I turned the conversation to their daughter.

"Dorothy has been great company these past few days," I said. "It's been fascinating watching her come into her own as a journalist. She was doing interviews with people across the country."

Dorothy spoke up. "I was able to edit my piece into a three-minute feature that I just fed to the network. It went up on the website about an hour ago."

So far, so good. We hadn't gotten into the coup. Part of me—a big part—was dreading getting into it. I didn't want to have a fruitless argument with the Rathers about "fake news" or the elephant-in-the-room coup. And yet it would inevitably come up, and when it did, I would need to muster every diplomatic impulse I had to make the Rathers into allies rather than enemies.

Once again, Bea turned the spotlight onto me. "Tell us a little about yourself, Lark. What an interesting name. Is it a nickname?"

"No," I chuckled. "It's the real deal. According to Chadwick family lore, when I was born, my mom said, 'She's happy as a Lark,' so the name stuck."

"Are you from the DC area?" Jerry asked.

"I grew up in Wisconsin, migrated to Georgia for a stint as a cops and courts reporter at a small daily paper before moving to DC a few years ago to join the Associated Press."

I used the beat-and-a-half of silence, to turn the tables and get them talking. "How did you two meet?" I asked, looking back and forth between Bea and Jerry.

She spoke first. "We met twenty-five years ago during Jerry's senior year at West Point. It was a blind date."

"Were you immediately smitten?" I asked her, but Jerry answered instead.

"*She* wasn't, but *I* was."

"True," Bea said. "He was very persuasive."

"Long courtship?" I took a sip and sat back, enjoying the story.

"Opposite," he said. "I was about to ship out to Afghanistan, so I needed to work fast. Convinced her to marry me within a week after we met."

"Whoa. That *is* fast." I turned to look at Bea. "It's none of my business, but didn't you have second thoughts?"

She smiled. "Those came later."

I decided to steer away from any possible marital strife which I'm sure eventually plagues every marriage. I pivoted. "And then little Dorothy came along."

"Yes," Bea said simply, still smiling.

"And that's when second thoughts became third, fourth, and fifth thoughts," Dorothy laughed.

"Not at all, dear," Bea said. "You've been a delight."

Dorothy scowled. "Until I decided to join the dark side and go into journalism."

Uh oh. Let's not go there. I thought. I said, "You have a beautiful home. How long have you lived here?"

"About five years." Jerry placed a piece of Gouda cheese onto a cracker. "Was able to afford it when I took my company public."

"I.T., right?"

He nodded. "Lots of government contracts."

"Is your specialty communications?"

"Uh-huh. The technology keeps changing, so it's a growth industry."

I decided to push the envelope a bit. "Are there any government contracts that you have in the Coeur d'Alene area, or does most of your work require you to travel?"

"Both," he said. "I'm on the road a fair amount, but there's a place just out of town I recently had to set up communications for."

"Is that northeast of town on County M?"

He looked surprised. "Yeah, actually, it is. How do you know about that?"

"Dorothy and I drove past it earlier today as we were doing some back-roads meandering. It was heavily guarded." I decided not to add "by Secret Service agents."

"Yeah. It's pretty hush-hush. I can't talk about it."

Soon, Bea maneuvered us to the dining room.

Dinner was excellent and light, nothing extravagant, but sumptuous.

Jerry refilled my glass and I felt myself relaxing into the conversation, yet I was still on guard.

"I see you're taking good care of yourself by not drinking alcohol, Lark." Bea nodded at my barely-a-bump tummy. "When are you due?"

"November." I'd almost said "August," but that was the end of the second trimester when I'd have to make up my mind about abortion. *The less you say, the better*, I said sternly to myself.

"We just heard a marvelous teaching at church this morning about abortion," Bea continued blithely.

I held my tongue and lasered my focus on a piece of lettuce on my plate.

"The guest preacher was from somewhere in Kansas," she continued, even though I offered not a hint of encouragement. "One of the things he said really got my attention."

"Oh?" I said reflexively. To myself, I added, *Shut. Up. Don't encourage her, Lark!*

Bea continued. "As you're no doubt aware, the constant refrain in pro-abortion circles, is 'my body, my choice.'"

"Pro-choice."

"Excuse me?"

"I don't think anyone is pro-abortion. That's a painfully difficult—and personal—decision. The issue is choice."

She waved a fork. "Whatever. It's semantics. But the point the preacher made is—"

"A man, right?"

"Excuse me?"

"The preacher was a man expounding on what a woman should do with her body, correct?" *Lark!! Shut. The fuck. Up!!*

"Yes. But that's hardly the point."

"It sort of is, but go on." *Jesus, Lark. You are your own worst enemy. Shut. Up.*

"Anyway..." She sighed at my interruptions but tried to remain pleasant. "The sermon was right before communion. He pointed out something I'd never noticed before. He noted that Jesus used the same words of the pro-abortion movement." She paused, deliberately baiting me into a response.

For once, I held my tongue. Partly because my tongue was busy savoring a divine bite of cucumber.

Bea, perhaps a little disappointed by my silence, continued. "Jesus said, 'This is my body which is sacrificed for you.' But the pro abortionists have twisted it: 'This is my body so I will selfishly sacrifice my baby.'"

"Whoa!" Dorothy exploded. "Mom. Talk about semantics!"

"I'm just saying. I found it to be a very interesting rhetorical juxtaposition. Don't you, Lark?"

"Oh, indeed. Fascinating." *Frightening,* I thought to myself. *Jesus, get me outta here.*

I gave Dorothy a rescue-me look.

She picked up on it right away. "So, Dad."

"Yes'm?"

"What do people here think of the coup?"

He turned the question back onto her. "What did the people you interviewed tell you?"

She said, "I was surprised to learn that most people don't seem to give a damn. I haven't done any interviews here, yet."

"My guess is that's not the case here," Jerry said.

"Really?" Dorothy asked, "You have to guess? Don't you know?"

"Yeah. I know. Most people, myself included, think it's long overdue."

I put down my fork. "Here's what I don't understand, Mr. Rather. Maybe you can help me. You took an oath to defend the Constitution against all enemies, foreign and domestic. You served your country in a war zone overseas. Thank you for your service, by the way."

"You're welcome."

"But I don't understand how it is that you're in favor of a domestic enemy who has removed the duly-elected president from office and then has shredded that Constitution, the one you took an oath to defend."

"The answer is embedded in how you phrased the question."

I scowled. "How so?"

"You said it yourself: 'domestic enemy.' Gannon is a domestic enemy."

"Really? Do you really believe that?"

"I do."

"In what way?"

"Gannon was right on the edge of a major push to disarm the citizenry."

I shook my head vigorously and was about to protest, but Jerry Rather powered on.

"He was right on the cusp of institutionalizing any so-called 'crazy' person who wouldn't fall into lock step with his national pro-abortion plan."

"What evidence do you have to support your assertion?"

"History."

I raised my eyebrows.

"Nazi Germany, to be specific. The erosion of freedom is like bankruptcy: gradually, then suddenly. Tomlinson saw what was about to happen and saved this country before Gannon could pull a Hitler."

I took the deepest breath I could, gritted my teeth, and did my best to push down the rage that was building inside me. "Look. I don't want to get into an argument with you. I know you have strong and very sincere beliefs, but will you let me make my case?"

He spread his hands magnanimously and nodded for me to continue.

"I find it ironic that you use the example of Hitler to make your case."

"Why's that?"

"It's true that Hitler was one of history's worst mass murderers. But don't you see that the very thing Tomlinson was supposedly trying to prevent is actually being accomplished by utilizing Hitlerian tactics? I worked with Will Gannon every day. I helped write the speech he gave right before he was arrested. He was calling for an international *conversation* on mental health. He is the antithesis of a dictator, yet he was removed from office *by* a dictator."

Jerry Rather listened to me thoughtfully, his chin cupped in his hand. "Yes. I see the point you're making."

"But do you agree?"

Before he could answer, the doorbell rang.

"I'll get it," Jerry said, obviously stalling for time. He got up and went to the door. A moment later, I heard him say, "She's in here."

Jerry re-entered the room accompanied by two Secret Service agents, guns drawn.

"Lark Chadwick?" one of them said, continuing before I could even answer. "You're under arrest for kidnapping the children of Will Gannon. Come with us, please."

Dorothy exploded. "What the hell!?" She jumped to her feet causing the dining room chair to tip over.

Before I could protest, the agents roughly pulled me to my feet, handcuffed me, and marched me toward the front door.

Chapter Sixty-Two

I actually recognized one of the Secret Service agents from Gannon's detail the previous weekend at Camp David.

"Really, Mitch? You? A traitor to your country?"

He tightened his grip on my arm but remained tight-lipped.

Two Cadillac Escalades, motors idling, were parked in the Rathers' circular driveway.

"Be strong, Lark," Dorothy hollered from the front door.

When I turned to look, she was pushing past her parents who stood at the top of the steps.

Dorothy yelled, "I didn't know this was going to happen. I'm so sorry." She brought her iPhone to her face, pointed it at me, and began filming, doing her job even if she didn't seem to like the event unfolding before her eyes. I assumed that within the next few minutes news and video of my arrest would begin to spread.

The guys arresting me were pros, not goons. Mitch placed his hand protectively by the side of my head so I wouldn't bump it getting into the vehicle, my hands cuffed awkwardly behind my back.

As I settled in for the ride to who-knows-where, I silently chided myself for being so naïve. I had avoided being recognized during our entire cross-country trip, but just as I was feeling the most relaxed, I should have realized I was in the most peril.

I should've listened to that small voice inside urging me to be wary of Dorothy's dad. But she and I had both believed, falsely, that his support of the coup was wavering. I could only imagine the content of their conversation now as I was driven away from the Rather manse.

No one spoke during our drive through town. I had to admit—Coeur d'Alene is beautiful. No wonder people here were afraid of outsiders besmirching their oasis amid the encroaching diversity of all The Others who also want a piece of the American Dream.

But apparently these people believed the American Dream was for whites and straights and Christians only. Sure, a few outsiders were tolerated. There had to be worker bees to do the grunt work.

It only took a few minutes for us to drive to the redoubt Dorothy and I had driven past earlier in the day. *At least*, I thought ruefully, *I'll get a look at the place.*

We drove down a dirt road bracketed on both sides by tall pines. I had no idea what to expect but was surprised when we came to a stop at nothing more than a log cabin. It was in a clearing adjacent to several other similar-looking buildings.

Armed guards were everywhere. So were several other Escalades.

A white panel truck with *Rather Communications* stenciled on the side was parked in front of a cabin with a tall cellular tower sprouting from behind.

Mitch, who had been sitting next to me in the back of the Escalade, got out when we came to a stop. He walked around to my side, opened the door, and helped me out. He then led me to the front door of the cabin where he frisked me and confiscated my phones.

An armed guard, AR15 at the ready, stood at the plain-wood front door. All the windows I could see were covered by iron bars.

Mitch removed my handcuffs, opened the door, and gave me a gentle shove.

Once inside, it took a moment for me to adjust to the dim lighting. But once I became accustomed to the light, there standing before me was a smiling, but haggard, Will Gannon.

Chapter Sixty-Three

Until this moment, I'd been resigned to my fate. Part of me knew it was inevitable that time would run out and I would eventually be hunted down and hauled off the street by the security forces of the Tomlinson junta.

Now to see a living, breathing, *smiling* Will Gannon was wonderful beyond my wildest dreams.

"Oh my God!" I shouted and ran toward him.

"Stop!" he commanded. He pushed his hands toward me, his smile morphing into a scowl.

I stopped. "W-Why?"

"There are security cameras all over this place. Probably microphones, too. They'll be able to turn even an innocent hug into literally a federal case against me. Against *us*."

I let out an exasperated sigh but kept my distance—at least twenty-five feet. "Well, it's good to see you, Mr. President."

He smiled again. "Good to see you, too, Ms. Chadwick."

He wore an orange prison jumpsuit and flip flops. His hair was mussed, and he had a dark five o'clock shadow that was working overtime.

For a moment we stood in stunned silence facing and appraising each other. Finally, I spoke. "How are you?"

He nodded thoughtfully. "Better than I thought I'd be."

"Are you being treated humanely?"

"Surprisingly well."

"What have you been told?"

"About what?"

"About anything. Do you know what's happened to the rest of the government?"

"No. I was hoping you could tell me." He looked around and waved a hand. "But remember, this place is probably bugged big time."

"Got it."

"How are Grace and T-Thomas?" His voice broke.

I took an instinctive step toward him but caught myself. I whispered, "They're well and safe at, um, an undisclosed location."

Will laughed.

"In fact, that's why I'm here."

He gave me a quizzical look.

"I'm accused of kidnapping them."

"Well, if you did, thank you." He smiled.

"No comment."

"And the government?"

I shook my head slowly and mouthed, *I don't know.*

He turned serious—and silent. He began to pace as he considered the gravity and enormity of the Tomlinson coup.

As he turned away from me, I noticed a bloodstain seeping through the back of his jump suit above his right shoulder blade.

"Will!"

"What?" He turned to look at me.

"You're hurt. There's blood on your back."

He looked over his shoulder briefly. "Oh. That."

"Yes. That. What happened?"

He scowled. "I suppose I can tell you now. As soon as they arrested me, while we were still on the way to the airport, they removed the GPS chip from my shoulder. It was a pretty crude job. And painful."

"So, Lionel was right."

"What do you mean?"

"He thought you might have gotten the chip when you were elected."

Will nodded.

"Let me take a look." I moved toward him.

He backed away. "Nah. It's okay. Don't worry about it." He resumed pacing.

I decided to let it go. For now. I looked around and took in my surroundings.

For all practical purposes, we were being held in what could easily pass for an Airbnb mountain cabin. There was a sofa, a couple bulky easy chairs, even a dining room table with four straight-backed wooden chairs, and a kitchen with a stove and refrigerator.

I ambled into the kitchenette. The drawers were empty of utensils, the cupboards had no dishes, and the refrigerator only had a couple plastic bottles of water.

On the other side of the living room area was a short hallway. As Will paced, lost in thought, I investigated. The hallway led past a bathroom and ended at a point where doorways on either side opened into small bedrooms. The doors of each room had been removed from the hinges. Each room was Spartan, containing only a small bed, but no other furniture, not even a dresser.

I checked the bathroom. The empty medicine cabinet had no door, either, which meant there were no glass mirrors anywhere.

The only reading material I'd seen was a Bible on the dining room table.

So, the place where Will and I were being held was no supermax prison, but it was no Club Med, either.

When I returned to the main living area, I saw Will standing at the window looking thoughtfully into the distance.

Before either of us could speak, I heard a key rattle in the door which then opened and in strode two burly Secret Service agents followed by Charles Tomlinson.

Chapter Sixty-Four

Tomlinson was dressed in combat fatigues and carried in his two outstretched hands what looked like a folded orange jumpsuit, a white towel, and flip-flops—presumably, my prison attire.

The two agents stood imposingly in front of the door while Tomlinson strode to the dining room table, placed what he was carrying onto it, and pulled out chairs for each of us.

"Sit," he commanded.

"I'll stand," Will replied, ice in his voice.

"Very well." Tomlinson shrugged and pointed to the table. "That's your prison garb, Lark."

I held my tongue—until I couldn't any longer. "Fuck you," I snarled.

Tomlinson smiled. "Lovely. Such vile words from such a pretty mouth."

"Double fuck you."

He shook his head. "But such a limited vocabulary." He waved a hand in an I'm-through-with-you gesture and turned to look at Will. "Here's the plan."

He was about to say more, but I took a step toward him.

That prompted one of the agents to leave his post at the door and bolt to a menacing position next to me.

I snarled, "Tell us what's happened to the vice president and everyone else in the line of succes—"

In a flash, Tomlinson backhanded me in a stinging slap across the face.

"Ow."

"Shut. The fuck. Up," he roared.

Will clenched a fist and started to swing at Tomlinson but the Secret Service agent grabbed his arm and wrenched it behind him causing Will to cry out in pain.

"All right, children. Let's settle down, shall we?" Tomlinson moved away from us and leaned against the back of the sofa. "Do you want to know what happens next, or don't you?"

"I'd like to know how you were able to pull this off, Charles," Will said.

Tomlinson gestured at the agent. "Let him go, Mitch."

Mitch released his grip on Will.

"It's been in the works since you were elected. It took a while to identify the true patriots who'd be loyal to me and put them into position."

"What about the line of succession?" Will asked. "The veep, House Speaker, Speaker Pro Tem of the Senate, my cabinet?"

"All neutralized."

"Murdered?" I asked.

"Neutralized."

Will shook his head. "You'll never get away with this."

He laughed. "I already have."

"So, what *is* the plan?" I hissed.

"I thought you'd never ask." Tomlinson pushed himself off the back of the sofa and began to pace in front of the doorway, gesturing grandly. "Tomorrow at noon you'll both go on trial. It will be touching for the country to see you both together again, but this time pleading for your lives."

"Don't get your hopes up, you asshole," I said.

"There you go again, Lark. Maybe I should have you bound and gagged at your trial so you'll be less likely to embarrass yourself."

"Do we get to have counsel?" Will asked.

"You're a lawyer, Will. You'll do fine. But, sadly, not fine enough."

"Judge? Jury?" I asked.

"At your service. And chief executioner, I might add." He bowed.

Chapter Sixty-Five

Neither Will nor I got much sleep that night. Mostly we talked.

After Tomlinson, Mitch, and the other agent left, locking the door behind them, Will and I looked at each other in horror.

"Well, this sucks," he said, then gave me an impish grin. "Do you want to work on Rose's biography?"

I snorted, then walked to the table, grabbed two wooden chairs by their backs and dragged them across the floor to the sink.

"What are you doing?"

"Let's talk." I turned on the faucet and the garbage disposal. "A little white noise," I explained.

As the water hissed and the disposal growled, Will took a seat in one of the chairs and I sat facing him in the other.

"We should whisper, just to be safe," I began.

"Okay."

"How are you really?" I asked.

"Really? I'm okay. I'm even better now that you're here. But it pisses me off that you've gotten dragged into this." He nodded toward the front door. "I could wring that bastard's neck."

I brought Will up to date on how I was able to smuggle Grace and Thomas out of the White House and safely to Lionel and Muriel's. "Octavia and the children were magnificent," I said.

Tears filled Will's eyes. "Thank you," he managed to say.

I told him about Tomlinson's Oval Office declaration of martial law and my impromptu address to the nation from Black Lives Matter Plaza.

"Good for you," Will said, beaming.

I also filled him in on the next day's Oval Office interview with Tomlinson conducted by Roland Roberts. "Tomlinson seems to have a lock on control of all the levers of government and a plan to rule by fiat," I said.

"Amazing," Will breathed. "But there must be at least pockets of resistance."

I nodded slowly. "I hope so. But the confusion within the military chain of command brought about by Senator Carmichael's hold on promotions seems to have worked to the advantage of the coup."

Will nodded.

"How about you?" I asked. "What happened after I saw Tomlinson take you away?

"I was whisked to a private jet at Reagan National Airport and we were airborne within minutes of my arrest." He looked around. "Where am I, anyway?"

"You're . . . *we're* . . . at a remote redoubt just outside Coeur d'Alene."

"Idaho?"

"Yup."

"Wow. I'm *way* off the grid. No wonder the military hasn't been able to launch a rescue effort. They don't know where I am."

"They do now, though."

He raised his eyebrows. "How?"

I told him about Dorothy, her dad, and our cross-country trek based on my hunch that he was out here, and our discovery of the redoubt when we'd followed Nora. "Before Dorothy's dad turned me in, I was able to tip off General Jackson, so there's every reason to believe help is on the way," I concluded.

"Yeah. I hope so, but I don't want to get our hopes up too high. She's a capable leader but rescuing us will be no slam dunk."

"Why not?"

"She still has to determine who she can trust to carry out a rescue plan."

"Uh-huh."

"Traitors can be brutal, as you well know."

I rubbed my still-sore jaw. "Yeah. I know."

We were silent a moment as the white noise of the running water and groaning garbage disposal continued.

"How are we going to get out of this, Will?"

He rubbed his chin. "I don't know that we will."

"You're not giving up, are you?"

"Hell no."

"We have to resist."

"Agreed."

"But how?"

"Well, telling Tomlinson to go fuck himself was a great start."

I blushed. "Thank you."

"But I don't recommend that as a defense on national television."

"Yeah. You're probably right, but it sure felt good."

Will stood and paced a bit before returning to his chair across from me at the sink.

"Do you have a plan?" I asked.

He shook his head. "Not yet. Do you?"

"I think it's safe to say we're not gonna be able to break outta here."

"Agreed. You didn't bring a gun, did you?" His tone was mock chiding.

"I hate guns."

"Me too."

"But admit it—in your day job you had nukes."

"True. Busted."

"Seriously, though, I do see a couple reasons to have hope."

"I'm listening." He leaned closer.

Chapter Sixty-Six

Neither of us slept much, but we both tried in separate bedrooms across the hall from each other.

Bright sunlight was coming through the window when I was rousted from sleep by a gruff female Secret Service agent.

"Wake up," she commanded. "Put this on." She held out the folded orange jumpsuit I'd meticulously been able to ignore.

Agent Mitch stood at my bedroom door, AR-15 at the ready.

"A little privacy, please," I snarled.

The agent turned and nodded at Mitch who backed out of view.

I threw off the thin blanket and swung my bare feet to the floor.

While the female agent watched, I shed my hoodie and jeans and stepped into the jumpsuit that was at least one size too large. *Federal Prisoner* was stenciled on the back.

Satisfied that I'd complied with her order, the agent walked to the door and turned to look at me. "Breakfast is on the table out there." She nodded toward the living area.

"Thanks. What's your name?" I tried, for once, to sound friendly.

She hesitated and her demeanor softened for just an instant. "Angela." Then her tone hardened, "but that's none of your fucking business."

"C'mon, Angela. You're better than this." But my words were fruitless. She was already walking away.

Before heading down the hall, I stopped outside Will's room and knocked on the door jamb. "You up?"

"Yeah," came a muffled response.

I feigned a snooty tone: "I'm told breakfast is served in the dining area."

"Be right there."

"I'm gonna make a pitstop first."

"Okay."

There was no door to the bathroom, so I did my best to make it quick and quiet, then headed to the main room.

Will used the bathroom next. The sound of him urinating drifted all the way down the hall. Moments later, he joined me at the table. He looked haggard, not presidential.

Breakfast consisted of a runny pile of ersatz scrambled eggs and a piece of white toast (no butter) on paper plates with plastic forks and two bottles of spring water.

In the roughly two minutes it took to eat, our breakfast banter consisted of, "How'd you sleep?" and "Okay, I guess."

If the digital clock on the stove could be believed, it was eight o'clock in the morning. We still had another four hours to kill before we went on trial.

While I bused the table and put our detritus in a garbage bag beneath the sink, Will picked up the Bible and began turning pages.

"The Bible," I said cleverly. "Did you see the movie?"

He smiled. "The book is better."

"Got a favorite passage?"

"Lots of 'em."

"Pick one."

He pawed at the pages until he found what he was looking for and began reading out loud. "I am convinced that neither death nor life, neither angels nor demons, neither the present nor the future, nor any powers, neither height nor depth, nor anything else in all creation will ever be able to separate us from the love of God that is revealed in Christ Jesus our Lord."

"Wow. Where'd you find that?"

"Romans 8:38." He looked at the spine. "New International Version."

"How'd you know where to find it so quickly?"

"When I was a kid in Sunday School, we had what were called 'sword drills.'"

"What's that?"

"In my church, the Bible was called 'the sword of the Lord,' so we were trained in scripture memory and how to look things up fast. We'd stand against the wall, each of us with a Bible in our hand. The teacher would call out a verse and the first person to turn to it won. Sword drill."

I laughed.

"Corny, huh?"

"Yeah. Maybe. But it came in handy today, of all days. What denomination did you grow up in?"

"Southern Baptist."

I winced.

He picked up on my body language right away. "I know. I'm not as rigidly dogmatic as I used to be as a kid, but there's still a lot of comfort and wisdom in the good book." He hefted it for emphasis. "What about you?" he asked.

"Episcopalian," I said simply.

"Did any of it stick?"

"I love the music."

He nodded.

"Kris, my grief counselor, gave me some mindfulness literature to read when I first started meeting with her after Doug died. It came in handy after I was kidnapped. Now, instead of an Episcopalian, I call myself a Buddha-palian."

He laughed, then turned serious. "It's none of my business, but do you believe in God?"

I nodded. "I think so. But sometimes I wonder if He—or She—believes in me. What about you?"

"Absolutely. No doubt."

"But *what* do you believe?"

"Oh, that's complicated. Seems like the more words a person uses to describe God, the smaller God becomes until He—" he nodded deferentially toward me, "or She—is reduced to the confines of a small box."

"Did you ever consider going into the ministry?"

"Yeah, actually. When I was a teenager, the pastor gave a sermon entitled, 'You Ought to Become a Pastor."

"Really?"

"Pretty subtle, right?"

"Geez. Kinda manipulative. What'd you do?"

"The pastor said, 'If you think I'm talking to you, come see me.'"

"Did you?"

Will nodded. "At that age, I rarely paid attention to the sermon, but that one really did seem like it was directed at me. I went to see him, fully expecting he was going to pressure me to sign on the dotted line."

"Did he?"

"Surprisingly, no. He confirmed my hunch that he was directing his comments at me, but he just said, 'Pray about it and see what God says.'"

"What did God say?"

Will laughed. "The pastor's comment got my attention because I didn't think God said anything."

"Did you pray about it?"

"Yes. But my prayer was, 'Look, God. I want to be a lawyer and run for president. I really don't want to go into the ordained ministry. What do you think?'"

"And what did God say?"

"Nothing. Or at least nothing in so many words. But, again, the Bible helped give me some clarity."

"How so?"

Will opened the Bible again and quickly turned to the page he was searching for. "Here it is: 'Delight yourself in the Lord and God will give you the desires of your heart.'"

"And apparently God did."

"Absolutely. God gave me a wonderful woman in Rose and a successful career in politics. My prayer was a simple declaration of the desire of my heart. And it came to be."

"Lemme see that." I reached for the Bible.

Will handed it to me and pointed at the verse in Psalm 37.

"Look," I said excitedly. "It goes on to say, 'Commit your way to the Lord; trust in Him. He will bring forth your righteousness like the dawn, your justice like the noonday sun.'" I looked at Will. "Our trial's at noon." I continued reading. "'Do not fret when men prosper in their ways, when they carry out wicked schemes.'"

Will pulled his chair next to mine and I pointed at the line.

"'Do not fret,'" Will read, "'it can only bring harm.'"

I read the next verse out loud. "'For the evildoers will be cut off, but those who hope in the Lord will inherit the land.'"

We got into the rhythm of each taking a turn reading a verse out loud. When we got to the end, my heart was racing.

Me: "'Though the wicked lie in wait for the righteous, and seek to slay them . . . .'"

Will: "'. . . the Lord will not let them be condemned.'"

Me: "'Wait for the Lord and keep His way, and He will raise you up to inherit the land.'"

Slowly, Will closed the Bible and looked at me. His eyes were gleaming with tears.

Mine were, too. Tears of hope.

Just then, we heard the key clatter in the lock. When the door opened, Angela and Mitch entered, both carrying a set of handcuffs and leg irons, chains jangling.

Chapter Sixty-Seven

The cold metal of the chains chafed my wrists and ankles. Angela cuffed my hands close together in front of my waist. The chain stretching between my feet was only a few inches in length so I could barely walk, only shuffle.

A longer chain, attached to the shackles between our feet, stretched between Will and me and bound us together, making it even more difficult to maneuver—or run away.

As Mitch knelt to complete the task of binding my leg irons to Will's, the president tried to engage his former bodyguard.

"Mitch. Don't let Tomlinson get to you, man. You're not obeying lawful orders. You know better."

The muscles in Mitch's jaw tightened, but he said nothing.

When Will and I emerged from the cabin, the bright sun made me squint. The sweet scent of pine trees was almost overpowering. I breathed in the smell as deeply as I could.

We shuffled in tandem across the dusty courtyard toward the log cabin where the day before I'd seen the Rather Communications van. To my right, embedded in the dirt a few feet in front of a plywood wall, I saw two wooden posts, each about six feet high.

Is that where we'll be shot? I wondered.

Will and I shuffled into the "courtroom" which was actually another log cabin with a floorplan identical to the cabin where Will and I were being held.

The room was brightly lit for television and two cameras were positioned on the right side of the room. Behind each were uniformed members of the military. I presumed they were from the American Forces Radio & Television Service (AFRTS).

One of the cameras focused on us as we entered the room; the other was pointed at Charles Tomlinson, wearing his bemedaled dress blues. He stood at attention behind a podium with the presidential seal affixed to the front.

As we shuffled into the room, our leg irons scraping against the wood floor, Mitch grasped Will by the left elbow while Angela gripped my right elbow. They guided us to two straight-backed wooden chairs at a table facing the podium, a single microphone perched on the center of the table.

The room was warm and deathly still, almost solemn. I presumed the event was being broadcast live to the rest of the nation—and the world.

Neither Will nor I had any idea what to expect, other than a sham trial of false allegations.

Once Will and I were seated—still shackled—Tomlinson picked up a small gavel and rapped it.

The suddenness of the sound made me flinch.

"This proceeding is now in order," Tomlinson announced.

I sensed Will stiffen as he sat up straight in his chair and rested his manacled hands in front of him on the table.

"Will Gannon, you are charged with treason. How do you plead?"

"Absolutely, positively not guilty." Will's voice was strong, and he spoke slowly and deliberately. "And for the record, I have not been provided with counsel, something that used to be a fundamental right in the United States of America."

Tomlinson turned his attention to me. "Lark Chadwick. You are charged with kidnapping and seeking to overthrow my government. How do you plead?"

"Take a breath," Will whispered to me, his lips barely moving.

I took his advice. The pause allowed me to gather my thoughts rather than to follow my initial instinct which would have been to tell Tomlinson on live television to go fuck himself. Instead, I said, "I have nothing to say to you." I then spat in his direction.

"Charming, as always," Tomlinson said.

The guy operating the camera off to my right chuckled.

"Now, then," Tomlinson continued, "the charges against you both carry the death penalty."

I leaned toward the mic. "And yet you claim to be pro-life."

Tomlinson glared at me. "You will speak when spoken to, Miss Chadwick."

"It's *Mizz* Chadwick, you pompous prick."

Will nudged me gently with his right leg. "Careful," he whispered.

Part of me knew Will was wise and right. But the anger and indignation I felt were so strong, I was having a struggle keeping my roiling emotions in check.

In that instant I was reminded of times when I used to play tennis. Tennis is as much a psychological battle as it is a physical one. Sometimes when I'd blow an easy shot, I'd get angry at myself and at the situation. Other times, I'd dig deeper and my silent resolve would result in a measured recalibration of my game. Often choosing that route resulted in a comeback and a victory.

But it was the times that I gave full rein to my anger that my cussing became self-defeating, and I'd end up losing the match.

The stakes now were much higher than a game of tennis.

Get a grip, Lark, I said sternly to myself.

Amazingly, Tomlinson ignored my insult and continued. For the next thirty minutes, Tomlinson presented what he called "evidence" of our crimes.

I had to admit, the evidence was compelling. Perhaps the most damning evidence against Will was the recording of the phone conversation between him and the Chinese president. It was clearly Will's voice on the tape, but he would never have said what it sounded like he was saying.

When asked for his response, Will, his face crimson, but his voice steely and controlled, replied: "What you have just played is Artificial Intelligence at its most nefarious. You have used so-called deepfake technology to take my voice and have me say things I have never—and would never—say, all to serve your own evil and selfish agenda."

The "evidence" against me included the moment during my Zoom news conference in which little Thomas Gannon had burst into the room, his image captured briefly behind me, "proof," Tomlinson said, that I had spirited the Gannon children out of the White House.

I was also stunned when Tomlinson played a video of Will and me sitting at the sink the night before, our heads nearly touching as I was bringing him up to date on what had been happening in the country after his arrest.

Even though no microphone would have been able to overhear our conversation because of the white noise of the running water and garbage disposal, an A.I. rendition of my voice had me telling Will, "I took our children to a safe place and once I'm able to overthrow Tomlinson, you and I can be together."

When Tomlinson asked for my response, I stood.

Angela, who had been standing off to the side, moved closer to make sure I wouldn't do something violent.

"All I can say is that you have a lot of nerve to present evidence against me," I nodded toward Will, "against *us* that is a manipulated and manufactured mishmash of falsehoods. I said nothing remotely like that last night and purposely ran the garbage disposal and the water so our voices wouldn't be picked up by the secret recording devices you planted in that room. You *should* be ashamed, but you obviously have *no* shame."

I sat, breathing hard.

"The defendants will stand to hear the judgment of this court."

"This kangaroo court," I muttered as Angela took me by the arm and lifted me to my feet.

With Mitch's help, Will stood, too.

"It is the judgment of this court that you, Will Gannon, and you, Lark Chadwick, are guilty of the crimes with which you are charged. Furthermore, at dawn tomorrow, you both will receive the sentence of death by firing squad. Do either of you have any final words?"

Will spoke first. "If this had been a fair trial, I would have addressed you as 'Your Honor.' But you are not an honorable man. You have disgraced your uniform and betrayed the Constitution you once took an oath to defend."

Will turned to face the camera to the right of the podium.

"Instead, I address the American people. You are seeing in real time what the Founders of this country sought to prevent. This country was created to resist and repudiate being ruled by a dictator. The founders put into place a system of government filled with checks and balances so that no one person would be in charge.

"My final word to you, my fellow Americans, is to take back your government. Resist being ruled by this man, or by any one person who seeks to make you conform to their will. Bring back 'we the people.'"

"*Miss* Chadwick?"

I directed my remarks at Tomlinson. "I echo everything just articulated by Will Gannon, the duly-elected President of the United States of America. Also, you, *Chuck* Tomlinson, are supposedly pro-life yet you are willing not only to execute me, but also kill what you consider to be my unborn child. What a hypocrite."

Tomlinson flushed, gritted his teeth, but said nothing.

I desperately wanted to raise my two middle fingers in a fuck-you salute. Instead, I, too, turned to the camera.

"It's entirely possible that Will Gannon and I will die at dawn tomorrow. All I can do is to call on the millions of good and decent people who I'm sure are still out there to find a way to replace tyranny with Democracy."

In a moment of inspiration, I added: "We are being held in a secluded redoubt on County Highway M, ten miles northeast of Coeur d'Alene, Idaho."

"Nice try, Miss Chadwick," Tomlinson sneered, "but these proceedings are on a five-second delay."

He pounded the gavel. It sounded like a gunshot.

Chapter Sixty-Eight

Our trial was over in less than an hour. As Charles Tomlinson stood at attention behind the podium, Mitch and Angela escorted us from the room.

The only sound was the chain linking us together dragging against the wooden floor as we trudged to the door and back into the sunlight of an Idaho afternoon.

It felt good to be out of the claustrophobic confines of our cabin courtroom. Even though I was choking back tears, I lifted my head to the tops of the pine trees that encircled the clearing of our redoubt. The forest was alive with the sounds of birds, including a couple crows cawing as they circled high above us.

The sentry standing at the door to our cabin-prison opened it for Mitch and Angela who led us into the room. Once inside, the door closed behind us and our two Secret Service captors uncuffed and unshackled us, neither of them speaking.

Once again, Will tried to appeal to Mitch's sense of duty and patriotism.

"Mitch. Thank you for your service to me and our country. I've enjoyed getting to know you during our travels. I know you're a patriotic young man. I honestly don't get why you've allowed yourself to be used by Tomlinson. Can you help me understand?"

Mitch ignored the president and turned to Angela. "You done?"

"Just about," she said.

"Angela," I tried. "I don't understand, either, how you could let yourself get sucked into doing what you're doing. Don't you see that Tomlinson is overthrowing Democracy? Don't you care?"

Angela stood from where she'd been crouched at my feet taking off my leg irons. She pulled a cell phone from her back pocket. Looking back and forth between Will and me, she said, "You each have five minutes to place a goodbye call to a loved one."

I reached for the phone, but she held on to it.

"What's the number?" she asked.

I gave her Lionel's number, she dialed it, then put the call on speaker while she continued to hold the phone.

"Hi, Lionel." My voice felt puny.

"Lark!" Both surprise and elation were in his voice.

"Before you say anything else, I want you to know that our guards are listening. This is NOT a private call."

"Got it."

"Is Muriel there?"

"I'm right here, Lark," she said. "It's so good to hear your voice."

"Were you watching?" I asked.

"Oh yeah," Lionel said. "I don't care if Tomlinson's listening to this call. You nailed him by calling him a pompous prick. You go."

"Thanks." I was already sniffling. A torrent of tears would not be far behind. "I suppose you know why I'm calling."

"Yeah. I suppose," Lionel said, his voice husky.

"I don't believe in goodbyes, Lark," Muriel cut in. "You stay strong."

"I'm trying, Muriel, but this might be the end of the line."

"Nonsense," Lionel said. "Yogi Berra was right: it ain't over 'til it's over."

I chuckled. "Well, just in case it *is* over, I want to say what you probably already know."

"Yeah," Lionel said.

"I love you guys."

"We love you, too, Lark," Muriel said.

"I remember the first day I met you two. Muriel, you were so warm and welcoming. And Lionel, you were so . . . so . . . *scary.*"

He laughed. "It's my most endearing quality. It took a long time to cultivate, I'll have you know."

"I just want to thank you for everything. You've both always been there for me. Always. You're the parents I never knew."

I couldn't go on. The only sound coming from the phone was heavy breathing and sighing as they both came to grips with their emotions.

"I need to go, but I want you to know that tomorrow morning, just as the sun is coming up, I'll be thinking of you both. I love you guys."

"We love you, Lark," Muriel said.

"Yeah," Lionel managed.

Angela ended the call, then turned to Will.

"May I have privacy?" he asked.

"No, sir," Angela said. "You may call anyone you wish, but I'll hold the phone and they will be on speaker."

Will gave her the number and, in a moment, Octavia was on the line.

"Octavia."

"Mr. President. It is so good to hear your voice."

"Are the children there?"

"Yessir. I will get them."

"Before you do that, I want you to know that this is not a secure line. People are listening. Do you understand?"

"Yessir."

During the pause while Octavia went to find Grace and Thomas, Will looked at me, smiled, and wiggled his eyebrows, a gesture I interpreted as *Let's hope the kids don't make a mistake and give away that they're with Lionel and Muriel.*

Octavia spoke again, but her voice was muffled. I presumed she had her hand over the phone, telling the Gannon children not to give away their secret location. Then she was back on the line.

"Here they are, Mr. President."

"Hi, Daddy," Grace hollered.

"Hi, Dad," shouted Thomas.

I glanced at Will. He was struggling to remain composed. Clearly, his children didn't know this would be their last conversation, but Will knew, and it was tearing him up inside. I, too, wished I could say something to the two children I'd come to cherish. But this was Will's precious time with them. I backed away to give him space, even as Mitch and Angela hovered.

"Hi, guys," Will began. "How are you doing?"

I held my breath. Would they blunder into revealing who they were with?

Octavia spoke, "We've been having fun playing, haven't we, children?"

"Oh, yes!" Grace gushed.

"I have something to tell you," Will said. "I want you to listen very carefully. Can you do that?"

"Yes," Thomas said.

"I'm going to be going away for a very long time. I don't really want to, but I have to."

"Where are you going?" Grace asked.

"It's a secret place far away."

"When will you be back?" Thomas asked.

"I-I don't know," Will said, his voice breaking. "B-but I want you to know that I love you v-very very much and I'll be thinking about you all the time I'm gone."

"We miss you, Daddy," Grace said. "And we miss Lark, too."

"And we miss Mommy," Thomas added.

"Before I go," Will said, "I have something very important to tell each of you, okay?"

"Okay, Daddy," Grace said. "We're listening. Thomas! Put that down. Daddy has something very important to say."

"I'm listening," Thomas said defensively.

Will took a deep breath, then continued. "I want you both to always tell the truth."

"Okay," Thomas said.

"Also," Will went on, "always be kind to other people."

"What does kind mean?" Thomas asked.

Grace said, "It means to be nice and to do good things for other people."

"That's right," Will said. "Very good. Thank you, Grace."

"What else, Daddy? This is fun talking to you." Grace said.

"I love you," Will said.

"You already said that," Thomas said.

Will laughed. "Yeah. I guess I did, but I love you so much, I had to say it two times."

Thomas giggled.

"I have something to say to you specifically, Grace, honey."

"Okay. I'm listening."

"Your mommy and I always tried our best to guide you so that as you get older, you'd learn to know yourself really, really well. I want you to do your best to, to . . . ." His voice faltered and he looked around for me. When he saw me, he gestured for me to come closer.

"Help me out here," Will said to me.

I leaned closer to the phone. "Hi, Grace."

"Hello, Miss Lark."

"I think what your daddy is trying to say is to be careful that you don't let anyone else tell you to do things that you know deep down are wrong. As you get older, all kinds of people will think they know what's best for you. But, in the end, only *you* get to decide that. Do you understand?"

"I-I *think* so."

"Tell me what you think I just said."

"Well . . . um . . . I think you mean that the better I know what I like and don't like, what I believe, and don't believe, the less I should let people boss me around."

"Exactly," I said.

"How'm I doing?" I asked Will.

"God, you're good," he said under his breath. "Is Thomas still there?" he said into the phone.

"I'm here!" Thomas called.

"I have something special to tell you, too, my big man."

"Okay."

"I want you to understand, Thomas, that girls and women are extra special people."

"Like Grace, and Octavia, and Lark, right?"

"Right. I want you to promise me that you will always, *always* treat them with respect. Do you know what respect means?"

"I think so."

"What do you think it means?" Will asked.

"I think spect is sort of the same thing as special."

"Good," Will said. "So, if a girl like Grace or a woman like Octavia is special, how should you treat them?"

"Like I'm not better'n them."

"Exactly. You got it. Can you do that?"

"Oh sure. That's easy."

"Your time's up, sir," Angela said. Her eyes glistened.

"Okay. I've gotta go, guys. Please take good care of each other. And know this: I will always love you." He was barely able to choke out the last words.

"Bye, Daddy," both children said in unison, with Grace adding, "We love you."

Will turned away from us, walked to a window on the far side of the room, buried his face in his hands, and sobbed.

Chapter Sixty-Nine

As our guards headed to the door to leave, I approached them.

"Angela?"

She stopped and closed her eyes, bracing for another verbal barrage.

"Do you think you could get a couple of yellow legal pads and pens for the president and me so we can write some letters? And a handful of envelopes, too?" I asked.

Her eyes opened and her face relaxed. "Yeah. I'll see."

Then she and Mitch were gone, and Will and I were alone together again.

Both Will and I were too distraught to speak for a while. We spent the next hour or so alone with our thoughts.

After a short while, Will stopped sobbing, but paced back and forth in front of the barred window that looked out at the clearing and trees behind the cabin.

I sat on the sofa, crossed my arms, and took stock of my life.

I'd never known my parents.

The mental problems of Annie, the aunt who'd raised me, had been so profound that I had to be a mother to her.

I grew up feeling like an outcast geek. The sexual assault encounter with Ross, my college English professor, so rattled me that I'd had a difficult time trusting men.

The relationship with Jason ended before it could get off the ground.

Same with Doug. But, with him, I'd made the mistake of trusting a person with a crippling addiction. Consequently, I'd gotten pregnant.

But, by the time I knew I was pregnant, Doug was dead. I'd never know what kind of man—and father—he would have been had he been able to get into recovery and kick heroin.

My thoughts turned to Lionel and Muriel, truly the only two people who brought stability and purpose into my life. As I sat on the sofa, I was grateful that I'd been given the unexpected opportunity to say to them how much they meant to me.

Despite my agnosticism, I found myself praying for them. I kept it simple: *God, thank you for Lionel and Muriel. Please bless and comfort them. They've lost so much. They've been through so much. Please be with them and continue to bring them closer to each other.*

And then there was Will. He now stood defiantly, hands on his hips, looking out the window.

I'd first met him when he was running for president, but it was his wife, Rose, who first connected with me when she gave me an unexpected compliment for the no-nonsense questions I'd asked him after an event in Columbia, Georgia.

I was with Rose when she died. Now I had a strong sense of her presence, and her approval to be her surrogate as a source of encouragement for Will in the last hours of his life.

My reverie was broken by the clicking of the key in the door.

I got up.

The door opened. Angela stepped inside and the guard outside closed the door behind her. She carried a couple yellow legal pads, two stubby pencils, and a handful of envelopes.

"Your request for writing materials has been granted," she said, "but know that any political manifestos will be destroyed. Also know that you are not to seal the envelopes. If you do, they will be opened and the contents scrutinized to make sure they are of a personal, not political, nature."

"Thank you. Is there anything I can say to change your mind about what you are participating in?"

Slowly, she shook her head. "It's too late for that." She paused a nanosecond before adding softly, "I'm sorry."

She then turned on her heel, knocked sharply on the door twice, and exited when it opened.

When Angela left, Will ambled over to me from the window.

"What's up?" he asked.

"I prevailed upon Angela to get us some writing stuff."

"Good idea." He took a pencil and one of the legal pads from me.

We walked over to the wooden table and sat down.

"She gave us a bunch of envelopes, too," I said.

"Do you think I got too preachy with the kids?" His voice was hesitant.

I smiled. "If ever there was a teachable moment, that was it. And what you said was very important."

"But will they remember? Especially Thomas?"

"That's why I asked Angela for the extra envelopes."

"What do you mean?"

"I suggest you write age-appropriate letters to Grace and Thomas to be opened on, say, their tenth, fifteenth, and twentieth birthdays. Something like that."

"Ahhhh. I see. Speak to them as if they are that age."

"Exactly."

"I like that. Thank you."

"I don't know if you heard, but Angela said the letters will be scrutinized to make sure they're not political screeds."

"Got it."

We spent the next several hours writing, sitting across from each other at the dining area table.

Will wrote feverishly, without even having to pause to compose his thoughts, they just poured out of him and onto the page.

Lionel and Muriel are the most important people in my life, so I wrote to them. I simply built on the comments of appreciation and love I'd spelled out during our brief phone call.

I then added specific bits of nostalgia and even a few admonitions.

To Lionel, I wrote:

Thank you for being my champion and my journalistic guide. I've learned so much from you. Thank you for being so patient with me. You were always there for me.

I'm especially proud of you for owning your alcoholism and turning your life around. As you do, I urge you to continue to listen to and love Muriel. She knows you better than anyone else, yet she loves you anyway. ☺

To Muriel I wrote:

In my letter to Lionel, I ordered him to listen to you. Here's hoping he does because he should. You're wise and wonderful and loving. You were there for me when I lost Annie, then Jason, and finally Doug. Thank you for being my rock.

I wish I could be there for you now. But I pray that God will provide you with surrogate children and grandchildren to love.

I remember that you once told me that you see your life as an artist's canvas. Rather than destroying it when something ugly, or unwanted, appears, you "paint over it" and try again. Your words guided my life; may they now continue to guide yours.

Long after I'd finished writing my letters to Lionel and Muriel, Will was still busy writing to the older incarnations of Grace and Thomas.

I got up from the table and lay down on the sofa to ruminate, and to take a power nap.

It was getting dark when the sound of the key in the door woke me up. Mitch and Angela entered with what amounted to our last supper. Nothing special, just thin soup.

I only took a couple spoonfuls, but Will wolfed his and the rest of mine when I pushed my bowl over to him. Immediately, however, I felt queasy and had to make a quick dash to the bathroom to throw up what little was in my stomach.

"You okay?" he asked when I returned.

"Yeah. Hormones. It's a pregnancy thing."

He nodded, and finished eating in silence, decompressing from all the time he'd spent pouring his heart onto the page, but as the darkness outside became complete, we migrated over to the sofa and sat next to each other.

An omnipresent single garish light glowed from the ceiling, illuminating the room for the benefit of the security cameras keeping an eye on us.

Will spoke first. "Well, this is it, I guess."

"Yeah. I guess."

"How are you doing?"

I sighed. "Even though I've cheated death more than once, I always thought I'd live a longer life. I'm not ready for it to be over."

He nodded.

"What about you? How are you?" I asked.

"Coming to accept my fate."

"Are you giving up without a fight?"

He shook his head. "I've said what I needed to say. It's out of my control now."

I thought about this, then nodded when something inside seemed to click. "Yes. I know what you mean."

"How so?"

"In these last few hours, there's a certain, I don't know, a certain grace in being able to contemplate one's mortality."

"What have you learned?"

"I've learned that I've been very blessed. There was a time when I almost killed myself."

"Really?"

"Yeah. I came close. But I'm glad I didn't go through with it."

"Why? When? What happened?"

I waved a hand. "The details aren't important. At the time, the pain was too much. I had tunnel vision. I couldn't see what I see now. Lionel and Muriel helped me have hope."

"Do you still have hope?"

I laughed. "Not for myself anymore. I don't see how in the hell I'm gonna get out of this one." I turned to look at Will. "What about you? Hope?"

He snorted. "Not for me. But I still have hope that somehow the grownups will prevail, and Democracy will be restored. But for myself personally? No. This is it. It's over."

"Why am I not hearing despair in your voice?"

"Because I'm resigned to my fate."

"Aren't you afraid?"

"Woody Allen said it best: 'I'm not afraid to die; I just don't want to be there when it happens.'"

I laughed, then turned serious. "But a firing squad. That's grim."

"Only for an instant. I've heard it's painless. Death is just a sting and then it's over."

"What do you think happens next, after you die?"

He chuckled. "Getting metaphysical on me, huh? Always the curious reporter."

"It's not an idle question, Will."

He sighed and thought a minute. "I don't know, Lark. I really don't know."

"Heaven?"

"Sure. I'd like to think so, but I don't know what that would mean." He turned to me. "What about you?"

"I don't know either. I do think our spirit goes on, though."

"Yeah. Me too."

"Maybe it's wishful thinking, but maybe I'll meet my parents."

"For me, Rose will be there, I hope."

"What about God?"

"Sure," he said. "Why not? But this is all speculation. We'll find out soon enough. And I mean *really* soon. I'd love to sit down with Jesus and have a conversation with him."

"Oh yeah. That would be cool. I've got soooooo many questions for him."

"I think he'd be your toughest interview."

"Why?"

"Because in no time, he'd turn the tables and get you talking. I bet he's such a skillful questioner that without even realizing it, you'd be answering your own questions for yourself."

"Huh. I'll have to think about that."

As we talked, without realizing it, we'd both inched closer to each other. It no longer felt to me that he was The President. He now just felt like My Close Friend Will.

It goes without saying that I'd always been physically attracted to him. But so had just about every woman in the world. In the days after Rose died, I felt that he and I had a certain electrical energy connecting us. If he felt it, too—and I believe he did—he never acted on it. And neither did I. Our mutual and recent losses were still too fresh.

But this moment felt different—at least for me.

Then Will turned to me and smiled.

Chapter Seventy

In that instant, I wanted to press my hands against the side of his face, pull him toward me, and kiss him passionately, hungrily, on the lips.

The impulsive Lark would have done that. But that was the old me.

Will leaned toward me, but he went for the top of my head, not my lips. He kissed me, then put his arm around me.

I leaned against him and took one of his hands in mine.

He sighed deeply.

I did, too.

"I'm glad I met you, Lark Chadwick."

"Same here, Will Gannon."

There was nothing more to say.

* * *

I was dozing against Will's chest, his arm still around me, when the sound of the key in the door behind us woke me up.

"It's time," Mitch announced loudly.

Will's body twitched as he awakened. He took his arm from around my shoulder and sat up straight.

Mitch and Angela walked around the sofa and into view carrying our shackles.

Will said, "I'm not going to plead for my life, Mitch, but I'm appealing to you to save your soul."

Mitch winced but, hands trembling, began fiddling silently with Will's cuffs and chains.

"Angela," I tried, "It's still not too late. You and Mitch can put an end to this."

"That would be suicidal," she hissed.

"Don't speak to them," Mitch spat.

Their task complete, Mitch and Angela brought us to our feet."

"I've got to pee," I said to Angela.

"Tough," Mitch said.

"No. Really. I'm not stalling. I've really gotta go." My voice was earnest. "It's been a thing ever since I got pregnant."

"I assure you," Mitch growled, "two minutes from now it won't be a *thing* anymore."

They led us away from the sofa.

Through the open door, I could see that the dirt courtyard was bathed in white light. A single snare drummer tapped a dirge-like beat.

When we got to the threshold, I saw that television lights were illuminating the scene. A camera sat atop a tripod in front of the door of the cabin where our trial had been held the day before. The camera was trained on Will and me as we emerged from our captivity.

Faint streaks of peach sunlight painted the clouds.

The snare drummer, in an Army uniform, stood to our right and I found myself involuntarily falling into step with his slow, rhythmic tattoos.

Will stood tall, his jaw set defiantly as he looked first at the camera and then toward the posts in front of the plywood wall where we'd be shot.

When I saw the posts, my knees buckled, and I faltered.

Angela's grip on my right elbow was strong and kept me from falling to my knees.

"Be strong," Will said under his breath.

Intense emotions were surging inside me. I felt my jaw tremble uncontrollably. Sobs were struggling to get out, but I gritted my teeth and kept them inside.

I took a deep breath. Then another. That helped.

As the drummer continued his measured cadence of rolls and staccato strokes, we trudged toward the execution posts, our chains clinking.

Charles Tomlinson stood at attention and had the nerve to salute as we came closer.

Another camera off to my right focused on the wooden posts.

Mitch led Will to the post on my right and Angela led me to the other one. They positioned us with our backs against the wood. We were close enough to each other that the chain between our leg irons didn't need to be removed.

At least in death we'll still be connected to each other, I thought ruefully.

In a ritual Mitch and Angela must have practiced, they simultaneously uncuffed us, then re-handcuffed us with our arms looped around the posts behind us.

I've never felt more helpless, hopeless, or vulnerable. My legs were rubbery.

I glanced at Will. His face was defiant. He glared at Tomlinson, jaw muscles tensing.

When they were finished handcuffing us to the posts, Mitch and Angela used safety pins to affix huge white paper circles onto our orange jumpsuits in front of our hearts.

Angela's head was so close to me I could smell her shampoo. Her fingers fumbled with the safety pin and she accidentally jabbed her finger.

"Ouch," she said under her breath.

Meanwhile, a squad of four uniformed riflemen marched two-by-two from behind the courtroom cabin and took a position spread out next to each other about twenty-five yards from Will and me.

The enlisted men carried bolt-action rifles. Their faces were impassive. Each wore a uniform of a different branch of service. The Marine and Army representatives stood opposite Will.

Apparently, I would be killed by representatives of the Air Force and Navy.

When everyone was in place, the drumming came to a sudden stop.

The only sound was of the riotous chirping of birds in the trees surrounding the clearing.

The sky was lightening, but had it not been for the television lights, the clearing would still be dark.

I wondered if Lionel and Muriel were watching. Something told me they were, despite their revulsion at what was going on.

Charles Tomlinson was about to make an example out of Will and me. A sobering message to the country about the fatal consequences of standing against his authority.

Mitch and Angela, who'd been standing at attention flanking us when the execution team assembled, now each extracted a single cigarette and lighter from their pockets.

"Cigarette?" Mitch said to Will.

"No thank you," Will smirked, "it's bad for my health."

I smiled. His quip helped me relax a little. I merely shook my head at Angela's proffered smoke.

Mitch and Angela pocketed the cigarettes and lighters, then whipped blindfolds from their suitcoat pockets, but before Angela could move behind me to put it around my head, I stopped her.

"Don't bother," I said in a loud voice.

"Same," Will said to Mitch.

They pocketed the blindfolds and returned to their positions ten yards on either side of Will and me.

Charles Tomlinson walked stiffly, formally, to a place to the left of the line of executioners, a spot where the camera would easily be able to focus on him.

"Will Gannon, you have been found guilty of treason and are to die by firing squad. Do you have any last words?"

Will spoke in a strong, firm voice: "May God have mercy on the *United* States of America." I could see his breath in the early morning chill.

Tomlinson turned to me. "Lark Chadwick. Your plea that I would extend mercy to your unborn child has touched my heart. Therefore, I am delaying your execution until after your child is born."

My jaw dropped.

"However," Tomlinson continued, "you are hereby ordered to be a witness to Will Gannon's execution as a lesson in how my government deals with traitors."

Tomlinson nodded at Angela who quickly unlocked the chain linking my feet to Will's.

"None of this is right," I shouted.

Angela unshackled me from the post, then re-cuffed my hands in front of me.

I made eye contact with the president. His face was a mix of surprise and horror.

"Be strong, Will," I said as Angela pulled me off to the side.

Tomlinson turned to the riflemen. "Gentlemen, at my command."

The snare drummer began a sharp, sustained roll.

"Ready!" Tomlinson shouted.

All four riflemen brought their weapons to their shoulders, barrels pointed at Will.

He turned to look at me. "I love you," he said.

"Aim!"

Will turned to the guns to face his fate.

Chapter Seventy-One

"Oh, God," I whispered and jammed my eyes shut.

KABOOM

My body convulsed. My knees buckled. My ears were ringing.

I opened my eyes.

Will was slumped in a heap at the base of the wooden pole, but the riflemen had dropped their weapons. Two of the men had fallen to their knees, the other two were staggering, disoriented.

Charles Tomlinson had his hands at his ears. He, too, appeared to be confused.

The ringing in my ears obliterated all other sounds, but movement above Tomlinson caught my eye.

Heavily armed paratroopers were rappelling down ropes attached to a helicopter hovering about forty yards above Tomlinson.

Will began to stir and was trying to sit up. I saw no blood. He appeared to be uninjured, but dazed.

Mitch and Angela were also on the ground, incapacitated, not dead but thrashing about in agitated agony.

Gradually, the ringing in my ears subsided and I could begin to hear unintelligible shouting.

In the distance, I heard gunfire coming from where I presumed additional paratroopers were engaged in a firefight with the Secret Service agents guarding the front gate.

Charles Tomlinson began to reach for his sidearm in the black holster at his hip, but before he could draw his weapon, a paratrooper threw him to the ground, tossed the weapon aside, and zip-tied his hands behind his back.

A volley of tracer bullets from the hovering helicopter found their mark on a perimeter guard I hadn't seen before. The soldier had just begun to regain his wits after the flash-bang stun grenade had gone off. Just as he was taking aim at the helicopter, the bullets tore through him causing him to writhe and fall.

Four paratroopers rushed toward Will. Two of them disarmed and zip-tied Mitch and Angela before they could resist. The third used bolt cutters to sever Will's handcuffs and leg irons while the fourth veered toward me and did the same.

They then hurried us to a position beneath the chopper.

Additional paratroopers were flooding into the clearing from all sides, their weapons at the ready.

I could now hear the whir and feel the downdraft from the helicopter hovering above the clearing.

A paratrooper grabbed one of the ropes dangling from the chopper, clipped it to the harness he wore, gave a thumbs up, then enveloped Will in a gigantic bear hug.

As a winch in the helicopter hoisted Will and the paratrooper off the ground, the other paratrooper secured me in the same way. In a moment, I, too, found myself being lifted above the chaos below.

From my vantage point in the helicopter, my last view of the redoubt below revealed a swarm of paratroopers in the brightly lit clearing rounding up and securing the remainder of those who had been loyal to Tomlinson.

I caught sight of a paratrooper bringing Nora out of the courtroom cabin, her hands tied behind her back.

Then the motor revved and the chopper whisked Will and me away to safety.

Chapter Seventy-Two

The next morning, newly-restored President of the United States Will Gannon and I entered the White House briefing room.

Will, now showered and shaved, wore a cool navy-blue suit, crisp powder blue dress shirt, and a blue and white polka dot tie.

I, too, had cleaned up well. My usually wild hair was now behaving, and I wore a dark blue pantsuit over a white blouse and two-inch heels.

The room was standing-room-only jammed. Everyone was on their feet applauding.

"Please be seated," Will said.

I stood next to the podium to Will's right as the reporters with assigned seats sat down. Credentialed reporters crammed both side aisles, standing along the north and south walls, eager to hear what Will and I had to say.

Will began, "I know that it's highly unusual for reporters to applaud a president. I take it that you are showing your appreciation for our survival," he gestured toward me, "but not necessarily approval of my policies."

Several reporters laughed and nodded.

"I'm sure we'll be back to the traditional—and inevitable—adversarial relationship in no time. But thank you just the same for your warm welcome."

As Will spoke, I scanned the faces in the room. Thankfully, Roland Roberts was nowhere to be found.

"Mr. President?" The voice belonged to the Associated Press correspondent who now occupied the front-row center chair Paul Stone and I once took turns sitting in. I pursed my lips, missing my old friend.

Will nodded and the reporter continued. "What have you been able to learn about the extent of the coup and how it was able to be carried out?"

"We're still sorting out those details, but here's what we know so far: Charles Tomlinson, the former chairman of the Joint Chiefs of Staff, had been able to take advantage of the turmoil in the military caused by some conservative members of Congress. Those Senators—and they were men—opposed abortion rights for members of the armed forces and were stalling what would otherwise have been routine promotions. The result was confusion in the ranks and in the chain of command.

"Apparently, several of my policies incensed General Tomlinson including my naming of Air Force General Mildred Jackson, a gay African American woman to a seat on the Joint Chiefs. Lark's friendship with General Jackson ultimately led to our rescue, but I'll let Lark tell that part of the story in a minute."

Will turned to look at me briefly and I smiled at him.

"It turns out," Will continued, "that General Tomlinson was of the delusional belief that America was founded to be a White and Christian nation. Over the years, as he saw what he believed to be those values replaced—" here Will raised an index finger and pointed for emphasis, "and the operative word is 'replaced'—by people of diverse races, religions, and political views, he gradually put into influential positions in the military people who reflected his White Christian Nationalist views."

"How widespread was support within the military, sir, and how was Tomlinson able to succeed?" the reporter asked.

"We're still assessing that but at this point it appears, because of Tomlinson's position as Joint Chiefs Chairman, support for the coup was wide—across all branches of service at the top levels—but not necessarily deep. He'd also been able to seed my Secret Service detail with agents sympathetic to his philosophy and cause.

"Tomlinson's coup was able to succeed initially because when I was arrested, I was whisked away to Reagan National Airport, placed on a private jet, and flown to a White Christian Nationalist redoubt in Idaho. Because the U.S. military had no idea where I'd been taken, Constitutional Loyalists within the military were unable to launch a counter-offensive."

"What about other government officials who were in the line of succession? What happened to them?" asked the reporter for *The New York Times*.

"The coup was executed with lightning speed. Amazingly, there was no loss of life. Everyone in the line of succession, from the Vice President,

Speaker of the House, and on down, were immediately and simultaneously, put under house arrest, unable to communicate with the outside world."

One of the network correspondents sitting in the front row on my side of the room turned to me. "Lark, what role did you have in bringing this to an end?"

The president stepped aside and let me stand at the podium. As succinctly as I could, I recounted the events that led me to believe that Will was being held in Idaho, being able to confirm that hunch, and alerting General Jackson to the place where Gannon was being held.

I continued, "Because of the turmoil within the U.S. military, General Jackson contacted her counterpart in the Royal Canadian Air Force. The rescue mission was led by Canada, our NATO ally to the north, by a unit based at Canadian Forces Base Suffield in southeastern, Alberta about 450 miles northeast of Coeur d'Alene, Idaho."

"Mr. President," another correspondent asked, "will you be seeking the death penalty for Charles Tomlinson and the others who were actively involved in the coup?"

"No," Will said firmly, retaking his position behind the podium. "When it comes to the death penalty, I am decidedly pro-life. I believe in mercy, not revenge; justice, but not retribution."

"Lark," the NBC reporter asked me, "on your first day as White House press secretary, you were asked rudely if you were planning to have an abortion. I'll broaden the scope of my question to ask what your personal plans are going forward?"

I stepped to the podium, leaned toward the microphone, paused (a pregnant one), smiled and said, "That's classified."

Epilogue

Charles Tomlinson was tried and convicted of treason. He was also convicted of hiring Cletus Bauer to murder Ron McClain.

FBI investigators found traces of Ron's blood on a hammer in Cletus's Virginia home workshop. The FBI made the connection after I'd told the president about Clete's hammer tattoo, his carpentry business, and that he was an ex-Marine. Bauer, it turns out, had served under Tomlinson in Afghanistan.

They are now serving life-without-parole sentences.

At her trial, Nora Tomlinson's defense was that she was trying to extricate herself from her husband's influence, citing her tip-off to me that Gannon might be in Idaho. That didn't fly with the jury, however, especially when I testified to Nora's lie to me that she was in DC when I saw her on the phone talking to me in Idaho. Her real motive for the tip-off was to smoke me out of hiding.

Nora, along with Secret Service Agents Mitch and Angela, were all convicted of treason, each receiving sentences of up to ten years in prison and ten-thousand-dollar fines.

Bonnie and Cletus were convicted on both federal and state charges of kidnapping. She won't be getting out of prison for at least twenty-five years.

Lionel and Muriel Stone won a five-million-dollar wrongful death suit against Roland Roberts and the Christian Newswire for publishing a false story about their son Paul which led to his death.

The White House Correspondents' Association stripped Roland of his press credentials. The Christian Newswire fired him not long thereafter, then it went out of business when subscriptions dried up.

Last I heard, Roland is having a hard time as a used car salesman in Catawba, Ohio.

A jury found Paul's killer, Arthur Van Doren, not guilty by reason of insanity. He is institutionalized at St. Elizabeth's Hospital in Washington, the same place that treated John Hinkley, the would-be assassin of Ronald Reagan.

Dorothy Rather got a promotion at CBS. She is now a segment producer for "60 Minutes." We've become close friends and meet regularly for coffee. She is estranged from her parents.

Lionel and Muriel are meeting separately with grief counselors at the Wendt Center for Loss and Healing in DC. In addition, Lionel regularly attends AA meetings. Will has designated them as official surrogate grandparents for Grace and Thomas, so L&M are regular visitors to the private residence of the president at the White House.

Will has been working at a frantic pace to shore up relations with Congress and within the military. The DOJ, FBI, and the Judge Advocate General's Corps (JAG)—the justice arm of the U.S. military—have all been working overtime to identify and weed out those people in uniform who actively supported and advanced Tomlinson's coup.

All branches of the military have also intensified their training, empowering members to discern and refuse to carry out unlawful orders.

Sadly, however, Senator Carmichael continues to hold hostage all military promotions until Will agrees that the federal government will no longer pay the travel expenses of personnel who seek to have an abortion in states where the procedure is still legal.

Air Force General Mildred Jackson is the new Chair of the Joint Chiefs of Staff. Will helped persuade enough GOP senators to support her nomination which easily passed the Senate.

Will has also reinstated his mental health emergency. He is working intensively to mobilize everyone in all sectors of the country to find ways to enhance, support, and sustain a society that is mentally, emotionally, and psychologically stable.

As for Rose's decision to have an abortion and keep it a secret? Will believes—and I now agree—that it should not be a part of her biography. "Sure, it would sell a lot of books," Will told me, "but it would also be a violation of her privacy."

As for my plans, that was Item One on the agenda when I met with Kris, my grief counselor.

"I was watching your news briefing with the president this morning," she said as I took my seat in her office. "So, what *are* your plans?"

I positioned the cushions around me on the sofa before I answered.

"Will has convinced me to stay on as press secretary, but only until he finds someone to replace me. He has promised to have someone in place within the next month."

"Then what?"

"Then he and I will continue to work on finishing the book I'm helping him write about Rose."

"What about career plans?"

"For now, I'm liking this ghostwriting gig, but I'm continuing to give serious thought to getting a degree in psychology and maybe going into practice."

"And then there's the elephant in the room," she said, pointing at my baby bump.

"I'm not getting *that* big, am I?" I asked in mock horror.

She laughed. "I'm speaking metaphorically."

I said firmly, "I've decided *not* to have an abortion."

"Okay."

"But I've also decided not to be a single mom."

Kris nodded. "So, that means . . .?"

"Adoption."

"I see." She cupped her chin in her hand and leaned forward. "Tell me more."

"I like the idea of an open, or semi-open adoption."

She furrowed her brow. "How would that work?"

"I've got the next few months to figure that out. Wanna help?"

She smiled. "I'd be delighted."

Acknowledgments

In many ways, *Enemies Domestic* was a collaborative effort.

Usually, I plot out my novels before I write them. This time I was pretty much making it up as I wrote. My wife Cindy was my canary in the mine for each chapter.

In addition, many beta readers took all or parts of the manuscript on a test drive, then gave me their helpful and constructive criticism. They are: Jenna Bourne; retired Army Lt. Gen. Michael S. Davison, Jr.; Joyce Woolsey Davison; Lowell Mays; Beth Morrison; Carolyn Presutti; and Christine Talbott.

I workshopped some chapters during the writing classes I teach at The Writer's Center (Bethesda, Maryland); The Loft (Minneapolis); The Muse (Norfolk, Virginia); and the online writing community of Scribophile. Thank you to students Jennie Brzezinski, Valerie Getsinger, Rose Goldberg, Kader Gumus, E. Kho, Beth Morrison, Kal Nossuli, Terri Pease, Sarah Peppel, Jonathan Phillips, Dwana Pinchock, and Blanche Vest.

A special shout-out to the students of the "From Novice to Novelist" class I taught during the summer of 2023 at the Chautauqua Institution in southwestern New York state: Elizabeth Colledge, Shaunie Eminger, Michele Fletcher, Jeffrey Long, and Alexandra Polchek.

I'm indebted to Kristen Keyes and Teri Murrison for their help as I researched White Christian Nationalism in Western states like Idaho.

Important sounding boards on the project were my long-time neurologist friend from high school days Dr. Steve Rasmus and his wife Diane, a retired ICU nurse. Diane's insights are already seeping into the upcoming (eventually!) Book 7 in the Lark Chadwick series.

I met Laura Cifelli at a critical point during the creative process when I was speaking at the Pikes Peak Writers' Conference in Colorado Springs in 2023. Laura, now a freelance editor, was an acquisitions editor at HarperCollins and other big NYC publishers. She listened patiently as I struggled to get Lark out of the corner I'd painted her into. Laura's feedback was so wise that I hired her to edit an early draft of the manuscript.

My thanks, also, to publishers Kurt and Erica Mueller at Speaking Volumes for championing this project.

For a deeper understanding of the themes explored in *Enemies Domestic,* I strongly encourage you to read the following books:

Preparing for War: The Extremist History of White Christian Nationalism by Bradley Onishi.

Pastels and Pedophiles: Inside the Mind of QAnon by Mia Bloom & Sophia Moskalenko. I interviewed the authors for my "One-to-One" podcast on YouTube.

How to Stand Up to a Dictator: The Fight for Our Future by Maria Ressa (co-winner of the 2021 Nobel Peace Prize). I was one of Maria's editors when we worked together at CNN.

Democracy Awakening: Notes on the State of America by Heather Cox Richardson. Her daily history/politics essay on Facebook is a must-read every morning for Cindy and me.

Fascism: A Warning by former U.S. Secretary of State Madeleine Albright.

The Exvangelicals: Loving, Living, and Leaving the White Evangelical Church by NPR National Political Correspondent Sarah McCammon.

Oath and Honor by Liz Cheney.

Enough by Cassidy Hutchinson. This young woman has Lark's courage.

    Finally, a big hug to my agent Barbara Casey. *Enemies Domestic* is our sixth book together, and 2024 is our twentieth year working together.

John DeDakis
Baltimore, Maryland
March 2024

About the Author

Award-winning novelist, writing coach, and manuscript editor John DeDakis (pronounced dee-DAY-kiss) is a former editor on CNN's "The Situation Room with Wolf Blitzer." DeDakis, a former White House correspondent, regularly leads writing workshops at retreats, literary centers, writers' conferences, and bookstores. He is also the host of the video podcast "One-to-One" on YouTube, Facebook, and LinkedIn. Originally from La Crosse, Wisconsin, DeDakis now lives in Baltimore, Maryland with Cindy, his wife of 46 years.

Website: www.johndedakis.com

Now Available!
JOHN DeDAKIS'
LARK CHADWICK MYSTERIES
BOOKS 1 – 2

**For more information
visit:** www.SpeakingVolumes.us

Now Available!
HAWK MACKINNEY'S
Historical / Fiction

Moccasin Trace was nominated for the prestigious Michael Shaara Award for Excellence in Civil War Fiction, the Writers Notes Book Award, and was a finalist for the Readers' Favorite Award.

**For more information
visit:** www.SpeakingVolumes.us

Now Available!
BARBARA CASEY

Power, betrayal, greed…
Conspiracy, deceit, murder…

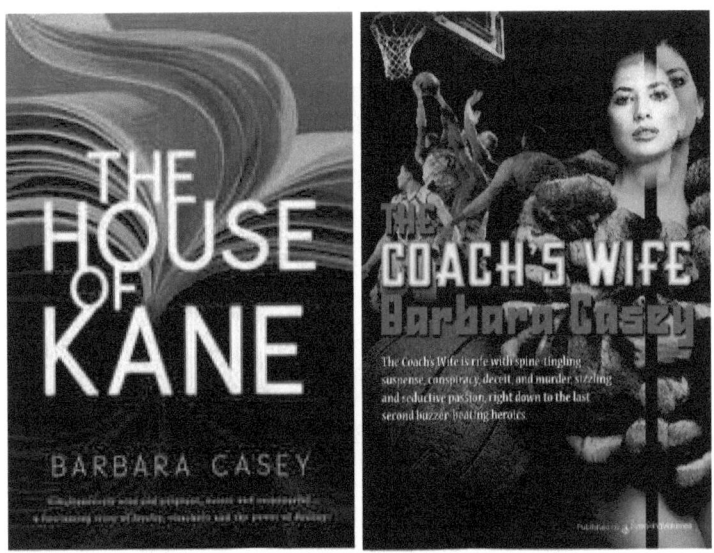

**For more information
visit:** www.SpeakingVolumes.us